Blood and Ink

D. K. Marley

BLOOD AND INK

A White Rabbit Publishing Book

Paperback edition published April 2018

www.dkmarley.com

www.facebook.com/dkmarley.author/

**FT
Pbk**

ISBN-13: 978-1986530392
ISBN-10: 1986530396

To my husband, Johnny,

for your love and my trips to England

and to my Grandmother, Naomi,

who gave me my first Shakespeare book.

I here beg for your clemency as I use the words of

Christopher Marlowe and William Shakespeare,

and expound on a tale needing to be told.

"The forbidden idea contains a spark of truth

that flies up in the face

of he who seeks to stamp it out."

– Francis Bacon

ROME, ITALY

April 6, 1616

*I savored dripping candle wax on the backs of spiders creeping
across my writing desk late at night. The occurrence happened
often, which speaks volumes of my supposed inspirational
surroundings. Guilt did not arise in my stomach watching them
writhe in the cooling liquid; only justice – justice that their ugly,
black, hairy existence was now encased immemorial and dotted
like small sepulchers before my eyes. To kill something appearing
to deserve death feels like divine justice; and yet, to kill something
of beauty, what does that say about a man?*

*Unfortunately, I know both. 'Tis amazing what envy will tempt
a man to do. Like the hot wax, the human spirit writhes and twists
beneath a liquid persuasion and your limbs flail to survive, to hold
on to the thing you hold most dear.*

*Envy moves men to covet, lie, steal, and, ultimately, kill. A
person never forgets the thing he envies if he lets envy encase him
– the dwelling, the longing, and the lengths he will go to obtain the
thing. 'Tis the fruit hanging from the tree, shiny and appetizing,
and forbidden. That one word, forbidden, awakens the monster
who crawls from the dark recesses of the mind to poke and jab any
decency a person has until he is transformed in to the beast itself.*

Thus, is envy the wax or the spider? Or both?

'Tis a shame, but those of artistic persuasion are the worst of the lot. Writers are the worst. Shall I include myself in the mix? Of course, and yet, the thing I envy does indeed belong to me. Words, words, words – ripped from me by another envious person and dangled like a fruit just out of my reach, forbidden to bear my name.

In truth, I bear the fault alone, for a writer longs to see his words come to life, especially as a playwright. What elation to see the characters you create in your mind come to flesh and blood on the stage. What delight strokes the vanity of a writer to hear the swoons of the penny-stinkers clamoring at your feet and calling your name. My name immortalized – so she promised me. A bitter lesson to learn that an educated man's vanity, when stroked with a promise of greatness, will cause him to sell his soul for any semblance of immortality. "Tis an age old lesson , yet to be learned by any of us; still, a writer never forgets the first promise, and the first taste of envy.

No matter. Did I not say: foul deeds will rise, though all the world o'erwhelm them to men's eyes. And ears have passed since I sliced the feathers from a goose quill, sharpened the tip with the dagger at my belt and scrawled those words across a waiting blank page. They are familiar ones to you, I know.

My name is there, just on your lips. Can you feel the letters roll off your tongue as familiar to you as if you spoke the name of your dearest love? Yea, perhaps you think you know me – the wave of my brown hair, the educated twinkle in my amber eyes, the audacious gold earring in my left ear; but wait.....

Perhaps you have imagined my tortured nights, my aching back bowed over the desk, the spent wax melting over a solitary pewter candlestick, the flame's shadow flickering and dancing with the movements of my hand across paper. These were the nights when my muse would not let me sleep as she filled my head with the sweet music of iambic perfection. More words, words, words....

Go ahead, speak my name. For what's in a name? That which we call a rose would smell as sweet by any other name? Ha! But you did not hear the irony flavoring my thoughts when those words first erupted from the fertile womb of my muse. 'Twas a sprinkling, a hint, a clue to the truth ,and those having "eyes" will see. Do you have the eyes for truth? Perhaps you will need the stomach ,as well, for my tale is not for those comfortable with lies. A curious soul is what I seek, and I promise to stroke your curiosity like a king of cats. When the curtains closes, I will charge thee to tell the world the true story of the great Bard of England.

How was I to know the outcome? I began as every man does, as a simple boy toying with lofty dreams and eating the air, promise-crammed. You think you know who I am, and yet, you are deceived.

Shall I speak the name with you? Come; let it fall. William Shakespeare. 'Twas easily said and now that I see you are settling in for a tale about the man you think you know – a twist.

I am not William Shakespeare.

Act One

1572–1579

"Why write I still all one, ever the same,

And keep invention in a noted weed,

That every word doth almost tell my name,

Showing their birth and where they did proceed?"

Sonnet 76

I

Lying in the tall silky grass on the bank of the Stour River, the wind playing tag with a willow tree, a muse blinded Kit Marlowe as daggers of sunlight pierced through the swaying branches. The first inklings of inspiration warmed his cheeks, not in the passionate sense, though, for his eight-year-old body still leaned toward the innocent pastimes of catching frogs in the swirling eddies. He relished the sudden prick of words as her soft, ethereal lips kissed his forehead and filled his mind with a lyrical rhythm.

He narrowed his eyes, watching her flowing chestnut hair dance and tangle in the breeze. Her imaginary form dissipated like sun-burnt fog as he opened them wider, and a small chirping sparrow clinging to a crooked branch filled the void of her fading figure. Kit edged his fingers through the grass and clasped the carved wooden handle of his slingshot. With quiet ease, he set a penny-sized stone, pulled back the catapult and slung. Just as the bird took to flight, the pebble found her breast, and she dropped to the ground near his feet.

The excited rush of killing rushed over him, puddled in his stomach and ebbed away with each beat of his heart, leaving behind a knotty fear in his gut. The imaginary voice of the muse echoed in the hollow.

"Poor innocent bird, Kit. God attaches special providence in the fall of a sparrow."

Kit heaved the slingshot into the river and looked up at the blue sky through the breaks in the trees. *Does God see her whispering,* he wondered, *and what is more, does he see me?*

He kicked the bird into the cat-tails and reeds at the riverbank, hopeful the waters might hide his mistake, and ran to join three boys in a game of hood man-blind in a hewed barley field on the outskirts of Canterbury. Yet, even in such a simple game, her words flashed bright and accusing in the darkness behind the cloth mask over his eyes. The words captured him, leaving him unaware of those boys laughing and pointing at him from the edges of the field. Rhymes flowed into his mind like the bubbling springs of Bath, just as a rock sizzled through the air and met the side of his head, striking him into reality. Kit reached up, pulled the cloth from his face, and dropped to his knees as he dodged more rocks along with a barrage of slicing insults.

"Idiot!"

"Fool! You are nothing but a cobbler's son," chimed like a common nursery song across the boy's lips as they ran into the woods.

Their laughter faded as he wiped his watering eyes with the edges of the mask. He felt alone as the sun touched her lazy head on the horizon and filled the rising mist with a shrouded yellow glow. His imaginary friend edged near to him and she lifted his chin with her fingertips. She tickled his neck and coaxed his crooked smile, the only adoring inheritance from his pallid Jute father. He closed his eyes and held out his hand, letting her lead him away from his bullying peers with their dirt-smudged cheeks and greasy hair, and to soothe him with whispers of greatness. *Yes,* he consoled himself, *I will become her prodigy with a quill.*

And he soaked in this love as it was the only he knew. His home lacked such affection, being just a boy squeezed between two older sisters and one younger. *'Twas none their fault,* he thought, *his siblings took the bread given them and taken from him.*

A shrew ruled their house, though to look at her, a person could not see past her curling brown locks falling over her shoulder and the spark of amber in her brown eyes. Kit's mother, Katherine, or as his father said with a twinkle in his eye, 'the prettiest Kate in Christendom,' governed the house like a stubborn nanny goat and led his father by the breeches. Kit felt a mercy of gaining her mysterious dark looks and not the sour disposition. His older sisters, Dorothy and Anne, leaned more toward the sunny side with golden hair and bright eyes, yet followed their mother's example with a biting tongue. As for Kit, the household considered him of little account, as just another mouth to feed. Though young, he never missed the words from his mother's mouth.

"Look at ya," she often scowled in her poor Dover drawl, as she pinched his ear, "my sad waif who, like his father, will never amount to anything. Lower than the mud on a sow's belly, is this one."

Time echoed forward, every year the same for Kit, and Michaelmas of 1570 swaddled in on the coat of Autumn, wrapping Canterbury in crisp winds and tumbling leaves, a collage of oranges and browns. The Marley house nestled tight within the parish of Saint George, tucked in a lane past the buttery and butcher; a simple wattle-and-daubed narrow with the second floor jetting out over the soured streets of the Shambles. Each day like another as Kit rose with the dawn, dumped the night pots into the street trough, toted buckets of water from the river Stour to refill the oak barrel near the hearth, and picked up his father's order of leather from the tanner. He loathed the last of his jobs, even more so than the night pot business, for the putrid smell of the cow hides aging in a vat of dog feces always made him retch, no matter how hard he pinched his nose. He hastened through his daily chores just to find a quiet moment to sit at the window of the small attic alcove perched above the children's sleeping berth, to nestle in the warm wheat rushes and wait for his imaginary friend's whispers. Yet, change blew in with the Autumn wind, approaching in the form of the Archbishop of Canterbury, Matthew Parker.

Two days after the feast of Saint Michael, John leaned over his cobbling bench and tooled designs on a pair of leather sandals. Kit huddled next to the hearth in his father's workshop and his right cheek warmed in the crackling fire as he scrawled a simple poem onto a slate. The wind and leaves blasted in as the door opened and closed, swirling the Archbishop's purple robe around the old man's legs and revealing his narrow pale feet in worn-out shoes. Kit looked up and smiled as Parker adjusted the small round cap covering the circle of his silver hair. The Archbishop's face lit up with a wide smile and he clapped his hands, as John held up the fine new shoes.

"Wonderful, Master Marley! I doubted my old sandals would last through another winter. How much do I owe you, sir?"

John wrapped the shoes in a length of undyed wool and held them out to the priest. "Take these, your Grace, without pay, if you kindly give me forgiveness for the past two times I have missed prayers."

The wrinkles on the priest's brow drew together. "Come now, John, thou knowest you cannot buy God with such things. He wants your love, not sandals."

John urged the shoes closer to the Archbishop. "But have I not heard from your own lips that Christ said if one shows mercy to the least of his brothers, then you have done it for him? 'Tis a mercy to receive such a fine pair of shoes for your Grace's feet in exchange for a wave of your hand in the air."

Kit coddled his chin in his palm as the Archbishop eked out a small laugh. "John, you make absolution sound so menial."

John wrapped the priest's hands around the parcel. "Pray tell, your Grace, is it not?"

Kit smiled at the two men as they laughed, and the Archbishop lifted his hand and struck the sign of the cross over John's head. After a few Latin phrases tumbled over his lips, the priest waddled over to the hearth and grunted as he sat on the stones next to Kit.

John stood near, wringing his hands, as the priest slipped the shoes over his calloused feet. "Are they well for you, your Grace?"

The priest stretched out his leg and arched his foot in the sandal, bending and easing the leather. "Ah, yes, and look at the clever scrolling designs across the top."

"Yea, sir, to match the scroll work across the pillar caps in the Cathedral."

"Of course, I recognize them now."

Kit clenched his tongue between his lips as he scrawled on the board, catching the curious stare of the Archbishop. Parker held out his hand to Kit, the gesture asking for the slate.

"What are you writing, boy?" Parker lifted the board as the firelight threw shadows over his shoulder, revealing the simple poem. His eyes perked wide. "This lettering is in Latin. Where is this boy schooling, Master Marley?"

John fidgeted. "Schooling, sir? Forgive me, your Grace, but Christopher is not to school. 'Tis difficult to afford on a cobbler's pay since we have three other living children to feed, and two others in the ground since his birth."

The Archbishop scratched his chin and narrowed his eyes at Kit. "No schooling? Then, pray tell, do you know this you are writing?"

Kit nodded, reached behind him, picked up a small leather book and held it out for the priest to take. The priest brushed his fingers across the spine, opened the cover and read aloud the title. "Metamorphose, Ovid. Where did you get this, boy?"

Kit frowned, wondering if he had done something wrong. "Mother gave me the book to keep me quiet."

The Archbishop mussed the boy's hair and smiled. "'Tis all right, boy, you have done nothing wrong. I only wish to know if you know the letters you are reading and writing, for the entire book and the poem is in Latin."

Kit took the slate and read aloud his words. "Si una eademque res legatur duobus, alter rem, alter valorem rei."

John cocked his head, and the priest leaned closer toward Kit. "And now, can you tell us the meaning, boy?"

Kit wrinkled his nose, glanced from his father to the priest, noting the confusion in his father's face and the exciting sparkle in the Archbishop's blue eyes. He took a breath and translated. "Of course, sir, it means if something of value is given to two people, then one shall have the value of the thing and the other shall have the thing itself. Sort of like new shoes and forgiveness."

Archbishop Parker drew his hand to his heart with a gasp. "Indeed! And how do you know this, boy? Is this a line from the Metamorphoun?"

"Nay, sir, 'tis a line of my own creation. I heard the words in a dream and she taught me the meaning."

The priest looked to John, arching his eyebrow. "Your wife, Master Marley, knows Latin?"

Kit tugged on the priest's sleeve. "Nay, sir, not my mother. My friend, the angel who visits me; she teaches me."

The Archbishop's mouth fell open, forming a circle, and he wrapped his hands over Kit's shoulders. "An angel visits you?" He paused and closed his eyes. Kit looked to his father as the priest collected his thoughts. John wrung his hands and interjected.

"Your Grace, just fancies is all. He has an imaginary friend. 'Tis just child's play, 'tis all."

The priest opened his eyes and curled his fingers around Kit's chin, raising his face to meet his wondering smile. "Master Marley, methinks I have found a way for your eternal salvation and to keep me in fine shoes for the length of my days. 'Tis may be a child's fancy and imagination, but methinks an angel has blessed your boy here, so he says. May be a devil giving him the ability to speak Latin without schooling, for such imps are potent with such gifts and look for young pliable minds. Who's to say, as yet? I have determined that young Kit here is to enroll in the King's School near the Cathedral, not only enrolling but even as a novice under my tutelage, so we may find the origins of his spiritual visitor. If an angel, then what better place to heighten his spiritual training; if it be a devil, then again, what better place to purge his soul till the claws release? You may pay for his schooling by delivering me a new pair of shoes yearly until my death. How does this sound to you?"

Dizziness swirled in Kit's brain as his father spoke. "Marry, well, your Grace! And where will the boy stay?"

The priest answered, keeping his eyes on Christopher. "There is a small dormitory where a few of the boys stay whose families live too far for them to walk home every day. We will find him a bed there." Kit's eyes widened and his stomach swirled with anxiety. "Tell me, Christopher, how like you to go to school?"

Kit considered, letting the thought settle on his mind with the images of books, vellum, slates and ink. He curled his mouth into a grin. "Your Grace, 'tis an honor I dream not of."

The priest laughed and slapped his knee. "Ha, good words! Such humility! The Kingdom of God belongs to such like ones, Master Marley. This boy could teach us a thing or two on how to lower our eyes and check our ambition. There is no telling what luminous future lies on the horizon for this clay-like boy."

Two days later, Kit's father lowered him off the haunches of his donkey, spurred the nag through the fallen leaves and never looked back at his son. Kit waved farewell to his retreating form, ever hopeful and quite naïve. His imaginary friend, whom he named Calliope, followed him there, and she coddled him like a proper mother as the days lengthened into weeks, the weeks into months. She daily ran her airy white linen-paper fingers through his brown locks and whispered inky words into his brain. Kit's heart craved her tingling presence to obsession, and she obliged him within those walls, teaching him to write in profound verse.

Each night as the shadows in the dormitory stretched long, his eyes strained in the candlelight, burning and watering, as he sucked the honey verses of Ovid like a greedy little bee. He read the passages over and over until the words oozed from memory in sweet lyrical simplicity.

His stare caressed over the ten other boys sleeping beside him, their beds spaced along the wall in the narrow room. Some slept in peace, some snored in awkward rhythms, and Kit imagined they dreamed of places other than school. *Not he, though.* He scratched his head, pondering the question of why he was the only one ever awake. *Did no one else have an imaginary friend? Did no one else taste excitement over words and language and learning within these sacred walls?*

Sliding out from under the woolen blanket, he knelt at the side of his bed and practiced his night ritual. The first: running his hand along the stone wall near the headboard. Kit adored the goose-flesh rising on his arm, as if knowledge seeped from every crevice and shivered against his skin. He breathed words. The second part of his ritual continued as his dug his fingers between the feathered mattress and the lattice of ropes, entwined to hold up the bed, to retrieve a small leather portfolio. A brief giddiness always rose in his stomach as he pulled the strings binding the book. Last, he reached for an ink bottle hidden in a niche in the wall beneath the bed and removed the cork from the mouth. The release made a popping sound and the pungent aroma of gall ink wafted into the air. He held the bottle beneath his nostrils and sucked in the acrid scent.

Calliope appeared everywhere, from the moment he opened his eyes in the morning to the dreams he dreamed at night. She walked with him through the garden gate, flitting in between the archways of the courtyard as she taught him to walk in verse. Kit's footfalls became poetry as he learned her favorite game, a game of counting. When his feet touched the floor, he counted his steps from there, along the corridor to the banquet hall, and then up the stairs to the schoolroom. She prodded words to the counting, words forming into verse, and verse into a tale. Every day a new one, and then, before closing his eyes to sleep, he penned them in the portfolio hidden beneath the mattress.

Two months after his eighth birthday, late into the night when the candle sputtered and melted into a small nub of wax, the portfolio overflowed with words and his left index finger stained permanent with ink. Thomas, his nearest bedfellow, tussled with a pillow and tangled himself in the bedclothes. Kit squeezed his eyes shut and prayed Thomas stayed asleep. He opened one eye and looked over his shoulder as Thomas wrestled, once more, and he noticed the candlelight in the boy's eyes.

"I cannot sleep, Kit. Can you for once go to bed? I can hear the scratching of the quill against the paper. 'Tis irritating!" Kit shrugged and ignored him as Thomas persisted. "Kit, where did you get that candle?"

Kit rolled his eyes behind his lids and answered. "Some stupid secret papist left a few at Becket's murder site in the Cathedral."

Thomas gasped and held the covers over his mouth. "I will tell Master Gresshop! That is blasphemy to steal the candles from the church."

Kit shrugged again. "I do not care, Thomas. God did nothing when he saw me take the candle and I don't think he will miss the one. Besides, Archbishop Parker hasn't said a thing. I think with his treasures supposedly in heaven he can afford to lose a ha'pence candle."

Thomas untangled himself from the blanket and padded across the limestone. He knelt next to Kit and folded his hands in prayer. Kit hated new students since their eagerness to attach to him irritated him. Words and his imaginary friend spoke simple truth; so often, real people did not. People unsettled him, especially the ones like this boy who invaded his space with his gangling limbs towering over him and whose cheeks caved inward as if he perpetually sucked air. Boys such as Thomas rarely survived the English winters, always coughing and always pale. Yet, from the first day, Thomas attached himself to Kit; following him, adoring him, and pounding him with questions on Latin, Greek, Seneca and Ovid. Kit and Calliope shared a quiet laugh while he reflected on the answers to Thomas, and then he spouted away as if the thoughts rushed upon him like an Elysium spring. Kit kept the quiet joke deep in his heart that he often lied to him for sport. The fool never knew, until he stood to recite a line before Schoolmaster Gresshop, assured Kit gave him the correct answer. Thomas' sallow cheeks whitened in his embarrassment, yet even in such a mortifying joke, he came back for more like a starving puppy.

Looking over at him, Kit laid the quill on his bed and folded his hands in front of him. "Thomas?"

Thomas' eyes scrunched together. "Hush, I am praying."

"Why are you praying?"

"I am praying for your soul, Kit."

Kit looked up toward the beamed ceiling. "'Tis not going to do any good, Thomas."

Thomas let his hands unfold and fall across the bed. His wispy blonde eyebrows arched upward like two emaciated caterpillars. "Why not? Do you not believe in forgiveness and that God listens to our prayers?"

Kit shrugged, took up the quill in his fingers and twirled the feather in front of his face. "Marry, the words please the ears, but are they true? Catholic or Protestant, Rome or the Church of England? Why do I have to care?"

"But, Kit, do you not pray?"

Wrinkling his nose, Kit answered him. "Yea, I pray, but not to England's God or Rome's God."

Thomas hurried to make the sign of the cross from shoulder to shoulder and head to heart. "You should not say such things, Kit. I wonder, if you have no faith and still you pray, then what do you ask for and from whom do you ask it?"

The questions vexed Kit. Thomas' quivering piety made him want to vomit, yet Kit obliged him a hint of his belief without revealing his imaginary friend.

"O, you are wrong. I have faith, and I pray daily that one day the world remembers me as the greatest playwright and poet of all time. That after I am dead, the schoolmasters begin their lessons with the philosophies of Socrates, the poetry of Ovid and the plays of Christopher Marlowe."

Thomas nudged him on the shoulder with one hand while giggling into the other. "That is just nonsense, Kit."

Thomas left him and crawled back across the floor and curled into the covers of his bed. Kit's glare followed him and just as the flame from the candle waned away, Thomas rubbed his eyes and mumbled, "Kit, tomorrow after class, I am going to the river to fish. Do you want to come?"

Kit did not answer him. Alone in the dark, he pondered the destinies of his sleeping peers. *How could Thomas call what he felt as nonsense? How can any of them understand what words mean to him?* His insides boiled with anger at their simple mindedness and he determined, at that moment, to tuck his feelings deep in the protective arms of his friend.

The moon peeked out from behind a cloud, glowing through the single window at the end of the chamber and casting cross-hatched shadows across his schoolmates. Calliope formed in the moonlight, sitting on the window frame, and her body collected together as if the stars fell from the sky and magnetized to each other in the shape of a goddess with copper hair and watery eyes. He imagined her skipping across the room, lifting him off the floor and cradling him in her arms. With his cheek pressed against her breast, her heartbeat sounded a rhyme in his ear. Da dum, da dum, da dum, da dum, da dum; five iambs, then again. The sound sang to him, calming the anger swirling in his stomach.

She lifted his chin with her finger and kissed his forehead. Her voice chimed clearer than church bells, more serene than a litany, and truer than a sermon.

"Christoper, forget these common boys. I chose you to bless. Never forget you are my special boy, the muse's darling. Never forsake me, Christopher. Trust me and I will give you your heart's desire."

His heart warmed to those words, "heart's desire," and he fell asleep to her singing, feeling safe within the protection of a mother's arms. In reality, he was nothing more than a boy, clutching his pillow and rocking himself to sleep with poetry in his head.

II

K it woke early curled around his pillow. The morning sunbeams warmed the chamber to a golden glow, tickling the bare sides, backs and cheeks of the boys through the mullioned glass. Like rote, they rose and dressed in linen shirts, tan doublets, laced breeches and black flowing over robes.

The morning progressed as always, filled with recitations of Latin phrases, ciphering in numbers, scrawling their answers across black slates, and burying their noses in worn horn-books. Master Gresshop weaved in and out of the tables like an ominous raven in his black robe and prying stare, glancing over shoulders, reviewing their progress and throwing an obtuse question to an unsuspecting boy to keep them quick and sharp.

Kit busied himself, perfecting the shape of the Greek lettering, when the sound of a leather horsewhip slashed across the table of the boy seated in front of him. The boys jumped in sequence as Gresshop glared down his crooked nose at Thomas. "You are idle, Master Thomas. Did you not hear me?"

Thomas shuddered and bit his bottom lip. The blood drained from his face, revealing he had not heard. Kit stood up just as Thomas' lips trembled upon his confession.

"Sir," Kit injected, "I will take the question."

Schoolmaster Gresshop smiled in Kit's direction and sliced the whip across the table for a second time. "Naturally, Master Christopher, I can always count on you. Thomas needs to understand the foolishness of being lazy. Idleness breeds discontent, it breeds rebellion, and we must purge the sin." Gresshop looked again at Thomas, whose eyes filled with water. "Tell me, Thomas, why are you idle?"

He shrugged, opened his mouth and before he confessed their

conversation, Kit cleared his throat and interrupted, once more. "Sir, please, Thomas is my nearest bedfellow and during the night I heard him moan and thrash. Twice I saw him grapple with his pillow. It wasn't till late in the night I saw him finally sleeping."

Gresshop grunted. "Hmm, dreams, Master Thomas?" Thomas nodded as he read Kit's pleading stare. Gresshop's face turned red as a cock's comb and his anger sprayed out upon Thomas in spit and words. "Dreams? Dreams are the children of an idle brain, the very coinage of your mind. We are not here to dream, boy, we are here to learn."

The statement unnerved Kit. He rubbed the spot between his eyes and tried to smooth out the perplexed crinkle. To question the schoolmaster often resulted in a palm thrashing with the horsewhip, so he curled his fingers over his palms and cleared his throat.

Gresshop jerked his stare toward Kit. "Do you have something to say again, Master Christopher?"

Kit whispered. "Nay, sir..... I mean, yea, I do, I think."

Gresshop leaned forward, clutching the horsewhip. "Then, pray, speak up, boy!"

"Master Gresshop, please, sir, indulge my ignorance. Has not Socrates taught us that the dream is also the ambition? Is not the substance of ambition the shadow of a dream?"

Gresshop squinted and scratched his chin through his burly silver beard. "Hmm, true, 'tis true, Christopher, the dream 'tis a shadow of humanity, yet oft times be it a shadow of ill. Ambition can warp a mind and set it to odds against a kingdom. Look to the history of our beloved England. Stories fill the pages of ambitious men and women who lost their heads. 'Tis a precarious quality to have and we must remember we are the Queen's subjects, so any dream stretching beyond her authority needs awakening."

Kit drew his stare out the window and across the green grass of the courtyard. Calliope urged his strong impulsive words. "Then are our beggars' bodies, and our monarchs and outstretched heroes the beggars' shadows. They clap us in to the crown. Our mind reaches past the head to heaven, and yet, they instruct us not to do so unless the Queen twists her ring. God gives us a lofty quality and usurps our ambition by appointment of rulers, thus binding us in a nutshell. By my fay, I cannot reason this."

Master Gresshop charged toward him and took Kit by the chin, his eyes making a straight line into Kit's face. "Heaven is the crown, and the crown is heaven. Dare you speak against our sovereign appointed by God to the throne and savior of the Church of England? Look to yourself, Christopher, that you may not dream of things you ought not."

Kit knew the words to say, placating words of Calliope to bring a smile back to the schoolmaster's face. Words to soothe his bugging eyes and stay the sting of the whip. "Sir, I dream only of England, for she is my love and my mother."

The corner of Gresshop's mouth twitched and curled into a smile. He looked awkward as the redness drained from his face. He glanced at the other young faces in the room, encouraging all by his gesture to look at Christopher. "Marry, well spoke, young man. Take a lesson from him. There is not a one of you who can match his prowess with words. This one has a future."

Kit smiled at Thomas, who glared over his shoulder and, for once, the spark in Thomas' eyes did not show admiration. *Do not speak for me again,* shadowed Thomas' look.

Kit should have recognized the isolation creeping upon him, but he did not. He was just a boy unaware of the common fault of friends clapping to you when advantage is there, and turning on you when they discover favors dry up like a dead dragonfly in the afternoon sun. Kit's fellow schoolmates clustered away from him, snickering into their palms, whispering and laughing as they cut their bullying stares toward him. He saw them, but his head soared too far in the clouds to notice the shadow of his future lurking behind their jealous mediocre smirks.

The boys filed out of the Almonry building, through the King's School gate and along the cobblestones to afternoon prayers, mimicking dark little mice scurrying to receive their daily cheese and unaware of the cat spying on them from the corner of the Cathedral. Shrove Tuesday burst over Canterbury and the apple trees showered the streets with soft white petals, a welcome after the dark mantle of winter. Canterbury Cathedral loomed over them as an ancient oracle, her gray Gothic arms jutting upwards into the blue sky, beseeching heaven for a blessing.

The boys knew the routine, so oft they had done it: no talking, hands folded, heads bowed; yet something gnawed at Kit as he stood in the nave. He lifted his gaze to the lofty heights of the ceiling. The spidery network and ribs of arches lifted high above their heads, weaving together like lace made from carved stone.

His perusing jumped from column to column, peering into shadows and sparkling stained glass until his eye caught upon a stirring. Across the aisle, a small black cat arched her back and rubbed against the trestle legs of a candle-anointed table. Her purr warmed the air like a prayer as she sat and looked up at Kit. A tiny mouse flailed in the trap of her teeth, squeaking and whipping his tail in her whiskers. She flicked her ear in irritation and released him to bat him back and forth between her paws. Kit continued to watch as the mouse fell over and stiffened to play dead. The cat drew her ears back like two pointed horns, displaying her boredom at the mouse, pawed him near her mouth and bit off his head. Kit gasped as the blood squirted across the stone floor. At that moment, a stranger, sitting in a solitary chair at the far end of the nave, and in eyesight of the cat, caught Kit's attention as he leaned back and snickered at the bloody mess. Dressed in a black robe with the hint of a white pleated collar haloing his neck, he held Kit's stare. Kit's stomach tightened into a knot. The stranger's grave-like eyes darkened, yet pierced like a sword dividing a soul and reading thoughts; reading Christopher's thoughts. The man tilted his head forward in a slight nod toward Kit and smiled. Kit felt caught.

The Archbishop, his purple robe rustling across the floor and the simple gold cross swaying back and forth across his chest, moved toward the man and leaned forward to whisper in the man's ear. The stranger nodded and never took his eyes from Kit.

Master Gresshop grabbed Kit hard by the ear and pulled him from the line. "Christopher! Where is your humility?"

Before Kit had the chance to answer, Gresshop pushed him to the back of the nave and shoved a prayer book into his hands. Kit dared not look over his shoulder at the man even though his heart dared him. Gresshop pointed his shriveled forefinger in Kit's face and gestured to the book.

"Perhaps an evening and a day spent reciting prayers will remind you of your place. You will be last before the altar and..."

His words faded away. The stranger overtook Kit's thoughts, and his left cheek warmed from the stranger's gaze boring onto his face.

The bells in the tower tolled the noon hour across Canterbury, resounding deep echoes in the nave. High above Kit's head, the vibrating tones sent roosting doves fluttering thought the sunlight. He fixed his eyes upon the book in his hands, wary of receiving a swift slap on the back of the head from the watchful schoolmaster.

When Gresshop moved away, he took the chance to bow his head and bend his gaze to the stranger. The man held his disturbing glare and curled his lips upward. Kit snatched his gaze away and scrunched his eyes shut, whispering to his imaginary friend as his stomach knotted more.

"Calliope, Calliope, where are you? Give me words to soothe me."

She remained silent and his supplication came too late. Fingers wrapped over his shoulder and when he opened his eyes, three men stood before him: Archbishop Parker, Master Gresshop and the stranger.

Gresshop's smile looked like a half-moon hidden in the storm cloud of his beard as he patted Kit on the back and nudged him toward the stranger.

"This, sir, is Master Christopher Marlowe, the boy you asked about. He is quite the wit for his age, but I must confess, he has a tendency for daydreaming and he flits between ambition and humility when the moment suits him. Nothing a horsewhip won't correct, I assure you."

The Archbishop lifted Kit's chin. "Gresshop tells me you are doing well in your studies and excelling well beyond your years. Seems I was correct to see to your schooling, yet his concern with your growing lack of humility is unsettling. Unfortunately, the results of education often has the effect of vaulting ambition. Hold out your hands, boy."

Kit obeyed, bulling up his courage for a sting of the leather. The stranger grabbed hold of Kit's left hand and raised it up in the air.

"His fingers are filthy with ink," then man snarled, his voice resounding as a nobleman, except, to Kit, flavored with a slithery air.

Gresshop popped him on the side of the head. "Did you not scrub your hands this morning? Speak up, boy!"

"Yea, sir, I did, but, you see, sir, I am a playwright and poet and the ink stains my fingers."

The stranger huffed. "You seem so sure of yourself to be so young."

The man took Kit hard by the arm and led him away from the Archbishop and schoolmaster. Fear blanketed Kit and tears stung his eyes, even more when he noticed the train of the man's robe brush through and smear the residual blood of the mouse. When they reached the other side of the nave, into the shadows and away from his schoolmates, the stranger pushed him against a stone column.

"So, boy, your name is Christopher? Yes, a good Christian name. And the Archbishop tells me you steal candles from the Church?" Kit eyes rounded and he swallowed hard as the man continued. "I suppose you wonder how he knew. The Archbishop has a clever eye, but do not worry, he also has an eye for genius. You do not have to fear, he will not scold as long as you stop the theft. I spoke for you." The man paused, waiting for any response from Kit. After a moment of awkward silence, the man pawed more. "You may wonder why I spoke for you and I will tell you. I am intrigued by your boldness, boy. Stealing the candles to write late into the night, your stained hands, they all tell me your ambition for the art is overwhelming. Tell me, what things do you write?"

Kit sniffed and wiped his nose across the sleeve of his robe. "Just stuff, sir."

"O, come now, poetry, sonnets, tales?"

Kit shrugged. "Yea, sir, poetry, sonnets and tales."

A laugh grumbled like soft thunder in the man's throat. "You answer so formally, boy. Are you afraid of me?"

Still keeping his eyes away from the stranger, Kit answered. "I do not know you, sir."

"Ah, I see. We have not had proper introductions. I am Sir Francis Walsingham, secretary and protector to Her Majesty, our good Queen Elizabeth. Do you know me now?"

Kit knew him and he lowered his brow in honor. All of England knew him and feared his taste for intrigue and torture. Kit's skin prickled as the man continued.

"Good. Now that the formalities are out of the way, perhaps

you can tell me of your pastime. I know you saw me watching you. You have little respect for this house of worship, do you?"

Kit shrugged and bowed his head while swaying and scraping his foot across the floor. Walsingham pointed toward a spot near the altar.

"Do you know who died there?"

"Yea, sir, everyone knows. 'Twas Thomas Becket."

Walsingham moved his fingers across the beard encircling his mouth. "Indeed. A meddlesome priest who defied a King. Sometimes a Kingdom undertakes drastic measures to protect the lives of sovereigns even if it means spilling blood on holy stones. Of course, the princes of a kingdom never knowingly command such murder. King Henry was clever to pretend his ignorance of the act his loyal servants undertook to protect him. 'Tis the same today. I live to protect my Queen and she pretends to stay oblivious to the many devices used to keep her on the throne. Do you know of what I speak?"

Kit shook his head, wondering only of why this man was speaking to him and of the poor mouse killed on the same holy stones.

"Of course, you do not," Walsingham continued. "You are innocent of such things. But, pray, tell me, boy, of your ambitions. Do you have aspirations for the pulpit?"

"Nay, sir, I wish only to write. I want to be the Queen's playwright one day."

Walsingham leaned forward, shadowing Kit like the moment before a cat pounces. "You know the Queen favors such pastimes. She is an avid patroness of the arts. She likes to surround herself with a young vibrant Court. A few more years and I might mention our chance meeting here today. You are a fair looking boy with your dark hair and golden eyes. I daresay she might take a fancy to you; if, however, you might indulge a few favors now and again for the safety of her Crown. What do you think, boy?"

Kit agreed, hoping his hurried answer would make Walsingham leave him alone. Yet, Walsingham continued. "A few years ago I took another lad under my wing. His name is Nicholas Faunt, and he has proved to be a fast learner and very obedient. Dependable. Loyal. All qualities her Majesty admires. Now young Nicholas is an invaluable tool traveling to far away places in the service of the Crown. He is doing this and fulfilling his own ambitions as well. Think of how your writing could expand as you fed on the spectacular sights of Court, feeling the wind break across your face as you stand on the bow of a ship bound for France, or Denmark, or Italy, or perhaps gabbing with other literary minds."

Try as he might to appear aloof, Walsingham's last words sparked a flame in Kit's heart. A question rolled off his tongue before he thought.

"Other literary minds?"

"O, yea, boy! Many, many poets, players and minstrels. You have heard of the Sidney family, of Sir Philip Sidney?"

Kit quelled his interest by biting his lip. He learned in class of the Sidney family. They were the foremost supporters and patrons of poetry and prose, and Philip led the way with his own lyrical verses. Walsingham edged closer.

"He is a friend of mine, Christopher. I will tell you what I shall do. 'Twas my thought to come here to Canterbury to seek another student to follow Faunt since his training is nearly complete, but a different idea has struck me. You want to be a playwright and I know Philip is seeking a pageboy. He is traveling with me at the end of this month to France and, perhaps, I can persuade him to take you on as his page. Do you see the connection, boy? Sidney can help you with your writing, you can serve him as a messenger; and both of you can attend me across the seas in service of Her Majesty. A delightful Trinity, would you not say?"

Kit remained silent although his heart pounded in his throat.

Walsingham pawed again. "Come now, boy, I saw your eyes stretching far beyond the subservience of being a mere school-boy. Your heart longs for lofty things. I understand this. Unbelievably, you and I are very much alike in that respect. Now, I suspect by the wrinkle on his brow that your Master Gresshop wishes for you to return to your place in the line. Run along, you will receive a letter from me soon."

Constraint swept over Kit and wrestled in the pit of his stomach with the prospect of freedom. Like the mouse, he felt batted between the paws of school-boy security and the impending adventure.

He cut his stare back over to Walsingham, who prodded him with his cat-like grin. "Do you not want to say your prayers, Christopher?"

Kit shrugged in a small childish way. "Not really, sir."

"Why not?"

Looking back up into the breathtaking vault, Kit answered. "I cannot think of anything to say to God, my Lord. I have done nothing wrong."

Walsingham reared back, cackling and coughing. "Ha! Good words, boy. Keep that wit and I perceive you will go far.

Early in the morning as the sun sliced the first hint of light, Christopher awoke and realized a night passed without writing in his portfolio. The rising sun glinted through the wavy glass and he held his hand over his eyes. A cloud passed by and in the moving shadow, Calliope reappeared on the windowsill. He waved to her and smiled. She tip-toed across the floor and sat at the end of his bed.

"My darling Kit, where have you been?"

Kit sank onto the pillow. The images of a disturbing dream during the night flashed into his mind. "Bad dreams, Calliope. Yesterday I met a mysterious man who promised me patronage with Sir Philip Sidney, and then, last night....'tis no matter. Surely it means nothing."

"Tell me of the dream," she prompted, as she ran her fingers through his hair.

Kit swallowed hard and closed his eyes. "I dreamed of the cat I saw in the nave yesterday. She smiled and wrapped her jaws around my throat. The more I struggled to free myself with my hands, the bloodier they got. There were no more words. I could not speak or write, there was only darkness. The more she tore, the less I could find my words. My heart hurts and I know not why."

Calliope leaned forward and whispered in his ear. "If your mind dislikes anything, obey it."

"Dislike anything? To leave school and become page to Master Sidney? Why should I dislike the prospect? I may dislike Sir Walsingham, but perhaps he is just a stepping stone."

Her smile disappeared. "A stepping stone to what, Kit? Be careful to whom you sell your soul for your art. Do you not trust me or are you like so many humans impatient for their reward?"

Reaching out and taking a tendril of her chestnut hair in his hand, he wrapped the curl around his forefinger. "I trust you."

She leaned over and kissed him on the forehead, then faded away as the cloud moved and the sunlight filled the room with golden fire. When he opened his eyes, his fingers clutched a downy goose feather which escaped from the pillow.

III

K it passed the months tucked away in innocence, saturating his mind with history, words and sharpening his Latin to translate Ovid's Elegies into English in secret. The talk with Sir Walsingham faded somewhat, yet still, from time to time, irritated him like an acorn in his shoe. Throwing himself into lessons eased the forgetfulness of his parents and the nagging vision of Walsingham's smile.

Philip Sidney came to Canterbury four months after that prophetic encounter in the Cathedral. He strutted into the schoolroom like a peacock, a spectacle in a green slashed silk doublet and shining yellow stockings blazing against the formidable brown Master Gresshop. This beacon of poets and pawn of the Crown swept Kit from the halls of the King's School and into his service as a page, just as Walsingham foresaw, filling his head with lyrical meters and vindicatory causes for the Queen. The 'just causes' took the form of upholding the continued reformation of England and tightening the Kingdom Elizabeth's father, Henry the Eighth, transformed months before her birth. Philip told Kit that Catholicism was soon to be a distant memory, and it was the duty of poets and playwrights to lure the common folk into an ambient sleep with words of such sweetness toward the Queen, her Kingdom and the new Church of England. So he said repeatedly, drilling Kit with the importance for a poet to make such well-placed alliances and setting the stages of England to support her.

"It assures success for us all," Philip repeated, "like cause and effect. The whole idea should make you happy, Kit. You need to stop walking around looking so sullen all the time."

Yet, something churned in the pit of Kit's stomach. Calliope flitted near, yet there was always something evil lurking in the shadows now whispering against his neck. *Something wicked this way comes.* Often his blood chilled in his veins when walking along a lonely corridor or when an arras breathed away from the wall.

Even his first taste of London felt like tallow on his tongue, the nasty remembrance of cheap wax his mother stuffed in his mouth when she wished for his silence. The harsh realities of a bright city of opportunity lorded over by the gleaming walls of Whitehall Palace blanketed his youthful imaginings. London reeked of filth and the acrid aroma of urine and sweat hovered over the streets like a fog. The narrow and cramped streets, lit with rush torches, hid much depravity from the bear-baiting circuses to the drab-occupying alehouses on nearly every corner. Sights sped by his eyes from the window of Philip's coach: fishmongers with their gut-smeared aprons, gentlemen in starched ruff collars, maids toting buckets of milk on their sun-burnt shoulders, ladies in velvet gowns and embroidered kirtles, horses neighing and defecating in the streets, coaches speeding by, scrounger dogs biting at the butcher's heels, and two dozen punts taxiing up and down the Thames.

Kit pinched his fingers over his nose as he soaked in the sights. Philip reached over and mussed Kit's hair.

"The smell gets easier to bear, I assure you. Before long and you won't even notice. It is a spectrum of sights for a writer, would you not say? This is just the skim of the city. The longer you stay, the more you will see beneath the surface and your writing will become deeper, richer and more experienced the further you delve into London's under croft. Look there, we are approaching Westminster, and there, further along the lane, you can see the gate to Whitehall."

The sight struck his heart. Her majestic walls shimmered in the sun; a true testimony to the Queen who walked within the veins of the corridors and a herald to royalty since William the Conqueror's mighty four-square Tower of London. Kit caught his breath as they wound around into the courtyard. The gardens stretched far into a royal park, dotted with yew bushes squared around pebbled paths and fountains filled with water lilies. A guard fitted in a scarlet tunic emblazoned with the letters E and R across his breast opened the door to the coach. Philip exited first. Kit followed, his stare fixated on the guard and Philip obliged his curiosity.

"This is one of Her Majesty's guards, a yeoman warder."

Kit's heart quickened. "Will we see the Queen, sir?"

Philip laughed and nudged him away from the castle and toward the looming hall of Westminster. "Nay, boy, not you. What would she have to do with you, you being just a page boy? She does not have time to sit and coddle you. We are on the way to see Sir Walsingham and his grace, Lord Burghley, in the Star Chamber. We have important matters to discuss before our delayed trip to France and I expect you to remain silent, respectful and an attentive little page. Do you understand?"

The former excitement froze upon hearing Walsingham's name. Kit lowered his head and his steps slowed to scrubbing through the rocks. Philip twisted Kit's ear.

"I said, do you understand?"

"Yea, my lord, I understand."

"Good, now pick up your pace. We mustn't keep members of the Star Chamber waiting."

When they entered the chamber, his insides jumbled, overwhelmed with excitement, yet mingled with foreboding. A sense of destiny, of glory and demise hung like a gloaming within the walls of the room. A thick oak door mortised with a massive iron lock opened to the private chamber. The only light breaking into the narrow nave-like room twinkled from candles perched on circular candelabras on each side of the dais. The golden initials of the Queen adorned a red velvet cloth draping the long table on the dais, and ten chairs sat in a row behind the table, empty and waiting for the next tribunal. Last, as his eyes perused the limestone walls, he lifted his stare and saw the reason for the heavenly name of the council. The beams of the ceiling jutted out like a rib cage supporting the roof in the peaks of Gothic arches and in between each arch, the plaster painted the color of the night sky and pocked with rosettes of golden stars. They appeared to twinkle as they caught the light from the candles.

At the back of the room, a door opened and two men entered. The first Kit knew and dreaded. Sir Walsingham nodded to Philip and presented the second man to him. They exchanged introductions as Kit studied the new man. Except for the fact he dressed in a black robe with a flat black cap on his head, only one word described him in Kit's mind. Gray. Gray eyes, gray beard and gray aura. He walked with a stick in his right hand and with each step, he let out a grunt. Philip bowed low before him and called him 'your Grace.'

Everyone ignored Kit, so he leaned up against the wall and squared his shoulders in attention as Philip commanded. Sir Walsingham's face looked sour as he spoke.

"Sidney, this, as you know, is Lord Burghley. He is interested in our visit to France. As you also know, things are collapsing there. We have much work to do for our Queen. That said, Lord Burghley will acquaint you with the details of what we must do."

Burghley motioned toward Kit. "Who is this boy?"

"This boy is my page, your Grace," Sidney answered.

Burghley's voice rumbled out. "Boy! Fetch me a chair before my legs give way."

Kit scurried as quick as his legs could carry him, taking a chair off the dais and setting it near the old man. Burghley sat with a grunt and grabbed Kit's arm as he turned to leave. "What's your name, boy?"

Walsingham interjected. "His name is nothing but Page, a blank page waiting for our mark. Isn't that right, boy?"

Burghley's gruff rattled in his throat. "Nonsense! Let me look at you." He curled his arthritic fingers below Kit's chin. "Yea, there is that ambitious spark in those amber eyes. I must say, Walsingham, you are clever to spy out such young ones. Speak up, boy, and tell me your given name and why you are here."

Kit swallowed the fear in his throat. "Christopher Marlowe, sir, and I am here to serve the Queen." He paused, and then, truth rolled off his tongue in a blast. "And I want to be her favorite playwright."

Lord Burghley's throat grumbled with laughter as Philip popped Kit on the back of the head. "Don't scold the boy, Sidney. He is ambitious and bold, qualities we admire and use. Stay the course, boy. Stay the course. With that boldness, I daresay to predict you will be a great playwright. Now, go away. Sit there at the wall while the three of us discuss our business."

Kit bowed and turned away into the shadows, far enough from

their faces, but close enough to hear the words.

Burghley cleared his throat and continued. "We have received news from Paris on the marriage of the Prince of Navarre to King Charles' sister. The festivities have begun as well as the rioting. Both Protestants and Catholic's rail because of this interfaith alliance. Two years have passed since the Edict of Pacification which ended the bloody war and resulted in a concession of Catholic France to allow toleration of Protestant worship. This marriage, this final act of reconciliation, fills the streets with Huguenot noblemen decked in their robes and hidden harquebusiers. Unfortunately, not only has the alliance brought out the Calvinists, but every religious zealot and fanatic screaming for blood and martyrdom."

Walsingman continued the story. "Yea, and the reports surge. Just last week, before sailing back to England, I heard of the account of a Catholic mob in Provence attacking and killing a group of Huguenots. They trampled their corpses, ripped out the pages of their Protestant Bibles and stuffed the pages in their mouths to muffle their screams. And the other side is not exempt from depravity. I have heard hundreds of Protestants are using the Catholic dissolution as an excuse for murdering anyone who protects the host or holy wafers."

Philip scratched his chin. "What of the Pope? What does he say?"

Burghley's chair squeaked under his weight. He grunted and answered. "Ha! The Pope? He has condemned the marriage as an insult to God and a danger to souls, even as he continues to blast our own Queen, calling her a heretic and bastard."

"And the Queen? What are her thoughts?"

Walsingham answered. "Her Majesty recognizes the importance of this marriage. The Edict must hold and the alliance between France and England must stand despite this posturing from fanatics. We must be very careful and clever. The threads weaving between these two religions are dividing families, governments and souls. A tip of the scales will send us into an age of religious war judging and weighing every man's movements, from pauper to Prince."

"Pray tell, what is the next move," Philip asked.

Walsingham spoke, "'Tis this: over the past few months I have been negotiating a marriage between our Queen and one of King Charles' younger brothers. At first we hoped for an agreement for Henry, the Duke of Anjou, but his crazed antics and his disgusting affinity for those of his own sex have prevented the match. Something Her Majesty discovered on his visit here, but, that is a story for another time, gentlemen. Now, we have only the Duke of Alencon. I am fighting a battle for Her Majesty. The Spanish Ambassador and the Papal Nuncio in Paris are wrangling me at every turn. Not only that, but here in England we have an enemy to her marriage."

Burghley laughed. "Indeed! Never fear him, Walsingham. I have my eye on Robert Dudley. He has placed his ambitions on wedding and bedding the Queen, but with my voice in her ear, it will never happen. He seeks to keep her close, but men such as he crumple under their own aspirations. The succession of Queen Elizabeth's throne is everything to the Church of England. I do not envy you, Walsingham, for these negotiations are full of perplexities."

"Well spoke, Lord Burghley. My private life has made me utterly unacquainted with that skill that the dealings in prince's affairs require. But I am learning the stealthiness of watching and listening and keeping quiet. S'wounds, I am learning!"

The long chamber door squeaked open upon the iron hinges and the flurried noise of laughter and silk rustled into the room. A jeweled hand lifted a lantern blanketing the room in a glow with the candlelight and her presence. Kit tucked himself deeper into the shadows as the Queen's white face blazed through the darkness. She giggled and nudged a stranger trailing behind her. No stranger, Kit saw, as he came up beside her decked in the cheerful golden doublet of a courtier. Robert Dudley took her by the hand and bowed before the three men seated in the chamber. Elizabeth caressed her fingers across his hand, then weaved in between those seated until she stood before Walsingham; the corner of her mouth curled in a mischievous grin.

"Pray tell, Master Secretary, what are you learning?"

Walsingham bolted from his seat and bent over her hand.

"Learning, your Majesty? I am learning what it means to humble myself in your presence."

The Queen's laughter rolled out in a deep wave as she stood

amid the men. She twirled around and wiggled her finger at each of them.

"Humble yourself? Ha! Which of you knows the meaning of the word? There is not one of you in whom ambition does not burn in your heart," she narrowed her eyes at Dudley, "or in your loins." She sat in the chair Kit fetched for Burghley, her watery blue gown cascading from her tiny waist like a waterfall.

She flicked her fingers for the men to stand before her, her lilting voice transforming into the authoritative air of her position. "Tell me, Lord Burghley, are you discussing the question of our marriage to the Duke of Alencon?"

Burghley lowered his stare and answered her. "Your Majesty, the topic arose briefly."

She glanced over at Dudley whose brow wrinkled upon the mention of the marriage. "No more talk of that today, sirs, for we have other things on our mind. Tonight, at Court, we will announce our wish to visit the Earl of Leicester at his home in Kenilworth soon, but before we will consent to a visit, it is our wish for Dudley to see to the rumors of Catholic factions forming there and to check the loyalties of our subjects in the surrounding villages. Walsingham, are you not supposed to be attending to your duties in Paris as our ambassador?"

Walsingham bowed before her. "Yea, your Majesty."

"Then, pray tell, why are you still here with the marriage of the Prince of Navarre to the King's sister so close on our heels?"

Kit leaned out of the shadows, amazed at the power emanating from her words, bending these men to her will.

Walsingham answered. "My Queen, I came to continue acquiring useful tools for your protection."

The Queen looked to Sidney. "And are you one of those useful tools, Master Sidney?"

Sidney's words trembled over his lips. "Yea, my lady, for whatever purpose to serve you."

The Queen spat out a sigh. "We thought you merely a simple poet, Master Sidney. Are you going to write us a sonnet giving us your opinion of our marriage to the King's brother?"

Philip kept his stare to the floor. "Nay, my lady, for my opinion is of no account to your ears."

She flicked her hand to dismiss him. "And so let it remain for you."

Try as he might, Kit could not keep his feet from tingling to sleep. He scrunched his eyes and stretched out his limp legs, unaware the movement swayed the arras and revealed his hiding spot. As he opened his eyes, the Queen's eyes peered toward him.

"We see, sirs, that we have a little rat spying on us from behind an arras. Come here, boy."

Kit stood on wobbly legs and removed the felt cap from his head. The Queen took his small hand in hers. "Who are you, boy?"

Walsingham, again, spoke. "This boy is a page to Sidney, your Majesty."

She arched her eyebrow. "Indeed? Can he not answer for himself? Tell me your name, boy."

Kit's words cracked over his tongue. "Christopher Marlowe, your Majesty. I am to be your favorite playwright one day."

The Queen cut her eyes to Dudley and laughed. "My favorite? Ah, Robin, seems you to have a rival for our attention." She lifted Kit's chin with her fingertips and peered into his eyes. "You are so sure in your words, young Marlowe, and we might even believe it. There is something behind those clever golden eyes of yours. Tell me, Walsingham, what are your plans for this boy?"

Walsingham answered, his words bent toward leaning the Queen's thoughts. "Nothing more, your Majesty, than to attend Philip in Paris. Philip is accompanying me as an honored guest in my house in the Quai des Bernardins. We will have an excellent view across the Seine as the marriage of the Protestant Prince of Navarre takes place beneath the shadow of Notre Dame. Philip will serve as a witness to the events unfolding there and I wish for my page, Nicholas Faunt, to tutor the boy as a provocateur. Nicholas is waiting for me in Dover. He will shuttle messages between your Majesty, Lord Burghley and myself. Somehow, as Lord Burghley, we foresee this boy as a useful tool in service to her Majesty, even if is by use of his skills as a writer. The quill can be a mighty voice in swaying the minds of a nation."

The Queen mussed Kit's hair and pinched his chin between her thumb and forefinger. "We will have to keep our eye on you, Master Marlowe. For your boldness, you have quite captured our notice. Be obedient and loyal to your tutor Sidney and to my servant Walsingham and we daresay you will rise like a sparrow on the wind."

Walsingham turned toward Kit. In the candlelight, he glared that noxious smile again. Kit's stomach knotted as Walsingham directed his words toward him.

"What say you, boy, are you ready for your first ocean voyage?"

IV

The heat of August sweltered Paris. The city appeared ravished, even more than London, beneath the strains of religious metamorphosis. As the coach passed through the South-western gate of the city wall, poor women in rags clutched their rosaries and called out for mercy and bread in one breath, revenge and blood in the next. In truth, with a King and royal family leaning more toward familiarity with the Holy Father, the Catholics appeared to be winning. And winning meant trouble for England, so Philip taught to Kit on their journey across the Channel.

The firm earth felt a blessing beneath Kit's feet. The voyage across the ocean, his first experience on a ship, taxed his young body. Most of the trip he spent in bed, a small cot allotted to him in the same quarters as Nicholas Faunt, the young lanky twelve-year-old spy with golden hair and dark eyes. Young, to be sure, Kit noted, yet so mature, so quick, so astute to his assignment that no one ever noticed his age. Kit learned from Philip that Walsingham picked him from the streets of London where he honed his skills as a thief. He disliked him from the first, more so since Nicholas spent the trip making fun of him as he vomited in the chamber pot.

Kit shrugged against the open window of the coach as they sped past Le Louvre Palace, up along the Seine, near the unfinished Pont Neuf and arrived at the English Ambassador's house on the Quai. The city gleamed beneath the summer sun with her plastered palace and mansard roofs, still Kit peered in desperation for his "friend." The wheels bumped along the cobblestones forming a rhythm in his mind as he counted the number of days since he last wrote. Ten days. Ten days since feeling the warmth of her presence and the comfort of penning a verse. He wondered if she even knew where Paris was.

The coach halted at the entrance to the embassy. Walsingham's wife, Anne and daughter, Frances, stood in the pebbled courtyard waiting to greet the entourage from London. Kit thought the scene odd to see a moment of gentleness in Walsingham's face as he leaned over to kiss his wife's cheek and pat his daughter's head. 'Twas a brief gesture and his face returned to its mysterious air. Walsingham came near to Nicholas, who stood next to Kit at the coach.

"Nicholas, you know your duty. Report to me anything about the matter of the marriage and of the State. Go now. Tomorrow is the feast day of Saint Bartholomew and my skin crawls with a premonition."

Nicholas bowed and vanished back through the iron gate into the streets of Paris. Anne scurried her husband, Philip and Kit into the manor, directing trunks and persons to their respective rooms. She assigned Kit to a small anteroom attached to Philip's garderobe, nothing more than a hovel with a rag-stuffed mattress on the floor. Contentment swept over him, though, when his small trunk arrived and he opened the lid. There, cradled in the pillow of his only cloak, lay his portfolio and a bottle of ink. When he popped open the bottle and held the pot to his nose, the hairs on the back of his neck tickled under her breath. Calliope formed right behind him and wrapped her arms around his shoulders.

The queasiness faded away along with the fear and he fell asleep on the mattress. The moon ambled across the sky, glowing through the windows like God's lantern on the secrets in the streets and illuminating upon the embassy three hours before dawn. Kit awoke deep into the night to the distant sound of bells. Footsteps scuffed through the hallways of the manor and Philip's room blazed with candlelight. He rubbed his eyes and padded into the garderobe, just in time to hear Walsingham's voice whisper through the air.

"Philip, come along to the council room and bring your page. The bells of Saint Germain l'Auxerrois peal and Nicholas has returned with a breathless report. The King's Admiral, de Coligny, almost lost his life two days ago when fired upon after leaving Le Louvre. I just received an envoy from Lord Burghley sent shortly after we left London. The letter says that King Charles reported to the French Ambassador in London that the act stemmed from nothing more than enmity between the house of Coligny and his brother, the Duke of Guise. As I suspected and with Nicholas' report, there is more to this matter. Come at once. We will be safer if we gather on the second floor."

Philip grabbed Kit's arm and the three of them sped through the corridors, their shadows stretching like long arms from the flickering candle in Walsingham's hand. As soon as they reached the council room, another barrage of church bells cried across Paris. Walsingham threw back the arras covering the window and stood as a dark specter gazing out across the Seine. Through the hazy glass, the unmistakable pop of gunfire pierced the air along with the building roar of a rioting crowd. Nicholas rushed into the room, slammed the door against the wall and fell at the feet of Walsingham.

"My lord, there is more news! The King sends word of rioting in Saint Germain, but he has it under control. Also, the Admiral is safe and guarded by his own men. He sends a guard to your home, my lord, with the message that you and your household are under his protection."

Walsingham eased the door shut and looked at Philip, his eyebrow arched upward. "Under his protection? If all is well, then why does this house need protecting?"

Philip nodded in agreement. "You think there is more to this?"

"Indeed, there is," Walsingham replied.

Kit's heart throbbed in his ears while they waited. The sand in the gilt hourglass on the mantel sifted away as the household sat in silence. Anne and her daughter huddled together on a divan tucked away in a dark corner of the room. Walsingham and Sidney convened in private whispers near the window and Kit balled up in a wide-eyed mass on a chair near the fireplace with his knees pulled up to his chin. Kit jumped from his seat as the sound of pounding echoed through the manor, the words rushing to his tongue.

"Master Sidney, the front door!"

Walsingham grabbed hold of him and slapped a hand over Kit's mouth. "Shut up, you stupid pox. Listen...."

The pounding grew louder, vibrating the oak door. Walsingham made no move toward responding to the pleading requests of a fist against the door frame. Philip walked to the window and pulled the arras back across, blanketing the room in darkness.

Kit whispered a question. "Why, my lord, what is happening?"

The back door of the council room opened and Marie, the scullery maid, broke the darkness with a candle in her grip. Behind her a stranger appeared dressed in the common clothes of a horse groom, his wide eyes stricken with pain. Sir Walsingham stepped forward as Philip reached for his dagger.

"Present yourself, sir!"

The man removed the flat beret from his head and bowed, his English words soaked in a French accent. "Sir Walsingham, I am Seigneur de Briquemault, lieutenant to the King's Admiral, de Coligny. I came at my own peril across the rooftops of Paris and down the river Seine to report to you what has happened. Nay, what is happening. De Coligny is dead. This morning, a group of men claiming allegiance to the Duc l'Guise burst into the Admiral's room and speared him through with a pike. The Duc stood in the street below, waiting for the assailants to open the window and throw the Admiral's body out. Hundreds descended en masse upon the body, dragging and hacking him through the streets. The crowd delivered his head to Le Louvre Palace. His murder done, the ringing of the bells of Saint Germain signaled a slaughter. It is upon us, Sir Walsingham. The Swiss Guards have taken to the streets and the Huguenots are being massacred. The mob is growing to include any commoner with a dagger, torch and sword; and, I fear, they are intent on divesting Paris of all Protestants. There are rumors this slaughter is happening upon the King's command with the blessing of his Holiness."

Walsingham closed his eyes and scratched his beard in thought. "This is most distressing. We thank you for the risk you took to tell us this news. You are safe in my home. Nicholas, go carefully back into the streets to see what more you can learn. Christopher, take Seigneur de Briquemault and see him bestowed with a place to rest his head."

Just as Kit turned to the lieutenant, a blood-curdling scream shivered through the room from outside the window and an ominous glow seeped below the tassels at the bottom of the arras. Walsingham grabbed the edge and snatched back the tapestry until everyone in the room gazed upon the spectacle in the courtyard—a concise message before the Protestant Ambassador's eyes and a message to England. The dead littered the street in front of the house. Crazed Catholic sympathizers swarmed like locusts, eyes raging, brows furrowed with anger, daggers flashing, as they stacked wood against the stripped trunk of the young elm tree near the pathway to the front door.

Kit could not look at the flames. His eyes rested, instead, upon a pair of turtle doves cowering in the eaves of the safe house. The glow of the fire turned their white breast feathers into pink, the warmth closing their eyes into a dreamy sleep. They coo-ed an airy peace midst the cleansing madness sanctioned by the holy father of Rome, Gregory XIII. Still, he felt the heat warming his own cheek through the thin glass. The smell of burning flesh singed the inside of his nostrils, the nauseating scent drifting from the inferno raging right below the window. Without knowing why, his eyes fell upon her. The woman, the Protestant sacrifice, writhed in a horrid dance with the flames, her face contorting and looking to heaven for relief. She burned too slow, a common practice assigned for heathens, for heretics and now, for Huguenots. *Too much wood and consummation burned too quick,* he heard them yelling. *Their skin and bones needing to purge for their sins and the sins of their fathers.* Without a thought to the others in the room gathering behind him, or to those fierce-faced zealots yelling and brandishing their fists toward Walsingham's house, he leaned forward and rested his forehead against the blown glass. His stomach retched as he watched her skin char into black, her hair sizzle away, and her whole being melt away like wax into a bubbling pool of blood and ash.

He traced his fingers along the cross-hatched leaded patterns as Calliope sparked the hint of a play in his mind. He whispered, "This will be a night of remembrances, dear lady, dear Paris. Your death will not go unnoticed. I will write of this for you one day."

A chill crept over Kit as tears filled the corner of his eye and trailed down his cheek. He looked over at Philip, who walked near and placed a hand on his shoulder.

"It is enough, boy."

Kit's words shivered across his trembling lip. "Look at them all, sir, lighting the streets of Paris like torches and bloodying the Seine as sacrifices. Sir, what do you think she thought of when she took her last breath? Do you think she thought of her sins or her blessings?"

Philip placed his palm on Kit's head and mussed his hair. "Come, now, boy, I said enough for you. These are things which need not trouble you."

"Please, sir, answer me."

Walsingham revealed himself from the shadows of the room, pulling the arras back further from the window. He grabbed Kit by the shoulders and faced him again to the window.

"Stop coddling him, Philip. This is our just cause, boy. This is what we are fighting against. Yea, the tide has shifted and now France will side with her Catholic sisters of Rome and Spain. A fell wind is stirring into a tempest that will rage against our Queen, sending out lightening in the form of assassins who will plot until she is dead. Your training begins at a momentous time, boy. Write this in your little portfolio, that you were present to see history unfold. So, answer the question for yourself, boy; what would you think on if you took your last breath?"

Nine years of his life passed by in a sigh. He had seen too much of the world out the window and yet, knew so little. There were too many memories to pick just one and they opened before him like a fan, and he found himself hurrying through them as if at any moment a Catholic soldier of Christ might rush upon them, tie him by the wrists and slice his throat. Yet, in his memories, he could not tell which were the sins and which the blessings.

His words slipped from watery to dry. "I remember my first book."

"Tell me, then, what was it," Walsingham pawed.

"'Twas Ovid's Metamorphoun, the only thing my mother ever gave me. She gave it to me to keep me quiet, yet from the moment I opened the pages, words have filled my brain. There are neither sins nor blessings, only words."

Walsingham turned to Sidney and shook his head. "Another poet I must harden. Yes, it is enough for you, boy. Philip, write an envoy and I will send Nicholas post haste to the Queen with the news of Paris. The Huguenots are ravished. You must leave in secret in the morning with my wife, daughter and your page. Paris is no longer a safe place to be, especially if King Charles ordered this fray. I myself will follow upon the will of my Queen. Now, boy, let your mind fix upon these base matters, for this sight will fit you for the day when you shall revenge these bloody deeds with your own bare hands."

The thought of revenge sat ill with Kit, and a chill quivered his bottom lip. "But, sir, I do not want to kill, I want to write."

Walsingham towered over him, the dying flames casting shadowy lines across his face. "More matter with less art, boy. All things will come in time. Remember my words I spoke to you in Canterbury. Have patience and your Queen will give you your heart's wish, if only you do these necessary things for her. She admires the boys of England who devote themselves to her so entirely and I am sure when you have done a few things to acquire her notice, she will grant you anything you desire. Perhaps one day when you are older and have proven yourself, you will be her court playwright. Remember the notice she gave you at Westminster?"

Kit's gaze progressed from the tiled floor upward upon Walsingham's black robe and held upon the firelight glowing against the white lining peeking out inside of the sleeve. The color fixed his eyes as words to describe the shimmering satin flashed in his mind: devil red, scarlet red, bloody red.

Walsingham shook him hard until their eyes connected. "I said, would you like that?"

Kit touched the tears stinging his cheeks, and he sucked in the air as the tears and snot gathered and rattled above his lip. His voice squeaked as he answered Walsingham in innocence. "I want to go home, sir."

Walsingham's eyes narrowed and his smile stretched, like the cat about to bite. "Home, boy? You are home."

Kit turned to Philip, who kept his stare away from the boy. "Please, sir, I want my father and my mother."

Walsingham knelt until they were eye to eye. He clasped Kit's arm in his grip, wrapping around and tightening until his fingers almost met.

"Boy, England is your father now, and Elizabeth, your mother; and I am your guardian upon her request."

Kit snatched his arm away and yelled, "My name is Christopher Marlowe, not boy!"

Walsingham grabbed hold of him again and tossed him onto the floor like a poppet. "Your name means nothing, boy. You are a blank page for me to write upon, a purchased pawn to use and dispose with as I wish. I bought and paid for you, so be glad, for your birth parents sit comfortable at their fire with ducats to spare for sacrificing their son."

Kit rubbed his arm and caressed the tender bruising beneath the skin. Lifting his stare, he caught Philip's sad glare. "Sir, 'tis not true. My father did not sell me..."

Kit's words trailed away as he saw the answer in Philip's eyes. He clenched his teeth as the tears filling his eyes dried into a stone coldness. He felt as if he were vanishing, burning away into ash. Truth and innocence sucked into a void from which, when lost, no man can claim again. At that moment, he knew there would be no more splashing in the puddles after a spring rain, no more catching frogs on the muddy banks of the Stour, and no more safety of a home with a warming fire. *Bought and sold.* Now, the puddles turned bloody and the frogs into treasonous Catholics whom Walsingham will flay and spike. And, as always, and for the rest of his life, words filtered into his mind.

Change invokes change, shock upon shock... betrayal is wormwood, indeed, and knows no age.

They sat at the ready, prepared to leave, for the next three days. The King ordered the city gates locked as the rioting and slaughtering continued. No one could leave or enter. The death of the Protestant Admiral sparked a craving for blood slashing the streets of Paris like the red strokes from an artist's brush. Briquemault stayed in the house, flinching as a scared mouse at the slightest movement. He had reason to fear, Kit knew, for the crowds raged for De Coligny's men. Nicholas drifted in and out of the house like a phantom, keeping Walsingham informed of the news. He told the story of the remains of De Coligny's body, now swaying from a gibbet in Montfaucon, and how the bodies of those slain littered the banks of the Seine downstream from Le Louvre. He said there were stories that the King feasted over the gore, raising his goblet and announcing to the mob that the smell of his dead enemy wafted sweet and delightful to his nose.

Walsingham tapped his fingers on the table and thanked Nicholas for his service. He looked across at Philip as Kit poured more ale into Philip's cup.

"The Edict crumbles," Walsingham sighed, "as well as any
prospect of the marriage of our Queen to the Duke of Alencon.
Even if peace returns and our Protestant brothers given assurance
by the King that no more blood will spill, the toleration of their
worship is done. We must assure every survivor that England will
welcome them and give them sanctuary. A new age has begun,
Philip. We must become crafty and train these clever boys, like
your page, to slice the throats of Rome's pawns, delving one step
below them all and blowing them to the moon."

Kit could take no more. He ran to the garderobe and spewed
out the croissant and clotted cream he ate for breakfast. Yet, there
was so much more he wanted to vomit from his insides. Leaning
over the chamber pot, he retched until blood mingled with his
saliva and snot. And then he cried. Not a simple whimpering, but a
wail surged from a dark place deep inside his gut.

No one came to check on him, no one except his friend, who
lifted him off his scraped knees and laid him on the cot. She
wrapped her arms around him as he shivered hard against the floor.
He felt so alone and lost, the first of many to shadow his life.

She dried his tears with her hair, took the quill out of the trunk
and curled his fingers around the slender shaft. He sat up and
wiped his nose across the sleeve of his shirt, leaving behind a
streak. She lifted his chin with her fingers and looked deep into his
eyes.

"My darling Kit, betrayal and pain are gifts to a writer. Take
this experience, take this pain and use it, for in these tears and
blood is the meat of a mighty play. Always remember this, life is
food to a writer filled with thousands of characters. Your
experiences woven into your words will speak your name for
generations. They will be tiny morsels, clues hidden like
sweetmeats tucked in a pastry. Now, dry your tears and write..."

The first line opened as a cocoon, morphing the simpering boy
into the outstretched wings of a poet. As if the city of Paris wept
onto the page, he began the play with the deceptive words of a
King, yet he knew years would pass before he had the courage to
finish, to recall the blood of that evening. He scrawled the title on a
clean page.

The Massacre of Paris

Before dawn on the fourth day, Philip, Anne, Frances and Kit raced in a coach through the north-western gate of the city. They sat in silence, jostling below the starless night with the curtains on the coach window drawn tight, and praying no one stop them. No one did.

Still, none of them breathed a sigh of relief until they reached Calais. Kit pulled back the curtain to peek, thankful to see the ripping waters of the Channel before him and thankful that in less than a day, his feet would tread those mossy shores of Dover. His hopeful heart prayed things might return to normal once when he breathed English air.

V

Kit fidgeted near the doors of Canterbury Cathedral while Philip talked with the Archbishop. Looking across the dirt road at the swans floating with the current on the Stour river, the city looked like a stranger. Nothing felt the same since leaving Paris. A gray veil covered his world.

Two schoolboys ran past him, laughing and kicking up dirt as they volleyed a small leather ball between them. Kit ignored them. His youthful interest in such pastimes died in Paris.

Philip and the Archbishop disappeared through the doors, leaving Kit alone on the portico. He looked to the left, his eyes tracing the path of the street veering southward to his father's house. With no thought in his head, his feet followed his gaze.

Leaving the crisp green grass around the Cathedral, Kit reached the rank bustling streets of the Shambles. Past the sweet aroma of the butter market and the soot of the blacksmith, the mud streets baked in the sun and the toothless shopkeepers called out for customers. Even in the distance, the green barley fields on the verge of bursting into gold brought nothing but flatness to his heart. His ear did not bend to the baaing of black-faced sheep penned in the butcher's yard, nor could he taste the sweetness of the ocean spray misting in the breeze. Sadness weighted his every step, and more so as he rounded a bend in the road and lifted his stare to the house where he once lived.

Frozen in time and as he remembered. The two-story narrow with her thatched roof draping over the eyes of the windows, the garden overrun with blue hollyhocks, a stone gray milk cow grazing in the side yard, and the cobbler's wife bobbing up and down along the rows of her weedy vegetables. Unrefined, but almost perfect.

The picture showed his father absent, yet a small lantern swayed from a hook near the door of his shop. Kit stood at a distance and watched his mother. Age had overtaken her once fair face, leaving behind trails of wrinkles and silvery hair peeking out from under her linen cap. She looked leathery and brown, much like the brown hide used by his father as he stretched a new pair of boots. He took a step forward, then froze in his tracks as she rose and wiped her apron across her brow. Their eyes connected for a moment. He felt the urge to wave and the corner of his mouth twitched to smile as he waited for a sign from her. She held her hand over her eyes to shield the sun, flicked away a buzzing fly and picked up a basket of leeks. As she turned away and sauntered toward the house, a small girl with reddish-brown ringlets toddled behind her.

Jane, he thought, *the little sister who used to snuggle beneath my arm.* His gray mood returned. His mother did not recognize him, or chose not to acknowledge him. Kit knew they forgot him and had moved on with their life. There was no love or pining for him in that house. He turned back to the city and kicked a rock into a puddle. He stood for a moment to watch the pebble sink and disappear into the murky water.

By the time he reached the Cathedral, the sun hovered just above the horizon and blanketed Canterbury in a hazy orange glow. Philip met him on the pathway and grabbed him by the cloak, jerking him toward the entrance to the church.

"Idiot boy, where have you been?"

Kit winced from the tightness of Philip's fingers twisting his collar. He dragged Kit into the nave and pushed him hard onto a chair.

The Archbishop appeared from the darkness and tossed a portfolio next to Kit. Kit recognized the familiar worn leather as his own and he grabbed it up, holding the pages against his chest.

"Master Sidney has obliged me with snippets your poetry. I must say, I am quite moved. Your verse technique is different. Tell me, are you still visited by your angel?"

Kit's heart fluttered thinking of Calliope. He knew they would never understand, so he answered with a lie. "Nay, sir, that was just childish fancies. Everything I have learned is from here at the King's School and from Master Sidney."

The Archbishop gruffed in this throat. "Nay, I do not believe it. There is something more to you. Something Sir Walsingham has seen, as well as your Master here. Tell me, Philip, what is this quality setting him apart from his peers?"

Philip threw back his cloak over his shoulder. "In truth, your Grace, he possesses that passion that every poet aspires to gain; he was birthed under a rhyming planet. That is why our bargain is well-placed. We must encourage his skill, for I foresee a brain used in service to our country. King Harry used playwrights and players to show the people of England the vices of the Catholic Church, thus entertainment became the Crown's means of propagating the new faith. Who knows, perhaps one day, the realm will esteem him as her highest mind, as long as he continues in the correct direction."

The Archbishop raised Kit's chin until their eyes met. "Yea, between the three of us, we will keep any ambition he may have in check. Tell me, boy, do you have anything binding you to Canterbury anymore?"

Kit paused before answering, thinking again of that rickety house and his parents sitting at their hearth: his mother darning socks and father straddling the cobbling bench tapping iron pins into the bottom of a new pair of shoes. Perhaps she told him of the boy she saw on the roadway near the parish church. Perhaps they pondered the possibility of the boy being their dear lost son. Kit shrugged at the pretty thought, succumbing to the shivering reality of truth.

Kit answered him, his stare falling to the floor. "Nay, sir, there is not."

Philip reached across in front of Kit's face and handed the Archbishop a small velvet pouch, the kind a nobleman ties at his belt to carry coin.

"See, Archbishop, 'tis settled. I will continue to patron this boy and see to his tutelage and education. Since nothing binds him here, then we are off to the continent. Sir Walsingham wishes for him schooled in languages and the art of diplomacy. Everything you did to set the boy on the proper path I will tell to the Queen. Just remember, Archbishop, 'tis Walsingham's wish that the boy matriculate to the University, perhaps with your blessing as one of your own scholars? His attendance at Cambridge will offer a double purpose when we return. Not only will he continue to excel in his own skills, but he will keep a squinting eye on any of those educated boys whose ambition directs them toward plotting against our Queen. Lord Burghley tells me in his last letter that suspicion grows and is well founded since the massacre, that Rome will stoop to using espionage to infiltrate and coerce our University boys with promises of money and glory. We must balance their delving by placing our own loyal pawns."

The Archbishop smiled as he rattled the coin pouch in his fist. "Then a Parker Scholar he will be, sir."

Kit could not wrap his thoughts around the course his life took after they left Canterbury. His stomach cramped. Philip's demeanor softened on the way back to Dover, even stopping the coach at a farmhouse near the forest of Castle Coldred so Kit might get a fresh cup of milk. Philip smiled at Kit and brushed his finger over his lip to wipe away the cream collecting there. Kit even managed a sideways curl of his lip; small, but enough. With his belly soothed and the coach swaying back and forth along the road, sleep weighed down his eyes. They flickered and fluttered as the images out the window zoomed by, and the night came fast swathing the countryside in gloom. His eyes drew to slits and through his lashes he saw a small sparrow. The bird lighted out of an elm tree and banked against the breeze, rising higher and higher until the fog rolling in off the ocean enveloped her.

Philip nudged him awake as the coachman reined in the horses. Kit rubbed his eyes and gazed across the beach. The fog broke, and the moon cast out her shimmering silver jewels across the breaking waves. A massive three-mast ship rocked off the coast, silhouetted against the sparkling water. Philip opened the door as the soft light of a lantern lighted upon the familiar face of Nicholas Faunt. Philip took the lantern from his hand, latched it near the door and motioned for Nicholas to take a seat.

"Nicholas, how is your master and my friend?"

He bowed to Philip and cut his eyes toward Kit. "Sir Walsingham is well, sir. He sends his greetings to you and bid me meet you here with this letter."

Philip took the letter and broke the wax seal. His eyes brushed across the words and he handed the page to Kit. "Here, boy, time to earn your keep. Read it aloud for us."

Kit rubbed his eyes, trying to wipe away the stinging tiredness. Clearing his throat, he began:

"To my most honorable friend, Philip Sidney. Dispensing with pleasantries, things here have sunk into such an oubliette of darkness that any hope of salvage vanishes into the pit. Nicholas is bearing a complete rendering of the happenings here in Paris to Lord Burghley and to the Queen. Since you left, the mob dragged Briquemault from my protection and slaughtered him. I escaped only with my life and am now in hiding. King Charles has now become so bloody that it is impossible to stay his thirst, even at the expense of quenching it in innocent blood. The King sent for me to his Court and after listening to his protestations of guilt, adding that the massacre was a necessary action against a power hungry conspiracy to seize his throne, all backed might I add, by his mother, Catherine de Medici. O, how well we know of her poisonous hands! Yet, there is more. More that concerns you, Philip. And I pray you will accept this assignment most heartily. I have received an entail that the dark knights of Christs, the Jesuits, were behind this bloody deed. I am inclined to believe this and I fear since they have now overtaken France and joined her back to Rome that now their attention turns to England. We must strengthen our allies, our Protestant brothers on the continent. I know you travel there for much less weighty matters, but I beseech you to use your influence among our Lutheran friends in Germany and Italy to strengthen our Queen's arm. The Jesuits fight with a bloody passion and even our young messengers are at risk now.

I expect young Marlowe to expound his mind upon these matters, for one day I will ask a great favor of him. If he wants not to feel the dagger's point, then payment is due. I am sure you will acquaint him with what it means to be a pawn of Her Majesty. Times have changed, Philip, and if it means for me to look evil in the eye, I will do so while smiling. I have a new motto: Video et taceo. Men will reveal their hearts through their transparent eyes. See and stay silent, for knowledge is a mighty sword. The Queen's ever humble servant, Sir Francis Walsingham."

Kit's eyes widened, and the words tumbled out of his mouth. "What does he mean that payment is due? I have no money!"

Nicholas huffed and slouched against the leather seat. "You

are so stupid. He means you owe him your life. He will keep you alive as long as you please him and the Queen. The moment you are no longer useful....," he drew his fingers across his throat in a long slice, "... off with your head. And he'll feed your entrails to the Jesuits on a silver platter."

Philip thumped Nicholas on the side of the head. "Nicholas! No need to frighten the boy. We will all do what we must because we love our Majesty and the pains she goes through to protect her subjects from the evils of Rome. You may leave us now, Nicholas, and continue on to the Midlands. The Queen is on Royal progress there and awaits word from your master. Come along, boy, for I see the torch light from the skiff at the shoreline waiting to bear us to the ship."

Another journey across the sea. Kit's legs and stomach felt more sea-worthy on the crossing back to Calais, this now being his third voyage. He settled into his days as Philip turned most of their conversations into a lesson in poetry. That made Kit happy. Even Calliope reappeared in his quiet moments, his alone times when Philip slept. His patron even gave him a gift of high quality vellum and a new bottle of ink for the trip. Mussing his hair and pinching his cheek, Philip told him he expected the pages soaked with words, phrases and notes from every place they visit. Along the road to Lorraine, the French countryside swept past them through the coach window filled with windmills, milk cows and French maids toting lavender-filled baskets along the lanes. Philip instructed Kit in the German language anticipating their arrival in Frankfort within a fortnight.

The nights continued to be less peaceful to Kit though. The darkness always brought the blood of Paris, the screeching mouse in the sanctuary and Walsingham's smile. No matter how long Kit tried to keep his eyes open to stay the night, the images always came. And always, as his eyes closed, the bitter flavor of wormwood singed his tongue, sending his dreams into bloody depths. He hated sleep.

After two weeks of traveling, the coach arrived in Frankfort late in the night. From the first, the city frightened Kit, and he hated learning the words. The language did not dance for him, but broke across his tongue in harsh meaty syllables; and the faces in the street appeared stern and formidable. Although Frankfort resembled London in the stench and the buildings, something lurked in the architecture. Smiling gargoyles strained their necks, perched high along the spire of the central Cathedral, overseeing the strangers entering their city. Other eyes glared from the corners of houses, strange dark goblin faces carved into stone and supporting eaves upon their heads. A memory flashed in his mind of the elfin figures carved into the beams below the roof line of his own father's home. The goose flesh raced down his arm. Philip leaned his head out the window of the coach and pointed toward the church.

"Look, Saint Bartholomew's Cathedral."

Kit shivered and repeated the name, recognizing the familiar namesake as the momentous day of the massacre. He looked over at Philip who raised his head toward the moonlight and closed his eyes as he spoke.

"With how sad steps, O Moon, thou climb'st the skies! How silently, and with how wan a face! So like the face of my sorrowful page. What ails you, boy?" Kit shrugged and cowered against the seat as Philip continued. "You are definitely a dark little thing, aren't you?"

The coach came to a halt before a narrow four-storied building, the upper stories overhanging the street and supported by massive pitch beams. Lantern light moved across the window and the front door creaked open. Philip unlatched the coach door and sprung to his feet to greet the lantern-toting man. They exchanged laughter and handshakes as Kit climbed out of the coach. Philip motioned him forward and presented him to the man.

"This is Kit Marlowe, my page. Kit, meet my dear friend, Master Languet. We will spend this year with him before we leave for Italy. He has an exquisite collection of books and if you are a good page, perhaps he will oblige you his library."

Languet bellowed a laugh and his large belly rolled beneath his nightshirt as he answered Philip in broken, German-soaked English.

"Nein, Philip, what would this boy want with my books. Come, come inside. We have so much to catch up on. Much meat to chew on."

Philip and Kit settled into the cozy house and into a routine. Kit kept to his studies, writing letters for Philip, and attending him in secret meetings with fellow reformists. The seasons passed by transforming the gray city twice over in the thawing greens of spring, the heat of summer and the russets of fall. Over the following few months of his eleventh year, as the snow swallowed the city, Kit remained enveloped in warmth at Master Languet's home. The fire in the main hearth always glowed, the arrases covered the windows, and Kit snuggled below the wool blankets on his goose-feathered bed in the room next to Philip. Despite the gloom outside the four walls of the house, he almost felt at home after more than a year of Philip's attempts of succoring alliance with England.

One evening after supper, with his belly full of mulled wine and crusty meat pie, Kit tucked himself in a tufted chair near the hearth. Philip and Languet sat at a trestle table across from him filling their tankards and throats with warm beer. Keeping his eyes closed, his ears pricked upon the mention of his name. He listened to their conversation.

Languet spoke first. "The boy, Kit, what will you do with him?"

Philip answered, "O, he is meant for great things, methinks. However, it is not I who wish to use him. He is for the Crown's use, more specific, for Walsingham. He is not the only one though. Walsingham is developing a scheme for England, an underground spy ring for the protection of Her Majesty and he is molding many such boys as his special soldiers, selecting them at a young age so they are pliable. Unfortunately 'tis a necessary step as the Jesuit faction spreads. So many are selling their souls to the Catholic church, thus my continued visitation to assure our brothers here of England's support."

"Indeed, my friend. And Germany is no different, I fear. There are many scholars and professors of Wittenberg who continue to express a public denouncement of Luther and his reformation. Books are burning on both sides, Philip, and some of our highest minds are selling their souls. The stories are getting grander by the day. Since you have been here, have you heard the story of Johannes Faust?"

"Faust? Nay, I have not."

Languet belched. "Hmm, I am surprised. The story grows wilder each day. There are rumors he has sold his soul to the Devil

himself who has, in turn, endowed him with incredible gifts.
Power, money and glory. In truth, I think the devil wears a pontiff
robe and sits on Saint Peter's throne. They say the Pope made him
sign his name in blood. As I said, the story is grand, but at the heart
of it is the truth of what means the Pope will stoop to eradicate
Protestantism. Chinks go a long way to motivate a person to switch
sides. I have learned there is much truth in art and literature, as you
will attest to tomorrow, my friend."

"Tomorrow? What, pray tell, is tomorrow?"

"Ah, tomorrow we will see a new play. The play is
Callimachus and has much of the same flavor of the story of Faust.
You told me earlier the boy wishes to be a playwright, then this
will be a good lesson for him in politics, as well as prose."

Later that night, Kit dreamed. This time instead of a black
smiling cat, a hunched back dwarf climbed down from the eaves of
Languet's house and poked him in the side with a cane. He jabbed
Kit over and over, prodding him to read aloud a parchment letter in
his hand. After reading it, and without knowing why, Kit dabbed
the end of a quill in an ink pot and signed the bottom with his
name. The letters, as he formed the 'C' to begin his name,
transformed from black ink to the scarlet hue of blood. Kit raised
his gaze, and the dwarf morphed into the figure of Walsingham.
Calliope stood in the distance, her face wet with tears as the words,
"I write in blood to write in ink," resounded in his ears.

He awoke on the floor next to the bed, cold and stiff, with two
sheets of vellum scattered next to him, wet with fresh ink. He
picked up one page, holding it before his eyes. His first inklings of
Faustus on paper. A mighty line glared back at him; a prophetic
line. He spoke the familiar words aloud.

"Si una eademque res legatur duobus, alter rem, alter valorem
rei."

Philip came into Kit's room and took the page from his
fingers. His eyes moved across the paper and he handed the page
back to Kit.

"If one thing is willed to two persons, one person will have the
thing itself, the other the value of the thing. Is this something new
you are working on?"

Kit shrugged. "I remembered writing that a long time ago,

back when the Archbishop first met me. I do not know why, but I dreamed about writing it again last night."

"Very interesting. And the other notes show a play of Faust. So, you were listening to our conversation last eve?"

Kit managed a small smile. "Video et taceo, sir."

Philip laughed. "Well spoke, page. You are learning and Walsingham will smile at your progress. Now, come help me dress for we are off to visit a few of Walsingham's connections before we attend a play this afternoon. But, you know that as well, don't you? We are to see Callimachus written by the Countess Hrotswitha of Gandersheim."

"A woman playwright, sir?"

"Yea," Philip answered, "and why not a woman? A woman can be a mighty writer, as well, boy. My sister, Mary, is quite skilled with the quill. Her education matches mine and the lofty standards of our Queen and counts herself among the intelligent ladies-in-waiting to Her Majesty. Perhaps you will meet her when we return to England. For now, fill your brain with more words to enrich your play of Faustus. Tell me, what will you call your play?"

Kit answered him as he dipped the quill and scrawled the title across the top of the notes. "Doctor Faustus, sir."

Callimachus turned out to be a miracle play. The miracles and the mysteries, plays of Kit's childhood, all designed to persuade or dissuade the common folk's simple brains—the state propaganda of the day. He learned quick that gore or laughter had the same effect off the stage, both swayed thoughts and betrayed hearts. Callimachus was no exception, filling the boards with lust and love, exchanging souls for money, and death. When they returned to Languet's haven, Kit sped to his room to jot notes for his own eventual play. As his quill raced across the paper, Philip entered, his arms wrapped around two large book volumes. He placed them on the corner of Kit's desk and tapped his fingers on the cover. Kit reached across and traced the hand-painted lettering.

"'Tis the Legenda Aurea and a book of the history of Wittenberg University. The Legenda is rich with stories you might transform into plays, such as the story of Theophilus which is very like the tales being told of Faust. I thought you might like to have something to read on our journey to Italy."

Kit place his palm over the books and smiled. "Thank you, sir. We are leaving soon?"

"Well, as soon as the snow melts, we are off to Venice and to Padua. More food for your muse to fill your prodigal mind. First, I have a letter to dispatch to Sir Walsingham about my success here in Frankfort. On your feet, boy, and speed this to Robin Poley. He is another young one hired by Walsingham and ordered to wait for my messages at an inn called the Cock & Hen one block southerly from the Cathedral. You will know him by his red hair and the lazy eye. Now, go to it."

Kit snatched the letter from Philip's hand and sped out the door. The winter wind blasted his face and within ten strides, his cheeks stung from the frigid air. Through the soft dusting of snowflakes, the gray spire of the Cathedral loomed before him. He wound through the streets and along the Rhine River to the destination, pausing once to watch a group of boys slide across the icy banks and across the frozen waters. A verse formed in his mind as he imagined Calliope's hazy figure form beneath the bare branches of an oak tree. The words flowed off his tongue as he continued the trek, committing each word to a footstep and memory.

"When I behold the violet past prime,
And sable curls all silver'd o'er with white;
When lofty trees I see barren of leaves
Which erst from heat did canopy the herd.... thank you Calliope. I'll mark that down, for there is more there to come."

Kit looked up and the painted sign of the inn swayed in the wind. Seated outside on the top of an empty beer barrel, his breath frosting in spurts between his pale lips, a red headed boy waited. Kit kicked his frozen toes on the back of his shins and approached him.

"Are you Robin Poley?"

The boy gruffed and tore off a bite of stale bread in his hand. "What's it to you?"

Kit held out the sealed letter. "I have a message from my Master Sidney for..." Before he could utter another word, the boy hopped from his perch and slapped his hand over Kit's mouth. He pulled him into the alleyway at the side of the inn and, after taking the letter from Kit's grip, threw Kit into a bank of snow.

"You are so stupid! Keep your mouth shut! Do you not know who may listen? Do you want our necks sliced?"

Kit stood and brushed the flakes from his breeches. Feeling the heat rising in his neck and tired of being called stupid, he charged Poley with both hands balled.

Poley laughed and tripped him back into the snow. "Well, now, you are a rounder, huh? 'Tis a good thing to have if you do this bit of work. What's your name?"

Kit brushed his breeches, once more, and bit his lip. "What is it to you?"

Robin snickered and held out his hand to Kit. "Fair enough. Are you hungry?"

"What?"

"Here," the boy said, as he held out a piece of the bread. Kit took the offering and chomped on the morsel, watching his odd companion as he sat in the snow and leaned his back against the side of the alehouse.

"So, you are another of Walsingham's pigeons, I take it."

Kit wiped his mouth with the back of his hand and nodded. Robin continued, "I thought so. Yes, my name is Robin Poley and I am fifteen. My family is from Coventry, but I was living with my uncle in Bishopsgate in London when Walsingham recruited me. What about you?"

"I am from Canterbury and I am eleven. Walsingham did not recruit me, he bought and paid for me like a slave when I was eight years old."

Robin rolled a huff between his teeth. "I guess it matters not how we were acquired for the fact remains that 'tis done and our lives now rest upon whether Caesar Walsingham turns his thumb toward heaven or hell."

Kit scuffed his foot through the snow until the wet cobblestones beneath his feet shined in the sunlight. "And what happens of those whom he turns down his thumb? Have you ever seen him murder?"

Robin stood back up, patting his chilled backside with his palms.

"Plenty of times. Too many to recall. Walsingham has a clever way of winning a boy to his confidence and then, if he discovers the boy to be inept, sloven or a betrayer, he has sliced the boy's throat himself. Yet, now all he has to do is to reveal the name to some underground spy of Rome, France or Spain, and they are ready to take out these fledglings of Walsingham. You know, I have learned you can never be sure of who is working double."

Kit rubbed the ink spot on his forefinger. "Well, 'tis not going to be that way for me. I will not remain a pawn for Walsingham or anyone else."

He caught Robin looking at his fingers and he ceased the gesture. Robin snickered. "So says every boy whom Walsingham captures in his web. What makes you any different?"

Kit lifted his chin. "I am Christopher Marlowe, one day favorite courtier and playwright to Her Majesty."

Robin folded his arms over his stomach and belted out a laugh. He reached inside his doublet and held out a sealed letter. "Then, here, Sir Christopher, take this straightaway to your Master Sidney, for it is a message from your lady."

Kit snatched the letter. He could still hear Robin's laughter as he tore back through the streets toward Languet's home.

VI

Philip opened the letter and the corners of his mouth sagged. "She wants me to return. I am summoned to Court and given instructions to attend Her Majesty as her cup bearer." He crumpled the letter in his fingers. "Her cup bearer? What nonsense! Her silly command means she is unhappy with my pursuits here on the continent, thinking them of little use." Philip looked over at Kit and shrugged. "And so, I am sent for and as I scrounge for crumbs from her table, I go. And you, boy, will continue to attend me. You have grown since last she saw you and now, it seems, you will get a taste of Court life. Ah, I see that ambitious glint in your eye, but do not be so hasty to win her favor. She takes as easy as she gives, just look at me."

ଈୠ

Kenilworth Castle glowed like a blissful bride on the day of her wedding. Kit heard from Sidney's own mouth that Dudley's intentions were to have the Queen arrive during this yearly royal progress across the Midlands with thoughts of marriage on her mind. The Queen's entourage trained through the villages from London loaded with twelve ebony coaches to carry her Court, majestic white palfreys decked in hand-tooled golden bridles and a row of red-coated warders leading the way. They snaked through the countryside, stopping often at a dairy farm for the Queen to give alms, taking a night's rest at Hampton Court, again at Windsor, onward to Coventry, until, lastly, the turrets of Kenilworth, decked with the royal standard of the Queen alongside the green and yellow banners of Sir Robert, topped over the trees.

Kit cowered behind Philip as the Queen's coach stopped at the hilltop overlooking the vale where she demanded a glass of wine to toast her arrival. The setting sun popped in her eyes like flashes of mica in a dark riverbed and her words bubbled full of giddy girlish delight, almost as if she might consider the prospect of becoming Dudley's wife. Almost, but not quite, Kit heard Philip tease to Lord Burghley, although Sidney favored the prospect since the match would make him a Prince, being Dudley's nephew and only male heir. Kit saw the first flash of ambition in his master's face.

Kit leaned out the window of Philip's coach as the train wound across the grassy knoll. As they approached the main gate, the Queen opened the door to the coach and dismounted with her ladies. Their presence twinkled in the evening like multicolored stars against the July sky. A small woman, with hair like spun gold, dressed in an ethereal white silk gown and the dusky blue half-moon tattooed on her forehead as herald to the mother goddess, approached the Queen and knelt before her. Kit caught his breath in wonder as the woman announced the Queen's arrival and prophesied a long and prosperous reign, doing so in a lyrical and poetic manner he recognized. The Queen turned and waved her hand, the gesture ordering all in the coaches to exit and follow in her steps.

Crossing through the gate, the blaring of trumpeters upon the battlements and players dressed in the costumes of the Lady of the Lake and her nymphs, adorned in flowing silks and floating in a barge across the large fountain in the courtyard, greeted her. The drums pounded, the fifes sang, guns blasted and, as the Earl of Leicester knelt before her and kissed her hand, the darkened sky lit up in a flurry of spidery fireworks.

Kit's eyes caressed the spectacle as Philip leaned over to him. "A sight to behold, is it not?"

"Yea, my lord," Kit answered in wonder.

Philip snickered. "Well, who knows, boy, you may be witnessing the historical betrothal of Elizabeth the First, and with it the elevation of the Sidney family. 'Twill be well worth remembering tonight."

Kit's lips form a circle as the torches blazed around the garden pool and along the towers of the castle. A thought sparked in his mind—the spectacle of a grand wedding attended by oracles and fairies, by courtiers and peasants, presenting a web-like fantasy drifting on the edges of a midsummer dream. He knew one day he would present this play as a gift to his Queen.

The Earl of Leicester, standing next to the Queen like a sure peacock, lifted his hand to quiet the gasping crowd. "You are all welcome to Kenilworth and the Queen honors us by her presence with us. Tomorrow we command feasting and dancing, music for your ears, plays for the eyes, bear baiting and hunting, whatever your heart desires. Come and we will see your Court delivered to their chambers."

Kit could not sleep for the excitement although Philip collapsed into slumber the moment his head touched the feathered pillow. The torches burned through the high arched window, glowing across his rush mattress on the floor at the foot of Philip's bed. Tiptoeing to the tufted seat at the opened window, the faint sound of a lute whispered through the night air. Quietly, he lifted his cloak, tied it around his neck, and made his way through the corridors of the castle until his bare feet felt the pebbled path leading to the outer wall. Covering his face with the hood of his cloak, he found the stone steps leading the battlements and made his way up to where the guards stood sentry. He crept across the walkway keeping his eye on the nearest guard, a stout man whose round cheeks glowed in the torchlight and whose attention bent toward the crowds gathering in the field outside the wall. Despite Kit's attempt at stealthiness, the guard turned on his heel and brandished the puissant pike in his hand; his jolly face transformed into a fierce frown. Kit froze as the blade touched his chest.

"Who goes there? Stand and unfold yourself!"

Kit's heart thundered in his ears. "A friend, sir, and servant to Sir Sidney."

The guard grabbed Kit's cloak and pulled the hood back from Kit's head. He lowered the pike and laughed. "Ah, and a boy, as well. You come too quiet upon the battlements; I could have run through your gizzard."

"Forgive me, sir, as I only wanted to see where the music came from and thought from this height I could discern the origin."

"Of course, of course, the excitement and festivities grows as the news spreads to the surrounding villages of the Queen's visit here. Lord Dudley gave permission for any of the townships to gather here in the south fields for the next nineteen days and to fill the days and nights with merriment and song. The lute player wanders though the crowd like a strolling minstrel dressed in a festive red jerkin adorned with bells. See there at the encampment where the fire burns the largest? He stands there now before the tent of Master Arden of Warwickshire."

Kit held his breath as the moon peeked out from behind a cloud revealing the field alive with a mixture of at least two hundred tents, wagons, horses and people.

"It almost looks like what I imagine an encampment before a battle."

The guard sighed. "You are right, boy, for I have seen and heard of many such scenes. The night before a siege, a camp whispers with soft talk and quiet laughter, so like the calm before a storm. My name is Bardolph and my third great grandfather fought at Agincourt and passed on the story of the night before the battle; how our fifth King Harry hid beneath a cloak and wandered the camp to gather the minds of his men. Now would be a good chance for our Queen to gather those same thoughts from her subjects for I warrant that not all gathered relish her visit to Lord Dudley or with the iron fist he has raised against recusants here in the Midlands."

Kit snickered. "Yea, but I cannot imagine Her Majesty doing such a thing. But, pray, tell me, sir, do you like such histories?"

"Very much, boy. Why do you ask?"

Kit shrugged. "Just a thought, sir, of how such a mighty scene might play on a stage."

The guard belted out a laugh. "The battle of Agincourt on a player's stage? 'Tis a folly, boy, to think a playwright might write a play to match Henry's victory, but if one could do it, then that one will be a masterful playwright."

Kit lifted the hood back over his head and turned to climb a wooden ladder descending the wall to the field. The guard turned to him.

"Where are you going, boy?"

Kit smiled and answered him as he made his way down the creaking slats. "You gave me a thought, Master Bardolph. To write such a play, and deliver dissenters to the Queen, would be very helpful. So, now I will give the camp a little touch of Harry in the night."

The guard's laughter tickled through the air as Kit's feet felt the wetness of the dew-covered grass. He slid down the embankment and scurried across the dry moat until he came to the gathering. Weaving through the crowd, his eyes soaked up the laughing faces in the moonlight, the camps dotted higgledy-piggledly in the battened-down tall grass aglow with firelight and lanterns, and his nostrils filled with the smells of strong ale and bubbling pots of onion soup. Finally, he heard the bells tinkling from the player's sleeve as the minstrel danced and plucked the strings of his lute.

Three wagons and a pitched tent made Master Arden's camp the largest. The low murmur of voices breaking with occasional laughter filtered through the cloth draping. Next to the fire, a young boy sat cross-legged leaning over a game of Nine Men's Morris, his chin propped up by his hands folded over the edges of his jaw. The boy sulked and cut his stare to the flap opening of the tent. Kit approached, his moonlit shadow falling over the boy.

"I will play with you if you need a partner," Kit said.

The boy looked up and smiled. Kit thought he looked a pleasant sort with big brown puppy eyes and dusty brown hair. The boy gestured for him to sit as he answered.

"Yea, for if I wait for my brother to come, he will be too soused with ale to play. What's your name?"

A thought tickled Kit's stomach as he conjured a name. "Harry Le Roy. What's yours?"

"My name is Will Shakespeare and my family is from Stratford on the Avon River. We came with my mother's cousin, Edward Arden of Park Hall. Where do you live? I have not heard that name around Warwickshire."

Kit curved his mouth into a grin. "Nay, you would not. I have been following the Queen's train since before the Midlands, since she left York."

Will's eyes widened. "York? That is a long way. Is your family following her progress?"

Kit's stare fell to the fire. "My family is dead."

"O, forgive me," Will answered.

Kit shrugged as they placed their pegs on the board. Kit won the first round, having reduced Will to two pegs. Will won the next after the clever move of hopping a peg across the board. Kit challenged him.

"You cannot do that! That is not a proper move."

Will grinned at him. "'Tis how we play it in the countryside. Flying to a vacant hole wins if none adjacent are available, thus giving you advantage. My father taught me this way to snatch up an opportunity when it comes."

Anger warmed Kit's cheeks. "That is just stupid! What are the lines on the board for if you can make up your own rules? You were not even going to tell me that that is how you played."

Kit knocked the board to the ground just as two men jostled out of the tent laughing, their beards wet with ale. Will glared at Kit and lifted his gaze to one of the men.

"Father, flying is a proper rule in Nine Men's Morris, is it not?"

Will's father, a course thin man, ignored Will as the other man, dressed in a fine russet robe of a gentry man, pulled him aside to continue the conversation begun on the inside of the tent. Kit strained his ear above the crackling of the fire to listen. Will's father spoke first.

"Come now, Edward, surely 'tis not as bad as you think."

The gentleman belched. "Nay, John, 'tis worse. You think I came here to see this spectacle to support this travesty. Not a whit! I do not care a pin's fee for the love life of the Queen, except for the fact that beyond those walls she now fornicates with that scoundrel Dudley. I am here to reacquaint with those who seek to displace her. They are all here, right among this gathering."

Kit's ears perked upon those words and Will kept tugging at his father's shirt. Kit took up the board from the ground and set the pegs again, eager to draw Will's attention away so the two men might continue their treasonous talk.

Kit whispered. "Come on, Will, we will play the game your way."

Will smiled and set the pegs as the two men continued.

John squeezed Edward's arm. "Edward, keep your voice low. You ought not talk of such things."

"Ha," Edward barked. "You cannot tell me, John Shakespeare, that you do not wish for the former days when England knew its place at the foot of his Holiness. There are many in the townships biding their time for the cream to once again rise to the top. Do you even remember the last time you visited our new Church of England?" John shrugged as Edward continued. "The Queen gave Dudley permission to harden a stance against recusants and men like he and John Whitgift clamor to take up the cause."

John's brow wrinkled. "John Whitgift? But he is just an archdeacon. What can he do?"

"Yea, an archdeacon with an ambition that has him salivating for the Bishop of Worcester's death. Mark my word, John; that man will keep climbing until he has the Queen under his thumb. But, we have an ally and perhaps a plan. Come, walk with me and I will tell you more."

Kit felt light-headed with information for the Queen and Will took his time to make his next move.

"Hurry, Will, I have to go."

Will moved a peg one notch and looked up from the board, his mouth in a puzzled frown. "But, why? Where are you going?"

Kit stood. "I have to get back to my family."

Will's frown extended to his eyes. "Your family? I thought you said they were dead."

Kit leaned over the board and flew a peg across the board, leaving Will without a move. He shrugged. "I lied.... and I've won using your own stupid device."

Kit laughed and ran as Will kicked the board across the campsite. Will chased behind him for a distance, but lost him as Kit wove through the crowds like a snake and dove into the tall grass bending over the edge of the moat. He waited a moment more, watching as Will appeared at the edge of the field. As Will sauntered back to his camp, Kit crept back to the outer wall and climbed back up to the platform. The guard, Bardolph, wavered as he extended his pike once more. Kit noticed a skin of wine shriveled on the stones.

"Ah, 'tis you again, I see. Pray tell, did you absorb the minds of the Queen's subjects?"

Kit shrugged and walked past the guard. "No such luck, friend, but only played a few games of mills with some stupid boy."

The guard blasted a burp and chuckled. "Well, 'tis just as well. Perhaps there will be other occasions over the next few days to listen and watch. Not all of us are as clever as a King, besides the glow-worm shows the morning close. I am sure Sir Sidney will call for his boy to fetch his chamber pot."

The guard's words angered Kit. *Ignorant drunken fool,* he assured himself as he stomped back to Philip's room. *One day all of them will know there is more to me than just the ability to dump my master's piss.*

Kit looked across the towers of the battlements, the stone crenelated teeth glowed gray in the morning air and the soft kiss of sunlight broke over the distant heathered hills. As he crossed the courtyard, the first rays of sunlight glinted on the windowpanes. Philip stirred as he opened the door. Kit fell to his knees and crawled across the cold limestone to his pallet, closed his eyes and waited for the gushing sound of urine to fill the hollow pewter bowl.

"Boy, come take this to the garderobe and fetch me my robe."

Kit obeyed, yet his insides surged, giddy with the spying he had done, and he felt hopeful for a reward. He helped Philip with his robe and then, cleared his throat to speak.

Philip turned to him. "Why the smile, boy? Do you have something to say?"

"I do, sir, but I beg your forgiveness for leaving you alone during the night."

Philip flared his nostrils and popped him on the side of the head.

"Leaving me? You did not have my permission to roam this castle."

Kit winced. "Nay, sir, but if you will listen..."

Philip spun around and crossed the room to his trunk of clothes. "I do not have time to listen to your foolishness. The Queen is holding prayers before breakfast and demands we all attend her. Come, help me dress."

Kit's brow wrinkled, but he stilled his heart to bide the right time.

Canterbury Cathedral dwarfed the small chapel at Kenilworth, yet the ribbed vault sprawled above their heads and the sun sparkled through the painted glass. The crowds packed the chapel to glimpse their Queen. Lord Dudley opened the gates and the church to those gathered in the fields and those of Her Majesty's court. Kit hovered behind Philip and Sir Walsingham, his stare falling upon the boy, Will, tucked in a corner behind his father and Arden.

The Queen finished her prayers, took Dudley by the hand and turned to Lord Burghley who hovered near her. Her firm voice echoed in the nave.

"So, Lord Burghley, you have news? We can tell by your anxious brow."

"Only this, your Majesty," he answered, "I wish to present to you the Bishop of Worcester and his archdeacon, John Whitgift, as humble servants to your great Church of England."

He waved to the two men standing at the altar—a shriveled white-haired man bent at the waist and a cunning-eyed man dressed in the black dyed wool of a priest. The Queen took the Bishop's hand.

"We thank you for your loyalty and allowing us to use our common prayer book."

The Bishop shook his head. "Nay, my Queen, for 'tis I must thank you for honoring Worcester with your presence and giving England's soul back to God."

Whitgift fell to his knees and kissed the Queen's hand, interrupting the Bishop's words. "Your Majesty, if there is ever any service I might do for you, then I am your most humble servant."

The Queen let out a throaty laugh, her stare darting from Burghley to Walsingham. "Ha, would that every man in our Kingdom took this approach. What is your name, sir?"

"John Whitgift, my lady."

She flicked her finger for him to rise. "I remember your name, Archdeacon Whitgift, for I have heard rumors you crave your Bishop's place."

Whitgift's eyes flashed. "Not so, your Majesty. I would never assume..."

She laughed again. "Nonsense, Whitgift, for every ambitious soul seeks the position of someone higher or are you so pious that those thoughts never enter your mind? Do not tell me nay, for I have heard my Scottish cousin Mary prays ten times a day while under her teeth she wishes me dead. Remember, man, ambition can make a man or break him depending on whose alliance you make.

Is that not right, Walsingham?"

Walsingham curled his lip into a half smile. Kit knew he must seize the moment; this moment. She continued along the center of the nave, pausing at decided persons to greet those of her court. From the corner of his eye, he saw Arden standing near the door waiting for an introduction to the Queen. Kit tugged on Walsingham's sleeve.

Walsingham glared at him. "What is it, boy?"

Kit swallowed hard. "Sir, you promised once if I did a good turn for the Queen you would see she give her notice to me as her playwright. Pray, listen, for I have something of importance to tell her."

Walsingham arched his brow and glanced to Sidney. "What is this? Has he told you of anything?"

Sidney shook his head. "Nothing but some frivolity of him sneaking out last eve."

Walsingham dismissed Kit with the wave of his hand, giving no further credence to his pleading. The Queen came closer to Arden and Kit grabbed hold of Walsingham's arm.

"Please, sir, will you not listen?"

Walsingham continued in the Queen's train as Sidney pinched Kit's ear, twisting until the lobe throbbed. "Sit you here on this chair, boy. You will not budge until the Queen leaves, do you understand?"

Kit did not understand. He suddenly felt small and insignificant, yet he had power in the knowledge filling his mind. *What do they know? I could seize the moment myself. Why do I have to wait? Am I not also the Queen's subject? Surely, she will listen to me.*

Arden knelt before the Queen, and Lord Dudley whispered something into her ear. John Shakespeare and his son stood at a distance from the scene; Burghley, Walsingham and Sidney stood like dull poppets behind the ladies-in-waiting; and all eyes adored the Queen's presence. Kit's heart raced and his breathing deepened as he rose from the chair and marched down the nave toward her. Before anyone could stop him, he threw himself at the feet of the Queen in between her cascading golden gown and Arden's leather boot.

Walsingham cursed and ran at Kit, tugging at Kit's arms as Kit clung to the Queen's skirt. The Queen took a step backward as the crowds murmured a gasp. Kit pleaded as Walsingham slapped him across the mouth and dragged him from the nave.

"Your Majesty, please," Kit begged. "Please, hear me... Arden... Arden seeks... he seeks... he seeks to kill you!"

Walsingham dropped him at the threshold to the church and pointed toward the castle wall. "Get out, your stupid pox! How dare you..."

"Wait," her Majesty announced. "Bring the boy back before me."

Burghley came up before the Queen. "But, your Majesty..."

She waved him away. "Quiet! I said bring him here."

Kit stood and wiped his bloody lip across the sleeve of his doublet. He brushed off his breeches and strode toward her like a courtier. She reached over and lifted his chin with her fingers.

"I remember you, boy. You were the bold one I met at Westminster several years ago. How long is it now?"

Kit's insides burst with excitement that she remembered him.

"Yea, your Majesty, 'tis three years. I am eleven now."

The corner of her mouth curved upward. "And ever so bold. You said Master Arden here wishes to kill me and yet, here he stands offering me his service. 'Tis a brash accusation to make within a church."

Kit lowered his gaze. "Yea, my Queen, but no one else would listen to me."

The Queen arched her eyebrow. "Indeed? Not your Master Sidney nor my servant Walsingham? 'Tis odd, unless the statement is frivolous." She turned to Arden whose face appeared a shade lighter than previous. "Tell me, Master Arden, before the boy interrupted us, our Lord Dudley whispered in our ear that you refuse to wear his colors during our visit. Is this true?"

Arden swallowed hard, and he forged a smile. "Your Majesty, he is correct that I am not wearing his color, for you see, my complexion pales against such yellows and greens. Give me the sturdy colors of your Majesty's countryside and my disposition is merrier."

The Queen smirked and eked a small laugh. "We suppose it is a small matter, for we ourselves disincline to wear colors which do not flatter, but the matter the boy speaks of, we will hear more.

Come, boy, and tell us why you accuse Master Arden."

Kit took a deep breath. "Last eve, your Majesty, I sneaked out of my master's room to view the festivities from the top of the battlements. On seeing the crowds gathered in the fields, I took it upon myself to walk among the camps and listen to the talk. You know, my lady, like your ancestor, King Henry the Fifth, the night before Agincourt?" A small laugh brushed through those gathered around the Queen and Kit could see Will edging closer to his cousin. Kit continued, "I stopped to hear the lute player playing at Arden's camp and set to play a game of mills with a boy there. While we were playing, I heard Master Arden tell one of his kinsmen he had come to Kenilworth to reacquaint with those seeking to displace you."

The frown on Walsingham's face transformed into a smile. The Queen lifted a finger to pause him and Arden fell to his knees.

"Your Majesty, this is a horrid lie!"

Her jaw moved back and forth as if she were mulling the thought over her tongue. "Boy, you best have proof to this."

Kit pointed one finger at the boy with whom he played the game of mills, Will Shakespeare, and smiled in victory. "I do, my lady, for he heard it all, and his father is the man to whom Arden spoke."

The blood drained from Will's face as the Queen set her stare upon him.

"Well, boy, what is your name?"

He bowed before her. "William Shakespeare, your Majesty."

"This boy says you played a game of mills and during the game he heard your kinsmen plot against us. What do you say to this?"

Will pursed his lips and raised his head. With the most honest eyes and plainest speech, he answered her. "He is a liar, your Majesty."

"To which part, boy?"

He looked straight at Kit. "To both parts, your Majesty. I do not know this boy. I fell asleep after the fireworks, you can ask my father."

Kit clenched his teeth. "He is lying, your Majesty!"

The Queen twitched her brow in irritation. "Well, now, look at the pair of you. Two little boys wrangling a lie before the Queen of

England. If we had a mind to it, we would lash your backsides; but as it is, we have not the time for childish games." She looked to Walsingham. "'Tis such a wonder to me that the male gender never tire of trying to trump one another. They learn it as boys and carry it with them always. Sidney, take your page and teach him a lesson. As for you Arden, we show mercy this day, for a Queen does not rely on the council of silly children; however, we will have a watchful eye on this county, so take heed our Lord Burghley not deliver us messages leaning toward such plots. You would be a very foolish man to take sides with my cousin Mary of Scotland. Do you understand?"

Arden bowed low as she strode out of the nave and the crowds followed. Sidney grabbed hold of Kit's arm, pausing in the doorway to speak to Walsingham. Tears stung Kit's eyes. He looked up and saw Will Shakespeare walking backwards behind Arden, a victorious smile on his face. Kit felt nauseous and angry with a knowing sense gnawing at his heart; a knowing that this would not be the last time he saw Will Shakespeare.

VII

John Shakespeare loved an opportunity. Every position vacant on the town council he filled with only one purpose behind his movements: to become a gentleman. Like the rungs on a ladder, he stepped—ale-taster, bailiff, mayor and alderman, with gloving on the side. The council even knew of his flair for brogging, and because he was so astute to the quality of wool as he pulled a single strand between his thumb and forefinger, they overlooked his not having a proper license from the Crown.

Yet, the problem with reaching the top of a weak ladder, William thought, *is the whole wobbly mess will collapse under the weight.* And his father's pride and head swelled daily as he made his rounds collecting levies, sipping beer and strutting through the lanes in his vibrant red robe.

Will's younger brother, Gilbert, would no doubt follow in their father's footsteps. William, however, found opportunities to sneak away to meander along the banks of the Avon with his head in the clouds. Ambition sparked in his heart, but not for the regular trades of a country shopkeeper. His heart yearned for the stage. When his father became alderman, he jumped at the opportunity to attend the Big School, not for the taste of education, but for the excitement to see the players perform on the stage of the guildhall on the lower floor beneath the school.

Since the festivities of Kenilworth, four years passed and John Whitgift became Bishop of Worcester. He started his pressure throughout the diocese and many were losing their positions because of failure to attend church. John Shakespeare's name glared among the lists. The resulting effect blanketed over the family as deep as the snowdrifts outside the window. The wind howled in the early morning light and the snow banked across the sky in harsh white streaks.

William blew his breath on the leaded panes, drawing circles and watching two of his fellow schoolmates scurry past his house with books in hand, their cloaks whipping around their legs. A year passed since last he trod Henley Street to the King's School next to the Guild Chapel. William's shoulders drooped. February shrouded with a discontented winter. John walked near to the window to spy whereon his son looked.

"Dost thou miss school so much?"

"Nay, father, not school. Just other things. The players are coming to the guildhall when the snow thaws, did you know?"

William relished the commotion the players brought; all the sights and sounds of the stage. He could almost smell the face paint and hear the words of Seneca - *Go on through the lofty spaces of high heaven, and bear witness where you ride that there are no gods!*

John laid his hands upon William's shoulder and turned him around. "There be more to life than school, Will. There be things I can teach you I'll warrant not taught at the Big School. And I'll not have thee sneaking off to watch a play whilst you need be helping me."

William dropped his stare to the floor. "Yea, father."

John scurried William to the back room. A fire in the hearth warmed the plastered walls and the morning light drifted through the window. Three pair of gloves laid on the worktable as if reaching for phantom fingers and the air filled with the pungency of well-oiled leather. John pushed the gloves aside and directed William to sit across from him. His father's face paled to an ashy gray as he spoke to William in soft whispers.

"Thou art an apt boy, Will, but I wonder, what have you learned from me?"

William knew this play well; the lines rehearsed and recited many times through the years. "Many things, father."

"Such as?"

William looked over the table. "Gloving?"

John stood and pulled a thin painted arras across the window as if the weaved cloth might keep his secret words from filtering through the pane.

"Nay, boy, not just gloving, but more. I want to know your

mind. Thou art schooled, so thus I ask you. What have thou learnt?"

Will fidgeted and twirled a thin strand of leather between his fingers. He knew his father did not know his mind, but he played anyway. "I know not what to say."

John huffed. "Pray, your youthful brow has not the skill enough to hide you know of what I speak. Hold not off."

William laid the leather back on the table, ran his fingers through his hair, and rested his palms over his eyelids, taking a moment to compose and transform. This role he played well, the one of the dutiful son. He laid his hands on the table and looked straight into his father's eyes. As he spoke, he could see the corner of his father's lips tremble.

"I shall not hold off, father, for I know what purpose you are seeking. You speak of the state of the state, which I know means the steps the Queen is taking to dismantle our old faith. I am not blind to the apathy in this household. You speak well of Protestantism, but only to a degree, and the oaths you keep are for the dark and secret places of the heart. There Queen Bess cannot touch. They teach us she is the head of the Church, that there is no other, but they teach us this in showy words for the daylight, as if playacting. But there are those wishing for the fair days before Henry the Eighth."

John clasped William's hands, his words breaking upon the joy in his throat. "Thou make me a most happy father! But I pray you that thou dost keep my counsel I shall speak tonight concealed. Can thou do it?"

William nodded like a good son and kept his ears alert. John reached within his shirt and unfolded a small parchment. The lettering handwritten by a skilled hand, not by his father who could only sign his name with an X, but the words revealed much as to his father's mind. At first, William's blood raced and his heart pounded, but with much control, he let the player again take over his words. His father spoke with breathy words.

"Know you what this is?"

"It says a testament, father."

"Yea, a testament, but know you what it means? Read it out loud."

William shook his head, at once afraid. "No, these words will put your head upon a block."

"Why, what should be the fear? My soul is immortal. What can the Queen do to that? Read it out, Will, for it speaks to not only my heart, but to many others, as well."

William rolled the parchment out on the table, rubbing his hands over the paper as if he were trying to rub away the words. He read:

"I, John Shakespeare, do protest I am willing, yea, I do infinitely desire and humbly crave, that this is my last will and testament..."

John pointed to a line. "No, read further down the page. Here, read here."

William continued. "I do pray and beseech all my dear friends, parents, kinsfolk, by the bowels of our Savior Jesus Christ, to do masses for my soul after my death."

John smiled and urged him. "Keep reading, more, the last. Read the last words."

William finished. "I do make a solemn promise I will patiently endure and suffer all kinds of infirmity, sickness, yea, and the pain of death itself, than to quit the most holy and devout faith of my forefathers."

William pushed the confession away from his sight. His insides churned as he watched his father glow with pride. "Father, know you what this means?"

"I do, my son."

William clutched his stomach. "The Privy Council will find you out or have they already done so? Is this the cause of your state now?"

William found it difficult not to blame his father for being ripped away from the Big School. John lost his positions in Stratford, both family homes in Snitterfield and Wilmcote sold, his application for a coat-of-arms denied, and now this.

"Father, tell me, do they know?"

John's face turned solemn. His eyes shadowed over with the answer. "Yea, they know. There are many of us here—John Audeley, Thomas Cooley, William Lonley, and more. They fined us a surety and commanded to present ourselves before the Queen at the Star Chamber this past June."

"Did you go?" John shook his head. "But why, father?"

John stood and pushed back the arras, letting the light fall across the table. "I paid the sureties. Why should I present myself to that Queen? Rome does not recognize her and neither should we who adhere to our faith. If I had gone, I would be to the Tower unless I gave to them what they wish, to give my testament to the Protestant faith. I did much against my conscience in saving my neck and for the glory, but 'tis enough."

William spat his words. "These words are not yours!"

"You are right," his father replied. "These are Campion's words, but they are mine now."

William stood, turning his back to his father, his knees trembling.

"Edmund Campion, the Jesuit?"

"The very man, William. He is soon to be a visitor at Arden's home. Secretly, of course. I met him when last your mother and I visited her kinsman."

A cloud passed across the sun, shadowing the room in gloom. An ominous foreboding filled William's mind. He turned on his father.

"Father, he is a hunted man and when Walsingham catches him, you will see his head on a pike. You must destroy this evidence of your ever having met him before the Council destroys you."

John matched him, his shoulders squaring. "You would have me denounce my very soul?"

"I would have you live."

John extended his hand. "And I would have my eldest beside me. You said my rules will guide you, so no son of mine will stand for this new religion, for this bastard Queen, nor for her jesters sitting on the Privy Council. Take thy father's hand, Will."

William's fifteen-year-old heart aged in a moment. His father stood before him like an actor playing a part in a play with too many characters each vying for center stage, each puffing with their own soliloquies; and yet, each no greater than the other. The idea amused Will but sorrowed him as well. The play would continue and William in his part. In all the comedy and tragedy of the lines, his father could not see how much in the seriousness of the real life, that he wanted his father's approval. Times changed since Kenilworth; darkened and deepened. Will should have recognized the coming long ago, back when his father first became alderman, or perhaps that day when his young eyes saw the results of the Queen's power and influence.

He recalled a day long ago, seven years before this day, of wandering into the Guild Chapel alone. The heavy oak door creaked open to his soft touch, and he padded cat-like across the black and white tile floor of the nave. Sounds echoed in reverent whispers and Will's eyes searched the timbered beams of the vaulted ceiling. Two turtle doves cooed and flapped their wings, sending soft feathers floating through the muted sunlight.

His eyes adjusted to the room, soaking in the first sunbeams breaking through the vacant windows where the colored glass used to spill out a rainbow across the aisles. His fingers traced along the mortar lines of the stacked stone walls and the faint painted pictures hidden behind a lime wash. He paused, letting the whiteness fade away from his eyes revealing the edges of forbidden images.

He conjured them, vivid and blazoned on every inch of the nave: Saint George shining in his silvery armor battling the great dragon, the ecstasy in Helena's face as she discovered the true cross, and the Holy Rood, high above the archway between the nave and chancel, with Christ on his rainbow sending the dead to heaven or hell.

The doves fluttered again, aware of the shadow falling over William's shoulder. He gasped as a gloved hand folded around his arm. His father's voice thundered to the rafters. "William, thy mother is sick with worry. Get thee back to the house this instant."

Will remained still, his gaze fixated on the green eyes of Modwenna seeping through the white paint near the chancel screen. "Father, the boys at school jeer at me. They say you did a terrible thing. Did you whitewash the pictures here in this church?"

Will watched his father's face as he looked around the room. His gaze looked disconnected, like a stranger in a foreign land. John reached for the crutch of a nearby chair.

"Whitewash the church? Yea, I did so, my son, the year before your birth." His words chopped across his confession. "It has been many years since I have paused here in the nave. It lost the sanctity for me the day I slopped the lime across Christ's face."

Will scooted near his father, his small fingers playing with the frayed edges of his father's coat. "But if thou knew it to be wrong, then why did you?"

John's mouth twisted in a frown. "Why, indeed? My son, it was for survival. We live in wicked times, William, a time where what you believe may send you to heaven or hell, to glory or to the block."

He took Will's face in his hands, rubbing his cheeks with his thumbs, and Will drank in the brief adoration.

"Son, will you be ruled by me?" Will smiled and nodded. "Then remember this well. Do whatever thy can in thy life to survive. Let not anyone tempt you to reveal the secrets of thy heart. I whitewashed these walls, but did not whitewash my heart. I followed the command to save my flesh from the fire, but God knows where my heart lies. Now, speak true, my son, what have you learnt?"

Will gazed over his father's shoulder, once more attending to the Holy Rood above the arch. "'Tis not your fault, father, surely Christ will see that. You did what you needed to do to survive. Can the Crown expect any more of sinners?"

John mussed his son's hair and smiled. "Ah, good words, my son. In there lies a lesson. Tender thy words and as night follows day, so then reward will follow compromise. See here, dost thou think I wear these robes for naught?"

Will watched his father as he stood and twirled in the middle of the nave, the light catching the shimmer of the red velvet folds of his alderman's robe. Glory lay across his father's face like sunlight. He skipped and pranced into the chancel and stood upon the altar. Will's mouth fell open as he heard his father's words.

"This Protestant church means nothing, my son, to my Catholic heart. 'Tis games our rulers play, and if you play it right, then you will have thy heart's desire. Our Queen Mary said death to the Protestants, and we did such as faithful followers. Our Queen Bess says death to Catholics and we follow suit like good little sheep. They rule our heads but not our hearts. Compromise with thy head, William, but betray with thy heart. Look at me, standing in this holy place where the papists are no more, now an alderman, a bailiff and mayor of this fine city, and all for taking the brush in my hand and covering over our sins. 'Twas a simple thing and our Queen extended her favor. Are you learning how to play, my son, and how to grab opportunity?"

Will's eight-year-old mind did not understand. He swung his legs back and forth beneath the seat of the chair watching his father's happy face. Will gnawed on his bottom lip, stretching his smile across his face. He stood and crossed the aisle, taking his father's hand in his, answering him in innocence.

"I am, father, I am."

William looked over at his father as he recalled the memory. Time had streaked John's hair with gray. Since that day in the Guild chapel William sought his father's approval, following his lead, leaving school when told, working the fields or in the shop, all the while ignoring any urging of his own heart.

"If I do not take your hand this time, father, will I still have your approval?"

John let his hand drop. "You will not."

William took a breath and swallowed. "Then it is done. You have never known my mind, but I will warrant a day when you will be proud to call me your son. Mark me. I may not give you my hand and pronounce my testament, yet there will be a day when all will know my mind. I have my faith here in my heart, same as you, and if there be a God, he will judge me soundly. Campion and Elizabeth demand pledges because of power and wish to save their own necks. Power hides fear. If you wield a strong hand, as you once displayed when you were alderman, father, then no one will ever see the tears you shed in the dark. But remember, father, it never lasts and it can only go one way. Either Elizabeth will win or the Pope. Either way, heads will topple. I intend on keeping mine."

"Then you give in to this Protestant church?"

William mused for a moment. "Compromise, father, implies someone must promise me something as well. Silence is the key. You are the one who taught me that when I was only a boy. Remember the day we sat in the Guild Chapel? You taught me that someone may assume you compromise if you are silent, but secretly you may not have done so at all; and yet, it brings reward nonetheless. If I am useful to the Crown, yet silent, then no one will take notice that I have not sworn and because I am useful, they will not care."

"Bah," his father snorted. "They will call you to account. As you said, it will not last. Look at me."

William scratched his chin. "Yet, the question goes, if you had remained silent, would you still have your lands? Would you still be alderman and be able to say Mass in secret?"

John slapped his hand on the table. "It was a lie to which I submitted. A lie is a lie, William. You speak like an ignorant boy, for I now know the closer you get to death, the more you want absolution."

William squinted. "And yet, if you speak a lie for a good reason, then what of it? Peter lied three times to save his life and Jesus forgave him."

John started from his seat and stoked the glowing embers of the fire. "Peter repented of the sin."

"And yet," William added. "He still saved himself."

An exasperated sigh rolled off John's tongue. "Bah! Your head is full of nonsense. You best go help your brother pack our things. We are off to visit Edward at Park Hall. You have learnt none of this from me, and besides all this, when would you ever be of any use to the Crown?"

William leaned back in his chair and smiled. "O, dear father, I warrant there will be a day. I will make the day."

VIII

"That stupid priest will be there," William snarled. He looked across at Gilbert, his brother, who shrugged his shoulders and closed his eyes. William dreaded the trip to Park Hall, for his father's insistence betrayed one purpose: to show further support of the Catholic cause in trying to atone for his supposed former sins. Will knew the secrets could not go on forever, something would uncover them and send the conspirators to the block.

The wagon clacked along the road to Birmingham. The large elm trees canopying over the road fell away, and the sun blazed across his family. His father and mother sat in silence on a bench at the front of the wagon, his father clicking his tongue every so often to spur the lazy mule; Gilbert dozed against a wool-stuffed bag and his little brother, Edmund, leaned over the side to count the number of bugs crushed under the wheels. William cringed as they rounded the bend, taking the left fork away from the lane leading to Kenilworth.

Four years since the Queen's visit to the Earl of Leicester's castle, that faithful day when he lied to save his father's neck. He wondered how many more times he would have to do the same. He nudged Gilbert with his foot and leaned near to him to whisper.

"Gilbert, do you even care the reason we go to visit mother's kin? 'Tis not just a friendly visit, I warrant you that."

Gilbert rolled over to face away from William. William slouched against the side of the wagon, his thoughts sparking upon the boy he met at Kenilworth. He wished he had learned more about the spying little knave. All he could remember is that wicked smile on the boy's face when he revealed overhearing Arden's conversation with his father. That and how quick the boy learned the trick of flying a peg across the mill board. A clever boy fooling

William with his obvious fake name and quip about his dead parents. William shivered when he thought that is all it would take again for a quick spy in the mask of a common man, perhaps a dairyman, or smithy, or even another pasty-cheeked boy, to listen close to his father's conversation. *What a cast of players,* he thought, *strutting across the stage of England.* He closed his eyes and said a brief prayer, praying his father's life not end in tragedy.

The wagon wheels clattered across the sparse cobbled lane leading up to Park Hall. John pulled back on the reins and William's mother, Mary, waved to the gardener plucking weeds in the flower garden. William jumped off the wagon and gazed up at the manor. Giant oaks and majestic ash trees draped their heavy arms across the waters of the River Tame flowing past the gardens, shadowing the fine brick and mortar farmhouse. William visited here many times, but none of the visits felt like this one. Edward greeted his cousin, Mary, and kissed her on the cheek as he threw his arm around John's shoulders. William watched as his family filed into the entrance, their laughter and words fading as the door closed shut.

A shadow fell across his back. William turned to see the gardener standing near to him and leaning on a scythe. William nodded to him.

"Greetings to you, Hugh."

The man smiled. "And to you, Master William. Will you not follow your family? Your uncle has apple wine from the redcoats harvested from his own apple trees. 'Twould be refreshing after your journey."

William shrugged. He did not want to go inside the house. He imagined them greeting the Jesuit, shaking his hand, kneeling as he blessed the air over their heads with the sign of the cross and calling them faithful servants. William wrinkled his nose at the thought and looked over his shoulder at the bubbling stream.

"Nay, sir, I will drink a bit of that liquid instead."

He walked to the edge and knelt over the waters, cupping a handful to his lips. The gardener sighed on the grass beside him. William glanced over and the man took a cloth from his pocket and wiped the sweat from his brow.

He looked harmless enough, William thought, *nothing special, the ordinary working sort with his gray hair and smooth white skin.*

William's mind sparked upon the sudden realization that the man's skin was not the sort for a gardener by trade. He turned his head away and kept his stare on the bubbling eddy forming near his feet. The man cleared his throat and spoke.

"You have gotten tall, Will. I can remember when I first came to Park Hall; you were just a small sprite. Sometimes your mother would lose you in the sunflowers. How old are you now?"

William pulled his knees to his chest and buried his mouth in the crease between his two legs. His answer muffled out.

"I'm fifteen, sir."

The gardener slapped his knee. "Marry, I thought so! My, my, fifteen years and more since I have been here. So many things have changed. I can remember when I was your age. 'Twas King Harry the Eighth then, and he was a sight to see, to be sure, and the ground trembled when he spoke a word. My, my, how things have changed. You know, your uncle is having a feast this evening. A piglet is roasting on the hearth and I caught three coneys in a trap in the vegetables."

William picked a blade of grass, set it between his two thumbs and blew. The blade trembled and his breath rang out in a whistle. Hugh, the gardener, plucked a blade, but only blew spit. William snickered.

"Look here, you are doing it wrong. Have you never blown a kecksie? Here, tighten the blade and purse your lips."

The man tried several times, gave up and strung a dandelion stem between his teeth. "You know this evening is a special occasion. Did your father not tell you of the guest?"

William cut his stare at the man, trying to ignore him with his continued whistling and feigning ignorance. "Guest?"

The man smiled. "Yea, 'tis Edmund Campion. He has stopped here on his way to Wales. 'Tis an honor to have him bless this house."

William threw the blade into the water. "An honor? To whom, sir, or are you set to capture me with a trap, as well?"

The man whistled out a laugh. "Trap you? Why would I do such a thing? You would only speak that way if you thought me a snitch bent on delivering such news to the Earl of Leicester. He would be most eager to hear the report. So, your wariness towards me tells me only one thing, you do not know who I am, do you?"

William's skin creased between his brows. "I have known you, as you said, since I was a boy, as Hugh Hall, gardener of Park Hall. But a boy does not notice when a gardener's skin tans in the sun, as would be the case if you were who you say you are."

Hugh pulled back the sleeve of his shirt and chuckled. "To be sure, Master Will. Thus you have discovered me, but you think me to be a spy."

William lifted his eyebrow. "My suspicion is founded, sir."

"Yea, it is, for the Earl of Leicester and the Bishop of Worcester are intent on scorching the ground to run the hiding Catholics out of the underbrush. So, we hide in any form we can."

William pushed his hair back behind his ear. "You are a papist?"

The man reached in his other pocket and held out a rosary. "Not only a faithful one, but an ordained one. I am a priest, William."

William rolled his eyes and propped his head up with his hands. The priest continued. "I take it from you sigh you are not fond of our old religion."

William shook his head. "'Tis not that, sir, only I fear for my father. When he wraps his mind around a thought, he will not shake it loose. My father is a simple man, sir, and has not the wit to become involved in the plots Campion plans. He will become a dispensable pawn, a neck to sacrifice in protecting more important people. He does not know the depth of the pit where he plays."

Hugh smiled. "You are a good son, Will. I will relay your concerns to Edmund. What of you? You are a bright boy. Campion could use a boy like you to further the cause."

William stood up, glaring at the priest. "Nay, you will not have me. My ambitions lie far away from the religious games played. No one will use me. I will have what I want and no one will break me from my course."

A serene look shadowed over the priest's face. "Then you are your father's son, wrapping your mind around a thought and not loosing no matter the shaking."

William flared his nostrils and ran. He stomped away along the bank, splashing though the shallows to the other side and weaving through the towering ash trees until he could no longer see the priest or the house.

He found a spot where the river widened and the water broke into a small gurgling fall through two or three boulders peaking their shiny heads above the surface. The ground felt mossy and cool to his touch.

My father's son, he scowled as he laid his head in the tall grass. *I will be a great man, even a legendary player bringing the name of Shakespeare to every man's lips—more than my father ever did.*

The sun sliced though the bare branches in narrow beams, lighting across his face and drowsing his eyes. He found it hard to keep awake with the sound of the water and the summer sun heating his angry cheeks. He felt his thoughts swirl away as his eyes fluttered and closed.

William woke with a start, sitting straight up and gazing around him. The forest had darkened and tiny fireflies twinkled in the haze mimicking the few stars he could see though the breaks in the trees. He rubbed his eyes and spoke aloud.

"Oh no, how long have I been asleep?"

Two women's voices whispered over his shoulder like the melodious chorus of two nightingales. "Only a short time."

He spun his head around, gazing into the vacant darkness of the forest, but recognizing the familiar voice of his imaginary friends—his constant companions since his early childhood, his playmates of the stage.

As the breeze blew through the mist, two figures formed and stooped in the grass before him. Two nymphs, one with golden hair, the other with dusky brown, dressed in gossamer gowns shimmering like spider webs in the starlight and their faces hidden behind golden masks, one smiling and one frowning.

William's flesh tingled as the smiling friend spoke first. "We have watched you, William Shakespeare, and we tell you of your heart's desire. Know this, you will be the greatest actor ever known to man. For generations people will speak your name, perhaps as something more than just an actor."

Then, his frowning friend finished. "But, be wise, for if you are not careful, all may not end well. There will always be another who will wish to destroy you, and one may succeed if you are not clever."

William shook his head, trying to figure out if the dream and the words were real. "What do you mean? Who will seek to destroy me?

The smiling nymph looked at her sister and laughed, her laughter sounding like the bubbling of the water over the rocks. "O, the comedy and tragedy of life!"

William rubbed his eyes. "Am I dreaming?"

They whispered in unison as they faded and their voices trickled away into the breeze. "Yea, William, you are dreaming.... and now.... you must wake...."

William opened his eyes, feeling the mossy ground and the tall grass tickled across his arms. He sat up and looked around him. A fog rolled through the trees, yet the sunlight still peeked though the canopy. Nothing else stirred except two silvery moths flitting and lighting on a cluster of rue. He wiped his hand across his brow, thinking of the dream and a shiver breathed across his neck. He darted back through the trees, across a small barren barley field, though the apple orchard and threw open the door at the back of the manor.

Gilbert and Edmund sat on a bench near the kitchen hearth along with two of their cousins, Bess and Jane Arden, with their lips circled in cream and crumbs. The scullery maid, Nan, poured more milk into their wooden cups as William closed the door. Gilbert caught William's eye.

"O, you are in such trouble! Where have you been? It has been three hours since we arrived and Father has been looking for you."

William huffed and picked up a cup for Nan to fill. "I fell asleep. Why does he want me?"

Gilbert wiped his mouth with his sleeve. "He wants you to sit beside him at dinner. Edmund and I are not allowed. We have to eat here in the kitchen."

Edmund smiled and added in his childish way. "'Tis only for grown-ups."

Gilbert motioned toward the door leading to the main part of the house. "You best be going. Dinner started a while ago."

William pressed his lips together and strode into the small dining hall. All eyes turned toward him when he entered. There his family sat at a long oak table lit with pewter candlesticks, feasting on roasted piglet and rabbit. His stomach growled smelling the sweet carrots and leeks. William thought the scene a dark secretive gathering midst the dark paneled walls and coffer ceiling. His father frowned at him and pulled the chair out next to him.

As William sat, his father popped him on the back of the head and spoke to Edward. "Forgive me, Edward, for the tardiness of my son."

Edward guffawed and William looked up to see his mother's cousin wink at him. "No matter, John, he is not too late to hear our report. William, meet our guest. This is Edmund Campion."

William cut his glare to the end of the table. Campion acknowledged him with a sly grin. William did not like him from the first. Something about his round piercing eyes and pointed chin unnerved William. He dressed like a gentleman in a fine slashed black velvet doublet, yet his cropped hair gave the image of a monk. He addressed everyone at the table and William detected a slight Italian flavor to the words.

"Where were we, Arden? Ah, yea, I remember. I was telling you of the recent developments in Rheims." William noticed the man cut his pork in large pieces, stuffing them into his mouth as he spoke. "There is a report there that Walsingham is preparing to infiltrate the seminary to silence our soldiers before they have the chance to strike."

"Do you think he will succeed," Arden questioned.

Campion guzzled a pint of ale and answered. "Perhaps on a small degree, but then again, all of us who are faithful to Rome must accept the possibility martyrdom may come. We know he has been gathering a great number of boys from the Universities to help with Elizabeth's cause against us. And many of the youths are clever."

William stuffed a chunk of bread in his mouth and swallowed hard as he spoke. "I met one."

Campion lifted his eyebrow in curiosity. "Met one? When?"

John pinched his son's arm. William flinched and glared at his father. "I did meet one, father! Do you not remember the day of the banqueting in Kenilworth? The boy who accused you and Edward of plotting against the Queen?"

Campion gripped his knife between his fingers and leaned

forward. "What of this? Arden, you did not tell me this story."

Arden coughed. "Yea, I suppose I had forgotten it. 'Twas a trifle. The boy heard me complaining about Robert Dudley, nothing more, and he thought to reveal the words to Her Majesty; but you could tell neither she nor Walsingham believed his antics. I cannot imagine there was much to him to worry about."

"Yea, you might think that," Campion added, "but it is boys such as he Walsingham molds. Many of them turn out to be skilled at killing and lying way before they turn twenty. What was the boy's name, William?"

"He said it was Harry Le Roy."

Campion smiled and slapped his hand on the table. "See, what did I tell you? Clever boy! The boy used an alias, of course, for most of the common folk would not know Henry the Fifth used that name the night before the battle of Agincourt. No doubt he is educated which fits with the modus operandi of Walsingham."

William wrinkled his brow. "Then, what was his real name?"

Campion shrugged. "We may never know, William. Walsingham trains these boys to conjure characters in a snap, and some, depending on their education, are more adept to it than others. But, no matter for now, for we have our devices. Even now as we speak in secret, Rome is preparing several avenues for our lady in Fotheringhay Castle."

Mary Arden crossed herself and drew her fingers to her lips. "Dear Queen Mary. She will be our salvation." Mary Shakespeare patted her on the arm.

John looked across to his wife and his eyes rounded. "You speak of the Scottish Queen?"

Edward answered. "Yea, we do. Campion told us earlier before you arrived, it is Rome's wish Mary of Scots take the throne of England as the only legitimate heir from the Tudor line. Rome does not recognize Elizabeth and never will since her excommunication."

John turned to Campion. "Then what will we do to further this business?"

William grabbed hold of his father's arm and whispered, "Hush, father, for you do not wish to tangle yourself in this web."

John snatched his arm away. "Leave me be, boy. Some of us are more inclined to uphold the faith of our forefathers in any way we can."

William looked past his father and noticed Campion's sly grin. The man directed his next words to William. "We could use young clever boys as you, William, the same as Walsingham does. You cannot tell me you have no ambition for coin in your purse."

William pursed his lips, pushed away from the table and stood. "Do not presume to know my mind, sir. This all seems foolishness and I cannot see how anything I might do will matter one way or another of who sits on the throne of England. I have one ambition, Master Campion, and it does not include plots that may lead me to losing my name or my life." William bowed to his mother and Lady Arden. "Please, excuse me, but I have lost my appetite."

Campion chuckled as William marched from the room. William heard his words as he ran up the stairs.

"You have quite the ambitious son, John Shakespeare. I warrant we will hear more from him."

Act Two

1579-1583

IX

K it's hand trembled as he clutched the leather handle of the dagger, his palm damp with sweat and the sound of his own heartbeat throbbing in his ears. Walsingham called these necessary things "the wet work of spies" and now, this necessary thing he feared now faced him across the narrow alleyway in Southwark. Kit tried to swallow, but fear dried his throat and his pasty tongue stuck to the top of his mouth as a raspy young voice questioned him in the darkness.

"Are you ready to die, boy?"

To be or not to be; to kill or be killed. This was the fulfillment of the dream haunting his nights in Frankfort and the climax to the schooling beneath the molding hands of Walsingham. Adjusting his eyes to the darkness, beneath the starless night, he looked from side to side for an escape. Nothing. The buildings crowded tight, hovering over his head with their witnessing windowed eyes.

So much changed in four years, not only in the increase of plaster and beamed houses or stone buildings crowding together along the Thames, but also in Kit's packed heart and mind. After Kenilworth, he and Philip basked for a year midst the bards of Ireland where he filled his portfolio with sonnets; and then, they traveled on to soak in an ocean of knowledge for three years in Italy. Philip gave Kit a new name, calling him Speed, in commendation for the fast deliverance of messages back and forth between spies on the continent. Philip thought Kit's quickness came from obedience when, in fact, Kit hated the job of a messenger. Still, in the job, he was learning he could trust no one, not even some boys in Walsingham's service, such as the one now urging him toward his first blood-letting. On more than one occasion did a message go astray, falling into the hands of Catholic insurgents; and more than once, did the failure end in finding of one of Walsingham's lackeys in an upper room with his neck sliced from ear to ear or face-down in the water near the bank of the Thames.

Kit learned wariness and cleverness, biding his time, watching faces and turning his ear to Rome's henchmen, keeping his back from their daggers and avoiding the day when he himself would become a murderer. With the sand draining out from the hourglass and nowhere to run, Kit closed his eyes and tightened his grip on the dagger.

The hidden boy near to him breathed a sinister laugh. "Never thought this to be you last day, huh, Christopher?"

"Walsingham will know of this," Kit answered.

"Ah," the boy's voice raised, "you think he will even care where your body lies? You must be young to not yet know you are merely his chattel."

Kit knew, but did not reply to the boy's taunting. The boy laughed again. "Come now and let us put an end to this."

Kit's eyes flew open as he heard a footstep toward him. He plunged the blade into the darkness in front of him. Another laugh.

"I can sense Walsingham has yet to train you in the wielding of a knife. I thought you to give me a little scuffle, but 'tis no matter; this kill will be easy."

Kit wiped a tear away with the back of his hand and slumped to the ground. The boy was right. Walsingham sent him the gift of the dagger three years earlier on his twelfth birthday, but being in the service of the poetic Philip did little to his becoming skilled with the knife. Philip stretched Christopher's training in history, loaded him with books and indulged his moments of writing. By the time their ship cut back across the Channel to England, sights and sounds of the continent inundated his brain. He carried a trove of fodder for his plays in the form of blackamoors and harlots, lords and ladies, scoundrels, knaves, lawyers, soldiers, apothecaries, players and minstrels, Venetian canals, Paduan universities and Veronian street fights.

A thought sparked his brain as he thought about the street fights where he learned surprise was always the key to winning. Kit lowered himself further and stretched out flat on the ground, hoping the secret boy would not think to watch his steps along the path, perhaps even passing right by him.

Another step, closer now, and Kit steadied his breathing. One more and Kit could smell the leather of the boy's boot standing within inches of his face. Kit knew he had a choice at this moment. To kill or to be killed. The quandary - whether the boy might wait at the entrance to the alleyway to plunge his dagger into the side of Kit's neck as he exited or if he would pass on into the night - puzzled Kit's will. Kit did not want to kill, and yet, the desire to live, the wish to continue his writing, overwhelmed him. He closed his eyes and whispered in his mind.

"If it be not now, yet it will come. The readiness is all." A vibrating spark rushed upon him and he clutched hold of the boy's boots, sending him sprawling across the cobblestones. Kit gritted his teeth and dove forward, vacating all thought in his head as he lifted the dagger above his head and bore down upon the wriggling boy. The blade found a soft spot, and the boy released a painful sigh.

A fervor swept over Kit and he dug deep, twisting until a gurgle crept from the boy's throat. In the pitch blackness, Kit's breath shivered over the fear in his own throat, heaving into the air as he waited for the boy's clenched fingers around his arm to loosen. When the boy's hand thudded to the ground, Kit pulled the dagger from the fleshy sheath and fled into the night. He never even saw the nameless boy's face, but the heat of the warm liquid as the blood bubbled across his fingers forever flowed into his mind.

He told no one of the murder, nor of his simpering wails as he rushed to the muddy bank of the Thames to vomit into the waters, nor of how many times he tried to clean his hands of the blood in the garderobe basin. Philip never noticed the change, but Walsingham knew. Somehow, without even a word, Kit's guardian gave him a knowing wink and a smile. Kit gazed into his own reflection in the wash bowl, wondering if Walsingham could see the fleck of murder in his eyes. *Without a doubt,* he thought, *for those with the same nature recognize their kin.*

Even more did Kit know that Walsingham suspected when the ambassador gave word to Philip to take his page on holiday, a brief reprieve in the countryside to clear their heads of thoughts of politics and intrigue, like giving a sweet to a child who scraped his knee.

As their coach clacked across London Bridge, Kit felt saturated and older for a boy of fifteen. Sidney, however, sulked since his failed mission for the Queen. There would be no reconciliation between Elizabeth of England and the Emperor of Italy. The fragile dance continued and Sidney no closer to being of any great use to her. Kit saw a change in his master. Philip appeared tired of wrangling supporters of England's religion and politics, as well as the delicate balance of keeping the Queen happy so favors continued. Philip sighed when the heathered plains of Salisbury appeared over the hilltop.

Tiredness enveloped him as well, and now, he was a stranger to his own self. He hoped the spring air might bring a few months of peace away from the sludge of Court and the haunting bloody image of his first murder. Philip looked over at him as he slumped against the seat.

"Christopher, I am thinking to write a letter to the Queen and discourage the continued talks of her marriage to the Duke of Alencon. Too many years have passed, and it is obvious she will never marry him nor my uncle Leicester, nor anyone it seems. Robert would not be a bad consort, methinks, but to convince the members of the Privy Council is another matter. Keeping a Queen happy is a tiring business, do you not think, Kit?"

Kit smiled, but did not answer. "O, well," Philip continued. "Perhaps we can just stay here at Wilton House and let all this nonsense just pass us by. Yet, we all dance around her like stringed marionettes, obeying to keep our hands and our heads. You know, you have grown tall and seen much, have you not, boy?"

Kit nodded, keeping his stare out the window. The white towers of Wilton House topped over the trees as they crossed the Nadder River.

Philip nudged Kit's leg with the toe of his boot. "Do not worry, boy, all of this will be over soon. Walsingham has given me instruction to have you back to Canterbury the first of September. He thinks you are ready to move on to the University at Cambridge, thus releasing you as my page after all these years. Christopher, I will be sorry to see you go."

Kit smiled at him as the airy blue skies and mossy green heaths sparkled with morning dew across the Earl of Pembroke's estate. Spring lusted with fertility in the bursting forth of heather, daisies, roses and the sweet tender leaves of the yew bushes in the knot garden.

Yet, to Kit, Wilton appeared nothing more than a sterile regal promontory nudged near a winding stream curving toward the willows and oaks. Her ancient and stoic square towers stood sentinel over the noble family in her corridors since the days of the Queen's father. None of the stone castle mattered to Kit, being just another place to serve Philip—making sure his cup stayed filled, his clothes arranged and messages from Walsingham delivered into his master's hand. The prospect of leaving Philip's service and setting off for the scholarly halls of Cambridge drew mixed emotions in his heart. All would be well if everyone left him alone to attend to his writing, but that old gnawing feeling returned hearing Walsingham requested the change. Kit knew there would be more to his schooling than mere book learning.

Kit wandered into the lower cloisters of the east wing, peering through the windows of the grand hall and ascending the marble Gothic stairs to the anteroom where Philip told him to meet him. The door squeaked open to his touch, and he hesitated in the opening. The image of a young girl standing near the window caught his eye. For a moment, he thought Calliope, his long gone imaginary friend, stood in the flesh. The sunlight streaming through the lead-encased glass glowed around her like an aura and her golden hair shimmered as she wrapped a curl around her index finger.

Philip waved Kit forward to present him to Sir Henry Herbert, the Earl of Pembroke, and to the young girl. She turned her head toward him as he entered and Kit sucked in his breath. Her delicate lips parted, and she smiled, filling Kit's mind with words and a mystery as to her identity.

During the journey to Salisbury, Philip told Kit of his sister. She prided herself on poetry, being from the foremost family of patrons, the echelon of Elizabeth's court, who favored music, art, literature and languages; her family denied her nothing from education to sweetmeats. Philip's passion for poetry was her passion, as well, and he told Kit she desired to inspire a poet with greatness. Kit wondered if this young girl with her lusty blue eyes was this sister and had those eyes found a hopeful prey.

Conversation ceased as he approached them. Philip motioned for Kit and presented him to his two companions. Kit bowed and lifted his stare, noticing how Philip and the girl giggled and nudged each other like two doting siblings. Philip exalted her beauty with a silly poem, stopping in mid sentence with a firm kiss upon her mouth. She giggled once more and pushed him aside.

"Dear brother, have I not told you to cease kissing me in such a way? My husband grows weary of his jealousy of my love for you and already you have the house staff whispering horrid rumors."

Philip laughed and led her by the hand. "Sister, dear, let them talk nonsense, for I have it on good authority servants have nothing better to do with their time than to create sensational stories of other people's lives, they themselves having none of their own. I was just telling your husband..."

The girl sighed and walked past Sir Henry, circling Kit like a hawk. "Pray, Philip, do not bore me with the details of your conversations with my husband. You have yet to introduce your friend here with the dark eyes."

Kit's cheeks warmed. Each time she caught his eyes with hers, he saw flashes of Calliope. She stood before him, and his mind etched her every detail—the softness of her eyelashes laying on her white skin, the cascades of golden curls weighting the pleated cuff collar haloing her slender neck, and the perfect oval pout of her pink mouth. Her lips curved into a smile as Kit's gaze darted back and forth between her and the Earl.

Philip circled his arm around her waist and obliged her curiosity. "This, dear sister, is Christopher Marlowe. He has been my page since he was eight, but soon will return to the University at Corpus Christi. Kit, this is my sister, Mary, the lady of this house."

Mary extended her hand. Kit bowed and brushed his lips across her knuckles. "My lady, 'tis an honor."

Philip continued. "Call him Speed, sister, for indeed he is so, speedy in wit, in learning and in service. He has already done great service to Sir Walsingham at such a young age."

Sir Henry poured brandy wine in several pewter cups and handed them out as he gestured for all to sit near the windows. "Service to Walsingham," Henry questioned. "Pray, boy, what would such a young one have to do for him; and what is your age, boy?"

"I am fifteen, sir," Kit replied.

Mary giggled a little. "Such a young age, you say? Only two years my junior! And you can count me an old maid, for two years I have belabored great service as well, being married to this old man since I was fifteen."

Kit caught the hard look between husband and wife. Before his eyes sat Sir Henry, an aged man bent with time, a man well known in Court from his years spent on former wives and mistresses and a man denied eternity from lack of offspring. Kit took the meaning in Mary's words that now the old Lord sought his legacy in his young fertile wife. She softened her husband's reproving stare with a coy biting of her lip and Kit watched the Earl shrug as if his body might melt into the velvet chair where he sat.

Her attention and notice turned back to Kit. "Would it surprise you, Speed, to know I already know of you? Pray, not at sight, but your name?" Kit widened his eyes as she continued. "Philip indulged my curiosity by sending me tasty pieces of your writings. I must say, Famous Victories, Lucan and Scanderberg show such promise. Pray, tell me, what are you working on presently?"

Kit's throat went dry as Philip disclosed the secrets of his portfolio. "Dearest, he is taking on the might task of translating Ovid into English. What have you to say to that?"

Mary licked her lip as if she stared at a comfit. "Indeed, a protégé in Latin and Greek? Hmm, you must have a quite trained tongue. I perceive you have a rare talent, Speed, which we must urge and patronize. Dare I say he will be a poet for a reckoning?"

"You perceive right, sister dear. In seven years he has learned six languages and his poetry and play writing is incomparable." Philip continued as Kit's stare fell to the floor, avoiding the amorous glint in Mary's eyes. "Come now, Kit, do not look so forlorn. There will be many who will wish to read your works. My dear sister, before you sits a youngling who has traveled the world, yet knows little of the world. Take not his darkness for sadness that you have tread upon his treasures without his consent. I have learned there is a depth about him I fear no one will ever be able to delve into."

Kit glanced up and Mary's face alighted with delight at the mystery. "No one? Pray, is it true, Speed?"

Kit's body warmed, once more, but not with adoration. Their eyes and words toyed with him, volleying their thoughts about his works like that old cat he once saw in the nave. Even the lethargic Earl who dozed into his cup sent fire into Kit's brain. He stood and walked to the open arched window, taking solace in the bending grasses at the riverbank.

Without turning to watch their faces, he spoke. "Enough! 'Tis enough! There is truth in what you speak, but you will not toy with me. Yea, I feel even I will not reach the depths of this darkness, but to say I know nothing of this world is false. I fear I know too much already and the knowledge sickens me. I feel the words rising," his voice lowered to a whisper. "With ink that's black on paper white, morning noon and eke at night, my fate, my life, my death endite." Kit looked over his shoulder as Philip raised his glass in the air.

"To thy words, boy, and to thy legacy. I toast my dark young poet friend who I warrant is the muse's darling. Now, let's to dinner, for I am famished." Philip nudged the Earl, who roused his slumbering head, and the two of them trod across the hall and disappeared down the staircase.

Mary brought herself between Christopher's stare and the window. She touched her hand to his chest and fingered the gold buttons of his doublet.

"Did you know I too dabble in verse?" She waited for a moment for an answer, for a moment to catch Kit's gaze in hers; still Kit looked beyond her out across the garden fountains.

"Kit," she urged. "Christopher?" She caught his look with the soft sound of his Christian name. In the sunlight aura, Calliope appeared before Kit again, but Mary's words filled her mouth. "I suppose you seek a muse, do you not? A patron of sorts? 'Tis the way, since many writers seek someone who can fund their days of sitting at a desk to ply their trade, but, as you know, many never find one and their art fades away. But, then again, there are few who possess fair looks and a pleasing tongue to catch the attention of a muse. You, dear Christopher, will not have that problem. We shall talk more of such things." She bit her lip again, sending a fiery chill through his heart with one word. "Privately."

X

K it was unsure what to think. Like the sudden sting of a bee, his skin burned with thoughts of her. There had been other moments over the past year when his blood raced; brief little encounters, inklings of the changes in his mind and body—the Lion's Head wench whose breasts boiled over the top of her blouse as she shoved them in his face and giggled, sending a ripple of laughter around the room when he stood up in a start and sent her sprawling on her backside. Even Philip chuckled in his beer and sprayed a foamy laugh across the table. And then, the dark-haired goddess he met at the Ambassador's home in Rome, who touched his hand during a masque dance at the Embassy. They stole away and hid behind a velvet curtain draping between the columns of the banqueting hall to share a moment pocked with deep kisses and declarations of sudden love.

Mary stirred different feelings; a distracting combination of the two experiences, and the distraction welcoming, yet unnerving, to Kit. She appeared the soft innocent angel on the outside, but when she narrowed her eyes, he saw flashes of a craving unfulfilled. An excitement fluttered in his stomach, still he thought it best, for now, to avoid any private time with her.

Two days passed without seeing her and he sought the refuge of a secluded place near the bank of the river to fill his mind with words. The breezy spring days melded into the hot days of summer, so Kit rose early just as the sun tinted the sky in soft pinks and oranges. Lord Pembroke obliged him with a young mare to ride and he spurred her from the stables, through the bank of sculpted yew bushes and towering cypress trees and across the temple bridge over the river. As he gazed out between the marble colonnade supporting the roof, the young Jennet pricked her ears and whinnied. Kit watched her nostrils flare and blow as he patted her on the neck and dismounted.

Through the willow branches draping across the ground and water, a familiar form appeared like Venus stepping out of the mist rolling off the river. Her image caused a fever in his brain and the first time the thought of her pricked a passionate verse in his mind. The mare pounded her hoof against the bridge stones and reared, causing him to lose his grip upon her rein. She bolted as the figure emerged from the swaying branches leading a jet-black stallion. Kit's heart fluttered as he realized the figure was Mary and not Calliope. Mary turned the stallion loose, sending the mare into a frenzied gallop, and then, ran to Kit, laughing and pointing as the two horses ran into the pasture.

"Watch how she plays with him and, all the while, she is actually seeking to yield."

Kit pondered the look on this young girl's face; her wild eyes, cheeks flaring red, her breasts rising and falling with her breathless anticipation. He had seen nothing like her. The marble statues of Aphrodite, adorning the streets of Rome, paled compared to the soft creaminess of her skin.

The two horses continued to kick and bite, which sent Mary into bubbling laughter. She grabbed hold of Kit's hand and pulled him into the veil of the willow branches. Suddenly, she spun around and pushed him against the tree, her mouth searching for his lips as if she were a starving wretch. He turned his face away from her, holding his hands against her shoulders. She laughed aloud and tripped him to the ground.

"Why do you resist me? Do you not see your muse is seeking you?"

The words filling his brain circled and surged as if in a crucible. Her face blurred before his eyes. He blinked several times to clear his vision, still the heat raced through his blood.

Mary knelt near him, wrapping her fingers over his shoulders and pushing onto his back. "Do you not recognize your muse?" She pulled away the tiny pins fastening the collar around her neck and tossed the pleated halo aside, and then, with boldness, pulled the top of her cinched bodice until her small rounded breasts ached to spill out. "See, my darling, my white skin is a blank page. One kiss from thy poet mouth is all I ask."

Kit's stomach surged with sudden fear and wonder at the same instance. His imaginary friend had never taken on such a lustful form, such a real form with touchable skin and pulsing veins. He pushed her aside until they faced each other. She stroked his face with her fingertips.

"Come, dear Kit, let me coax away the frown upon your brow."

Kit sat up in frustration. "Nay, Mary, leave me alone. You are a wife and your husband most likely looks from the top of the keep at the sport his wife makes."

Mary bit her lip, dropping her stare in a playful act. "Speak not on him, the poor fool. I am a Mary as our former Queen. 'Twould have been a miracle for contrary Mary's garden to grow by the Spaniard prince. I warrant his seed never grew there, and so, like her shall I die barren. And if I do not bear a child to this old Earl, he will rid himself of me. Our dear Queen Elizabeth bestowed a favor to him with this marriage, and she thought to bring a blessing upon me, her dear Robert Dudley's niece, but she has given me a curse instead."

Mary pouted and tiny water droplets formed on her lashes. Reaching across, Kit traced a tear down her cheek with his fingers. "Cry not, my lady. You are young and will have many children."

She lowered her eyes until her lashes fanned out across her cheek and curled her lip in a devilish smile. "Yea, I will, but not issue from the Earl of Pembroke. Our marriage remains unfulfilled for all he can manage now is to eat, drink and fall asleep. Two years have passed, Kit, and I crave poetry and passion and a soft mouth. I am but seventeen after all."

Her words renewed her quest, and she fell upon him as if her kisses would devour. Her lips found his brow, cheek, chin, and then circled again across his face. Still, fear prevented him from answering her with a willing kiss.

She narrowed her eyes. "Kit, the more you resist, the more beauty breeds in your eyes. I will not relent until you give me a kiss." She tried again to find his mouth, but he turned his head away toward the sounds of the river water surging against the rocks. She wrinkled her face and frowned. "You are a flint-hearted boy! 'Tis only a kiss I beg. Why are you so coy?"

Kit smiled, hearing a sonnet kiss his ear. In the dark depths of his mind, he noted the words.

She popped him on the arm with a tender slap. "Why do you smile? Do you jest at me?"

He wrapped his fingers around her chin, his stare melting into hers. "You may be the muse I seek, Mary, for in your words a sonnet I have found. I think this day will be one for remembrances befitting the forceful Venus."

"Indeed it shall if you will surrender your Adonis lips. Let me taste the honey words you have found and perhaps I will inspire your youthful quill to thrust words upon my unblemished pages."

Kit closed his eyes, surrendering to the spring senses: the breeze drifting across the riverbank as it rustled the tender willow branches, the morning lark singing out of tune, and the softness of her curls as they brushed across his cheek. In the darkness behind his eyelids, Calliope's lute played, and as he opened them, before him sat an inspiration. Words filled his mind and flowed out upon his tongue.

"Fair Queen, if any love you owe me, measure my strangeness with my unripe years. Before I know myself, seek not to know me. No fisher but the ungrown fry forebears, the mellow plum doth fall, the green sticks fast, or being early pluck'd is sour to taste."

Mary giggled. "Sour to taste? O, I think not. Shall I continue it then? Let me see... does the tender spring upon thy tempting lip show thee unripe? Yet, mayst thou be tasted? Make use of time, Kit; let not advantage slip. Beauty within itself should not be wasted." She picked a violet and held it up to his eyes. "Fair flowers that are not gather'd in their prime, rot and consume themselves in little time."

The word play delighted him and he felt the fear subside into a surging curiosity. "Mary, you could very well be my match. If you will say good day and let me part, then you will have a kiss, and only my kiss, for I sense a deeper meaning to your looks. Forsooth, you never thought you may have reason to fear unleashing the secrets in my soul."

Her goddess smile displayed victory. She nodded and said, "Good day," closed her eyes and waited for the reward.

He took a moment more to adore her face. His hand trembled as he ran his fingertips across her cheek. Words quivered inside him like rain adding to the river and forcing the rushing waters to overflow the bank. Her sweet coral lips stood ready and just before touching, he breathed another line.

"Shall I compare thee to a summer's day; thou art more lovely and more temperate."

The sweet first kiss melted away all resistance and the hot summer sun heated their bodies to a quick desire. She conquered as their mouths folded into one another and her hands fumbled to unfasten the buttons of his doublet. She brushed her fingers across the smooth skin of his chest. Kit shivered, pausing his kiss to look into her eyes. Her blue eyes softened as she bit her bottom lip. He rested his back across the mossy grass and she lowered her mouth to his ear.

"Perhaps you will write a mighty sonnet about this day," she whispered.

He closed his eyes and gasped as she kissed behind his ear. Like a thousand tiny pin pricks tingling across his stomach, his fever surged and his heart pounded until he could take no more of her caresses. He sat up, seizing her around the waist and crushing her mouth with his. He spun her onto her back, her voluminous silk gown gathering in a heap between them. His teeth shuddered as he yielded to her thirst, thrashing all reason away, forgetting shame's pure blush and honor's wrack. There beneath the willow tree, time paused as two poetic fires met and consumed one another, purging their passionate rhymes like waves breaking though a dam and flooding the virgin plains. She ran her fingers up his neck, tangling her fingers in his hair as victory quaked through her. His lip trembled when he caught the pleased glint in her eye. She sat up and pushed him aside, ironing the wrinkles of her crumpled gown with her palms as she smiled a knowing smile. She leaned over, kissed him hard on the mouth and darted away like a carefree doe. Kit rose on his elbow and wiped the beads of sweat on his brow. Elation and defeat took turns on each heartbeat, his mind pondering the rapture in his exhausted breath and confusion upon her quick departure.

Indeed, 'twas a love too early known and known too late, he thought to himself. The opposing feelings of lost and found mingled in his heart. He and Philip spent the summer at Wilton House, eighty sultry days mingled with nightly liaisons. The days filled with lessons of poetry, love and lust. Yet, Mary proved to be a brief muse, satiating her wish for a child and using Christopher as a willing pawn to her own end. When the first cool morning heralded the change of season and yellow kissed the leaves of the elm trees, Mary's affections turned likewise variable toward him, turning her stare out the window when he entered a room, yawning when he recited a new sonnet he wrote for her or finding more pleasure in embroidery than she did with his body. She sparked an anger in him as strong as his passion, and indeed, awakened the dangerous secrets of his heart.

He slid a note into her hand beneath the table during breakfast. Three weeks passed since their last crazed encounter in Mary's own goose down bed, an afternoon when the Earl snoozed in his library with a snifter of brandy wine and Philip hunted fox in the nearby forest, leaving the two of them alone with their poetry and delights.

She stood up from the breakfast table with her wine cup in her hand and walked to the window. The Earl and Philip watched her and Kit rested his cheek on his hand, pretending to be uninterested in her sudden rise from the table.

The Earl questioned with concern. "My dear, are you unwell?"

She kept her stare toward the gardens, unfolded the paper without notice and read. Kit felt proud of the lines; a lyrical verse oozing love from a shepherd boy to his secret lover. The lines spoke simple, an honest request to 'live with me and be my love.'

Kit looked up from his plate of bread and cheese and noticed the sly grin on the Earl's face. The old man nudged Philip on the arm.

"Your sister might have reason to feel poorly. I felt quite overcome a few weeks ago when she kept urging the wine on me, not realizing until later that my wife sought to complete our marriage after all these years. She is quite the spirited filly," he laughed, "well, a filly no more, I should say."

Philip snickered and raised his cup. "Then a toast to my sister and her husband. Perhaps soon there will be an heir to grace your Lord's table. What say you, sister, is this the reason for your humor?"

The heat rose in Kit's neck and he saw her flick her brother a glance over her shoulder. Kit pushed away from the table and rose, bowing to Sir Henry and Philip. "Sir, excuse me, please. I wish to finish up the letters you are sending to the Queen and Lord Burghley."

Philip waved him in dismissal and as he pounded through the anteroom doors, he heard her feign a headache and the hurried rustling of her gown as she came up behind him. He turned in a snap, grabbed her by the wrist and pulled her into a shadowed corner of the lower cloisters. Before she could speak, he covered her mouth with his. She gasped and tore herself away from him.

"Mary," he asked, "why are you avoiding me?"

She wiped her mouth with the back of her hand and lifted her chin, her demeanor transforming into the aloof noble lady of the house.

"Things have changed, Christopher."

Kit stomped his foot and blasted a huff. "Changed because you finally bedded the old blind courser?"

He saw her grimace. "That is none of your concern." She reached across and held out the note. "And I will have no more of your sonnets."

Kit snatched the paper from her fingers, feeling a sharp ache in his chest. "Pray, tell me one thing, Mary. Are you with child? Have you succeeded in your quest and now you wish to discard me?" Her face remained stone as he sought a way to soften her. "Please, Mary, come away with me. We could go to Ireland..."

"Ha," she bit back. "You expect me to leave my life as a lady of Elizabeth's court for an unknown and penniless poet?"

Her stab cut deep into his heart. "I thought you loved me, my muse."

She turned on her heel and stomped away, her answer cutting through the air as direct as a pointed arrow. "You mistook me."

Kit could not concentrate on matters of State, or missions or Philip's prying stares; nothing, but filling his portfolio with words to her. Late in the night, he opened the window to let the brisk air sooth his boiling blood, leaned over his desk, dipped the quill and penned:

"The expense of spirit in a waste of shame is lust in action;
and till action, lust is perjured, murderous, bloody,
full of blame, savage, extreme, rude, cruel, not to trust,
enjoy'd no sooner but despised straight,

past reason hunted, and no sooner had past reason hated,
as a swallow'd bait on purpose laid to make the taker mad;
mad in pursuit and in possession so;
had, having, and in quest to have, extreme;
a bliss in proof, and proved, a very woe.
Before, a joy proposed; behind, a dream.
All this the world well knows;
yet none knows well to shun the heaven
that leads men to this hell."

He left the sonnet in a basket of embroidery thread. The next day she wrote back with another thorn to his already bleeding heart. "Again, what are you that I should sacrifice my place as the Countess of Pembroke? Your name is nothing."

Kit crumpled the note in his hand, grinding his teeth and cursing the obstructed lust surging in his blood for her.

The first week in September, he and Philip loaded their trunks onto the coach. The Earl came to see them off, shaking their hands and wanting to know when Philip might return. Philip gave his answer, not until he helped settle the alliances on the Continent for Her Majesty, wrecking Kit's hopes of ever seeing her again. Mary never came to say farewell although Kit thought he saw a curtain flutter as the coach ambled down the drive.

And so, he dammed his passion and diverted the waters to spilling his thoughts on paper. In the days to follow, as they sped along to Canterbury, Mary blackened his dreams as a dark lady hiding beneath a scarlet cloak. During a brief stop for refreshment at the Harvest Inn near Surrey, he dipped a quill in the ink horn at his belt and scrawled the line: "in nothing art thou black save in thy deeds." He ground his teeth together and snapped the quill between his fingers as easy as breaking a twig. The sharp splinters sliced through his skin and a trickle of blood oozed across his inky fingers.

How was I to know, he thought as he cradled his head in his hands. *I am a foolish boy making rash decisions and not looking ahead.*

Yet, for all her betrayal and rejection, his writing blossomed in the experience. He determined to drive her from his mind, diving into the prospects of University life and studies with all the force he could muster. He even spurned Calliope from his dreams, blaming her for sparking the lust in his body and mind.

She giggled at him and whispered into his ear, "My darling, all such things will make you a better writer. Look at the mighty lines you have written. If you had never tasted the pleasures and the fall, would you know the words to use?"

She was right, of course. Still, the thrashing of the quill against paper did nothing to quell the pain. The darkness remained with him, hovering like a wraith over his shoulder.

XI

Old for his years at fifteen, he returned to Canterbury, his birthplace and home. Archbishop Parker welcomed them back, giving Kit a room at the far end of the tunneled cloisters. Yet, an awkward strangeness enveloped him, and even the sound of the word "home" across his tongue tasted foreign to him.

Leaving Philip and Parker alone to begin their business, he walked out toward the Stour. The clouds draped Canterbury in gray and gushed out a rain shower muddying the path as he trailed along the edge of the river. The city had grown, a few more timbered houses cropping against the water's edge, a new platform stretching out near the marketplace with a dozen or more skiffs bobbing in the current, and still the Cathedral threw her ancient founded shadow over his back.

He kicked a pebble with his boot, spurring the rock ahead of him and trying not to think of Mary. The crowds thickened and mingled with carts and horses as a young girl shuffled a gaggle of geese ahead of him. The sound of a blacksmith's hammer clanged against an anvil, bringing him from his thoughts, and he realized his feet, once again, found their way back through the alleyways of the Shambles like a prodigal son. This time, with more maturity and a gritty gut, he did not tarry at the corner of the parish. This time, he marched across the garden and rapped on the familiar dark-pitched door.

Even then, just before the door swung open, a hesitation churned in his stomach. He swallowed hard as the face of an angel appeared before him. The little sister he saw years earlier toddling behind his mother stood before him as the adolescent picture of an English beauty; fair face, brown eyes and dark copper hair. As she gathered up her apron in her hands, she revealed her small young body heavy with child. Kit bowed to her, took her hand and kissed the back of her fingers like a gentleman. She flushed, giggled and jerked her hand away.

"You must be Jane Marley," he said.

She answered in a drawl like her mother. "Yea, sir, I am. Can I 'elp ya?"

Kit managed a smile, his insides swirling upon the revelation.

"Well, my lady, I am here to see my mother and father. I am your brother, Christopher."

Her face lit up as if the sun broke through the clouds and shone only on her face. The door pushed open further and Katherine appeared. She shoved Jane out of the way and cocked her head at him.

"Get along upstairs, Jane, before someone sees ya. Well, well, if t'aint the 'igh-stomached boy come 'ome to 'is simple parents."

She fingered the edge of his velvet doublet and stepped aside to let him in the house. The familiar surroundings filled his senses —the pungent smell of soured rushes on the floor, a pot of bubbling leeks over the fire, candlelight flickering against the plastered walls, and his father tinkering at the bench. John raised his eyes as Katherine walked ahead of him.

"John, look ye at who is gracing us wit 'is presence."

He rose and nearly fell into his son, his hands clamoring at Kit's shoulders as if he didn't know whether to shake or hug him. Kit clasped his hands around his father's arms to steady him.

"Sir, I see you are well."

Katherine spat, "Not as well as ye from the looks of ya. I see ye 'ave the chinks now, so 'ow 'bout a little touch for ya ole' mum."

He helped his father sit in a chair and turned to Kate. "From what I hear, you are both doing quite well at my expense."

John found his voice. "Hush, boy! Dare you speak to your mother that way? You owe us respect."

Kit shook his head and laughed. "I owe you respect? I owe you nothing."

Kate walked over and stirred the contents in the pot, all the while clicking her tongue. "O, our Kit is angry that we sent 'im away with that poet fella. Tell me, love, did ya expect such a lofty education on a cobbler's pay? Seems to me you should be thankin' us."

Kit's jaw hurt from the grinding of his teeth. "Thanking you? 'Twould have been enough for me to cut my teeth in the library at the Cathedral, learning my Latin and Greek like an ordinary boy, but nay, you would not have it. You heard the rattle of coins in a velvet pouch and set my course. Do you have any idea to what you have sold me? For the rest of my life I am bound to this path. 'Twill never be enough just to write a pretty verse or delight the crowds with a play, but that I have to pay for it with blood. What kind of people would dispose of their own flesh for a bit of coin?"

John ran his fingers through his thinning gray hair. "We all do what we must, son. We thought you well suited for great things such as they promised us, such as the pulpit. What kind of life could I offer ya? The skills of a simple cobbler, or would ya wash tables at your sister's tavern for the rest of your life? And when the Archbishop suggested, along with the support of the Queen's own secretary, how could we refuse? 'Twas like getting a command from the Queen herself."

Kit spat back. "Ha! When have you ever cared for her? I know your Catholic leanings very well." Kate charged him and reared back her hand to strike him in the face. Kit grabbed hold of her arm and twisted until she winced. "Nay, Kate, there will be no shrewing with me. You set me on this path and now, I could send you both to your deaths for the things I know about you. No more toleration for papists, have you not heard? I saw what the likes of your kind did on the streets of Paris with my own tender eyes and will feel no sorrow at your demise. I did not come here for lost love, I never had that anyway, nor did I come for reconciliation. I came here to write the last act of this play. When I exeunt through this stage door, 'tis over and your penny-stinking faces will see me no more."

As he turned toward the door, Jane's shadow hovered near the kitchen. He paused, thinking to speak to her, but moved on as he heard Kate yell, "Good riddance to ya!"

The rain stopped, yet left behind a murky dampness. A fine misty fog rose off the heated cobblestones as he turned back toward the Cathedral. Emptiness settled in his gut as he rounded the street near the Meister Omers, stopping to read the plaque celebrating the Queen's visit four years ago during her royal progress through the Midlands on to Kenilworth. Kit conjured the spectacle she brought alighting from her fine coach to give alms to the poor and say prayers in the mighty cathedral and his mother among the gaping crowds wriggling her greedy fingers to receive a coin from the Majesty's hand. He clutched his hand over his heart. The void felt as wide and as deep as the waters of the Channel.

The nave was quiet and empty as he entered, no sound but the scuffing of his feet across the limestone and nothing filling his eyes except the sunlight breaking through the images in the glass window casting colors over the kneeling bench before the altar. Kit found the place where he sat all those years ago when he saw the cat eat the mouse and he sat in the chair. The stone vaults curving over his head, once again, amazed him. He closed his eyes and prayed to Calliope, prayed as he had never done before, letting the depths of his soul tear out into words.

"If this is thy will, then let me have the glory. If blood is what you require as payment for my gift, then so be it. Dear Calliope, take your prodigy and make me thy pawn. Mary had my body and has my heart, Calliope, you have my words, Walsingham has my hands; and yet, where is Christopher's soul? What should fellows as I do crawling between earth and heaven? I am bound in a nutshell and the king of infinite space."

The sense of a shadow crossed across his face. He bolted upright, his eyes touching upon a shrouded figure kneeling before the altar. The hairs on his arm prickled.

"Calliope?"

The figure turned, letting the hood of the cloak fall back.

"Nay, brother, 'tis your sister, Jane."

She came and sat near him and took from her pocket a snatching of rosemary. She took his hand and wrapped his fingers around the posy.

"Jane, what is this weed?"

Her eyes sparkled. "O, do you not remember? Rosemary is for remembrances. Pray, love, remember?"

He creased his brow in confusion. "Remember? What should I remember? I do not wish to remember anything of this place."

Her eyes watered and a small tear trickled down her cheek.

"Wilt ya not remember me?"

Kit brushed her cheek with his fingers. "Sweet Jane, you do not even know me, and yet, you give me tears? Why do you cry, sister?"

She stood up and twirled in the middle of the nave. Odd-like and disjointed as her words flew between melancholy and madness. "Do you not know, brother? I cry for the baker's daughter who can never return to 'er former state. See my swelling belly? A song, yea, a song. Do you know it? Young men will do't if they come to't, by cock they are to blame. Before he tumbled me, he promised me to wed... do you know this song?"

Watching her, he scratched his head and cradled his chin upon his opened palm. "Yea, sister, 'tis a common song. What means you, though?"

She scooted near him, sitting on the arm of the chair and took both his hands in her grip. "Dear brother, forgiveness is the key. God will forgive our indiscretions if'n we forgive others. I believe that. These things we must do before we swallow our last breath."

Kit spat onto the church floor. "Well, I do not believe such lies. Where has God been in my life? Where was he the day my parents sold me or the night of the massacre in Paris or even the day when my heart broke?"

Jane hummed and twisted her fingers in his hair. "Poor brother, your dark eyes 'old such sorrow and such 'atred."

He took her hand and kissed her fingers. "Look at you, Jane. I see the same dark hue in your eyes. What rejection have you felt living in my father's house that would send you to seek love in another's bed at such a young age? Your poor small body now misshapen because of your quest. Nothing more than a child with a child. We are a pair, are we not? Pray, tell me, Jane, where is the father of your babe?"

Her stare dropped to the floor and a small whimper escaped across her lips. "The priest read our bans, brother, and yet, I cannot chose but weep for he left me for another. Now ya know me, do you not?"

He wrapped his arms around her and held her to his chest. Her tears soaked his doublet, and she shivered as he rocked her back and forth.

"Hush, sister, hush. I am learning quick that sorrows advance not as single soldiers, but in battalions. I wonder, do all humans sell their souls in search of love or acceptance? My mind feels full of questions of late." She whimpered. "Hush, now, all will be well.

I promise, Jane, when my reward comes, I will send for you. We must stay strong and not let these shocks thwart our purpose."

Kit did not believe what he said, still the words calmed her. He remembered the nights when Calliope did the same for him, reassuring him all would be well—and then, of course, all was not. He barely knew the little girl tucked in his arms, but betrayal latched them together. The calmness broke as she sprung to her feet with her fingers on her lips. Her eyes widened as if a thought seized her. She giggled as she spoke.

"Ah, thank you for your good counsel. Good night, good night, good night. But we must sing it a'down, a'down. Come, dear brother, and fetch me my coach!"

Kit darted toward her and tried to clasp her slender arm, but she raced out of the Cathedral into the streets. The rain returned, streaking through the air in slanted stings. He called to her but the roar of the rain drowned out his voice, and her form disappeared into the heavy grayness. There was nothing more to do, so he returned to his room and shed his drenched clothes. He pulled the nightshirt over his head and took up the quill. The notes flowed out on a new vellum page, notes of his sister—crazed, betrayed, innocence lost, used and cast aside; all the things he himself felt. His female reflection in his sister. He scrawled a name and blew out the candle.

Ophelia

Philip woke him early, tugging at the covers. Kit struggled to stay hidden beneath the blanket, but his master's persistence won out.

"Boy, get up! There is a stirring by the river and the Archbishop wishes for you to report to him the commotion. We will meet back in the nave for morning prayers."

As Kit laced up his doublet and pulled on his boots, his heart beat faster with premonition. He pushed his hair over his ears, threw on a velvet flat cap and rushed though the arches of the cloister.

As he reached the edge of the churchyard, a gathering of villagers crowded at the bank of the Stour. He ran to the crowd and pushed through, oblivious to the gasps and sighs touching his ears. The crowd parted and his heart sank. All the eyes at the riverbank glared, but no one offered a hand to the sin staring up from the waters. A wail started deep in in the pit of his gut, traveling upward, catching on the painful knot in his throat and wiggling through until his tongue released the sound across his lips. Like the unearthly screech of a coney hare the moment before a hunter breaks his neck, so Kit's cry across Canterbury.

Jane floated before his eyes. She appeared beautiful to Kit; mermaid-like below the rippling waters, yet her bloated face held a bluish tint and her tiny neck scarfed with the tangling branches of a willow tree. Her mouth gaped open in an oval as if in permanent song. Kit dove into the river and tore the branches, bracing her body upon his knee. For all his shivering, for all the kisses upon her forehead, as he pushed back the reeds, clutching her body, shaking her and praying her eyes open, her skin drew no warmth from him, but remained cold, stiff and lifeless. Words formed in his mouth but sounded far off like distant echoes filtering through a cave.

"Sister, O, sister! Why, why, why?" He lifted her and sloshed through the crowded reeds, laying her body in the wet grass at the bank. The villagers formed a circle around her. Kit stood up, roaring his pain across the waters and his arms flailed toward them.

"Go away! What will you do for her now? All your stupid sighs and not a one of you offered to help. Get you gone, for I will carry her to the Cathedral."

Through the crowds, his mother stepped forward with a swaddled babe in her arms, her eyes dry and her lip upturned in a smirk. "Stupid boy, you cannot take 'er to church. She birthed 'er babe last eve and then took 'er own life and 'twill burn for it."

Matthew, the blacksmith, curled his fingers over Kit's shoulders, to which Kit jerked away, glaring at him and gritting his teeth. "I prithee, take your fingers from my shoulder, for I have something lurking in me you should fear. Hold off your hand!"

Kate took a step forward and snickered at the sight of her two children. "What cares ya for the soul of this silly little girl?"

Kit ran at his mother, yelling and pointing his finger straight into her face. "I loved Jane! Forty thousand brothers could not with all their quantity of love make up my sum. What wilt you do for her, mother? S'wounds, show me what you will do. What? No tears, no fight, no fasting? Will you not tear yourself or drink bitter vinegar? Do you not come to whine, to outface me by leaping into the water? Nay, I see the answer in your face. What is the reason you use me thus?" He gritted his teeth. "To think I loved you ever, but 'tis no matter. Go away, I say! I will see to her burial. You never cared for her, or for me, so why do we need your company at this last hour."

He cradled Jane in his arms and stumbled down the road toward the Cathedral. His arms ached under the weight of her water-drunk gown as he kicked open the massive doors. Philip saw him and rushed to support her as Kit collapsed in the aisle. He laid her gently upon the stones, patting her hair and adjusting her gown as the Archbishop stood over her. A few of the villagers stood stunned at the back of the nave, their whispering words of 'suicide' and 'sinner' floating on the air. Philip questioned Kit as he caught his breath.

"Who is this, boy?"

"'Tis my sister, Master Sidney. Will you help me bury her?"

Philip gasped. "Indeed? How did she come to this?"

One villager, Matthew, the smithy, wiped his sooty hands in his apron and answered. "She took her own life, your Grace. 'Twas obvious from the branches around her neck."

The Archbishop hardened his look and turned his back to her.

"Then we will not bury her. If she took her own life, then it is blasphemy to have her lying on these holy stones. Get her out of here."

Kit gritted his teeth. "If? We do not know, no one knows of the cause. It could have been an accident. The rain sliced heavy last eve and she could have slipped and tangled herself in the willow."

The Archbishop turned and glared at Kit. "We will give her rites as far as authority permits us, but because of suspicion of her death holds sway, she will rest in unsanctified lodging."

Kit wiped away the tears on his cheeks with the back of his hand.

"No more, sir? Will there be no more?"

"Nay, boy, for holy prayers spoken would profane the service over those who die a peaceful and sinless death."

Kit lifted her once more to his chest and cradled her in his arms.

"Sweet Jane, rosemary is for remembrances. Forgive me for not being there for you all these years. One day, I will make you immortal."

The Archbishop permitted her burial near White Horse Lane in an unmarked and unsanctified grave. Her name forever scarred, a pure innocent scathed by life, betrayal and her search for acceptance and love. Kit knew better and bitterness boiled in his stomach with one question ruling his thoughts. *When this sparrow fell, did God see?* So far, in fifteen years, nothing proved to him that he even cared.

Shock after shock until that last breath. Poor Jane, he sighed. He won and lost a sister in less than a day. Sadness enveloped him as he rested his face against the pillow that evening. Calliope came to comfort, but he sent her away to the dark recesses of his mind. He did not feel like writing. All thoughts of Jane he tucked in the corners of his brain, there next to his thoughts of Mary and of Paris. He knew one day he would retrieve them all; much later, when his reward came, when he became a renowned playwright and he would make the world weep at the massacre of a city, the death of a young girl, and swoon from the passions of a goddess. One day he knew a reckoning would come, but for now, Kit felt himself aging; and he wondered, what sorrows waited on the next sunrise—*another battalion? Another push across the mill board? Where would this all end?*

XII

The townspeople of Stratford welcomed the drizzly days of May. The ice covering the banks of the Avon melted and laughter came again to the waters beneath Clopton Bridge. William watched the children splashing and playing, jumping from the Roman stone wall holding the bridge in an arch. The wagon he sat upon clacked across the cobblestones, rocking his family from side to side. They were one short on their journey to Coventry this spring, and he looked to the spot where his sister, Anne, would have sat. Little Anne did not make it through the harsh winter and he missed the dimples in her face.

Gilbert nudged William from his dreaming. "I heard mother say this would be the last year for our trip to Coventry."

William shrugged his shoulders. "'Tis the same as last year."

Gilbert scooted closer and lowered his voice. "Nay, 'tis not the same. Father said the council in Coventry has banned the mystery plays. They see it as an old influence of Catholic Mary. You know, watch the plays and scare the common folk to confession."

"Well, if 'tis banned, then why do we go?"

Gilbert looked to their father whose back was to them as he rallied the horses to Coventry with a click of his tongue. "Father still clings to it, know you this?"

William frowned and pulled his coat close around his shoulders, still feeling a chill in his bones. Goose flesh raised on his forearms as he thought of his father's descent, the meeting with Edmund Campion and the testament he saw his father tuck above a rafter in his workshop three years ago. So much had changed since that talk with his father. Foremost, the capture of Campion.

William remembered seeing his father stagger in late from a tavern, his cheeks pale and ashy, but not from too much ale. John slumped in a chair, hanging his head over his hands. Mary and William gathered near to him, sitting on the hearth and urging him to speak. When the words came out, what a tale he relayed.

The lower lid of John's eyes reddened. "Walsingham arrested Campion, and many others. Edward sent word that his sources at the Tower reported for the past month they subjected Campion to thumbscrews and the clenching jaws of the Scavenger's Daughter before throwing him into a pit below the White Tower. There is more. Campion crumbled and delivered names to his torturers. After his confession, they dragged him to Tyburn where they burned his innards and quartered him into four parts. His head now sits as food for the ravens atop the ramparts of London Bridge. Edward fears for us all, for the Queen's wrath will descend upon Warwickshire, headed up by that sinister man, Walsingham. We must learn to suspect strangers in our midst."

William found it impossible to care about the death of the Jesuit. His thoughts continued dwelling on pursuing his nagging desire for the stage. A day did not pass without his mind tracing over the peculiar dream he had several years earlier in the forest at Park Hall. Yet, his family needed money and, as the eldest, he had to find work. In between tanning hides for his father's gloving work, setting traps for hares in Charlecote forest, and packing wool in woven bags, he managed a few chances to walk the boards at Burbage's tavern. The plays usually brief, always staying to the classic lines of Plautus or Seneca, but just enough to keep his blood stirring.

John Shakespeare hid well the cause of his fall from the rest of the family. The thought made William's skin crawl, for in his father's demise he brought them all down. His mother turned into a wafting specter, ashy and non-existent, while his siblings bumped about their lives grasping for semblances of their identities, the way for a family of an ambitious man whose star plummets. William squared his shoulders and jaw, setting down a promise in his mind.

I shall never travel that path. When I marry, my family will never suffer from my ambition.

Within the hour, the cart rallied around Wiltshire Wood where the oak tree girths widen and the whispering tales of thieves in the trees fill the air. They topped the hill overlooking a fresh culled wheat field just south of Coventry, green and lush with new growth, and the lilting music of days long past drifted on the wind. Old Celtic ballads plucked upon lutes and lyres, piping and drumming surged through the gathering crowds, beckoning their pagan past. William stood up in the cart and held his hand over his eyes, shielding the spring sun, and scanned the field for the stage. In the distance, past the maypoles adorned with a rainbow of dyed ribbons, two green banners flapped in the breeze embroidered with the arms of the Earl of Leicester. William's blood raced. He clasped his hands together and laughed, grabbing hold of Gilbert's shirt.

"Look there, 'tis Leicester's Men on the stage. If you look for me, there is where I will be."

William jumped from the cart and sprinted across the emerald field. As he approached, the sights and sounds of players drowned out all notice of the festival. Richard Burbage, William's long time friend, saw him from afar and waved to him.

"Will, come join us!"

William touched his hand to the stage, feeling the knots and the grain as he soaked in the sensation pounding within him. He watched the players as they walked around him. They were all there, the statues of his idolatry: William Knell, Tobias Mills and John Singer, decked in costume. Tarleton, adorned in white face paint and rosy cheeks, sat on the steps tapping upon a tabor. William nodded to him as he rounded the corner of the stage.

Richard came up to his elbow and nudged him. "What say you, Will, shall you join us for a line or two?"

A knot formed in his stomach as he cut his stare to Richard. "What do you mean? To perform with Leicester's Men? Surely they would not allow it."

Richard pulled a mask from his cloak. "Who is to know? 'Tis a masque we perform today. You know Sidney's masque The Lady of May?"

William huffed. "Know it? Has not every child in Christendom suckled on his works?"

Richard handed him the mask. "Then put this on and we will keep the secret. Master Wilson owes me a favor. I will have you in his mark, so come with me."

The groundlings gathered before the stage and roared at the clown Tarleton's prologue, his comic ambles full of religious slights tame enough to keep his head and wild enough to thrill the audience. The masque came next and William hit his cues with finesse, even falling upon the gestures and attitudes like natural rote. As the last exeunt passed and the final bow before a cheering crowd, William gazed out behind his mask upon the faces and heard his calling. His heart soared. At that moment, his eyes fell upon a golden haired maiden gazing up at him as Andromeda upon Jason. She tilted her head toward him, giggled and wove away into the crowd.

The May dance began. Hundreds of people gathered at the poles, clapping to the rhythm of the pipes and tabors and watching as maidens attired in white laced corsets and flowing blue skirts circled and braided the ribbons of the maypole, in and out, twisting the colors, as their voices soared breathless in laughter and song. William watched only one girl among the virginal flowers, her hair shimmering like struck gold coins dipped and cooled in water, and flowing down her back to her waist.

As she twirled near, William, in a burst of passion, clasped her hand and pulled her away from the dance. She ran with him to a shaded spot behind the stage where the hanging painted tapestries hid their conference from prying eyes, even as the mask on his face hid his desire.

She gasped as he pulled her near to him and held up his palm before her eyes. "Forgive my hand for its boldness."

She smiled and lowered her eyes, her eyelashes fanning out across her creamy cheek. "I forgive you," she answered with the voice of an angel. "Yet, your boldness was only in response to what you saw in my eyes. I watched you on the stage. Never has the Coventry plays stuck me so until I saw your eyes behind the mask."

William shivered. "Truly? So suddenly?"

Her pink mouth curved into a smile. "Did you not feel the same when you saw me watching you? Did you not wish to speak words with me?"

William snatched off his mask, throwing it to the ground. "Nay, sweet lady, 'tis not words I thought to seek on this pagan day."

He seized her around the waist, yet the sudden fervor subsided into a gentleness as their lips touched. Their mouths melded into one and William felt a tender awakening, an untouched soul discovering a faith surpassing words. As their bruised and breathless lips parted, they stared in adoration into each other's face. She touched her fingers to her lips and giggled. William's thoughts lightened and a dizzy fever seized him. The spring heat popped beads of sweat across his brow and he tugged at the tightness of his doublet collar as a sudden awkwardness filled the moment.

She turned away from him, retreating to the sounds of her mother calling her name. He grabbed hold of her hand, once more, before she left their hiding place.

"Where are you going?"

Her cheeks flushed. "My mother calls me presently and I must attend her."

"Tell me, then, are you a muse? Your smile makes me think so, and it inspires me to perform the entire play by myself."

She reached up and touched his cheek. "You shall have my inspiration if you wish. I gave it even before you did ask for it."

"What is your name and shall I call on you?"

"Those that know me call me Anne and I shall send to you of where we may meet again."

"Then, know this, dearest Anne, I shall forevermore be your Will."

The sounds of the May fair filled his ears as he watched her leave and his heart reveled in the festival. He slipped the mask back over his face, mounted the stage and drew the crowds around him as he fell into character. Through the sea of faces, all he saw was her smile, a smile inspiring him to strut and fret upon the boards until the groundlings shouted accolades upon his name.

As the sun faded, William slowed his pace along the narrow roadway into Stratford. A few of the young men of Leicester's troupe swayed and sang in a drunken chain ahead of him. He kept his eye over his shoulder, watching Anne as she walked in the other direction with her family. Richard ran up beside him and shoved him hard in the back.

"You showed me up today! I swear, Will, if you would only

come to London, I could get you an apprenticeship with us. I am thinking to build a theater there." Richard looked toward William's gaze. "Oh, I see now where your mind lies."

"What family is she," William asked. "Do you know?"

Richard shrugged. "I know only her father's name is Whatley from Temple Grafton, but anything else, I know not. Come now, Will, and lets to my father's tavern and drink our fill. Put aside your long face of loving looks and enjoy our pagan day."

William shook his head, his strides slowing with the heaviness of his heart. "I am enjoying our pagan day, but not with thoughts of drinking ale with you."

The other fellows of the troupe folded Richard into their pack with laughter and jesting. Richard threw his arm around Gilbert and looked at him with a sour face. "Your brother is sadder tonight, methinks. Cupid hath sunk his arrow deep and cleft his heart in twain."

His words sent the revelers into an uproar as they swooned and blew kisses into the wind. William crossed his arms and kicked the dirt with his toe. Richard put a scarf over his head and continued his prank.

"Shall we conjure her for you, Will?"

Richard poked him in the side, trying to coax a smile to William's lips with his winking eye.

William never smiled, but brought Richard to a peace with his words. "Get you gone, Richard, for tonight I find no delight in drink or in your merriment. I am sick in thought of my lady. I pray you, leave me be."

Richard slapped him on the back and motioned for the troupe to be away. "Very well, but take my advice, dear friend. With your heart bent on love tonight, go straight home. If you wish to stay faithful to this muse, let not this awakening and youthful humors lead you to another wench's bed to quench your unsatisfied desires."

William smiled then. "I take your meaning and will in all haste to my father's house."

Richard ran ahead to catch up with the troupe. "I shall drink a toast to thee tonight, and shall drink another on your wedding day."

William waved to them as they disappeared into the night. As he walked down the solitary path, his mind drifted back to the fair. Nearly the entire town of Stratford attended, and folk from as far away as Elmley, and as near as Shottery and Temple Grafton. Temple Grafton, the home of his new love. He pictured her at home sitting by the window, her golden hair lying on her shoulder and tied with a simple blue ribbon, and her chin upon her hand as her lips parted in a sigh, a perfect whisper as his name crossed her perfect mouth.

He stopped and skimmed a stone across Shottery brook. Sporadic rain droplets formed circles across the surface of the water, building until the clouds burst open. William cursed as he ran along the path toward Stratford, his clothes drinking the liquid and the path fast becoming mud. In the roaring downpour, he stopped in his tracks and listened. A woman's voice filtered from the forest on the other side of the brook. He looked ahead and saw candlelight flickering in the window of a nearby house. He hesitated, thinking of the warm dry fire at his father's house only a short run away, and then, he heard her again. He jumped across the brook and made a path through the trees.

"Ho? Who is here?"

The 'help' came muted at first, but increased as he found his way to the woman. He pushed back the branches and saw her sitting in the mud, her face wet with rain and tears and her brown hair stuck like dark tendrils clinging to her neck and clothes. He had seen her before, at the market in Stratford and at the fair. He remembered how she watched him as he strutted upon the stage and the uneasiness he felt, as each time he turned, she hovered in his sight behind Anne Whatley.

She wiped her face with her hand, smearing dirt across her cheek.

"Pray, please, help me. I came to chase away a fox that has been preying upon my chickens. I fear I have twisted my ankle when the rain began."

William bent down and helped her to her feet, still she collapsed again. "Hold your arms about my neck," he urged.

He lifted her and carried her back to the path. She bit her lip in pain and pointed to the candlelit window in the distance. William hesitated, wondering to leave her on the path or continue. The rain pounded stronger. Still in Will's arms, she opened the door, and he set her on a bench near the fire. Even in the firelight, he could see it was a good home; timbered and plastered with mullioned windows, painted tapestries, pewter candlesticks, and a sound four-poster bed peeking through the door leading into the next room. He placed another log onto the fire and stoked the glowing embers, reigniting them into a blaze. She handed him a cotton cloth to wipe his face.

"I am indebted to you. I very likely would have been there all night if not for your finding me."

"Your father would have missed you, surely."

She looked toward the bedroom door as if seeing a ghost. "Nay, my father died a year ago."

William looked to the door. "You live alone?"

She shook her head. "Nay, I do not. My brother lives here, but he is away to Worcestershire on a farm for a month. He found work there as a shearer."

Will twitched at the sudden awkward isolation with this woman. "I have seen you before, or rather, I saw you today at the fair."

She smiled, never looking into his face. "Yea, I have seen you many times. You are Will Shakespeare from Stratford. I am fond of you acting. I have been to the tavern many times to see the plays you have performed in." As she removed her shoe, she lifted her skirt to her knees. Her eyes caught his. The awkwardness surged and the chill of his wet clothes acute.

"I am Anne Hathaway."

William urged his feet and his mind to the door. "'Tis a pleasure to meet you, Mistress Hathaway." He watched her from the corner of his eye, seeing her face twist with pain as she rubbed her ankle. "Will you be all right?"

"Pray, please," she begged, "could you help me to the fireside?"

He turned back toward her, wrapping his arm around her waist and lifting her until they both sat on the floor near the fire. The emptiness of the room crept upon him like the shadow of a passing cloud at noonday, and he made a move to stand until he felt her hand on his arm.

"Will you leave me alone?"

Will's words fumbled across his tongue. "I must... make haste to my father's house."

Her eyes darkened into a deep well of enticement, filling and brimming over with a watery fire. "You would not run back into the storm when there is a fire to warm you here? At least wait until the storm passes." Her fingers on his arm traced the wet wrinkles of his shirt. He shivered under her touch and her words fell to a whisper. She leaned near to his ear, close enough he felt her words breathing upon his skin.

"How fortunate destiny has brought you thus to my house. I have watched you for so long, Will Shakespeare, strutting upon the stage, and I have dreamed of playing a scene with you. I have imagined this moment, two souls alone, finding each other in a storm. Can you conjure the scene? Me, an older woman, and you, a young vibrant actor sitting next to the warm fire and yielding to the softness of a sweet kiss." She brushed her lips against his neck. "Go ahead, Will, 'tis your cue."

As quickly as Richard's words flashed into his mind about finding shelter in another woman's arms, they vanished. In the darkness, like the sudden spark of a flame to a wick, restraint melted like candle wax, easily ignited and quickly fed. The firelight crumbled into embers and in the flashes of the lightening through the window they discovered each other, their lips crushing and devouring. They untangled themselves from their wet clothes and entangled each other. There on such a pagan night, a tempest raged outside the Hathaway home in Shottery and when the morning sun shook off the wet cloak of night, William glanced over at Anne Hathaway sleeping beneath the covers of that four-poster bed. He sighed and covered his eyes with his hands, feeling every bit an ass.

XIII

Bedded and wedded, in that order. William yawned and stared
through the crosshatched patterns on the window of the
Hathaway home. *His home now*, he cringed. The outlines of the
dark tree trunks of the apple trees in the garden formed slow as the
hazy light of dawn touched the horizon.

Six months passed quick from the first time he shared Anne
Hathaway's bed, six months full of twists and turns, entrants and
exuents, full of the smiles and frowns of those imaginary muses in
his dreams so long ago. The drama filling his days and nights
would make any muse proud of such a gifted actor for he spent his
time acting through life, playing the paramour in Shottery while
his true love waited in Temple Grafton; but as all tragedy plays
out, quick and sure, life came upon him with boos and hisses and
with tears.

He closed his eyes and conjured Anne Whatley's face: her
dancing blue eyes hiding behind blond ringlets as they fell across
her brow, skin as soft as goose down, and those delicious lips. His
heart sighed remembering how he lost her.

The memory swirled fresh in his mind. Their love sprung fair
in May, lilting on the breeze like delicate apple blossoms and dizzy
like honey-drunk bees. His love for Anne Whatley bloomed pure
and innocent and vows pledged both swore they would not forget.

William cursed himself under his breath. The heat of summer
approached fast on his heels and the innocence of Anne Whatley
could not contain such a heat, which led him to an older woman's
home and bed. He traversed a tangle and set to create a delicate
balance, even as intriguing as a game of mills, and one he amused
himself with like a foolish eighteen-year-old boy. Twice a week he
walked to Temple Grafton and sat with Anne Whatley at her

father's table midst her relatives, holding her hand and delighting in her blushing cheek as he pledged his troth to her; and then, twice a week, his desire led him astray on the path to Shottery as he pledged his body to Anne Hathaway.

Guilt never entered his mind until the day Anne Hathaway whispered a secret in his ear after an afternoon spent in her arms and bed. The words stung him like a potent wasp. He dressed in a hurry, darted out the door and sought the relief of a pint of ale at Burbage's tavern. As he slouched in a dark corner with his head in one hand and a tankard in the other, Richard plopped down beside him in a merry mood.

"Pray, William, this is what I have been thinking. Stratford will be a memory for me come next Whitsun. I am binding myself to London. I have already acquired a room at the lodging house in Holywell and my father is backing construction of a playhouse across from Finsbury Fields. O, Will, wait till you see the sketching. She is the woman of my dreams!" He slapped William on the back. "What? No merry smile for me, for I know you know this means you can follow me soon to ply your trade."

William guzzled the pint. "Richard, my thoughts are heavy today, forgive me."

Richard scratched his chin. "Ah, heavy with thoughts of the woman of your dreams. From your sour look I would think you have lost your maid, Anne of Temple Grafton."

"Nay, friend, I have not lost her, but I find myself surrounded by that name."

Richard chuckled and replied, "Well, 'tis good then! Thou art a happy man then."

"Nay, sadder, my friend, for in this hour my heart's dear love lay on the fair daughter of Whatley. We met, we wooed and made an exchange of vows, and thus she consented to marry me this morning."

Richard rose from his seat and lifted his cup, but William silenced his toasting words by placing his hand on his friend's arm and pulling him back to his seat.

"'Tis not the end of my tale, Richard; pray sit so I may confess to you."

Richard leaned forward, his brow knitted in confusion. "Will, I am not thy shrift."

William smirked. "I am not looking for forgiveness, only this; you spoke well as my friend many months ago when we left from Coventry. You spoke good and sound advice, but 'twas advice I did not heed. This is why I am sadder today."

Richard chuckled into his beer, the foam blowing away from his nostrils as he answered him. "You are not the first fellow to wreck his reed. So, little fair Anne hath given away her virtue to you and now you wish to confess it before you bind your hands?"

The dryness in William's throat knotted up his words. He leaned forward and coughed into the sleeve of his shirt. "Nay, not Anne Whatley, but Anne Hathaway. I have spent my days with my Anne of Temple Grafton and my nights with Anne of Shottery. And now, on the day my Temple Anne gives consent to marry does my Shottery Anne whisper she is with child."

Richard's chuckle turned into coughing as he inhaled the ale and the words. "With child? Does Temple Anne know of this? Does thy father?"

William pounded the table with his fist. "Nay, and none shall know of it. I will marry Anne Whatley before Advent Sunday."

Richard pulled him close, his words just above a whisper. "'Tis three months away, Will. By then Anne Hathaway will be heavy with child. How shall you avoid this?"

William shrugged his shoulders and held his head in his hands. "I do not know, my friend. S'wounds, I am caught in this game."

And so it went. For three more months he kept the secret, planning his wedding day to Anne Whatley, even having the license drawn up emblazoned with her name. The day came when he knelt at Anne Hathaway's knee and told her of his betrothal to someone else. She cried and pleaded and when she thought she lost, she did what any betrayed pregnant shrew might do, she rushed to the house on Henley Street and confessed everything to John and Mary Shakespeare.

Time fell away from William, the moment peeling away like the skin from an apple in one continuous ribbon beginning and ending with Anne Hathaway. He never saw Anne Whatley again, but on the twenty seventh of November, he rode in a wagon with his pregnant Anne to Worcester. The biting wind and the hint of snowflakes on the air stung his skin, and the frozen ache in his heart chilled his blood. He could not even look at her.

The Bishop of Worcester, John Whitgift, scrawled his name across the bottom of the license and handed the paper to William as Anne hovered near the entrance to the consistory court. Fulk Sandell and John Richardson, friends of Anne's father, stood like armed guards at the doorway with their arms crossed and brows furrowed to make sure that he, the boy who sullied their friend's daughter, did not bolt. William held the paper up to his eyes and huffed, noticing Anne Whatley's name still marked in black ink and no one had bothered to change it. *No matter,* he thought, *for Anne Whatley is my true wife. No need for me to mention the mistake.*

The Bishop glanced over William's shoulder and lowered his stare. He cupped his hand around William's elbow and urged him away from the group as a concerned priest, his voice quietening to a reverent whisper.

"Boy, the lady is with child?"

William bit his lip. "Yea, your Grace."

Whitgift patted William on the arm. "How old are you, my son?"

"Only eighteen, sir."

"And the lady?"

William glanced over his shoulder at Anne. "She is twenty-seven, your Grace."

The priest's eyes widened. "Ah, this explains the reason for the hasty marriage. I take it from your pale face you thought to avoid this path."

William nodded. "Yea, father, again you see things clear."

The priest shrugged. "Yet, sometimes we have to pay for our indiscretions. We will suggest the ban announced at the parish in Temple Grafton for reasonable secrecy from the prying ears and whispers of your neighbors in Stratford. The church's saint is Saint Andrew and thus you will marry on that sainted day as absolution for your sins."

William flinched at hearing his marriage would take place in the very city of his true love. Whitgift wrinkled his forehead. "Tell me, boy, do I know you? Your face looks familiar."

"Yea, sir, perhaps you remember me from years ago. My family visited the festival in Kenilworth and you stood before the

Queen's train when some boy accused my kinsman of treason."

Whitgift's eyes rounded. "Ah, yea, I remember now. And I thought I recognized your name as I read it on the license. Shakespeare of Stratford-upon-Avon. Yea, your father is John Shakespeare, methinks."

"Yea, it is, sir."

The priest grumbled in his throat. "Hmm, and your father's name has shown up several times on the list of recusants in Warwickshire. He places himself in great danger, you know. What of you, William, do you share his distaste for our Church of England?"

William scuffed his foot on the floor. "My father is a simple man, your Grace. You need not worry that he has the wit to form any plot against the Queen. I do not share the same passions with him and have no quarrel with the Queen or her church. I wish only to be a player on the stage. That is my ambition."

The priest smiled. "Ah, good words, my son. Then I am sorry for you this day. You tangled yourself in a web of your own making and detoured from your goal. Yet, there is nothing I can do but urge you to the right course and offer you forgiveness. As to the matter of your father, remember well that there are many eyes watching. 'Twill do you well to form alliances with those who can further your pursuits. All of us have aspirations, William, but only those who are on the right side will achieve them. Who knows, perhaps this is a fortuitous meeting between us and I will be in a position one day to drop a whisper in the Queen's ear to offer you a place with her troupe of players."

William bowed. "And, your Grace, perhaps one day I will be able to offer something of worth to you for your kind words and forgiveness this day."

The next day when he and his new wife emerged from the church in Temple Grafton, William scanned the faces in the crowded streets for any sign of Anne Whatley. Her form and her face had vanished from him, but he knew her memory never would.

William sighed at the memory. He rolled over and watched the blanket covering his wife rise and fall with her breathing as it rounded over her swollen belly. A moment passed when her breathing paused and he felt a sudden chill mingling with excitement. He gritted his teeth when he realized, for a moment, he wished her dead.

My detoured life, he pondered. *'Twas what the Bishop called my life.*

The thought gnawed his stomach. He stood up from the bed and blew his breath upon the windowpane. Two farmers sauntered behind a team of oxen pounding across the hade land, the furrowed ground already hardened by an icy layer of snow. A young man waved to them from the roadway and darted away toward town. The young man's face appeared carefree with eyes full of the future. Life walked past William on the other side of the window and he wondered if anything exciting would ever happen to him again.

Anne stirred as he crawled back beneath the covers. She coddled near to him, wrapping her arm around his waist and caressing her fingers over the small of his bare back. He closed his eyes and shivered as he rubbed a tendril of her hair between his thumb and forefinger. Behind his eyelids, he conjured Anne Whatley's face. He realized quite sudden he was acting a scene and Anne Hathaway merely played the part of a wife wearing a mask he could remove in his dreams to reveal his true love. He could even whisper the name Anne across his lips without notice. His wife would never know when he breathed the name like a lover that he thought of the girl in Temple Grafton. He leaned over her and kneaded his lips with hers, curved his palm over the roundness of her belly and fell asleep with her full warm breast pressed against his cheek.

William awoke with a start, sitting straight up in bed and glancing over at Anne. Darkness blanketed the room as if the sun forgot to rise. He adjusted his eyes to the pitch black and heard a faint giggle breezing though the unlatched and opened window. He pulled on his breeches and boots and strode into the main room. Still, no one stirred, nothing but the crackling of a steady fire in the stone hearth. He opened the front door, and the air felt strangely warm, more like a summer evening. Another giggle and he quickened his steps through the garden and around to the orchard. There, sitting amid the trees nipping on redcoats and caraways, sat the two masked women from his boyhood dream.

"I am dreaming," he announced.

"Yea," said the frowning maid, "sadness fills your heart, William, and we know why."

The other turned her smiling face. "But do not fret. You are not bound to this life. You have the courage, William, and change comes quick, if you are willing snatch hold."

The frowning one continued. "Listen well to this line: cowardice often makes calamity of great enterprises. For so long your friend Burbage teased you with the prospect of giving up your life in Stratford for a life in London, and you hesitated. So much so that now a ring binds your finger, a wife in your bed and a babe soon to feed. You forgot your childhood dreams, the day you dreamed of us in the forest of Park Hall."

William's heartbeat pounded in his chest. "But I thought I only dreamed then, that this is not real."

"Yea, this is not real," the smiling maid replied, "and you are dreaming only. But listen... I hear a player's cart wheeling down the lane. Will you go see, William?"

As he tried to get through the orchard, the briers thickened, snagging on his breeches and scratching across his bare stomach. He looked over his shoulder and the maids vanished. As he turned his gaze back toward the road, there in the field across the way, a player's stage sat with the red banners of the Queen flapping from poles at each corner. He mounted the steps, placing his hands upon his hips as he strutted across the boards. He pivoted as a hand touched him on the shoulder.

Bishop Whitgift stood before him adorned in the purple robes of the Archbishop of Canterbury, with an ax in his hand. Nausea settled in his stomach and his legs weakened as the Bishop's face morphed into a black raven, his words squawking out between the black beak.

"Do it quickly, William. Do it quickly and you will have your reward."

William lifted the leaded ax above his head, unsure of where to strike. The image of the Bishop faded away, leaving behind a headman's block in the middle of the stage. Chirping and in pain with a broken wing, a small sparrow sat in the middle of the block. The swing of the ax struck true, rushing by his ears like a blast of *wind. The sparrow sliced in two, but the blood pumped out from a human-sized heart, bubbling and gurgling out until the red liquid covered his boots. William backed away, then slipped and fell. He flailed his arms, coughing and sputtering as a bloody wave crashed over his head. The salty ooze smelled of wormwood. A cry crept up his throat, awaking him from the nightmare.*

William looked around the room and wiped the sweat off his brow with the back of his hand. The sunlight glinted through the closed window and Anne sat on a bench near the hearth with a pewter pitcher over the fire. The smell of warm wine mulled with anise seed filled the air and the window slammed back and forth letting in a cold wet spray of snow each time it flapped open. Anne brought him a goblet and motioned toward the window.

"You best be fixin' the window today, Will. You do not wish me to catch a chill with your babe on the way. The latch broke during the night. 'Twas quite a storm. Methinks the frigid air cracked a few panes, so you must fix those as well." She popped him on the leg, bocking like a mother hen. "Come on now, no more idle sleeping. Get up and get to work. And your father wants you to town to help him skin a few goats."

William frowned as he watched her scurry about the room folding blankets, stirring the wine, and strewing fresh rushes on the floor; the daily chores to go with his dreary married life. How different she appeared to him now from the dark temptress who tempted him toward this path during those heated days of summer.

Act Three

1583-1588

XIV

K it held the parchment pages to his nose and closed his eyes, breathing in the rich woody smell mingling with the sharp odor of the ink. Contentment swirled in the smell; a sense of belonging. *Belonging,* he thought and smirked as if the word were an aloof spirit, intangible and hazy in any physical sense. He rested his cheek on his opened palm and added up the days in his head. One thousand ninety-two days since he last saw Mary's face. He heard her name by snippets of gossip doled out to him from a line or two in Philip's letters. Three years parted them and three children to insure her state to her husband, and not a single kind word in Kit's direction.

No matter, he grimaced, *so far the women of my life, women of flesh and blood, have played the roles of shrew, slut, sovereign, simpleton, senseless and suicidal, all great fodder for mighty plays.*

Kit laid the page on his desk, dusted the front with powder and blew away the excess into a cloud of white. His heart glowed with pride as he read aloud the title.

"Tamburlaine. My mighty Tamburlaine, generations will hear your voice. And there you are in the stack, my Henry the Fifth, and Faustus, you, as well. O, what tossing in my bed in sleepless nights to set you to paper. How many nights did you rack me and not let me sleep? Too many to count. Even now the words cause my skin to crawl upon my own words." Kit looked to the window and shivered. "How many times did your pointed fingers drum against my window? I pray 'twas not prophecy I wrote against my soul." He looked into the surrounding air, his eyes scanning the room for a vision. Touching his fingers to his lips, he blew a kiss. "Thank you, my dear sweet muse, my one faithful woman."

Hearing the afternoon chimes of the church calling the students to prayers, he placed the pages into his leather portfolio, wrapped himself in the black University robe and crept out into the long empty hallway.

Another moment to enjoy the solitary walk to class, walking in step to iambic pentameter, the rhythm his imaginary friend taught him at an early age. As she whispered in his mind as he walked in and out of the shadows of the dark corridor and the bright sunlight streaming through the windows cast patterns on the floor. He paused at the window and watched a group of students struggling against the strong breath of Autumn, their black robes twisting about their bodies and the leaves kicking up around them, swirling in a vortex of oranges and browns. The ancient stone walls of Cambridge appeared to shiver in the wind through the wavy glass as she prepared herself for another English winter of dark grays.

"A tempest," he whispered, and then again, to his imaginary muse, "I will mark that down, thank you, for there is a story there somewhere. Controlling one's destiny is very like that."

A tug on his sleeve brought him back to where he stood. Two boys, students of his age and friends of his heart, mused at him with looks of curiosity veiling their faces. The smaller of the two, Thomas Colville, stood half way in the light and in shadow, and his lips crept into a forced smile.

"Kit, are you to prayers?"

Kit nodded, noting the malingering hue in their eyes. "I am, as all of you."

"Then you are not as we are, for we have a truant's disposition today. We are tired of these formal walls and need to seek dark ale and warm wenches."

The second, the one nearest to Kit's own height and complexion, John Penry, stood near to him in the light. He interjected, his feminine voice ringing high like church bells. "These are not my wishes, Kit. I will go with you to church."

Reaching across, he placed a hand on John's shoulder. "I know you are no truant, my friend. Who knows, John, if we exchanged doublets, perhaps you could stand in for me." Kit slapped him on the back and laughed. "Go along, I will join you both by and by, for a new patron summons me." Kit waved the portfolio in front of their eyes. Thomas and John grabbed for the book, eager to read the offerings from Kit's hand.

"Something new? Let us see," Thomas pleaded.

John tugged at the leather pouch, his eyes filled with adoration. "How do you do it, Kit? Words flow from you as if from the source of the Nile. I wish I had your gift."

Kit held the portfolio high over their heads, laughing at their eager fingers. "Nay, not yet. Perhaps soon you will see them on stage with the Lord Admiral's men and Edward Alleyn as the lead."

A shadow moved along the hallway in front of the boys. A cloaked man, his eyes beady and sullen, walked into the sunlight; his gaze pierced through the haze at Christopher.

Kit stepped away from Thomas and motioned to the man. "That man, there, who is he?"

Thomas shrugged. "I know not. Do you know, John?"

"Nay, I do not, but he looks upon you, Kit, as if he knows you."

Kit pushed by them until his face leveled with the man's stare. "Do I know you, sir? From your weeds, I can see you are no student, but you look upon me with disfavor. Who are you, sir, that you correct me with your eyes?"

The man's lips curled into a smirk. "Sir, you are looking for things that are not there. I am an alumnus from Cambridge, eight years your senior. You will know me soon enough."

Thomas stepped near to them, leaning his head to listen. He laughed, jabbing Kit in the side. "He is an admirer, Kit, who hath heard of your rare talent. Perhaps he is the new patron."

The man paused and cocked his head. "Talent? What talent? I am no patron."

Thomas continued to interject. "Christopher is a poet and playwright, sir, and the first one among us."

The man curled his lips again into a smirk and turned on his heel, slinking back into the shadows. Kit grabbed hold of Thomas. "You should not have done that. From his countenance, I gather you earned his scorn. He may be a new schoolmaster, did you not think?"

Thomas punched to the wind. "His scorn? He will earn my fist in his mouth if he crosses me."

Kit cut his stare in John's direction. "Thomas, be still. You are a weak fool for even a boy could pound you into the dust. 'Tis interesting that so far in my life, all my Thomas friends bear such a disposition. Go along, catch up to him and find out, if you can, the nature of his odd intrusion. I will meet you two at the tavern at five; until then, I must to my patron's door."

John and Thomas followed the man and Kit clutched the portfolio to his heart.

"Now, get you to my master's chamber."

Walking in the opposite direction, winding through the hallways and up staircases, he came to the library. The church bells chimed three, and he crept inside, pushing the oak doors with a heave. His eyes drank in the walls lined with manuscripts, folios and bound books ranging from hand-sized to arm-sized stretching twenty strides and as high as a small cathedral. Tall ladders rose to the upper shelves and long sturdy tables ran the length of the room. Taking in a deep breath of the bookish air, he soaked in the smell of the leather and paper.

The shadowed sun cut through the windows at the end of the room creating a dreary atmosphere for study. A solitary candle flickered on one end of a long narrow table stacked with books. He walked toward the light. The black velvet curtains adorning the windows moved, revealing a window seat, and a shadowed figure. Kit looped his finger through the curved handle of the holder and held the candle forward to light the face before him. Robert Cecil, the disfigured son and protégé of Her Majesty's Most Reverent Counselor, Lord Burghley, sat before him, frowning.

Robert spoke, his voice raspy and crooked as his back. "You came."

Kit's brow wrinkled. "Is there a reason I should not have come?"

Robert stood, straining to straighten. "Nay, I suppose not. Did you know it would be me you were to meet?"

Kit shook his head, still unsure of this private meeting. Robert motioned for him to follow as he waddled to a nearby study room. Kit obliged, listening to Robert's words as he walked. "I am only a pawn, Christopher, as are you, sent thus to direct you to your new patron."

"A pawn? Nay, I am not as you are, sir. Do you know this new patron?"

Robert turned to face him before pushing the door aside to reveal the secret identity. "Like a son knows his own father. He dotes on you, know you this? Like a son would want from his father."

He pushed the door open, letting it creak upon the hinges. Kit looked up, his eyes filling with the image of an old man with bristly beard relaxing on a velvet couch. One name fell from his lips.

"Burghley."

Burghley hacked a cough and waved his son away. "Go along now, Robert, I have things to discuss with this young Marlowe."

Robert's shoulders curved downward as he folded into himself, the hump at the base of his neck rising like a hill as he hunched. Robert's stare darted between Christopher and his father as he backed out of the room and closed the door.

Burghley's eyes were on Kit, piercing through as if he were reading Kit's thoughts. "I see you study men's faces, Christopher. Tell me, what do you see in my son's eyes?"

Kit walked near to Burghley and leaned back against a table, his fingers wrapping around the squared edge to steady himself. He held his words, letting them swirl upon his tongue. Burghley rested his own chin upon his hand, and Kit could tell the councilor's eyes searched for the answer in his face.

"Go ahead, boy, and tell me what you saw."

Kit's chest filled with air. "Shall I speak truth?"

Burghley chuckled. "Truth? All of us seek the meaning to the word truth. Answer me simply from this point onward, Christopher. Simplicity is something I adhere to, that I strive for, for if words lay simple on the tongue then they, more often than not, resemble truth."

The old man's words brought a smile to Kit's mouth. "'Tis true, my Lord, for I have found playwrights and poets often exaggerate, their words falling half way between truth and imagination. Shall I tell you simply, then, what I saw in your son's face?" He thought about his own father and answered. "I saw a son who seeks his father's approval."

Burghley grunted as he ran his fingers through the white and silver flow of his beard. "Indeed. Robert is a capable son. If not for his crooked back he might quite excel as a soldier."

Kit's stare fell to the floor. "I wonder, why is it fathers always look to their son's imperfections? Perhaps his mind does not crook as his back. Perhaps it is sharp, even a wit and deviser like Richard the Third."

Burghley leaned forward and chuckled again. "I see you are the wit. Do you always look for a new play or a new character in everyone you meet? Tell me, have you already formed one for me in your mind?"

Kit folded his arms and let his mind study the aged man before him, who sat before him perched on a velvet pillow with his chin tilted upwards as if an artist just commanded him to lift his face to catch the perfect glint of sunlight in his blue eyes. Burghley melded into the studious decor like a treasured book, noble, properly bound and tastefully gilded with a touch of gold at the edges. Admiration settled over Kit, yet he toyed with him to measure the distance between a simple pawn and a man who hovers behind the Queen's right shoulder.

"Perhaps I have, and perhaps my muse will indulge me and I will set it down one day. I remember you from long ago when first I saw you in the Star Chamber at Westminster. To my youthful eyes you were just an old man with a gray beard, wrinkled face, eyes purging thick amber and plum tree gum, weak hams and a plentiful lack of wit."

Burghley slapped the arm of the chair with his hand as he bellowed out a laugh. "You are indeed the wag. Your words echo a hidden wisdom beyond your years."

Kit's mind brushed across the rapid succession of memories aging his innocence. "Indeed, I have seen too much of the world for one my age. You yourself, sir, should be as old as I am if like a crab you could go backward." Kit walked his hand across the table top, outstretching his fingers like crab legs.

Burghley relaxed in his chair, lifting his gout-ridden feet to a velvet hassock. "There is a method to your madness, Christopher. Your replies are pregnant with meaning."

Kit walked behind a nearby leather chair and pushed it up to face Burghley. He sat before the old man and folded his hands over his lap.

"I choose this corner, your Grace, and will bait this bear. If there be method to my madness, I shall be in good company. Madness in great ones should not unwatched go, so like pretty poppets we will spy on one another and seek our own advantage."

Burghley's eyes squinted. "We seek only the Queen's advantage, boy, not our own. I would have thought you learned that long ago."

Kit leaned forward and matched his eye slits. "You think I will not seek my own advantage in this. After I have given Walsingham my life, my words and my faith? Nay, I will have more out of this or you will have nothing of me. I will not be a stupid pawn with no reckoning. Why do you think poets seek the patronage of those who can afford us? Do you think it is simply for the money it avails?"

Burghley's heavy body shook with humor as he chortled deep within his throat. "I see everyone has been right about you. Walsingham praises your astute genius, and Philip, your gift for perceptive jabbing. You will do well and go far, Christopher." His smile disappeared. "Now, to the meat of the matter. You have impressed me in this word play and I most heartily give you my patronage. Keep me supplied with your witty words designed to propagate our Queen and I will see them to the stage with a promise. My promise is this: I have a few missions I would like you to perform and if you do them well, then I promise to present you to the Queen herself, the ultimate patroness for a young poet. How like you this, Christopher?"

Kit leaned forward, his elbows upon his knees, as his heart filled with the edges of hope. "I hear the promises again and again, first by Walsingham, then by Philip, and now by you. Yet, it continues to be the chameleon's dish. I eat and eat and eat the air, promise crammed, yet nothing fills me. Tell me, what is it you wish for me to do?"

Burghley leaned forward toward him, their conference reducing to whispers. "This first, know you my son who was just here?"

Kit looked to the door. "You mean Robert? The one whom we spoke on before?"

"Marry, yes. I would have you keep an eye on him and report of his behavior. You will inquire everything about him and his friends; how, who, what means, and where they keep, what company and at what expense, what drabs he visits, what gambling, and such. You are a playwright, write the lines; and now you will play the spy, the provocateur, for me."

Kit looked down at his hands and rubbed the ink stain on his finger.

"Wherefore should you do this to him? I would know that before I take it. Why should a father want such liberties attached to a son?"

Burghley sat back in his chair, his voice returning to a normal tone.

"Here is my drift. You believe me to be slight of wit but this will prove you wrong. I believe laying slight sullies on my son amongst his friends, as you converse, will bring someone around to say 'aye, I know the gentleman. I saw him yesterday or such and there was gaming, there overtook in a rouse, there falling out at tennis', or perchance, he entered a house of sale, a brothel. Or perhaps, even there will be none of such talk, so then will I know my son's mind."

Kit leaned back, as well, the meaning filling his mind. "So, then, this bait of falsehood takes this carp of truth. By indirections finds direction out."

Burghley smiled and nodded. "You have it. I knew you would weasel the meaning. Do this and we shall see how cleverly and secretly you can delve. Then we shall to our next mission."

"Which is?"

Burghley stood and walked to the window. His bloated feet twisted under the weight. "There is a small town in the shire of Warwick. We believe there is a faction growing, a small insurgency which needs weeding. The Jesuit Campion hid in many of the homes there before his arrest, spreading his unholy messages and collecting together vermin intent on putting Mary of Scots on the throne. Remember this name: John Somerville. He has relatives in Warwickshire who have leanings toward Rome and he himself has voiced his opinion on too many occasions. We must watch him and any who befriend him."

Kit blew out a puff of air. "Unrest among the peasants, my liege?"

Burghley turned back to face him, his mouth turned downward. "You take this lightly with your sarcastic words. These are troublesome times for our Queen and a severe blow must fall upon any hint of treason. This is not mere unhappiness over plague-ridden bread; this is a Catholic insurrection. Do you not remember Paris? Would you have the same thing happen here?"

A passing cloud shadowed the sun beaming through the window behind Burghley's back. Kit's heart pounded in his ears as he remembered Walsingham's words tapping out to each beat.

This sight will fit you for the day when you shall revenge these bloody deeds with your bare hands.

Burghley stepped back slowly across the room and pointed to the portfolio on the table. "Is this your newest play?"

Kit's shoulders dropped as the portfolio shrouded in the shadow of the cloud.

"Yea, my Lord, there are many there."

"What do you call the plays?"

Kit curled his lip upward in a half grin. "I would call them the Mousetraps for by this encompassment does my Henry catch the conscience of a King, while my Tamburlaine and Faustus catch the conscience of men. Henry inspired men to fortify God's approval of his kingdom, Tamburlaine stimulates God from his sleep to look upon his stupid creation on Earth; and Faustus? He rouses the Devil himself to sell his soul in selfishness as most stupid men do."

Burghley grabbed him by the chin, his stare boring into Kit's face. "Watch your words, Christopher. If you play too close to the edge by your cutting remarks, someone may push you into the fire. Remember, we are a good Protestant people and your words can influence many to love or hate their Queen. Philip has given over your patronage now, so, remember this too, I can protect you from the Star Chamber, I can protect you from Rome, but I cannot protect you from yourself."

Kit jerked his chin away. Burghley reached inside of his robe and pulled out a velvet pouch. He dangled the purse in front of Kit's face, letting the sound of coins jangle in his ears. As Burghley wrapped his fingers around the portfolio, Kit held tight for a moment, his hand trembling upon the release.

"So, like a whore I shall unpack my heart with words."

Kit snatched the purse and Burghley finished the thought. "Keep the plays coming, Christopher. I will see them to the stage with each neck you bring and, unlike a whore, you shall receive more than what you are worth."

Kit bowed deep before Burghley, a servant's bow. Burghley flicked his fingers toward him, signaling his dismissal. With each step toward the door, Kit's eyes held fast to the portfolio in Burghley's hands. His heart trembled. As the door closed behind him, he leaned against the wall and wiped away a tear welling in his eyes. The words of his heart rang loud and accusing.

What have I done?

A passing shower wet the streets of Cambridge and his feet shuffled and scuffed through the mud, finding no solace in any rhythm. As he approached the pub where his truant friends soused with drink, Kit paused for a moment and gazed up and down the lane. His heart sensed a shadow, yet he shrugged away the feeling and entered the tavern.

The sour man he saw in the hallway earlier sat at a table far in the corner nearest the window. The setting sun filtering through the passing clouds cloaked him in a peculiar orange. Kit waved to the barkeep and slapped a gold coin onto a tabletop. "Come barkeep, some ale!"

The stranger crept up next to him and spoke. "I take it your patron liked them well?"

The barkeep approached and Kit slip the coin into his fingers. "A pint, sir? This coin is too much for a pint."

Kit spat his words. "A pint for Spanish gold? Nay, I say to keep the tankards coming until dawn."

The man prodded as the barkeep ambled away. "Spanish gold for your plays?"

Kit ignored him and looked about the room.

The man continued. "You look for your friends, John and Thomas. You know what a saint John strives to be. He went to church, confessing it is the pulpit for him and he cannot sully himself with wine and women. And Thomas? He is just the opposite and I believe him to be upstairs with the tavern wench."

The barkeep set two tankards on the table before them. Kit lifted one, toasted the air and downed the ale.

The man plied his comments even more. "You are in a foul mood I sense. Are you not happy for the good payment for your plays?"

Kit set the tankard aside and leaned forward into the man's

inquest.

"There is things more dear, sir, than gold."

The man laughed. "There are? Tell me so that I may know, for I have found nothing more dear."

"You would sell yourself so easily?"

The man leaned back in his chair. His lips curved into a revealing smile. "Do you know what your problem is, Marlowe? You think because of your gift you can hold the world in your hand, but arrogance deceives you. Some women birth a child to greatness, some achieve greatness and others have greatness thrust upon them."

Kit puffed out a small snicker. "I know not why you speak so bitter toward me. I do not know you and have never given you cause. I take it, though, you have gained greatness from one of the three? So, which is it, born, achieved or thrust?"

The man leaned forward again, his eyes dancing with revelation.

"Shall I tell you? Achievement rides on the back of ambition, thrusting a man into his future. One only has to follow the lead, and when the trail seems empty, you spy out another avenue. The end is the same if you will do what is necessary."

"What is necessary, indeed. And what if the price is blood? What then?"

The man spat a puff of air. "An odd question coming from a man who should know." He paused for a moment, waiting for Kit's reaction. The wrinkle on his brow proved his irritation as Kit continued to savor his second tankard instead of answering. "I followed you, Marlowe. I know who it was you met with. Your new patron? 'Twas Lord Burghley." The man paused for a moment as confusion settled in Kit's mind.

"To what end are you following me, sir?"

The man's face lighted with humor. "I shall tell you. My name is Richard Baines, and I have heard of you, Kit Marlowe, from the mouths of very influential men. Walsingham, Sidney and others. They speak of you with such admiration, like a gifted youth whose poetic words and quick hand lives and dies in the service of the Queen. Yet, you are not the only one who can capture the eye of those close to Her Majesty. I was in the room when you left Burghley. I heard the entire conversation and I know it is not only plays he wants from you. A provocateur, Christopher? So, you will be a spy for the Crown?"

Marlowe remained silent as Baines continued to bait.

"I came to Cambridge to seek you out, to see what all the fuss was about over this new young protégé. Walsingham recruited me the same as you, for I impressed him at a young age. I was cunning and slipped into a private meeting he held in London. When I revealed myself to Sir Francis, he asked me how 'twas so easy for me to hide. I said 'twas as easy as hiding a Catholic priest in the walls of a Protestant home. He laughed. You know, it does not take much to impress him, and with that, he offered me a place within the secret ranks of his spy circle. After he discovered you, he told me that with your wit and my cunning, we could make a very dangerous team."

Kit smirked. "So, you wished to be a spy?"

Richard wrinkled his mouth. "Nay, not so much. However, I do not wish for someone like you, someone who can bend an ear with a rhyming word and an eye with fair looks, to squeeze out my ascension to the glory that is rightfully mine. Both you and Sidney have your minds wrapped in poetry and prose; and what do I have? I have the gift of deception and will us it to the full. Is not that the way for those of us seeking the crumbs below the Queen's table? And what did you say to Burghley? Like pretty poppets we will spy on each other and seek our own advantage. Each step you make, Marlowe, I will be one step behind you. Faustus, see, I am thy Mephistopheles."

Kit eyes widened when he heard him refer to his play. He pushed the tankard away and peered deep into Baines' face, answering him with one line.

"I see envy is a green-eyed monster, sir."

Kit grabbed up his cloak, wrapped it about his shoulders and left Baines sitting there smiling a demonic smile. As he reached the street, he leaned against a torch post, his eyes devouring the last rays of sunlight. In the doorway of the inn attached to the public house, he saw her, his imaginary friend, hiding her face beneath a blue hooded cloak. Thoughts of Baines flowed out in her words as he whispered.

"Why is it that particular men that for some vicious mole of nature in them, these men carrying the stamp of their defect, being nature's costume and fortune's star, shall always choose corruption? Virtue is nothing. Even men of grace censure that quality to swallow vice. Aye, there is meat in these words and I will pen them tonight."

He bowed his head toward her, neither one of them smiling as he questioned her in silence.

What does everyone want of me? I am but a simple poet.

She answered in his mind. *Nay, not a simple poet, but you are my darling. You have opened your vein and those beneath you will suck you dry. Mark my words.*

Sadness ambled with Marlowe along the moody hallways of Cambridge back to his room. He went in, closed the door and sat upon the bed. The ink bottle on the desk still uncapped and the quill still wet from the final changes he made to his plays before his departure to meet Burghley. The former joy vanished and his "friend" sulked in the corner of the room.

Kit threw the velvet bag across the room, the coins spilling out onto the floor. Out of the corner of his eye, his stare fixed upon a package at the end of the bed. He reached across and untied the string, unfolding the linen fabric to reveal the contents. Before him, a doublet and breeches in a deep rich velvet, the color of burgundy wine. His fingers traced the trim at the collar and down through the black velvet slashes running vertical across the breast.

A fine outfit, he thought; *an outfit suited for a titled man or rather, a bought man.*

Tucked between the jacket and breeches, a letter sealed with Burghley's coat-of-arms. He pried open the waxen seal and read:

"Master Christopher Marlowe, here is a gift from your patron. I have arranged for a local artist of Cambridge to meet with you in the library to have your portrait painted. It is natural for a young man of your caliber to have his likeness hung in the student's hall. 'Tis your first gift, your first step to glory. 'Tis your first, but as I foresee a future in you, 'twill not be your last."

Marlowe walked over to the table and lifted the quill. He dipped once and let the words flow out onto a clean page. His muse lifted her head and sighed as he spoke the words aloud.

"Quod me nutrit me destruit. That which nourishes me, destroys me."

XV

Richard Baines sucked the last drop of his ale, leaned his head back and belched into the air. He pounded the empty tankard onto the tabletop and released a chuckle.

"Clever plan," he whispered. "Marlowe's rise will carry me now. There is nothing to stop me."

Richard felt pleased. He gathered a bit of information and barely revealed anything. In his world that meant success; although, his stomach knotted thinking about the pretty boy with his amber eyes stepping into a position which should have come to him. He was older than Kit by nearly eight years, more experienced in matters of espionage and strategy, and more suited to the art of lying and doing whatever necessary to conform to any situation. A perfect provocateur.

Walsingham praised him on his return from the seminary in Rheims, even astounded at how effortlessly Baines morphed into a chameleon. *Nothing to it*, Baines feigned to him. His conscience never tweaked during the years there, not a hint of sin when he, a devout Protestant and supporter of the Queen, lay on the stones before the high altar with arms outstretched to the side and accepted the ordination as a Catholic priest. And the progress continued, onward to his ascension as deacon and friend of the seminary president. He fooled them all and did it without the blink of an eye. No one ever guessed, and he did it without a whit of pause.

Once the fellows of the school, both new students and old instructors, accepted him and folded him into their confidence, he felt he could carry out anything in smiting the Jesuit breeding ground. His letter to Walsingham spoke to the point: his intention to poison the water supply of the entire lot. Thus, in one fell swoop, all Catholic hopes lost and he, Richard Baines, heralded before the glorious virgin Queen. He used to imagine her overwhelming gratitude, her flushing cheek as she cupped her palm around his chin and her pleading words that he might visit her in private.

He suffered much in his service for her, even submitting to the questionings and torture for eleven days when some little rat revealed his Protestant leanings. No matter, for his imprisonment did more to convince his jailers of his devout devotion to the Pope than anything earlier, ending in the most eloquent recantation ever written, one that would put even Marlowe's words to shame. Of course, 'twas nothing but a ruse, a bold lie to win his release. He felt sure he would find a Protestant priest to absolve him of those necessary things. Necessary things such as lies and, of course, murder. His stupid little room mate who snitched on his secret feasting on meat pies on Fridays in his room, a horror for any Catholic, now fed worms at the bottom of a nearby French lake.

Baines chuckled at the image in his mind. Yet, the humor subsided into a sigh. His hope for glory on his return to England did not go as he imagined. All his plotting and planning for the demise of the seminary failed and Walsingham pointed this out to him as he sat in a chair before the Secretary's desk.

He recalled Sir Francis scratching his pointed chin and lowering his stare to him. "Pray, tell, what should I do with you? I mean, you weasel into my counsel, acquire a position within my circle to which I allow you to go to Rheims to carry out this elaborate plan you concocted; and now, what do I have to show to the Queen? Nothing! You managed a few tidbits of information, a few names and rumors of messages between the Scottish Queen and her uncle, things we are well aware of, and now you wish for more?"

Baines fidgeted. "Yea, sir, for I still have much I can do for Her Majesty."

Walsingham stood and walked to the window, keeping his back to Baines. "I am not so sure, Baines; however, there is a snake in you that may still be of use. Give me a bit of time and we will work you in again. My mind is upon another at the moment."

"Another, your Grace?"

"Yea, another. I have watched him over the years grow into

quite a clever young man. He is an astounding wit with a quill, as well as cunning and malleable. He could very well mold the minds of this island with a mighty line and I perceive his passion for writing will work well with my need to protect the Queen. His quick hand with ink translates into a quickness to kill, one will feed the other and vice versa. I think he will do more for my purpose than you at the moment."

Baines sensed his dream fading into dark. He stood up and gritted his teeth. "You mean to replace me after my old gradation? Instead, advancement is gained by letters and affection than by the three years of service I rendered in Rheims, even subjecting my very soul to eternal damnation by taking the vows of a papal priest? This will not pass, your Grace! Who is this incredible youth bending your eye?"

Walsingham glanced over his shoulder with a wry smile on his face. "My, my, Richard, you show your envy too openly. The youth is a Cambridge student by the name of Christopher Marlowe. Lord Burghley is even now on his way to Corpus Christi to engage the boy to a mission. This gives me a thought. Methinks that with his wit and your cunning, you might be a very dangerous team. We will think on this. Stay here in London. Enjoy the hiatus and let patience guide you. There may be more for you to do."

Richard writhed at the thought of this boy shadowing over his dream. Stay in London, Walsingham urged, but his mind drifted elsewhere. He made a quick determination to hire a coach and speed a path to Cambridge to look upon the boy genius.

Two days passed since then. He followed Marlowe through the maze of corridors and cloisters, along the garden paths, hiding in doorways in the streets and cowering in hazy corners of taverns to watch him. Baines thought there was not much to the youth. He looked like the typical poet with the musing dark eyes, hair sweeping back and curling over the winged collar of his linen shirt, with a form to turn a wench's eye and a dreamy air to make her swoon. Marlowe's entire image made Richard want to vomit.

Typical, he also thought, for the Queen to instruct her Secretary and Counselor to reel him in near her. She always fixed her eye for those sorts. He knew the only way for the Queen to bend her eye in his direction would be from good service, for he lacked the beauty of those she favored. He cursed his mother for the inheritance of a weak jaw, splotchy skin and profound nose, those distinct traits from his ancestors near Cumberland.

Baines looked toward the tavern door and pondered his next thoughts.

Marlowe sped away much too quick for someone who has nothing to fear. I must find his weakness, yea, and even mold myself into a friend, a confidant, for if my instinct does not fail me, there is something dark in the boy; something I can use to my benefit and to his fall. Yea, this is well. He will scream when the bones in his back crush as I use him as a ladder. A snicker tickled his throat when he thought of how the boy's eyes flashed wide when he referred to himself as the demon Mephistopheles.

He curved his eyebrow and whispered to himself. "Perhaps that is the key. He fears death, damnation, and even perhaps, that his rise to glory will be at some great cost. Ah, yea, this piece of information will stew quietly until I can act upon it."

A tap on the shoulder brought him out of his musing. He turned to see Thomas Colville tucking his shirt back in his breeches, his doublet still all unlaced and open.

"Marry, you are the man who followed my friend in the hallway."

Richard nodded and ignored him. Thomas hopped onto the stool next to him and tapped a coin on the bar top. "Come along, barkeep, and give me something to quench my thirst." He guzzled a bit of ale and continued. "Prithee, sir, what was your interest in my friend?"

Baines slurped some ale across his lips. "Nothing more than curiosity, Master Colville. There is much talk throughout the University of his skill as a playwright and I wished to give a face to the talk."

Thomas wrinkled his mouth. "'Tis strange then that you creased your brow when I spoke of his rare talent. You acted as if you had never heard of his skills."

Baines snickered. "Thomas, you pick upon me like an unskilled surgeon on a festering wound. You should learn to delve without letting a person know of your intentions. Therefore, because you are so inept in questioning, I will ease your mind. My interest in Master Marlowe is nothing more than what I said. I love the theater and am eager to see his plays performed. Do you not feel the same?"

He knew Thomas' answer would be the affirmative, for Richard saw how he worshiped Marlowe like an idol, grabbing at his portfolio in the hallway and begging for a word. Again, Baines felt clever in his skill to turn the conversation to where he now had the upper hand.

Baines questioned Thomas. "Pray, tell me, Master Thomas, of your dear friend. What sort of playwright is he?"

Thomas smiled. "O, the best sort, sir. He is much traveled, knows six languages and is a prodigy in Latin and Greek. He completed translating Ovid's Elegies and gives us little snippets of lines he says one day will come out in a play."

Baines continued with his act of being only interested in Marlowe's writing. "Ah, how exciting! And you say he traveled to the Continent? Has he said how this has influenced his writing?"

"O, yea, sir. His family is from Canterbury and from the time he was eight years old he began as a page to Sir Philip Sidney. You should hear some of his stories. He attended Walsingham at the embassy the night of the massacre in Paris and a year in Frankfort while Sidney tried his hand at encouraging Protestant supporters there, and more. He lived among the Catholics of Ireland and Rome."

Baines prodded a bit more. "And all to expand his writing, I suppose?"

Thomas shrugged. "Perhaps, but I do think there may be more to his travels. He is silent to anything else. I have always attributed it to his being a deep thinker, a brooding soul blessed by the muses, nothing more."

Baines stuck in his last clever question. "Have you never given consideration that your friend may be a provocateur for the Lord Secretary Walsingham?"

Thomas laughed, spewing out some of his ale. "Kit? Not a chance! All he talks about is the chance to become court playwright to the Queen and for her to give consent to the Master of the Revels in London for the performance of his plays."

Giddiness rose inside Baines, for now he delved to the core of Marlowe's ambition and why he willingly gave his works to Burghley. He considered this more useful information.

Thomas downed his ale and tugged on his breeches. "Blasted wench! She had me all roused and then ruined it with talk. I might have had a decent time of it if she could have kept her mouth shut. But, I suppose 'tis interesting the information you can get beneath sheets with a wordy drab. She said she just came from London where the Queen declared her new Archbishop of Canterbury. Have you heard? 'Tis the former Bishop of Worcester, John Whitgift."

The news sparked Richard's attention. "Indeed? Whitgift? I have heard the man is hard-nosed toward recusants and even has a taste for inquisitional tactics not seen since Bloody Mary."

Thomas wiped his mouth with his sleeve. "You are correct, sir. If ever there was a man who rushed upon success with much speed, then it is he. Ambition is no stranger to him, and see, his ambition succeeds and he now has the ear of Her Majesty and the soul of England."

Baines rubbed the coarse hair on his chin. "Hmm, this is interesting." *Marlowe's family is in Canterbury,* he thought. He wondered what it would be like to be friends with an Archbishop. After all, he himself could claim the rights of a cleric, for he studied at Rheims and took oaths as a priest, so with right he could claim tithes and a parish. Whitgift might be just the man to be another stepping stone to his dream and might be just the man to execute a strong hand on a youth like Marlowe, not to mention what other tasty morsels he could learn from the family.

He slapped Thomas on the back and slid a coin across the table to him. Thomas' eyes flashed at the gold piece.

"I thank you for your conversation, Master Colville, and hope to see you at your friend's plays. Take this as a gift. Ask the barkeep for Molly, she is spirited and is a mute. As for me, I feel a sudden need for a pilgrimage to Canterbury to welcome our new Archbishop."

XVI

B urghley felt pleased with the reports Marlowe sent to him of his son. In truth, there was nothing much to say except to emphasize the words dull, studious, proper and witless. The only redeeming quality Kit found was that he possessed the same delving qualities as his father, otherwise Kit found the whole matter incessantly boring. Burghley tired with it, as well, and ordered him on to the next assignment.

Stratford-upon-Avon, a peaceful pastoral village hiding intrigue within the shadows. Kit knew his mark. Rumors gathered and spread like a brush fire through a meadow of the true leanings of many of the Warwick country folk, first and foremost, the Arden family. Edward Arden held to his Catholic stance, yet hid his secrets well, even though his kinsmen, Somerville and Throgmorton, railed and plotted against the Queen. Edward let his true opinion slip only once, nine years previously, when the Queen visited Kenilworth. A day the Earl of Leicester never forgot and a moment Kit could not erase as well. It was at that faithful festival that he encountered the stupid boy who lied to save Arden. Kit knew it did not matter, for Walsingham filed Arden's name away until the links in the chain melded together. The moment arrived with the first frost and with the arrest of Arden's son-in-law, John Somerville. Walsingham dispatched Kit to connect the chain.

Walsingham's coach clacked along the rocky road stretching between Banbury and Stratford. Only ten minutes into the ride from the inn in Banbury, late in the evening when the moon's face glowed full over the elm trees as they swayed in the breeze, Walsingham tapped the roof of the coach to bring it to a halt. He turned the latch to the door and motioned for Marlowe to exit. Anger surged up in Kit's neck, yet Walsingham's stare remained fixed and stern.

"Get out here, boy."

Kit gritted his teeth. "'Twill take me the rest of the night to walk to Stratford. Why will you not take me the rest of the way?"

Walsingham's arched his eyebrow with resolution, so Kit took up a leather satchel and swung it over his shoulder as he dismounted the coach. Walsingham tossed a lute through the window. Kit caught the instrument, holding it up in the moonlight.

"Pray tell, what is this for?"

"'Tis for your masque as a minstrel, boy. You will learn that hiding behind masks is the easiest way for enemies to ignore your presence, especially when playing the part of a fool or musician. 'Tis interesting what secrets people speak to such men."

Kit hurried to the brambles at the side of the road and Walsingham slammed the door shut. Kit's breeches leg tangled in a thicket of thorns as the coach sped away, throwing up dirt into a cloud. Doubt blanketed over him as the film of dust settled, yet his heart surged at the excitement of morphing into a player. For years he thought about writing the plays, now he had the chance to be the character. Still, he knew he could not simply walk into Stratford and the expect the people's confidence. Common people needed a sweet voice drowned with the wine of his words and a clever smile.

'Tis a job for a witty lip and the reward will be great. Great for him, not so for the stupid papists revealing themselves to him.

He pulled his leg from the stickers and strummed his thumb over the chords of the lute. Calliope giggled and skipped ahead of him as he turned a corner on the road toward Stratford.

The morning sun kissed over the horizon as he walked over a hilltop overlooking the town. The glow banked the tilled fields on each side of the road in a sweet gold. He breathed in the crisp air and his feet crunched against the frozen ground as he walked through the shadows and beneath the elm and oak trees of Arden forest. The road dipped and curved to the right entering the city, and his footsteps made icy impressions in the small drifts of snow as he crossed a wooden bridge arching over the Avon River.

The villagers stirred. He followed a boy herder clicking his tongue behind a drove of fat wooly sheep, wove between carters loaded with a mixture of animal skins and meat, casks of ale, candles, rush torches, and wool cloth. The bread cart caught his eye as his stomach grumbled, but the man pushing the meat cart drew his attention as he tipped his head to those he passed, greeting all who raised their hand to him with a 'Ho, Will' and 'What do you have today for us, William?'

He took note that everyone liked him, thus it would make sense he might know a thing or two about Stratford's persons. He continued to follow as the streets filled and the sun rose higher, somewhat melting the crunchy mud beneath the soft heated chill of winter. They approached the marketplace, and the lanes thickened with conversing crowds, wooden carts, baaing sheep, growling dogs fighting over a stolen piece of salted beef, and peasant children in woolen capes and felt boots tossing muddy snowballs at each other as their parents tried to buy wares from the barking vendors. Many in the crowd queued in a line in front of the butcher as he wiggled his cart in between the baker and ale-man.

Kit tossed pence to the baker, broke off a piece of dark rye bread, skirted through the line and perched himself on the top of a large weathered oak barrel. The ale-man furrowed his brow at him.

Kit held up the lute and flavored his speech with a slight French accent. "Do you mind if I play, Monsieur?"

The ale-man scowled. "Ah, 'tis too early in the morn to hear such squalling!"

Kit smiled and closed his eyes, conjuring the sweet tunes of his imaginary friend and answered the man. "Come now, sirrah, I am in good company in the market. Music is the food of love bringing forth buyers to satisfy their appetites at your booths." He opened his eyes and caught the butcher smiling at him. Kit strummed his fingers across the chords; his voice breathed out in the crisp air in a warm ghostly haze.

"I will sing a common song, here:
O mistress mine, where are you roaming?
O, stay and hear; your true love's coming,
That can sing both high and low;
Trip no further, pretty sweeting;
Journeys end in lover's meeting,
Every wise man's son doth know."

The butcher and ale-man paused and a small crowd gathered at their booths. The butcher smiled and nodded to him.

"Ah, you have a sweet and contagious breath, sir. Have you been a bard your entire life?"

Kit crossed his legs and leaned the lute against his knee. "I have, good sir, and taught by Calliope herself."

"Yea," the butcher replied, "I can believe that. And what shall we call you, minstrel?"

Kit cocked his head and sang his answer.

"I am but a clown for show,
but you may call me Henry Fagot,
for my mother was an English whore,
and my father a French troubadour."

The butcher extended his hand. "Then shake my hand, Henry, and stay at your pleasure. For look you, the crowds gather to hear your voice and thus brings much coin to my stall."

Kit plucked a few strings. "Nay, sir, 'tis not my singing but their stomachs bringing them to your venison and bunnies. Tell me, have you been butcher here in Stratford for a time?"

"Nay, sir, this work merely earns me a keep for myself and my wife. There is nothing to it touching my heart such as your living."

The butcher's words peaked Kit's interest. "Forsooth, sir? Then, what, pray tell, is the thing close to your heart? I will find a ditty to sing for your heart's wish."

The man's stare drifted upwards to the passing clouds. "My heart's wish? Ah, to be to the stage as a player, even in a troupe traveling from town to town as you do, sir. Perhaps even to perform at Court. Have you ever played at Court, sir?"

Kit released a small laugh. "Yea, too many times to count. I am a fool for those in high places."

The butcher wiped his hands in his apron and bent at the waist in a bow. "I am William, minstrel, and I say nay, not a fool, for I know the great clown Tarleton. I warrant that man has more wit than any soul in Christendom for he sees much and he veils heavy news with clever quips."

Kit plucked the strings again and lilted out a line in soft melody.

"Ah, let the jibes and ambles soften the truth.
Fools and players are the chroniclers of our time.
When you die, 'tis better to have a bad epitaph,
Than their ill report whilst you live."

While he played, two women came to William's stall and picked out a few fat hares. Kit remained quiet and listened for any papal leanings.

William wiped a bloody blade across the skirt of his apron, leaving a smear of red blazoned like a brand, and he transformed like a seasoned actor into the part of a butcher. The sun blazed at the noon hour and the market filled with men and women seeking to fill their bellies with fresh meat. Meat was scarce for the common folk since a rash of drought ravished the Midlands. Agnes, the wife of the blacksmith, and her sister, Blanche, laid their coins on the table.

"'Tis good, William. Tell me," asked Agnes, "how is it you have such a supply of fresh meat?"

William shrugged, bending his body into a bow befitting his acting skills. "Ah, 'tis a secret, dear lady."

Blanche leaned forward toward him, pulling him into her private conference. "You can tell us, Will. We will not tell a soul. Will we, Agnes?"

William whispered, enveloping them into his captivating smile and intrigue. "You see, my ladies, if I told you then it would not be a secret, and you would not visit me every week here at my stall. I would miss out on seeing your adoring smiles."

Blanche tapped and nudged him on the arm as Agnes' words tumbled out between giggles. "You are a devil! How does that wife of yours put up with you?"

William's mouth wrinkled into a smirk and Kit noticed a man lurking behind the women. William waved the man forward. "Come along, Richard, I see you there. What is your business today?"

Richard pushed past the women as they made their retreat, still giggling and glancing over their shoulders at William. Richard's glare darted between them and his friend. "The women love you, Will."

William shrugged as he tossed the remaining coney warrens into a basket. "Women are foolish. You say one pretty word to them and they are next wondering how they can lure you to their bed."

Richard chuckled. "I would think you have had enough of women."

William gritted his teeth. "One woman, you mean?"

Richard slapped him on the back and snorted a laugh. "How is your Anne?"

"Aging, my friend; she is aging."

Kit noticed the despair in William's eyes and the sadness furling his brow.

Richard urged him. "Come on, Will, your mind will be at ease again. We will have a play tonight at the tavern. Will you perform? Many are asking for you."

The corner of William's mouth turned upwards. "Of course, of course. There is my true love and I will always return to her bed no matter what the cost. What are we performing tonight?"

"Well, I had thought something touching a mystery play, but I fear that skims too close to the old religion. There are rumors of a secret infiltration of Walsingham's henchmen, so I was thinking perhaps something Senecan, something safe so no one will suspect any leanings in our case."

William frowned and Kit looked down at the lute so they could not see his eyes.

"What means this," William asked.

"Have you not heard?"

William shook his head and leaned near to hear Richard's words.

"There is talk that more Jesuits are near and are being held up in an estate in Warwickshire. The county swarms with Leicester's men and the Justice, Sir Thomas Lucy, is chomping the bit to search all the surrounding houses. Many fear an onslaught of raids backed by the Queen looking for sympathizers and traitors. It seems murder doth permeate the air here in Stratford. Such plot and intrigue even in our own small town with Catholic against Protestant and the like."

"Thomas Lucy? I think he best look to his own meadows in Charlecote. The only thing he will find in my house is his own coneys." Will lifted one rabbit by the long ears and smiled.

Richard placed his hand on Will's arm. "Seriously, Will, whether it be coneys or seditious papers, Lucy will stop at nothing to hang someone. I know they are looking for a singular person who is scheming plots against the Queen and funneling assassins into the country more fanatic than Campion."

Kit noticed the butcher-player rubbing his brow as if to brush away a bad thought. "Indeed, I think it would be best to retire to the airy heights of Plautus. We do not want to provoke curiosity, do we? And perhaps you will come this even, minstrel, and enliven our stage with a pretty tune? This is Master Richard Burbage. He is a player, as well, and his father is proprietor of the tavern here in Stratford."

Kit looked up and saw the two men staring at him. Kit knew Burbage from the stages in London, so he lowered his gaze so Burbage could not recognize him. "Of course, good sirs, anything for some coin in my purse and a belly of ale."

William extended his hand to Kit. "Then accept my invitation and hospitality and come home with me for a meal. And you, as well, Richard."

Richard shook his head and held up his hands. "Nay, please forgive me, but I do not wish to receive the wrath of your shrew. She nearly knocked me senseless last evening for bringing you home late from the tavern."

The three of them shook hands and parted. Kit followed William in silence along the road to Shottery. The trees parted to reveal a mushroomed house, squatty and cream-colored with the aged thatch trimmed like a pageboy's hair over the eaves and a slender gray ribbon of smoke streamed up from the chimney. A woman stood in the doorway with one arm clutching a baby and the other crooked in displeasure at her hip.

Kit noticed William's feigning smile as they walked down the pathway. "Dearest, this is Henry, a French minstrel I met in the market today. I thought he might play a lullaby to Susannah and ease her colic. Sir, meet my wife, Anne."

Anne threw a stern glance at Kit. He could tell by the wrinkles around her eyes, she was a quite bit older than William. She cocked her head and replied, "Well, I suppose I have no choice since he stands here at my door. And I suppose he will want something to eat as well."

She stood to the side as they entered the house. Kit glanced around the room and remembrances of his childhood home in Canterbury flashed in his mind: straw on the floor, stew boiling over the glowing coals in the hearth, the plastered and beamed home. An almost perfect English family. William took the crying baby and Anne scooped stew into two bowls, placing them on the table. William motioned to Kit to sit on the bench across from him.

"Forgive me, sir, for her crying. She is but five months old and suffers daily from a sour stomach."

Kit thought it was more like a sour mother the child suffered from, but he just smiled and remained quiet. Anne took the babe from William's arms and marched into the other room. Kit kept his stare into the bubbling rabbit stew in front of him, dipping his bread into the thick brown gravy and the two of them devoured their dishes. Kit leaned back and held his hand over his stomach.

"Madame, your dish has filled by belly and my heart. I thank you for your kindness."

William wiped his mouth and reached across to a pouch at the end of the table. He untied the strings and pulled out a familiar board.

"What say you, minstrel? Are you up for a few games of mills before we leave for the tavern?"

Kit's eyes widened when he recognized the board and his heart drummed in his ears. He lifted his gaze to William's face, and his mind formed the image of the stupid boy from the festival in Kenilworth, now a husband and father. An awkward chill crept over Kit, realizing this man in front of him was a player and would know the attitudes to portray to hide his memory of Kenilworth.

Kit stood up quite sudden and threw the lute over his shoulder.

"You must forgive me, Monsieur. I thank you most heartily for the meal and I will be glad of your conversation this even, but I do not know this game and also, I do not wish to continue to intrude on the kindness of your wife. Let me be on my way to gather coin in the village with my playing and I will see you again at the tavern."

William stood up, confusion enveloping his face. "O, sir, of course. I mean, if you must."

Kit looked to the door and saw Anne's shadow hovering across the door frame. "Yea, sir, 'tis for the best."

Kit tightened the lute strap across his chest and hurried out the door, leaving behind William waving to him in the doorway and Anne glaring from the window.

XVII

That night the shadows stretched across the dirt and cobbled streets of Stratford. The lamplighter, soused from too much ale, swayed from pillar to post along the roadway to light the torches and lanterns in the midst of the village. Along the alleyway nearest to Burbage's Tavern, a coach clacked across the cobblestones.

In the darkness, as Kit rounded the narrow alleyway to the side of the tavern, he collided into the drunk, knocking the lamplighter onto his backside. Kit stepped over him, nearing the window of the coach. The air thickened with whispers.

A raspy voice filtered through the heavy-curtained window. "Is everything in order?"

"Yea, all is in order, Sir Francis. The reports are verified and once you make the arrest, there should be plenty of incriminating evidence to find within the man's house. I warrant you and Lucy should be able to find what you need."

"Then, when the trap snaps, make haste to London."

The coach sped away, disappearing into the rising fog. Kit turned upon the lamplighter, watching as he tried to stand upon his drunken legs, and spoke to him in a whisper. "Get you gone, you stupid drunk."

The lighter stood for a moment and fell upon Kit with both hands as he tried to steady his crash. Their eyes locked. Kit smelled the foul, cantankerous breath of aged ale and stale bread. The lighter grinned a gapped smile, his nose blasting a pocked reddish hue and his large belly rising and falling upon the laughter he held within. He pointed into Kit's face.

"I know you, sir."

Kit pushed him, even as the man clung to him. "No, you idiot, you do not."

The drunk's back straightened from his inebriated dance. He squinted and his rolly cheeks trembled from the humor.

"I see you, sir, in your secrecy. You are the minstrel from the market, but I remember you as a boy in Kenilworth. See, the ale may have knocked me a notch from my service as a guardsman, but does not cloud my memory of the youth who climbed over the wall and spoke to me about the battle of Agincourt. Do you not remember Bardolph the warder? Spare me pence and I will speak of this to no one." He held out his hand to Kit, his fingers wriggling for a coin.

Kit pushed him with all his force, sending the round man rolling into a bank of muddy snow. The man groaned and clamored for a pile of wet leaves to perch his head as if he were oblivious to the former brief conversation. A moment more and the man snored. Kit looked from side to side, making sure no other eyes lay upon his face, straightened his jerkin and slipped into the tavern.

The tavern breathed in low hushed whispers as a dozen or more townsfolk sipped ale and supped on venison stew. The fire in the hearth, candles on the tables and torches perched along the wall illuminated the small establishment and a small stage at the end of the room.

Kit moved along the wall, edging around chairs and behind an arras until he reached a single table pushed into a corner; a perfect vantage point where he could see the faces of men and the performance. He listened, bending one ear to eavesdrop and the other to the stage. The conversations varied from the mundane to the scandalous until William walked out onto the stage.

Kit's gaze led him to this actor, and he took a moment to study the boy he knew, now the man before him. He calculated William's age as his own of twenty from the encounter of long ago. William's hair matching Kit's in length, tucked back over his ear and curling over his collar, and he bore the same light beard circling around his mouth. Kit thought him a fair looking fellow and one, if his acting skills played well, who might fit into one of the characters in his plays. Kit soaked in the words as William swept the audience into a scene.

Plautus' words tumbled from William's lips with such naturalness, as easy as breathing or conversing over the weather.

Kit's chest swelled with admiration, his heart moved with each attitude and gesture, and he let out a small sigh upon the last line. When the play ended, and the tavern emptied, Kit sat in silence and watched him. William walked out from a curtain at the back of the stage and shook hands with Richard.

Kit called the barmaid near and placed a coin in her hand. "Give Master Shakespeare a pint and ask him to join me."

She curtsied and darted away, returning with a tankard and stopping to whisper in William's ear. William strode across the room and plopped down on a bench across from Kit. Kit raised his tankard in a toast.

"You are an amazing actor, Monsieur. I applaud you for 'tis not everyday you see Plautus performed with such skill."

William lowered his gaze and sipped the brew. "Thank you, Henry. Pray, tell me, sir, since you are a poet of sorts, do you have a patron?"

Kit smiled. "And if I do, are you seeking one?"

William's brown eyes flashed with hopefulness. "Perhaps. I am always seeking ways to further my acting skills."

A snicker crossed Kit's lips. "Here in Stratford, sir? If that is true, then why are you not in London? There are patrons there that could do you better service." As he spoke, he noticed William fidgeting with the ring around his finger. "Forgive me, Monsieur, I forgot life binds you here."

William twirled the band, removed the pewter trinket and slipped it into a leather pouch at his belt. "Nay, sir, I am not bound to Stratford. I am an actor and I am bound to the stage."

"Ah, a servant of Thalia and Melopmene, the fair muses of the theater. Pray tell, am I correct to perceive that you are the best of players for you perform even off the stage?"

William squirmed in his seat. "Why do you say such?"

Kit leaned forward toward the candlelight. "I know a little of what it is like to become someone else when your heart is elsewhere."

William's brow wrinkled. "Indeed, you are a player to audiences, as well."

"A player? You are correct, Monsieur, but are we not all players? We strut and fret for an hour, and then, when we leave this mortal shell, no one hears anymore of us."

William downed his ale and slammed the mug upon the table. The candle flame shivered from the force. "Nay, 'twill not do. 'Twill not be so with me. Generations will speak of me; mark me."

Kit leaned back into the shadows, pondering this free revelation of William's ambition. "O, we all want a legacy, sir, but at what price are you willing to pay? That is the question."

William motioned for the bar maid to bring more ale. He pushed a pence across the tabletop toward her and tapped the stamped image of Elizabeth with his forefinger. "Price? I will pay anything."

Kit reflected on the creature before him; his resolute eyes, his determined brow, and the way his jaw clenched upon opportunity. Over William's shoulder and within Kit's sight, he imagined the translucent image of Calliope whispering into the eager ears of her sisters. Thalia smiled and Melopmene frowned at the words flowing next from Kit's mouth.

"Do you have no conscience, then? For I have perceived conscience makes cowards of men because they fear the unknown laying before them. Have you not thus settled here in Stratford because you fear the leap from here to London? You incline to bear the ills you have than to fly to others you know not of, thus the native hue of resolution is sicklied over with the pale cast of thought, and your enterprise of great pitch and moment with this regard, their currents turn awry and lose the name of action."

William's face lit up with a smile. "You speak like a philosopher bard."

Kit downed his ale, steadied himself and ignored the vision of the three sisters. He shivered and adjusted his words as one adjusts the pegs on a game board. The nearness of William's words whetted his almost blunted purpose.

"Ah, as a minstrel I have become an observer of men's consciences. We live in a time filled with dilemmas, a time when men must decide what they will give up to survive or to thrive. I am sure you know of what I speak. Have you not seen unrest among your neighbors here in Warwickshire?"

William lowered his stare. "I do not know what you mean, sir."

"Come, come, sirrah. Surely as a player you are privy to the stench in the air. Players are privy to the pulse of a nation, even heralding forth tragedy and comedy depending on the state of church and state. You cannot tell me you have no thoughts to these things." Kit leaned forward and urged William with a lie. "Besides, 'tis easier to keep our heads without betraying our hearts here in the countryside. I warrant there are more of us waiting in secret for the cream to rise again to the surface."

William's eyes rounded, and he lowered his voice. "You are a papist, sir?"

Kit curled his lip in a deceiving smile. "I am French, Monsieur, what do you think? Are we not all, forsooth?"

William's stare turned toward the door as two men pushed into the tavern. The former resolution in his face drained away as one of the men approached. Kit recognized the men as William's kinsmen, John Shakespeare and Edward Arden. Kit pushed his chair back further into the shadows.

"William, come speak to your kinsman," his father bellowed.

William fidgeted and spoke to Kit. "Forgive me, sir, for I wish to continue our conversation." And then, to his father. "In a moment, father, for I am conversing with this gentleman."

John cast a glare over Kit, his dusky gray eyes peered out from under a bush of silver eyebrows and darted back and forth over Kit's face as he tried to decipher Kit's features in the darkness. John removed an embroidered pair of gloves and extended his hand. "Sir, shake my hand. I am John Shakespeare, William's father."

Kit accepted the introduction. "'Tis a pleasure, Monsieur. I was just telling your son what a delight it was to see him on the stage. He is quite the brilliant performer."

"Nonsense," John spat, "a frivolity, 'tis all. I would wish him to put his mind to meatier matters."

Kit arched his left eyebrow. "Indeed? He appears to put his mind to meatier matters as a butcher during the day, but are you not aware of the importance a play can do to change the views of the common man? 'Tis a tool used by many a sovereign to propagate modern thinking."

John's eyes squared and squinted. "There are better ways to change the views of the common folk. And who are you that you give your opinion so freely?"

"I am of no importance, Monsieur. Just a man who observes, 'tis all."

"You have not given your name, sir."

Amusement swept over Kit. "I am Henry, sir, Henry Fagot."

John's eyebrows arched. "Norman descent, are you?"

"You are quick," Kit answered, "for my father was Norman and the 'T' is neither here nor there."

John smirked and turned away from him and walked back toward Arden. Kit reeled William back into conversation. "Your father is very headstrong, I daresay. And the other man with him there, who is he?"

William looked toward them as he downed another mug of ale.

"You speak right about my father. He is as stubborn as a goat and he is very often in the company of my kinsman, Edward Arden, who is my mother's cousin."

Kit faked a gasp, for he already knew the man's face. "Edward Arden? Tell me, is he not the father-in-law of that Somerville the Star Chamber arrested and threw in the Tower? 'Tis a pity, but pray, tell me, I have heard rumors that Arden hides Jesuits beneath the floorboards of his own house."

William looked around the room and leaned near to Kit. "I would not think to tell you, but that you confessed your own leanings. That and the fear there is talk of spies in our midst. Yea, Edward fights in his own way for the Holy Father and hides priests in the walls and floors of his home. My own father met Campion there before his arrest and execution."

John waved to his son once more until William pardoned himself from Kit's company and left to greet his uncle. Kit's thoughts swirled in his head. He covered his mouth with his palm and whispered to himself.

"Ah, yea, William, I already knew the man by his reputation, but your words have bound him. Now shall the 'T' in Fagot become resolute and this bundle of sticks shall add to the fire he is about to feel."

Like a seasoned spy, Kit shifted from the table and made his way through the maze of tavern patrons, all the while keeping his eyes fixed upon William. He watched as the blood drained from William's face upon returning to the table to find him absent and the fear shadowing him as he grabbed his father's coat, urging him to the door. Kit kept himself invisible to William's sight, hiding behind the arras near them to listen to their telling conversation. As a spy, an arras was a useful tool, for through the weaved and painted threads, faces became transparent and words filtered without restraint.

William pulled John toward the door. "Father, we must leave this instant."

John yanked his arm away. "Nay, we will not leave. We have only enjoyed one pint and have many more coming. Is this not right, Edward?"

Edward nudged William with his elbow, guffawing into the ale and forming a ridge of foam along his burly gray mustache. "Indeed, John, indeed. Sit with us, William, and share a pint and a tale."

William kept pulling on their coats as his eyes darted toward the door. "Nay, come along, we will have a pint at home. Please, come along for I fear something is coming."

The two men laughed and shoved William as Kit edged out the back of the tavern where he signaled Sir Francis' coach waiting in the darkness. Kit hovered near the doorway as Sir Francis Walsingham and Sir Thomas Lucy strode into the tavern, their black cloaks rustling across the floor and collecting dirt along the hems. The conversations hushed, and the crowds parted. Walsingham marched straight up to Edward, looking square into Arden's round face.

"Edward Arden?"

Edward's laughter fell away as the fear crept into his voice and eyes. "I am, sir."

"Do you know me, sir?" Edward swallowed hard and nodded. Walsingham motioned for two yeoman guards to surround him. "Then you know why I am here. I hereby arrest you in the name of the Queen and charge you with treason before all these witnesses."

William's father rushed forward, knocking his stool to the ground.

"Treason? What means this?"

William grabbed his father's arm, his fingers squeezing and urging him to silence. Edward puffed his chest and his countenance relaxed.

"I am no treason master, Sir Walsingham. I am a loyal subject to Her Majesty."

Walsingham's lip bent in a sarcastic snarl. "Loyal to Her Majesty? Which majesty, sir, Elizabeth or the usurper Queen of the Scots?"

John Shakespeare lunged forward into Walsingham's face. "Dare you accuse my kinsfolk of such things!"

William pulled his father back as Walsingham surveyed each of their faces. "Such passion for a kinsman. I have watched you all since the festivities of Kenilworth, and now, shall I tell you of your kinsman's indictment? We apprehended Arden's son-in-law, John Somerville, at an inn near Aynho after he thrashed about a gun and declared our Queen to be a heretic and that her head should be upon a pike. He now sits weeping in the Tower. And yea, there is more." He glared at Edward. "Your wife is a Throgmorton, and we have her kinsman, Francis Throgmorton, in the Tower alongside Somerville. He is spending his days in the Little Ease for plotting to set the Catholic Mary of Scots upon our English throne. I have you, Arden, for even now your home is being searched and I warrant there is enough there against you. Your wife follows presently. In her sobbing she spilled the news of your gardener-priest Hugh Hall, so now shall I have a three-fold cord to deliver to Her Majesty." He leaned further into Arden's face as the beads of sweat popped out on Edward's forehead. "Shall I tell you of the Little Ease? Shall you become acquainted with the stone box so small a person can neither stand up nor lay down? And the days will pass where your aging and creaking bones will cry for relief. Tell me, Arden, how like you the chance to occupy the space? Or shall I take in all of your family to get to the truth? Surely one of them will crumple under my form of persuasion."

Thomas Lucy's wrath bore down on William. "And you, boy, we have no papal evidence against you, but I ought to take you to jail for the rumors of you pinching deer and rabbits from my property in Charlecote. Perhaps a few weeks would soften your resolve to confess something of more weight against your family."

William gritted his teeth. John's face turned pale as he spoke to Edward. "What shall I do?"

Arden turned to look into John's face. "Be silent, John. I will not have you or my cousin, Mary, tangled in this misunderstanding. I will go in peace and all this matter will unraveled properly."

Walsingham grinned. "Properly, indeed. Our Queen wishes to face all the Catholic rebels."

Kit slid out of sight as the guards bound Arden by the hands and led him out to Walsingham's waiting coach.

XVIII

The Queen of England allowed Kit to walk with her into an anteroom of the Guildhall. Walsingham and Burghley followed behind, tossing smiles at their young protégé. Kit soaked in the approving glow on the Queen's face. Walsingham gloated and Burghley beamed, *and all for me,* Kit mused.

Burghley whispered to Walsingham, "This one is much different from the Earl of Leicester. Dudley is too full of self, too full of a house vying for royalty and the chance to breed a royal heir. I see a future in this young one for he can mold minds with words like no other. He has proven to sway thoughts and moods with a sonnet and betray conscious with a soft rhyme. He is gifted and sly. We must keep him close and on the right side else he might topple the whole of England."

Marlowe seeped out a quiet snicker. He heard all of Burghley's words for the old man's whispers were like the buzzing of a bee's wings, low and deep yet discernible to an attuned ear.

The Queen extended her hand to Kit. His hand trembled under the power emanating from her fingers and his heart pounded. Inspiring words surged through his blood racing and ebbing until his head ached from the excess. He was sure this lady was the muse haunting his dreams, for from the touch of her hand flowed music, sonnets and poetry. She sat at the window seat and Marlowe knelt before her, his eyes fixated on the gold embroidery at the hem of her skirt.

She spoke. "So, Walsingham, 'twould seem you did well all those years ago in gaining this young man, this illustrious playwright who hath saved England's life."

Kit cheeks flushed at her compliment.

Walsingham bowed. "Yea, your Majesty; my suspicions well

placed."

She studied Kit. "You have grown to be quite a handsome young man, Master Marlowe. Pray, tell me, how old are you now?"

"I am twenty, your Majesty."

She brushed the back of her forefinger across his cheek. "Ah, twenty? 'Tis a pretty age. I remember when my Robin was twenty. We used to shock my ladies at Hatfield with a spirited dance or a stolen kiss. He was not a poet of words, but he possessed a poet's soul. I have found over the years, quite often, bookish playwrights and poets are dull and unattractive, having to woo women with words rather than by form, but you are quite different with your mysterious eyes. We are pleased."

Marlowe took the compliment to his heart, which gave him the courage to raise his eyes toward her. Every detail etched in the volume of his mind to one day write upon a page: the fiery red of her velvet gown; her royal hands clasped and slender fingers weighted with golden rings, signets and jeweled; the tiny red ringlets circling her whitewashed face; and her eyes, those bold and powerful seductive eyes like two dark warm springs melting snow, a trait from her lusty mother, Anne Boleyn.

"You are not what I imagined either, my lady."

Burghley turned and gave Kit a harsh stare, but Kit detected the humor in the corner of her upturned lip.

"Am I not? And how often do I pass through your imagination, Master Marlowe?"

Kit paused. He stepped carefully, choosing words to inspire. For a moment, his thoughts drifted back to Mary, the Countess of Pembroke. No other since her had inspired in him such words and heated blood. He fell back upon words Mary once inspired.

"Shall I compare thee to a summer's day? Thou art more lovely and more temperate."

The Queen's amusement turned into deep laughter. "Indeed? You are clever and entertaining, but we wonder..." she responded, as her face changed to sternness at the pondering of her next thought. "We wonder where a poet's loyalties truly lie. For so often, a poet seeks only to ally himself with someone who can afford him, but does that really speak to how his heart feels. He writes to fill his pocket, thinking naught of serious matters. My father thought it a matter of state as to what stories play on the stages of England. We liked the law well to establish a Master of Revels over the playhouses, but now the likes of Burbage are building theaters beyond the jurisdictional walls of London. We wonder if it is to promote subversive speech, perhaps even as a pawn against our throne. Pray, tell me, Marlowe, where are your loyalties?"

"I serve you, my lady."

She sighed and turned her eyes away. "Easily said. You serve Walsingham and Burghley because of the advantage it avails you, and we wonder if it shall be the same with us. Where is your faith, sir? What are your leanings? If given a choice between life and death because of your words, would you compromise and live or adhere and die?"

Marlowe smiled. "I know on what you speak. You speak of whether I have Catholic or Protestant leanings. It matters not what I think or feel, for I have no quarrel with you or with Rome. I am a simple playwright who wishes to write and to see my work upon the stage. That is all, my Queen."

Elizabeth stood up and turned her back to him. "Oh, no, my dear Marlowe, you mistake. There is nothing simple about you. And it does matter, for you see, poets have the ability to mold a nation's thinking in this day and time. Have you not seen the things written and posted upon the church doors? What you write about and the subjects displayed upon the stage could cost you your life whether it is from our throne or from Rome." She motioned to Burghley for him to take Kit from the room. "He is too young. Clever, to be sure, but arrogantly stupid. Did you not tell him we cannot protect him from his own arrogance? Why is it we must surround ourself with such stupid haughty men?"

Walsingham stepped forward and urged Kit to his feet. "Your Majesty, if I might suggest, perhaps I should send him on some errand where he might have time to come to his senses, and in the meantime, write you a play?"

Kit snatched his arm from Walsingham's grip, confusion filling his heart. "But, your Majesty, I have already written three plays needing your approval to go to the stage. Burghley promised..."

She lifted her hand to demand silence. She turned toward Kit, the former adoring hue now a pale coldness. Her teeth ground behind her lips as if she chewed upon the thought.

"Yea, 'twill serve us well. Send him back to Cambridge or on another mission. You say you have written three plays for our amusement, Master Marlowe? You are quite presumptuous to think you have earned our patronage. Tilney is our servant for the stages within the verge and it will take the promise of payment before Burbage or any other player will back your plays outside the city walls. We will see your plays, but not yet. There are more rats to find. Arden is a nice catch, now, find us something better. Leave us. We have things to discuss with Lord Burghley before Arden's trial."

Kit bent to a bow. He backed out of the room with Walsingham and just as he crossed the threshold, he lifted his head and caught her stare. A bold smile passed across his lips catching her by surprise. Before the door closed, she returned a look with a small grin of approval. Kit knew he had won her.

In the hallway, Walsingham stopped him in the shadows. "You did well, boy. Continue to please the Queen, but remember, she is a woman. Her mood is fickle and changes like the wind. Open your sails, Kit, and let her guide you. Follow where she leads." Walsingham stretched out his arms until his black cloak billowed. "Look at me, I have free reign to devour as long as my Queen smiles and feels protected."

Kit's smile ceased to a frown watching him. He felt no humor in his feelings for Walsingham, only dread, fear, anger and blood. The approval of the Queen made his words bold.

"I am convinced, Sir Walsingham, that no matter who sat on the throne you would find a way to devour and find advantage."

Walsingham grabbed his arm and squeezed until his knuckles turned pale. "Watch your words, Marlowe, for I hold your life in my hands. Do you think a smile from the Queen will keep you from harm? Who do you think keeps your name in her ear or from revelation to Rome's spies?"

Walsingham released his grip and walked into the darkness. Nausea swept through Kit's gut. His head swam in a crucible of approval and doubt, glory in advancing his art and despair for the price he daily paid. He stepped out into the arches of the main floor of the Guildhall. As he leaned against a stone pillar, he caught sight of William Shakespeare weaving through the gathering crowd.

ℰꙘ

William pulled his coat about his shoulders. The morning air bit and his breath frosted from his mouth. His eyes fixed upon the building before him.

She rose like a mighty temple, three stories high, creamy plastered and tar-beamed in a profound octagon. Richard looked at Will's face and smiled.

"She is a work of beauty, is she not?"

William agreed as two enamored words fell from his frozen lips.

"The Curtain."

Richard urged him forward. "Shall we go in for a moment?"

William shook his head. "Nay, not now. Later, perhaps, when I can drink her thespian essence. The thoughts of my kinsman's trial at the Guildhall distracts my brain. Take me there, Richard, for I wish to know what will become of him."

William kept his gaze over his shoulder while his feet crunched along Curtain Road toward Hogs Lane through the frozen puddles and icy mud. Her powerful presence loomed behind him, teasing him and beckoning him. As they made their way southward on Norton Folgate Road, a dark figure opened and closed the door of the actor's lodging house. Through the fog rising off the Thames, William's eyes locked with the stranger. Something familiar passed between them. The figure paused and looked down at the cobblestones and vanished, swallowed up in the thickness of the mist.

Richard nudged William in the side. "Did you see him?"

William's brow wrinkled. "I saw someone, but could not discern the face. Who was it?"

"'Twas the newest playwright here in London. His pages are already being distributed at Saint Paul's Yard. He is so young, your age even, but his words hold an age and wisdom far beyond reasoning. The muse blesses this one and actors such as Alleyn fawn to enact his characters. 'Twas Master Christopher Marlowe."

"And his plays, when will they see the stage?"

Richard rubbed his fingers together. "Ah, as soon as he can get the chinks and the approval of Master Tilney, and Tilney cannot flinch without Her Majesty's nod."

William looked again into the fog as it swirled into a slight breeze. A chill shivered down his neck.

Richard patted his shoulder. "Will, are you well?"

"In truth, I do not know, Richard. There is something about my brain. Perhaps 'tis just this business with my uncle." He pondered the veiled look between him and the stranger through the fog. "I do not know, perhaps fancies is all. My mind is abuzz with these sights and sounds of London."

Richard chuckled. "Ah, 'tis as I said all along, is it not? I knew when your feet touched these cobblestones you would sense the muse. Come along, let us get you to the Guildhall and settle these matters so your mind settles upon the Curtain's stage this eve."

The sights of London filled William, the repulsiveness and drawing taking turns upon each heartbeat. They trudged down the narrow lanes weaving in and out of Cheapside, rank lanes smelling of urine and befouled with the plague pocked poor. William, in a way, missed the airy spaces of Stratford and the earthy smells of Charlecote forest, but then, as the streets widened and his eyes filled with the splendor of the Guildhall, the surface filth evaporated. The Guildhall looked down over the city, her windows peering like judging eyes, melding out law within her gray stone walls, and rising from the muddy streets to the south of Cripplegate. A light dusting of snow drifted from billowy white clouds, a pure delicate innocence covering London and freezing on the cobblestones in an unholy muddy and yellow slush. The shivering crowds gathered and filled the hall, some to view the Queen in her royal splendor, some to feed on the fervor of gossip and others to soak themselves in the soon spilled blood of a traitor. William positioned himself to the left of the hall, his eyes within range of his cousin's face. The trial commenced in less than half an hour; more of a show to the common people and, to Will, appeared more like an entertaining play bent to scare any other Catholic pawns from showing their intent. Edward Arden, his wife, Mary, John Somerville and the priest Hugh Hall stood before the counsel. The words 'hanged, drawn and quartered' floated through the air and scorched William's ears. Mary Arden fell to her knees and wept into the hem of Elizabeth's scarlet gown as the herald read the order for her to hang and burn at Tyburn. Elizabeth rose and placed her pale hand upon Mary's head, stroking her dark hair and lifting her chin in her fingers until their eyes met.

Silence fell upon the hall as the Queen spoke. "Tears do not move us, Lady Arden, but only by the fact you leave your children orphaned when you die do we reprieve you of your sentence and pray you search your heart toward your Queen. We give forgiveness only once, do you understand?"

Mary stood and curtsied, backing away as the Queen ordered the next three traitors forward with the flick of her finger. Archbishop Whitgift, now a member of the Privy Council, completed the announcement of judgment.

"As for these other traitors, the sentence will conclude at Newgate in three days as an example for all. According to the custom for treason, a hurdle will drag you through the streets to the platform at Smithfield where you will hang by the neck, and being alive, cut down and laid before the crowds. Your privy members will be severed, your bowels taken out of your belly and there burned, you being alive. Lastly, your head cut from your shoulders and piked upon the ramparts of London Bridge as a warning to all."

William nudged Richard with his elbow and he pointed toward the Archbishop. "Look there, do you know who that is?"

Richard shrugged. "Yea, 'tis the Archbishop of Canterbury."

"Yea, that it is, but I know him also as John Whitgift. He was Bishop of Worcester not long ago and signed my marriage license to Anne, and now, look at him. He has come to his reward very quickly. You know what he told me that day? He said when he came to his glory he, perhaps, could render me a favor."

"Pray, William, I think it be too late to ask for a pardon for Edward."

William closed his eyes and sighed. "You are probably right, but I will remember his promise. Only three days hence and a great blow will strike our family. I fear for what is coming next, but now I know he is Archbishop, perhaps I can use such knowledge if ever needed." He thought of his father and the secret testament hidden in the rafters above the workshop. As he opened his eyes, other figures entered from the right of the hall and stood before the Queen as the prisoners exited from her view.

Walsingham came forward and kissed the hand of the beloved Virgin Queen. Elizabeth's smile displayed satisfaction and approval of the man, her eyes doting upon the excellent discovery of these would-be assassins. Burghley bowed next. The power of the small lady whose hand he kissed overpowered his large frame. William peered with quiet interest as Burghley stepped to the side and motioned for another adoring creature to step forward. William recognized him at once as the minstrel he met from Stratford the day of Edward's arrest.

He turned to Richard, his face wrinkled with betrayal. "I knew my fears spoke true, Richard. S'wounds, I am the one who gave him up. 'Twas I who revealed him."

Richard clutched his arm. "What do you mean?"

William motioned toward the young man receiving the reward of Elizabeth's approval. "Do you remember, we performed Plautus the night of my cousin's arrest. That same day, do you remember the minstrel we met? After the performance, he kept prodding me with compliments and conversation, and I remember him making some very odd statements and asking questions. I think it was one of Walsingham's spies and I am sure it was the man standing right there next to the Queen."

Richard chuckled. "You mistake, Will, for the man there is the same one we saw earlier, the one who darted from the lodging house in Holywell. 'Tis Marlowe, not some minstrel, besides he looks different from the man we knew as the minstrel for I remember him to be a Frenchman."

William's body shook. "'Tis the same man, Richard, I would swear to it."

Richard pulled William by the arm into the street. A thick fog shrouded the city, and the snow subsided into a cold misty rain. They took shelter in a nearby doorway and William buried his face in his hands.

Richard steadied his friend with his arm around his shoulder. "Will, 'twas not Marlowe. He is a playwright 'tis all, not a spy for the Queen. He is clever, to be sure, but for him to play the French fool is unfounded. The man is a genius, William, not a provocateur. One would have to be mindless and soulless such as

Walsingham to play such a part, and that, Marlowe is not."

William wiped his face on his sleeve, clearing away the raindrops along with the tears. "I suppose you could be right. My insides are in turmoil with these sights and sounds, talk of religion and politics and executions. There is nothing more I can do for Edward. I have done enough."

"You knew Walsingham might learn his secrets, William. 'Twas only a matter of time."

"Yes," William replied, "he would, and yet, still I fear for the rest of my family. Surely there will be more searches."

Richard patted William on the back. "Of course, 'tis the way of things. But there is nothing to be afeared of if there is nothing to hide. I know your family and I see nothing to reveal any treachery toward the Crown. All of us knew of Edward and his leanings, and all of us kept silent. There is nothing more, is there, Will?"

William's eyes flashed, afraid the answer revealed itself in them. He quickly looked away, burying his stare in the fog. "Nay, my friend, there is nothing."

Richard urged him toward the theater. "Be at peace, my friend. We will have a pint at the Mermaid and see a play this eve and perhaps, if you are lucky, Kit will be at the tavern and you will see the man up close and see he is not the minstrel."

William and Richard sauntered along the streets of Cheapside. The people along the streets passed by wet, haggard and worn like the cobblestones; tracked on, pounded on, and drinking in their days mixed with slick rain and human waste. William held a rag over his nose as a fat pock-ridden woman steadied herself in a doorway. She wiggled her stubby finger at him and bared a toothless grin.

"Come inside, love?"

William grabbed Richard's arm and sped his footfall. His voice breathless behind the cloth. "This is not the London I imagined, Richard."

Richard chuckled. "Is it not? You look at it all wrong, my fellow, for within these streets are a treasure of material and groundlings wanting to see us perform. It may surprise you to see how many of these worthless souls will scrounge up pence to see a play. Remember to look at all things as the actor you are."

Richard urged William through the door to the Mermaid.

"Come, we are here, the premier spot for actors and playwrights to mingle before and after our performances. I will make introductions for you to those who can advance your state on the stage."

They stepped into the shadowy darkness of the tavern. The torches gave off a dusky orange glow, lighting the faces in the dusty room. William breathed in the thespian air and listened to the familiar words passing from mouth to mouth. Every word spoken reeked of the stage. He held his hand over his pounding heart as his gaze jumped from face to face, finally resting upon a man whose face glowed in the candlelight flickering before him. The man leaned against the bar, his eyes downcast as he twirled a quill between his thumb and forefinger. Richard's jovial laughter and handshaking caused the man to look in their direction.

He bears the semblance of the minstrel, William pondered, *yet he is clean-shaven whereas the minstrel bore a beard; and his hair falls just below his ear, not the long locks of the minstrel. Still, what is it I see?*

Their eyes locked in a long stare and something unnerving passed in the look.

XIX

The Mermaid Tavern on Friday Street in Cheapside swarmed with literary minds and arrogant actors; hoveled, but cozy, with her warming hearths, low beamed ceilings and strong ale. Kit stepped into the candlelight of the tavern, taking in the faces of a dozen of the Queen's Men, players of the highest caliber and blackguards to boot. Tarleton, the clown, slouched in a corner strumming a tabor, Edward Alleyn teased a barmaid about his prowess off the stage, and Henslowe played chess with Burbage's father.

No one knows me, he thought, *not yet, but soon.* He conjured the images, as he slid onto a stool at the far end of the bar, of those around him nodding their heads and raising their mugs to him in a toast.

He lifted the tankard to his lips and let the warm heavy ale flow down his throat as he closed his eyes. Something about being in a room with the players felt comfortable. Almost like a home. Calliope hovered near him and he sensed her invisible presence as he reached inside his cloak, removed a quill out of a hidden pocket and twirled the white goose feather between his thumb and forefinger. A tap on his shoulder brought him out of his momentary daydream. Kit turned to see a young man standing before him in raging yellow stockings and padded doublet, which seemed to compensate for his wiry frame and pale skin. He reminded Kit of the clinging schoolmate at the King's School in his younger days. The stranger held out his hand for Kit to shake.

"Sir, I am Thomas Kyd. I think I know you."

Kit's eyebrow arched in excitement to think the man might know his name. "Do you, sir?"

"Yea, sir, I see you are a writer because of the ink stain on your finger and the quill in your hand. I am a writer, as well, and new to the London scene. What is your name, sir?"

The excitement slugged to disappointment. "O, you know me as a writer only. I see, sir, my name? I am Christopher Marlowe."

Thomas's eyes rounded, as did his mouth. "Marlowe? You are Kit Marlowe?"

Kit's heart thumped in his chest. "Yea, sir. You act as if you do indeed know me by that name."

Kyd turned and waved his arms to quiet those in the room. The crowd hushed and looked to him as he spoke. "Kind sirs, shall I introduce to you all Master Christopher Marlowe?"

One by one, each man and actor of the Queen's Men pushed away from their tables, stood and raised a cup toward him. Edward Alleyn trudged across the floor and clinked his tankard against Kit's cup. Kit's mind swirled in disbelief and the quill trembled in his fingers as Alleyn spoke.

"We welcome you, Kit Marlowe, to the ranks of the London stage."

Kit pushed back the hair from his eyes and rubbed his brow, imagining he still daydreamed.

"Thank you, Master Alleyn, but how do you know me?"

Laughter rolled across the room as Alleyn reached inside his doublet and removed a rolled pamphlet. He unfurled the printed pages and tossed them onto the bar. The black words blazed against the creamy whiteness of the page, filling Kit's soul with pride, wonder and confusion.

Alleyn answered. "Your Tamburlaine, Master Marlowe, is being sold at Saint Paul's bookstalls. We have all read the work, sir, and forthwith entranced with your blank verse. I would be honored, sir, to play the mighty Tamburlaine when it comes to the stage. You should come see us perform this afternoon. We are enacting a mighty feat, taking on the battle of Agincourt on the boards."

Kit's words caught on the lump in his throat. "Agincourt? What is the name of the play?"

"Ah, 'tis the Famous Victories of Henry V."

"And the author?"

Alleyn shrugged. "Actually the play came to us rather anonymously. We have adjusted some scenes and lines, but 'tis a fair piece."

Kit curled his lips into a smile. "Yea, a fair piece for a youth. 'Twas only a first draft of what is coming. I forgot the pages were in the portfolio I gave to my patron."

Alleyn's eyebrows arched. "You are the author? O, then this is most providential you are here among us this day."

One name flew into Kit's head, one explanation—Burghley. Burghley arranged this. Even though the Queen did not give her permission for the performance of his plays within her verge, the good old man gave Kit's words the wings to fly. Kit's gaze brushed across the floor and lifted, his eyes moistened as he saw the tankards raised before his face. Alleyn made the toast.

"To Kit Marlowe, whose blank verse astounds us all. His mighty sounding rhyme will breathe life unto the stage and sweep the groundlings of London into a swoon."

The patrons of the pub concurred and Alleyn thudded onto the stool next to Kit. Kit watched him as he guzzled his beer. *Yea,* he thought, *he will be a superb Tamburlaine, for his presence evokes confidence from his tall commanding stature to his lusty blue eyes. The groundlings will follow him with adoring eyes as he pounds the boards in my play.*

Alleyn slammed the empty cup against the bar top and let out a low burp, following it with a question. "Pray tell, Marlowe, when will Tamburlaine come to the stage?"

Kit shrugged, thinking of the Queen's words. "In truth, I do not know, Master Alleyn. My patron demands me back to Cambridge, so I cannot say when I will see London again. Unfortunately, I am bound to my patron's will for he supplies my keep. I will remember your request, sir, and know my final revision of Henry V will do justice to your acting. I think, though, you will be an excellent Tamburlaine."

A barmaid filled Alleyn's tankard. "Then we will pray to the muses they herald you back swiftly. We understand, sir, for the chinks always have the command over poets and players. Speaking of the chinks, here comes one now."

Kit looked over his shoulder. Through the haze of the candlelight, Richard Burbage entered and following him, another man in a simple brown doublet and worn boots. Marlowe recognized him straightaway as the man whom he had seen with

Burbage near the Curtain theater, and as the boy from Kenilworth and the Stratford butcher-player, William Shakespeare. An ill knowing crept about his heart. Closing his eyes, he retraced his steps until the picture became clear. Just before seeing William through the fog in Holywell, as he stepped from the doorway of the actor's lodging house, his boot crunched upon the tiny bones of a sparrow upon the path. She laid there dead in the mire, her beak gaping open and her feathers askew. He scanned the cobblestones for any caustic traces of her end. None. The remembrances of a scripture and of the bird he killed as a boy formed in his brain and his gaze flew heavenward. Ravens dotted the thatched tresses of the theater and they squawked at his intrusion. No other sparrows graced the sky that day.

As Kit opened his eyes and caught William's stare, he whispered to himself. "There is a special providence in the fall of a sparrow."

William inched his way toward Kit, shaking hands with actors of Leicester's Men. Marlowe rose as the two of them approached. He shook Richard's hand as the actor bowed to him.

"Kit Marlowe, Master Alleyn pointed you out. 'Tis a privilege to meet London's newest and brightest playwright. Your words will give us all employment."

Kit bowed his head, aware of William's eyes on him. "Burbage, I hear 'tis good to have you back in London and that your theater is complete. You have been on the road?"

"Yea, Master Tilney closed the theaters for a time because a rash of the plague, so we took to the countryside from fair to fair and castle to castle, whatever stage would take us."

Kit laughed, wondering if anyone gauged the hint of apprehension in his voice. "No one would refuse you, Master Burbage, I am sure." Kit looked past Burbage into William's face. "And who is this new face amongst us?"

Richard stepped aside. "This, Kit Marlowe, is William Shakespeare. He is an actor of the finest stock. Perhaps 'tis destiny for you to meet him here at the Mermaid. I will wager a bet he will knock Alleyn from his perch. 'Twould do well for you to consider him when your plays come to the stage."

Kit sniffed nervously and rose to stand before William, face to face. They eyed each other as if they weighed each other's soul, measure for measure.

William spoke first. "Have we met, sir?"

Kit knew to what he referred, the encounter in the pub in Stratford, the foggy gaze in Holywell, and the ancient game between two boys, but Kit steadied his words and answered. "Nay, Master Shakespeare, for I am sure to have remembered your face."

William clenched his teeth. "Indeed, sir, I remember yours."

Kit turned away and sat back down at the bar, sucking in the air until it reached the bottom of his lungs and readying himself for the revelation.

"How, sir, since we have never met before now."

"I saw you today at my kinsman's trial. You delivered him to the Queen."

Kit smiled, knowing already how to play the pegs William set. "Yea, I was at the trial, but only at the Queen's request. You see, I am her new Court playwright and she has commissioned a play from me. I do not know your kinsman and would have no reason to deliver him to Her Majesty."

William's jaw clenched. "I know you, sir, I would swear to it."

The walls of the tavern seemed to close around Kit. He knew if he stayed any longer Shakespeare would discern his face. He stood and brushed by him, pausing a moment near William's ear.

"Master Shakespeare, you are new to London, sir, and I would caution you. If you are indeed the caliber of an actor to which Burbage recommends, then I advise you this, your weaknesses are showing. That is a dangerous thing for a man here in London."

Kit skirted out of the tavern, leaving William with a frown. Kit pulled his cloak tight around his shoulders as he stepped out onto Friday street. The air bit cold and the soft flakes of snow billowed down, blanketing the city in a white out. He paused for a moment, not sure of which way to turn, and thoughts of Burghley swirled in his mind. He owed the man a gesture of gratitude for seeing to the publication of his plays.

As he wove through the shivering and sparse crowds in Cheapside, making his way through the narrow alleyways toward Westminster, a chill crept across his skin. He stopped in his tracks and threw a glance over his shoulder. About ten paces behind, Thomas Kyd walked along in his same path. Thomas glanced up, and seeing Marlowe peering at him, waved and jogged up beside him.

"Master Marlowe, I hope you do not mind, but I was following you."

Kit raised his eyebrow. "Indeed, sir, I can see that, but the question is, why are you following me?"

Thomas puffed, trying to catch his breath. "Forgive me, sir, but we really did not have much of a chance to talk earlier. I do not want to delay you from where you are going and the snow is increasing, so may I walk with you?"

Marlowe shrugged. "As you wish, sir."

Thomas blew into his hands as they walked. "The reason I wanted to speak with you is that, as I said earlier, I am a writer, as well. I read your Tamburlaine. It is a wonderful piece of work, sir, and I was wondering..."

Kit sensed his hesitancy. "Go on, speak."

"S'wounds, I am pigeon-livered or else this cold is unnerving my resolve. Please, sir, I was wondering if you might look at what I am working on at present. There are many among those at the Mermaid who do not take kindly to an unlettered fellow matching any of the University wits, so my own wit is somewhat quelled to the fact that maybe I do not measure up to the standards of a playwright."

Kit stopped in his tracks and smiled. "And what makes you think I am any different?"

Thomas's brow wrinkled. "Marry, sir, I do not, but only that you are new to the London literary scene, as well, and you have received many compliments from a certain friend in my circle."

"Friend? Do I know your patron?"

"Nay, sir, my patron is Lord Strange. He has read your Tamburlaine, as well, but also keeps his distance from those that patron you."

Kit snickered. "You mean Strange has his reasons for distancing himself from those on the Privy Council, men such as Burghley?" Thomas nodded. "Interesting, Thomas, that a Lord of Elizabeth's Court would do such a thing. Anyway, no matter. My question then is, if not your patron who commended me, who is the friend?"

Thomas gestured for them to stand beneath the shelter of a thatched overhang. The small lean-to stall banked up against the stone wall of a residence where a ragged merchant roasted chestnuts in a pan over a fire. Marlowe gave the man pence and warmed his hands over the flames.

Thomas leaned near to Kit's ear and whispered. "Do you not know, sir? 'Tis the Countess of Pembroke who praises your work."

Kit's blood warmed at the mention of her name. "The Countess of Pembroke? And she is an acquaintance of yours?"

"Yea, sir. She is often here in London at Court in company of the Queen. She is doing much to expand the enveloping arm when it comes to art and literature, so much like her brother Sir Philip Sidney. Her home at Wilton has become an academy of sorts for all kinds of artists. I, myself, have been there several times."

Kit cracked open a shell with his teeth and let the warm meat swirl on his tongue. He smiled and handed Thomas two chestnuts while wondering how this man might be his link back to the woman who, even now, inspired such passion within him.

"Then 'tis destiny that we met, Master Kyd. You honor me to review your work. What, pray tell, are the titles of your work?"

Thomas's cheeks glowed from pride and the chill. "Thank you, sir. I have a small bit of work called King Leir, but I have made little progress on that one; and then, the one that is becoming my heart and soul called Hieronimo or the Spanish Tragedy. I cannot decide about the title as of yet."

"O, let it be the Spanish Tragedy. Titles can do much to prepare an audience and that one draws the ear. When may I come to your lodging?"

Thomas grabbed Kit's hand and shook it heartily. "O, sir, this is most grand! Anytime, sir, and if ever you need lodgings yourself, please, I have room and would be glad to have you as a friend and fellow playwright."

Kit noticed the shadow even before the words were spoke. Before Thomas finished his acclamation, Kit's skin shivered with premonition and a sense of something wicked creeping up behind him. A firm slap on the back confirmed what he feared. He turned to see Richard Baines and another stranger blasting the snow like two dark ravens. Richard acted as if coincidence caused the meeting, but Kit knew the truth.

Richard cut his stare toward Thomas Kyd. "Pray tell, Master Kyd, are you seeking to befriend the new illustrious playwright of the time?"

Thomas frowned. "Who are you, sir, that I should answer your question?"

Kit lifted his hand to silence Thomas. "He is of no concern, Thomas; just an acquaintance of mine, 'tis all. What do you want, Baines?"

Richard's smile and slivered eyes gave off an air of pure knavery. "O, Master Marlowe, I do not want a thing from you. Our common patron, Lord Burghley, sent me to find you and bring you forthwith to Westminster."

Marlowe reached up and fingered the dagger at his belt, holding back his cloak for Baines to see the gesture. "You may go along, Richard, and tell Burghley I am coming by and by."

Baines smiled a crooked grin, looking down at Kit's dagger. "I am sent to escort you, sir, and will say so with you."

Kit took a step forward. "By and by is easily said, sir. I know my own way to Westminster."

The man behind Baines chuckled. Kit pulled the dagger from the sheath and pointed the blade at the stranger. "Are you here for a quarrel, sir? Obviously, your master did not tell you I am adept with the dagger as I am with the quill."

Thomas grabbed hold of Kit's wielding arm. "Come along, Kit, and I will walk with you to Westminster. These knaves are not worth any days in a cell."

Kit sheathed the dagger, and they scurried away from the two chuckling men. Thomas leaned near Kit. "That man with your acquaintance is Master William Bradley. He is an arrant knave of the lowest kind and will attach himself to anyone who tosses a few crowns in his way. I have seen him many times at the Mermaid boasting claims of his playacting skills and prowess as a poet, but to my mind, I have seen nothing to confirm the claims. I think him to be more like a leech."

Kit's harried breath puffed out in steamy clouds. "Then he has found a willing vein in the likes of Richard Baines."

When they reached he gates of Westminster, Thomas shook Kit's hand and bowed. "Master Marlowe, I thank you once more for your interest in my work. You are welcome anytime at my home in Norton Folgate."

Marlowe bowed. "Yea, 'twill be an honor, Master Kyd. Please, give my warm greetings to the Countess of Pembroke."

Burghley waited for him in Walsingham's office, and both men's countenance filled the paneled room with an air of irritation. Kit strode inside with his own nonchalant manner and plopped onto a couch near the windows overlooking the stretch of trees and lanes between Westminster and Whitehall.

Burghley hobbled across and popped Kit on the head with the back of his hand. "Where have you been? Do you not know that 'tis necessary for you to keep us informed of your whereabouts, especially since Arden's trial?"

"O, forgive me," Kit touted, "I forget I am not my own person."

Walsingham glared at him. "You also seem to forget we are here for your protection, boy."

Kit sighed. "Protection? Then why do you insist on shadowing me with that idiot blackguard Richard Baines? He has more on his agenda than serving any of you or the Queen. He would see my head on a pike."

Burghley grunted down next to Kit and Walsingham hovered near the window as Burghley answered. "Yea, he has more on his agenda, Christopher, and that is why we want you near to him. 'Tis almost like the balancing of the scales. He has the street sense and you, the poet's nous; thus, you can do much to find out more about him and get to the heart of his loyalties. We have determined for the two of you to go the seminary in Rheims and sniff out any plots forming against Her Majesty."

Kit's eyes flashed. "To Rheims? With Baines? O, this is hire and salary! I am clapped to a fool who has an intent to thwart me, do you not see that?"

Walsingham answered. "Yea, sir, do you think us the fools, as well? We see Baines' designs and will use him as we see fit. Either he will crumple under his own ambition or he will soar under your tutelage, and either way we will reach our own goal. He has his assignment for the Jesuit breeding ground for he knows his way and knows the communion. We will give you an assignment, as well, and we will decipher much from how each of you play."

Burghley interrupted. "And the Queen has told me if you play well, she will give Master Tilney permission to back your *Tamburlaine* for production. You are happy the play made publication?"

Kit's irritation softened. "Yea, your Grace, and I wanted to thank you..."

Burghley raised his hand. "Hush, now, no need for that. We do not wish for you to think we care not for your own aspirations, Kit. You have to remember that you are on the threshold of your success. 'Tis a common thing for a man to reach the pinnacle on the back of doing favors for those in high places. Do not fret over this small thing. Now, Walsingham and I have discussed your next more, and it is this: go back to Cambridge for a time. Ease into your studies so as not to raise suspicion to your absences and when the time is ripe, we will send for you to go to Rheims undercover as a secret papist with the intent on taking orders and joining the Jesuit cause. Baines has already been there before and can acquaint you with those you need to befriend."

Kit sat up and kicked the couch leg with his boot. "What choice do I have, for you keep dangling the carrot in front of my asinine eyes."

XX

"You have twins, Master Shakespeare," the midwife announced as she came down the stairs carrying a bucket and soiled cloths.

William propped his elbows onto the scullery table and cradled his head with his palms. "Dear God," he whispered, "I am becoming my father." He wiped his brow and looked up at the round woman standing in the doorway. "And are they well, Meg?"

Meg pursed her mouth in disapproval. "I was a wonderin' if'n you were goin' to ask about them. Yea, they are well. A fair girl and bonny boy. The mistress thought to name them after her friends, the Sadlers, Judith and Hamnet."

William stared out the window and sighed. "Yea, that is well. Shall I see Anne?"

Meg furrowed her brow. "You will do nothin' of the kind. Anne needs her rest and little Susannah will help with the babes. You may see them in the morning. Anne will have her churching for a month, complete isolation from you, Master Shakespeare, for 'tis well known after the last weeks of pregnancy and restraint from a husband's bed, how a man's fever burns for his wife's flat belly. Nay, you will not see her, for she needs not a new seed planted in such a freshly razed ground. The babes will likely be marked in the church register sometime in February."

William wanted to laugh. No fear of that, for he was of the mind to never plow that ground again, if he could help it. He lifted a pitcher of apple wine and poured the golden liquid into a wooden cup, took a sip and considered his life. He, Anne and Susannah moved in with his parents and siblings in the house on Henley Street, and commotion reigned in the house; children cried, spouses argued, too many elbows at the table and too little bread to share.

The past year passed by as miserable and drear as the wet gray winter, and as slow as the current of the Avon river. Country life wrapped him like a cocoon around a fly and he dangled and waited for the spider to suck him dry. Not only the day-to-day toil, but the trial of his cousin, Edward Arden, stuck with him and troubled him. He and Richard attended the execution at Smithfield. He was not sure why he felt compelled to attend, but for the fact he disbelieved the horrid tales and rumors of the brutality, and to honor the blood he shared with the man.

William remembered holding his sleeve over his mouth as the torturers dragged Edward on a hurdle through the streets. He looked so dignified, so proud and calm like a martyr; calm until they tied his arms and legs to an iron cross and ripped open his belly with a ragged hook. William retched as Edward's cries squealed out like a slaughtered pig while his insides burned before his eyes.

When William returned home to Stratford, the tirade grew in Warwickshire. Sir Thomas Lucy searched all the homes, jotting down notes and names in his journal. Thankfully, his father escaped any suspicion for the pamphlet testament stayed hidden and secure in the rafters of his Henley home. William, however, did not escape a small smattering of Lucy's anger.

When the winter settled in, so did the famine. Groups of beggars clustered to Stratford from the countryside bringing in women in tattered clothing, old men with canes and shoeless children with blackened and bleeding toes, all of them always standing at the edges of the frozen roads with extended hands. The almshouse near the Guild chapel overflowed with them. William determined not to fall victim to the rash of starvation, so he passed many a winter, spring, summer and fall feasting on coney hares and deer he trapped in Charlecote forest, and selling the excess in the market.

A week after Arden's execution, William burrowed himself behind a small hillock near the road to Sir Lucy's estate, watching the hays and traps he set for the arm-sized rabbits. His mind drifted off to thoughts of the play he saw in London, a meaty piece called *The Famous Victories of Henry V* by the clever youth he met at the Mermaid, Christopher Marlowe. William stood watching the play in the penny pit, rubbing elbows with the sweaty drunks and corset-bulging drabs, as the battle of Agincourt raged on the stage. He craved to mount the stage and morph into one of Marlowe's characters, speaking those words, becoming a different man such as King Henry, walking among his men masked as Henry Le Roy the night before they thundered against a rousing French army.

William paused and whispered, "Harry Le Roy? Where have I heard that name before?"

A heavy wooden staff cracked over his back, bringing his musing thoughts to a halt. He rolled over and moaned, holding his hands over his eyes to shield the sun. The man above him stood in shadow, black and haloed with the sun's aura, but William knew the man at a glance. Sir Lucy grabbed him by the collar and clapped him in irons. For two weeks, William sulked in a cell tucked in the bowels of Lucy's estate home. After his release, he settled on earning a small keep by tanning goat hides for his father's glovery during the winter and carting wool to Birmingham during the summer. Nothing like the kind of work he desired, but it was enough to put food in their mouths. The last time he stopped in the market in Coventry, after buying three shearings from a shepherd in Balsall, the troupe of Leicester's Men performed at the tavern there. He ached to attend, but the blaring voice of his father and the stern look of his wife irritated him like an ant bite. *Burbage will be there,* he thought, *with the same old urging. How long before I break free, or more to the matter, will I ever have the courage?*

The sweet sound of a newborn echoed through the stairwell in double harmony with both babes voicing their presence to the world. Meg waddled back up the stairs with swaddling clothes and oak logs for the fireplace.

William took another sip of the wine and whispered, "How did I come to this? I am flailing my arms whilst I drown." He squeezed his eyes shut, willing himself to succumb to the darkness behinds his lids. "O, how I wish I could conjure the muses at my will. Come, Thalia and Melopmene, where is your promise?"

Beads of sweat popped above his eyebrows and he shuddered as something like warm breath crept across his neck. His eyes flashed open upon a resounding knock rattling the front door. He hesitated, looking to the stairwell. The babes quieted and the crackling of the fat wood sputtered. Another booming knock brought him to his feet, and he crossed the room to throw open the door. Two familiar faces greeted him, smiling with mirth and cheeks reddened from drink.

Burbage grabbed hold of William's shoulder and pulled him from the threshold. "Look at you, Will! Methinks you are the saddest of men!"

Tarleton, the clown, jiggled a string of bells and danced a jig in the middle of the street. "Come out, come out, and play with us!"

William's lip curled into a half-hearted smile. "Nay, sirs, I cannot. My wife just birthed twins this eve and I must stay to tend the house during her churching."

Burbage chuckled and gathered William's sleeve in his fingers. "O, nay, sir, you are not midwife nor housekeeper. We know of the custom of churching and will be many months before she will need your services again. Besides, I have news that will make you merrier."

William followed him into the street. "What news?"

Burbage looked at Tarleton with a victorious grin. "I have procured you a rank in with Leicester's Men, William."

William's heart skipped a beat. "Indeed? What rank?"

"Pray, William, temper your mirth for though it be with them, 'tis a mean rank, a novice and a serf's task, but a rank nonetheless."

William grabbed hold of Richard's arms and squeezed. "Go on, sir, for any rank with a troupe, any beginning is my beginning."

"Pray, 'tis only a server of sorts, as in running errands, a prompter and prop-toter, and perhaps in the rank of ostler from time to time. I cannot promise you anything on the stage for now."

The glow of the prospect radiated inside him. "O, Richard, 'tis no matter. I would do even less to travel with such a pack. When do we go?"

Richard chuckled. "So quick to depart from Anne, my friend? Look you how you should have heeded my counsel so long ago, then perhaps your apprenticeship would not be so late in the making."

William creased his brow. "No more scolding, Richard. I am not the first among men to pay daily for wrecking his reed and thus hustled off to matrimony at the end of a blade, and I warrant I will not be the last. The difference is this: I will not let this delay keep me from my ultimate goal. I will tread the boards of London and do so with all the skill, all the glory and all the awe-inspiring attitudes surpassing any actor before me. Mark me, sir."

Richard bent in a small bow. "I will mark you, William, and most heartily believe you. We will leave come mid-morning tomorrow for we booked a hall near Banbury. What do you think she will say?"

William looked up to the bedroom window. The candlelight glowed blurry yellow through the mullioned glass and he imagined her tucked beneath the quilted blanket his mother had made for them as a wedding present. "I do not know, my friend, but I best wait till morning to deliver the news."

Richard chuckled. "Of course, of course. Then we will wait for you at my father's tavern."

William could not sleep, volleying between dozing at the fireplace and pacing the kitchen in excitement. His nerves stood at the ready. He packed a small burlap bag with essentials—a black-dyed jerkin, one linen shirt, a loaf of rye bread and hard cheese. Meg cracked a layer of ice covering the top of the milk bucket, ladled out a cup and guzzled. Her brow furrowed as she looked at William with beady eyes over the length of the cup. She wiped her mouth with the back of her hand.

"You lady wants to see ya. I thought it not a good thing, and told her so, but she insists on it. So, ya best mind yourself and not rile her in any way. She had a tough time of it bringin' two babes into the world and is poorly this morn."

William saw her gaze fall upon the wool satchel. She blew out a puff and squinted her eyes. "Are ya leavin', Master Shakespeare?"

He set his jaw. "That, Mistress Meg, is something I will discuss with my wife, not you."

She took another swig of the milk straight from the wooden ladle.

"Then you best get to your business, but remember what I said. Your lady is weak. She might fall sick upon hearin' bad news, and I suspect you would not want to find yourself raisin' three children without a mother. Do you get my meanin'?"

William bowed his head toward her. "I do, Mistress."

He turned and alighted up the stairs, pushing the door to the bedroom with all confidence. A warm blast of air hit his face and a picture of pure domesticity. Susannah slept on a blanket near the blazing fire in the fireplace and Anne dozed beneath blankets of the tapestry-canopied bed, and in between the two, at the foot of the bed, a small wooden cradle glowed in the firelight. He crept near and leaned over the babies. They coddled next to each other like suckling puppies, their small pink mouths moving up and down as they dreamed of milk. Meg discerningly wrapped a narrow blue embroidery thread around the boy's wrist and a pink one around the girl. William tucked his hands around the swaddled body of the boy and lifted him into his arms. The baby squirmed and grunted like a happy little pig. William shushed him and patted his behind with a steady rhythm and the babe slept once more.

William felt a small tug on his heart as he touched his fingertip to the baby's cheek.

"My boy," he whispered, "my name carried on." He held the baby close to his face and breathed in the sweet newborn scent as he kissed him on the forehead.

Anne's voice broke the air as he set the babe back down next to his sister. "A son to carry on the Shakespeare name."

He turned toward the bed. The pillows and blankets propped Anne up and her ashy face paled against the dark wood of the headboard. William walked over and sat at the edge of the bed. "Yea, a son. Thank you, my wife. Are you well?"

Even in the gloom, he watched her face shadow over with spite. "So formal, William? Will you not kiss me?"

William hesitated. "Nay, my dear, for Meg has given me instructions to keep away from you during the churching."

Anne blew through her nose. "Ah, and you snatch up any means to keep away from me. But 'twas not so the night we conceived the twins, was it, William? Or was it simply that you were so soused with drink after a night with your mates at the tavern that 'twould not have mattered what wench you tumbled?"

William gritted his teeth. "Anne! Mistress Meg said you are to take care of your health for the sake of the babes. I will not have you talk to me in such a manner."

"O, will you not? Then, pray tell, what was the meaning of

Burbage's visit last eve? You will not have my anger up, but you will set a plan to leave me?"

William cut his eyes toward her. "What means you?"

"O, come, come, William, speak plainly to me. I know the players seek you and I know you crave the stage. I had Meg eavesdrop upon you and she told me all of what was said as she stood on the other side of the door. So, you are to leave with the troupe of Leicester's Men with me so newly birthed?"

William took a deep breath and steadied his gaze straight into her stern eyes. "I would think you might smile for me to take on a job to support you and three children."

"You can do that by working with your father or working the fields come summer."

The heat and her biting words warmed his face. "And what of my dream, Anne? Would you have me give that up forever?"

Anne winced as she leaned forward. "Your dream, William? Is it always your dream? What of mine? I had a dream, as well, but my dream was always of you. I dreamed of you and the family we would have when I saw you in the marketplace, when I saw you pass down the lane, when I saw you sitting with your family at Trinity Church, when...."

William held up his hand to stop her. "... and when you saw me playing the stage. You fell in love with the actor, Anne, and yet you will not let me be the thing for which you desired me most. Nay, I will not turn aside from this opportunity. Likely, 'twill only be for a month or so, during which time you will regain your strength, your purification during churching time will be complete and I will return home with money in my pocket and experience under my belt."

Anne snapped her fingers. "Ha! Under your belt, indeed! Just remember you have children enough to look after here in Stratford."

William's resolve strengthened watching her gray mouth purse and wrinkle. He shivered and wondered how he ever found a desire for those lips. The stage would be where he could forget his mistake with the words of a play, he could forget her shrill voice with the music of lutes and tabors, and he would remember how deceiving a woman can be behind the mask of firelight and lust. He bowed to her and walked out of the room.

XXI

Night came and winter settled upon the seminary chapel in Rheims France like a heavy woolen mantle. Kit rubbed his arms to encourage the blood flow and the warmth, pausing every few minutes to blow into his hands. His breath drifted out between his fingers in blasts of steamy fog as the seconds ticked away during his silent vigil. Walsingham said this will be a good kill, a slice upon the artery of Rome. Kit could not fail, nor was he likely to since many years passed as he practiced and honed his skill upon the necks of Rome's Jesuits. Those soldiers of Christ filtered into the halls of Cambridge like wide-eyed eager students, making friends, whispering behind their palms, and luring greedy boys with their pouches of Spanish gold and dreams of glory.

And thanks to me, Kit mused, *most of their necks sliced like butter.*

England's Queen remained safe and secure. The cold and hidden recesses of castles and keeps, the rank and festering hovels of rebellion-breeding alleys, and the hypocritical niches carved into the ancient crypts of churches were protective havens for Kit, hiding him from the murdering fingers of Rome whilst keeping his gargoyle eyes upon the bubbling plots rising to the surface.

He waited quiet and still. Still, yet shivering, against the cold quarried stone in the niche of a wall nearest an ancient marble tomb whose carved angels peered down upon him with vacant eyes and knowing smiles. An excellent vantage point to view the narrow nave where three priests gathered; an unholy trinity of holy men planning a three score attack upon the beguiling harlot of England, cackling and rubbing their palms together like plotting witches. Kit watched them through the darkness as their eyes filled with blood and candlelight. Another figure entered from the chancel, his robes bleeding through the dark night like a fresh sacrifice—the Archbishop of Rheims adorned in his scarlet red robes of the Catholic hierarchy. Their whispers resonated through the arches and the message rang clear into Kit's ears. He saw the man hand wax-sealed parchments to each priest.

"Here are your letters, signed and blessed by our Holy Father. Do whatever you must in our Lord's name and you will find a place beside him in his Kingdom."

Each priest accepted the scroll and knelt to receive the Archbishop's hand upon their head, the sign of the cross in the air and a kiss upon his ring. The Archbishop left the room quickly, dipping his hand into the holy water as he passed. He washed his hands of the meeting and the quest and brought his fingers to his lips to kiss them as if to bless and forgive them at the same instance.

Kit turned again to the priests, watching as each in turn removed his cowl hood as they knelt before the crucifix of the Christ and pledged their life to this will. Kit noted their identity and planned their execution.

The first came forward and Kit sucked in his breath in a quick gasp. John Ballard, Kit's roommate in the dormitory of the seminary, now bore the shorn circle on the top of his head and the simple brown robe of a monk. John kissed the feet of the Christ, took up his parchment roll, and shook the hands of his fellow assassins.

The next two followed suit, rounding out the triad. An Englishman, a Frenchman, and a Spaniard, bonded together to show unity to their papal cause. The cause of bringing England back to her senses, back to Rome and an end to the reign of the bastard Queen.

Each man absorbed himself into the darkness. Kit waited a moment more, having learned from experience not to thrust oneself so hastily into a killing. He needed a calm quick hand and mind, something he learned well from Walsingham. Even in the midst of his mission, his playwright words seized him and seeped across his trembling lips in a whisper.

"I have no spur to prick the sides of my intent, but only vaulting ambition, which over leaps itself and falls on the other. Yea, if not for this vaulting ambition, would I so hastily kill?"

Though the air, the hoot of a human owl floated on the wind. Kit took the cue and slid from his hiding place. He returned the tune, signaling a shadow at the other end of the nave. Baines appeared and Marlowe motioned for him to follow the priests, to which Baines nodded and disappeared into the darkness.

Kit stepped cat-like into the chancel, peering around a stone column which lifted the arch high above the altar. He held his breath, seeing two of the priests still in counsel near the doors to the churchyard. He pulled his dagger and crept along the wall, his fingers caressing the cold cheeks and silent lips of marble effigies as he passed, as he edged closer to their conference. A soliloquy shadowed and hissed in his mind as goose flesh formed on his arm.

I see the dagger, the handle toward my hand. Come, let me clutch it. I have it not, and yet I see it still. Are you not, fatal vision, sensible to feeling as sight? Or are you but a dagger of the mind, a false creation, proceeding from my heat-oppressed brain? I see you yet, in form as palpable as this which now I draw. You direct me to my purpose and such an instrument I am to use. Bah! There is no such thing; 'tis the bloody business which informs thus to mine eyes. Now over half of the world nature seems dead, wicked dreams abuse the curtained sleep, and the wolf who howls his watch, with his stealthy pace moves toward his design like a ghost...

The midnight toll of monastery bells pealed through the darkness as the priests separated, one moving close to him, the other to the confessionals on the right side of the chancel. The curtain closed. Kit could hear the breath of the priest as the man dipped a hand into the holy water. The parchment fell out of the man's robe and rolled near to Kit's foot. The monk knelt, searching for the lost scroll, unaware of the shadowy dagger looming above his head.

Marlowe, again, whispered. "I go, and it is done. The bell invites me. Hear it not, priest, for it is a knell that summons you to heaven or to hell."

He grabbed the monk from behind, his right hand clasped across the monk's mouth, his left hand holding the dagger nearest the vein beneath his jaw. He watched the rise and fall of the man's heartbeat beneath the steely blade, speeding up as he indented ever so slightly. Kit leaned his lips near to the man's ear, near enough to feel a tremble shiver over his skin.

"To be or not to be, that is the question."

The monk flinched, to which Kit tightened his grip and dug in the blade until a tiny droplet of blood formed on the tip.

Kit continued. "Nay, do not struggle, for I know what it is to kill a man. It would go well with you if you let it come easily."

The monk clenched his teeth. Kit loosened his palm, and the man growled out words flavored with a Spanish accent. "It is typical of Walsingham's man to kill from behind instead of facing a man."

"Typical, yea," Kit answered, "but not easier. I learned from the best."

Kit closed his eyes for a moment and readied himself for the kill. Behind his eyelids, he conjured the Queen's smile of approval. As he opened his eyes, the blood drops oozed a path down the blade and across his knuckles. There in the candlelight he saw his life as the red of his kill colored the inky spot on his left index finger. *I write in blood to write in ink,* he thought, and the thought brought forth a sting of tears.

Kit leaned in close again to whisper and a single tear trailed down his face and onto the monk's neck. "I may be Walsingham's poppet, but you are the Pope's. We are all players in this game. 'Twould have been the same for me if you were the one who held the blade."

The priest softened his voice, seeking immunity in the tear. "Dost thou weep as thou kill?"

The words sliced Kit's heart. "Aye, I weep as I kill, for you see, it goes so heavily against my nature."

The priest relaxed. "Then lay down your blade, for you seem not to have the stomach for this."

Kit's arms tightened, he muffled the man's mouth once more, and toyed with the blade against his throat until a glaze of fear welled in the corner of the man's eye.

Kit's words flowed bitter. "Seems, sir? I know not seems. I have a stomach for death, 'tis something I long for, for I wish for the death of the man I have become. With each kill I make, I am one step closer to mine own."

Marlowe pulled the man's head back to silence his cry and sliced, ear to ear, and let his body fall at his feet. Fresh blood bleeding upon an ancient grave. Kit stepped into the candlelight, looking once more down the nave at the towering Christ above the altar. He did not ask for forgiveness, but only smiled. The whispering prayer of the second priest still hummed through the air, signaling that his perfect skill at a silent kill did not raise alarm.

He approached, standing before the curtain. Without knowing where he plunged, he dug his dagger deep into the hovel. A shocked gasp, then a moan. Another plunge and a gurgle. The body collapsed, tangling itself in the velvet curtain. The man bled quick, his life force eating up the fabric like a cloth dipped in woad.

Kit leaned forward to remove the hood covering the face and whispered. "How now, Ballard? A rat? Dead for a ducat!"

The Frenchman's eyes lay open, fixed in a permanent startle. Fear surged into Kit's brain. John Ballard was at hand, an Englishman with English connections. He rolled the man over with his foot and ran into the churchyard. Baines cowered on the steps with his hand holding his head and a small trickle of blood seeping through his fingers.

Kit grabbed hold of him. "Are you hurt?"

Baines winced. "Yea, but I am not dead."

"And Ballard?"

Baines could not look at him. Marlowe shoved him and grabbed his collar. "Ballard? Tell me he is dead!"

Baines shook his head and moaned. "Nay, he overpowered me. He has fled, Kit."

Kit released him and walked into the graveyard. The crisp, icy grass crunched beneath his feet and his fingers caressed the headstones as he went from cross to angel as he walked. He looked over his shoulder at Baines who quivered from the cold and from failure. Kit's left hand clenched and unclenched the bloody dagger. Even in the midst of murder, those taunting words filled his brain, and he trembled to take up a quill.

He looked up at the moon, whose silvery head peeked out from behind a passing cloud, and whispered, "Now could I drink hot blood, and continue this bitter business the day would quake to look upon. I should kill him for his idiocy. Who would know? How could he let Ballard flee? Whereon does his loyalty lie? I must watch him for I fear his loyalty lies with himself."

Baines stood and walked across the yard toward Marlowe. He shrugged, still holding the wound above his eye. "'Twas a mistake is all, Kit."

Kit gritted his teeth. "A mistake, indeed. 'Tis the second time you have failed on your mission here in Rheims. Plead to Walsingham when next you see him and see if he will take pity on you. As for me, I must get the news to Faunt. My lady is in danger from this man you have released."

Baines' squinted his eyes. "Released? I did no such thing. You accuse me of conspiring with these?"

"Should I, Richard?"

Baines stomped past him, his mouth pursing together in a tight frown. He paused, turning his face to Kit, and bared his teeth. "Say what you think, Christopher."

Kit answered. "Only this, knavery's plain face is not seen till used. You would be dead if Walsingham were here. He would not and will not stand for one of his agents to be sloven. There is more at stake here than your advancement."

"Your advancement, perhaps," Baines cut.

Kit smiled then. "Ah, I see your green eyes, Baines. I have seen them since the day we met."

Baines grumbled and pointed his finger into Kit's face. "Pretty boys, such as you, with your witty words and your curving mouths will always get the head nods, weaseling in and squeezing out those of us who scrounge for the crumbs thrown at us. I despise you, Christopher Marlowe, but I work by wit as well, and not by witchcraft as you, and wit depends on dilatory time. You will know me, sir, as will all of England."

Marlowe scratched his chin as Baines disappeared into the forest. He dismissed the man's tantrums. Baines was always one to run and sulk and now was not the time for sulking, nor for chasing after him. The glowworm approached, the morning drew near and Ballard already two steps ahead. Kit went in haste to his dorm room and noticed Ballard's things missing. There was no time to delay. He opened the cap to the ink bottle and scrawled a coded poem on the back of the parchment roll.

It read: "Fair is foul and foul is fair, hovering through the fog and filthy air. The hurly-burly's done, the battle's not lost and won. Three met upon the pew; three said 'twill do, 'twill do, 'twill do.

Peace! The charm's wound up, two are silenced, a third one comes."

Before the first rays of sunlight kissed the horizon, Kit stole a horse from the seminary stables and bound for the coast at Calais, hopeful to reach London before the next dawn.

XXII

A ll it took was a beer barrel and three strokes to sever her head from her shoulders. *That and my services,* Kit mused. The Queen of Scots now rotted in a wooden coffin with her neck shredded after a monstrous beheading. That service courtesy of Walsingham and an inept executioner.

Kit stood sentry at the execution in the courtyard of Fotheringhay Castle, hovering behind the shoulders of Walsingham and the Archbishop of Canterbury. The disastrous first blow caught on the right side of her neck and a gash across her shoulder. She raised a bit, her mouth affixed in a silent oval and the shock of pain shuddering her eyes. The second made a path across the back of her head, causing many ladies in the crowd to faint and two noblemen vomited near the castle wall. The last and final stroke affirmed the butchery as the executioner took to sawing the last of her skin from the body. He lifted the head by the top of her red hair, declaring 'Long Live the Queen,' but the head fell free of the wig and rolled into a heap of blood-soaked straw. No one that day will forget Mary's lusty terrier breaking free of the lady-in-waiting's arms and his yelping cries, nor banish the image of the hint of a serene smile curling on the Queen of Scot's loose head.

As if she knew, at the last dying moment, what her death would bring like the flash of lightening before the thunder rolls and the spark of a flint before a raging bonfire. And it came, the storm and the inferno, and whipped Marlowe right into the stir.

From the time he left Rheims, hot on the trail of John Ballard, Walsingham maneuvered the pieces in place toward this end. Whatever means necessary to protect his Sovereign, he always told

Kit. Rumors spread for many years that it was he who cast the final stroke against Mary's own mother, the infamous and powerful Mary of Guise, luring the French seductress to take him to her bed and, sometime during the night, poisoning her. Kit found the story hard to believe, not that his instructor might kill her, but that the beauty would incline to take a man like Walsingham to her chamber.

Sir Francis was clever, to be sure, and the plot against the Scottish Queen flowed as easily and quickly as the Thames at high tide. Almost too easy, Kit thought at the time, as he switched aliases and masks to fit his different spy personas. He met with Walsingham on his return from Rheims, as did Baines, who gave him the job of spy upon spy, making sure those whom Walsingham placed near the Queen of Scots were not double-crossing him. Baines scowled as they sat in the Master Secretary's chamber while Walsingham paced in front of him and blasted him for his ineptness. With a flick of his finger, Sir Francis cut him loose from the fold. Kit gazed over his shoulder as he stood at the window and caught the fire burning in Baines' stare.

Richard stood and knocked the chair over he sat in, pointing his finger at Kit and cursing him. "You best watch your back, Christopher Marlowe."

Walsingham walked over and stood in the path of the finger pointing. "And you best remember who can send you to the block, Master Baines. I have my eyes in every cranny in England and France and my ears can hear clear to Rome, so you would show wisdom to reform your thinking. It would do well to take this hiatus as a chance to hone your skills. If you learn your place, I may take you back and you may still have the chance to turn Her Majesty's head."

Baines spun on his heel, his cloak knocking over a stack of books on a nearby table. "You are not the only means to win the Queen's favor. There are others."

Walsingham wrapped his fingers around the edges of his desk as he leaned back and answered him with a cold resolve. "Perhaps, but as for now, I am the only one who holds the scales of life and death. To whom do you think to run? To Archbishop Whitgift, or perhaps the rising star of the Earl of Essex? O, nay, sir, they will come to their own end most assured."

Kit snickered as a line tickled his mind. He glared at Richard and recited the snippet. "Let Hercules himself do what he may. The cat will mew and dog will have his day."

Baines grabbed hold of the door latch, yelling as he exited. "Yea, I will have my day, just you wait and see."

Walsingham sighed and collapsed with a gruff on the chair behind his desk.. Although Kit still abhorred the man's presence, he knew any alliance with him kept him safe for the time being. Safe until he could break free from the shackles of the bloody wet work.

Sir Francis motioned for him to take a seat across from him. "Take no heed to Richard Baines, boy. He has proved useful from time to time, but, unfortunately, his weak mind mingled with a misplaced ambition makes him a fool. I cannot imagine he will do much to thwart you. You did a necessary thing by reporting his failure in Rheims, and we thank you for your service there. As you know and have also reported, the news of John Ballard's penetration into the London underbelly is of great concern. We have received information that he stays in the company of Bernard Maude, one of my informants and a supposed friend of Ballard, at the Plough Inn. I am sending you as a backup to Maude, not only to watch Ballard, but to keep a watch on Maude for fear their friendship will influence him to switch sides."

Kit slumped in his chair. "Ballard will know me, sir, from our acquaintance in Rheims."

Walsingham blew out a laugh. "Ah, but you are so clever with your masks, Master Marlowe. How goes the other play you are enacting?"

Kit knew to what he referred. Since mid-winter, after his speedy quest from the French seminary, he found himself enveloped near the Scottish Queen. Walsingham, with unbelievable craft, arranged for another of his low-life spies named Gifford, a former Catholic loyalist, to offer his services in secret to Mary of Scots. The plot would be Walsingham's masterpiece in all its simplicity. He assigned Marlowe the menial task of taking on a role as a common ale-man dressed in a plain tunic, breeches, felt boots and a beard to hide his features. His job: to tote beer barrels back and forth between London and Chartley House, Mary's isolated prison castle in Staffordshire. Marlowe conformed into character with such skill that no one, not Gifford, nor Mary's jailer, Paulet, knew aught of him. He found himself smiling from time to time, remembering his old adage to Burghley of 'spy upon spy.' He watched the system work flawlessly as she placed small coded notes inside a corked tube into the beer barrels, wherein he delivered the barrels to Paulet. Paulet read the notes, and then back to Marlowe, on to Gifford who shuffled them to the French embassy in London and Walsingham's decoder, a man named Phellipes.

Kit thought her a pretty wench with her dark flowing red hair forming a perfect peak in the center of her high forehead. She, even once, brought a smile to his face when she referred to him as 'the only honest man among the throngs of deceivers' with a voice sounding like a French breeze blowing though a field of Scottish thistle. And his pockets felt the reward, as well, filling with crowns and angels enough to pay a troupe to take his plays to the stage. Now all it would take is a slip from Mary for Kit to receive the approval of Elizabeth for all of his plays to see performance. Mary was his ultimate offering to the Queen.

Kit looked up into Sir Francis' eager eyes. "All is going well, sir."

Walsingham leaned forward, his face shadowing over with seriousness in the candlelight. "We are so close, boy, to bringing down the source of these Catholic plots; thus, this means you are close to receiving the full bounty of your reward for all these years of faithful service to which Burghley promised you. Can you not feel it in the air?"

All Kit could sense was a creeping chill racing up his back. "And when I do this, what next, sir?"

Walsingham sat back in his chair and entwined his fingers. "O, we will discern your next move when you bring a report of Ballard's movements. Do you know where the Plough Inn is?"

Kit took and deep breath and stood, noting the question as his dismissal. "Yea, sir, 'tis in the precinct of Temple Bar."

Walsingham flicked his hand. "Then get to it, boy."

There is no stopping a rolling boulder tumbling down a hill, Kit thought, as he fidgeted in an alleyway across from the Plough Inn tavern, waiting and watching for the players to take their marks. Within an hour, after the sun settled far below the horizon and the moon played tag with the clouds, a dozen or more men filtered in and out of the tavern doors. None brought a familiar notice to Kit's eyes, at least none resembling Ballard.

He crept along the lane and eased up to a front window, gazing through the mullioned glass at the customers clinking mugs and feasting on crusty meat pies and moldy cheese. As he took a step forward, a hand wrap around his upper arm. He spun around with his fists balled. An older, but familiar smile greeted him.

"S'wounds, 'tis you," the man whispered.

Kit lowered his hands and creased his brow. He knew him at once. "Robin Poley?"

The man laughed and pulled him into the alleyway. "Yea, 'tis I! I have not seen you since our days in Germany and Rome. How fares you?"

Kit eyed him. Robin's boyish features had stretched into a man and his former mass of curled red hair retreated into a premature balding. Still, he held the spark of mischief in his blue eyes.

"I am well, Robin."

Robin arched his eyebrow. "And I see you are still playing in the shadows with Walsingham. I thought you would have found a way to ease yourself from that state."

Kit knew better than to even trust him, so he tempered his words with caution. "What do you mean, sir? I have come only to have a bite to eat and a pint of ale."

Robin snickered. "Forsooth? Do not try to play upon my frets, Marlowe, for I know the stops as well as any man. I know you are here seeking John Ballard, are you not?"

Kit swallowed hard. "How do you know?"

"Walsingham informed me to expect you. I am here for a similar purpose, but my mark is the man whom Ballard is seeking, a wealthy young Catholic by the name of Anthony Babington."

"Babington? I know the name. I heard Richard Baines speak of him when he was doing spy work at the embassy in Paris. He said the youth had a hatred for our Queen like no other."

Robin nodded. "Yea, and since the little plotting going on with your beer barrels, it seems the plan is lulling them into a comfort that they will succeed in overthrowing our Queen. Babington has been to my lodgings several times in the past month after I succeeded in convincing him of my promises to help the cause. He made a slip recently, saying he wondered if it was lawful to murder the Queen of England. I laughed it off and pretended I was drunk, but later reported the slip to Walsingham. Now, 'twould seem Ballard and a small group have taken Babington under their wing. I think they mean to use him and push ahead with their plan."

Kit scratched his chin. "And what is their plan?"

Robin shrugged. "That we do not know as of yet. But, is not that why you are here?" He pulled him by his sleeve to the window and pointed.

"Do you see that dark corner? Move along the wall until you place yourself there. I will infiltrate myself into the group and urge them closer so you can hear. Perhaps between the two of us we can discern what their next move is."

Kit creased his brow. "But Ballard is not even here. We could be waiting all night."

Robin chuckled. "Ha! Can you not see? He is there standing in the midst of the room and toasting his Catholic friends."

Kit squinted until the man's image formed. His face looked like Ballard, but his attire attuned to the antics of a French dandy with his gold-laced cape and a velvet cap with silver buttons. He was not at all the dour monk he saw in the seminary chapel taking an oath to assassinate the Queen of England.

"That cannot be the same man," Kit questioned.

"O, 'tis indeed. He has found an appetite for gold since his return to England, calling himself Le Captain Fortesque and declaring himself a papal buccaneer."

Kit shook his head in amazement. He patted Robin's back and crept into the tavern. Within the short time span of an hour, all the chess pieces moved nilly-willy across the board: pawns, knights, rooks and bishops; a white Queen and a black Queen faced each other. Kit heard all and reported the whole bloody plan plotted by the dreamy bunch.

Ballard urged Babington to write a ciphered note to the Queen of Scots assuring her that soon she would replace Elizabeth on the throne of England, backed by the Spanish ambassador's promise that Spain would send sixty thousand troops and herald an uprising by all secret Catholics throughout the land. With much urging, Babington agreed and within the week, Kit delivered the note in a barrel to Mary with the encoded plan announcing 'he would lead ten gentlemen and many followers to undertake the delivery of your royal person from the clutches of that heretic Elizabeth.'

Kit stood next to Walsingham when he received the envoy from his translator revealing Mary's answer. Walsingham laughed as he read. To Kit's own eyes there was no mistaking her word that they not deliver her until they assassinated Elizabeth, else her cousin might escape and resort to enclosing her forever in some hole. Kit's stare rested at the bottom of the letter where the translator scrawled a brief message and an artistic rending of a gallows. Checkmate.

Walsingham caught them and all suffered torture administered by the long reaching arm of the Star Chamber: hanged, drawn, and quartered. Kit heard that Ballard and Babington screamed like march hares caught by their ears.

ℴ)Ж

Christopher Marlowe stood behind an arras to the right of the stage at Blackfriars touching his fingers to his cheeks as he held back the tears welling in his eyes. From his vantage point, he watched Edward Alleyn morph into the daring infidel Tamburlaine, blasting mighty lines and soliloquies over the heads of the gawking crowd. The Queen kept true to her promise.

Even though she railed for a few weeks after her cousin's death, presumably from a hint of guilt over killing an anointed Queen and a kinswoman of her own Tudor blood, she rallied and gifted him with the approval of Tamburlaine at Blackfriars with the verge of the jurisdictional walls of London. Not a court production before her own eyes, but a stepping stone nonetheless.

And the crowds stood amazed with nary a blinking eye, no nodding head or yawn, no shifting feet or folded arms, just a quiet reverence at the final act bursting in an applause filling the theater like the rumble of thunder. Kit felt humbled and proud at the same measure. He walked out onto the stage when they called for the author and stretched out his arms as if to bank on the breeze of the clapping hands. He caught the smile of Her Majesty's Councilor, Lord Burghley, seated in a box to the left of the stage. Kit walked to the edge of the platform, lifted his hand to Burghley and bowed in a long sweeping motion. As he rose, his eyes jerked and his heart jumped at the sight of Richard Baines standing at the edge of the penny pit. His eyes glared with purpose, and just as Marlowe backed away, Baines drew his fingers across his neck in a threatening slice.

A sudden churning swirled in Kit's stomach and he backed through the center stage entrance, wiping beads of sweat as he leaned against the stage wall. The back room swarmed alive with laughter and accolades, players aglow with success, a pocket of coin and an opening night revelry waiting for them all at the Mermaid.

Alleyn approached Marlowe and shook his hand. "Thank you, Master Marlowe, for such meat to chew. Tamburlaine is hard to match, but if ever you need me to fill another character's shoes, I am your man."

Kit's smile felt uneven, wrestling between the happiness of the play and the taunts of Baines. "You are most welcome, sir. I must need thank you for portraying my vision in my head with such perfection. I daresay when people speak your name, they will follow it with, 'yea, there stood Tamburlaine'."

Alleyn nudged him on the shoulder and laughed. "Come along and join us as we spend our chinks on warm ale and wenches."

"I will be along by and by. Give me a moment alone."

The troupe filed out, along with the dispersing crowds in the pit. Kit looked around and saw no sight of Baines. He walked out and stood center stage, just a moment more to remember the awe-struck crowds and the cheers.

Yea, this is what the entire struggle was for. All the blood spilled and all the games played. For this....

He lifted his eyes to the faux heavens of the stage and imagined his muse, Calliope, sitting there on top of the column. She winked and faded as a tug pulled on the lower hem of his velvet doublet. A ragged little boy with a dirty face and torn breeches held up a crisp yellow parchment letter for him to take.

The seal, the unmistakable misshaped red wax poured, cooled and stamped with the Arms of Pembroke. Kit's eyes flashed upon the boy.

"Where did you get this?"

The boy pointed in the direction of the Blackfriar's entrance and scurried away. There, standing the doorway banked in the last dusky rays of sunlight, the Countess of Pembroke removed a black mask from her face, a novelty worn by the noblewomen to hide their identity. She lowered her eyes toward him and disappeared into the retreating crowds. Kit stood there in confusion and delight. She looked the same; the same angelic face, the same golden hair, yet her eyes appeared older as he soaked in her presence.

Kit sat down at the edge of the stage and held the paper near his lips. He closed his eyes and conjured that summer at Wilton House, letting the pages caress across his cheek as if her own lips lingered. He opened his eyes and broke the seal.

XXIII

K it pounded his fist on the desk of Walsingham, sending the ink pot skirting across the table.

"Why was I not told?"

Walsingham shrugged with an uncaring manner, which infuriated Kit.

"There was much more for you to do. Even now, what does the news benefit you?"

Kit lifted the letter to his nose and breathed in the sweet aroma of lavender kissing the pages. His eyes traced over the waxen seal embossed with the arms of Pembroke. Mary Sidney Herbert. He caressed the name over his tongue and his eyes reviewed once more the painful words she wrote:

' *I did not think to write to you, but after your unusual absence*
and the lack of letters of condolence, I thought to scold you.
My brother accredited you with the highest of regard,
remembering you fondly for the years you spent in his
service as a messenger.
I would not think you so capable of such cold cruelty,
but as it is, you are, after all, the sculpture chiseled by
the hands of Walsingham. 'Twas a mercy that Walsingham's
own daughter found happiness in the arms of my poet
brother. He died as he lived, with hopes of glory in the
shadow of Elizabeth; and as always, with the kiss of
poetry upon his lips.'

Marlowe cringed and his words burned across his tongue. "All this time, Master Walsingham? After all Sir Philip did for me, you did not think it would benefit me to know that the man and friend, who afforded me all the knowledge of literature and languages and poetry he could, had died? Now, his sister thinks me the most arrogant and conceited of knaves; that his death meant naught to me. How can I answer this now?"

Walsingham tapped his fingers on the table. "Marlowe, men die all the time. 'Tis the way of life. Even the Queen did not find it necessary to carry on after Sidney's death for, if you recall, we were all embroiled in the Babington fray. Sidney was a good man, to be sure, and he served Her Majesty well in our cause in the Netherlands, but I have learned in my aged wisdom that it does no good to persevere in obstinate condolement. It shows unmanly grief and a will incorrect to heaven, for we all know this to be common. All we that live will die, passing through nature to eternity like dew on grass. I, like Sidney, feel the chill creeping upon me all the time."

Kit found the thought almost amusing and revealed his humor with a smile. Walsingham narrowed his eyes.

"O, do not think to wish death upon me so quickly, Marlowe, for I shudder to think what ills will befall you when you no longer have me to protect you from Rome. More so if your patron, Lord Burghley, shuffles off this earthly stage. What will you do then? I warrant you will become a cowardly hermit, afraid of even the hint of death, bending over your desk as you live your life off the pages of your plays. Right now you are young and bold because you cower behind the protection of your Trinitarian idol: me, Lord Burghley and the Queen. 'Twill be quite interesting to see how the play ends."

The heat rose in his neck. "I am no different from you hiding behind the skirt of the Queen. Pray tell, Walsingham, what will you do if she dies?"

Sir Francis smirked. "O, perhaps I will retire to a quiet life in the country. But you do realize that 'tis treason to speak of the death of our Sovereign? 'Tis a sore subject with her the older she gets without an heir, but I take it Lord Burghley spoke to you of the matter of Her Majesty's closest possibility now that Mary of Scots is no longer a viable threat?"

"You mean Mary's son, James?"

"Nay, I was speaking of the young beauty, Arabella Stuart. She is the great-grandchild of Margaret Tudor, sister to Elizabeth's father, Henry the Eighth, and therefore, bears the same blood."

"What of her?"

"I thought Burghley would have spoken to you of the lady. It is his wish for you to tutor her. Since her father's death, Burghley took her as ward in hopes to groom her for the throne. You see how the old man continues to think of your future welfare, for if she does become heir she will bestow great gifts to those supporting her. You will be right among those in her favor. What do you think?"

Marlowe walked to the window and leaned upon the sill as he gazed out over the courtyard. *Such games,* he thought, *a continuous hopping from advantage to advantage like playing Nine Men's Morris.* He blew a sigh through his nose and turned to give his answer. Both he and Walsingham jumped as the door blasted open, rattling upon the hinges and shuddering against the wall. Elizabeth's imposing figure stood in the doorway with her fists balled and her cheeks flushed with anger, yet Kit discerned a hint of fear flashing in her eyes. She strode in, her emerald green gown rustling across the floor as Burghley followed close behind her. Her councilor closed the door and turned the key in the latch.

The Queen pounded her fist on Walsingham's desk. "I suppose you have already heard, Master Secretary, of the great enterprise Spain is taking upon our Kingdom."

Walsingham bowed. "Yea, your Majesty, remember we discussed the matter in our last council meeting."

She flicked a knowing smile at him. "Ah, then you have not heard? Can it be our ears have received news ahead of my own spymaster? They are upon us, Master Walsingham. Sir Drake sent news of a fleet of a hundred and thirty ships on route from Cadiz and are now flying toward England with utmost speed."

He held up a letter before her. "Yea, your Majesty, he has informed me, as well."

Elizabeth grabbed hold of the letter and tore the paper to shreds, gritting her teeth at him. "And you stand there so calm whilst your Queen and country are at peril?"

Lord Burghley threw a glance to Kit as he approached the Queen.

"Your Majesty, all is at hand. When the watchmen spot the ships coming near Calais, they will light the beacons. Sir Drake and Sir Raleigh have already engaged them and Leicester's garrisons rally at Tilbury...."

She raised her hand in interruption. "Silence! Repeating a thing to us does not ease a Monarch's conscience. There must be more we can do...." She paused and placed her fingers to her lips in contemplation. As she turned, her stare rested upon Marlowe. Kit bowed before her.

"Ah, Master Marlowe, we did not see you there. Pray, tell me, what do you think of all this melee?"

"Forsooth, my Lady, I think little of it for I must return to the University soon else my absences count against me."

She snapped her fingers. "Ha! You would consider such trivial things when your homeland and your Queen are under such vicious attack from King Phillip?"

Kit shrugged. "'Tis a job for fighting men, my Lady, not for poets."

The Queen curled the corner of her lips and her eyes veiled with a thought. "For fighting men, you say? Ah, you give us an idea, Marlowe."

She spun around to Lord Burghley and Sir Walsingham. "Prepare my coach and warders. We are leaving for Dover Castle to stand against this attack as if to stare like a hawk upon Philip's rat-like ships. We have much fight in us as any man. England will not fall whilst we are alive and if it means our life, then we will do so like a soldier." She looked over her shoulder at Kit. "And you, Master Marlowe, will watch the battle from the deck of a ship."

Kit flinched and his mouth dropped open. "But, your Majesty, to what end shall I do this?"

She stomped her foot. "Because we wish it! Use what you will to write words of this, for I foresee history in the making, sir." She lifted her hand to silence him and left the room. Burghley threw a look to Walsingham and the three of them followed her retreating form.

Burghley whispered to Kit. "We will expect you in the courtyard within the hour. By the way, you might like to read this letter I received from Cambridge this morning."

Walsingham and Burghley trudged behind the Queen, leaving Kit alone in the hallway. Kit broke open the seal, holding the letter close to an iron sconce on the wall and read:

'In response to your commendation and intervention, as well

as the Majesty's pleasure, explaining the reasons for
Christopher Marley's absences touching the excellent service
he hath rendered in protection of the Crown, we express our
ignorance in the affairs he went about and hereby do
administer and grant the letters and degree of Master of Arts
with utmost willingness.'

Kit gasped, and he looked up to see Burghley standing at the end of the hall banked in the sunlight of a nearby window with a proud smile across his face. Kit bowed his head in thanks. Another reward from his patron.

By the end of the week, Spain warred against England as a retribution for the execution of the Catholic Queen of Scots. Even Marlowe knew King Phillip had his own agenda against Elizabeth, having nothing to do with Mary and more to do with his own ambition. Kit stood on the deck of the *Nonpareil*, the most stalwart of her Majesty's ships, gazing across the Channel at the force of dark Spanish galleons rocking in the choppy waves off Calais. The wind blew in England's favor and he could see the iron anchors dropping from the sides of the Spanish ships in a frantic attempt to keep them from smashing against the shoals.

But the black clouds rolling and shuddering over the waters and the fiery hell-ships loaded with pitch and gunpowder bore down on the galleons like the finger of God. Their crescent formation broke in retreat from the inferno, scattering like yelping dogs scorched by the lighting of their tails. The waves deepened and formed yawing valleys and breaking whitecaps, roaring and splashing in answer to the thunderclaps. An odd time, as he wrapped his fingers over the railing of the wet wale, to think of a play. From his view, the carved image of the ship's figurehead charged, her long flowing hair and naked body diving into the waters as the bow rose and fell, the image of a muse chiseled by human hands in tiger oak.

The rain sliced hard, stinging his cheeks, and two dozen mariners scurried and yelled behind him, hoisting sails and rolling barrels of ammunition. The day pumped alive with sounds of war, and yet, all he could think of were words. She was right to send him here, for where else could he imagine such a scene. As the rain pelted harder and his hair stuck to his face, the *Nonpareil* lurched forward, readying for the attack along with ten other companion ships. The crack of gunfire and the booming of cannon shot pounded his ears, and the warmth of the fire ships glowed against his skin.

The captain, manning the helm, pointed toward the bow and yelled, his voice muffled in the wind and rain. "Hold for the ramming!"

A quake shuddered the ship and the noise of splintering wood reverberated along the deck. Grown men, former steely Spaniards shrieked and cried like babes as the *Nonpareil* gutted a gash in the side of their ship. Kit fell to his knees and grabbed hold of a rope flailing in the wind, watching as a dozen or more of them spun into the waves. His ears filled with their last Spanish words.

"Mercy on us! We split, we split, we split!"

Another crack, the whistling of a flying cannonball and the railing blasted into a thousand shards above his head. He fell to his stomach as his heart thundered in his chest.

"S'wounds! I would fain die a dry death!"

He grabbed hold again to the rigging, held tight and closed his eyes to the surrounding violence, letting the words take over as choppy and harsh as the crucible surrounding him.

…. like fiery dragons taking to flight and meeting, and from their smoky wombs sending grim ambassadors of death.... the hideous noise was such, as each to other seemed deaf and dumb.... the sea purple and the channel filled fast with streaming gore.... gushing moisture breaking through the crannied clefts of shot planks.... a head flew there away from the trunk, mangled arms and legs tossed aside as the whirlwind takes the summer dust and scatters it to the air. O, that this ship, this might Nonpareil, might hold!

A roar filled his ears and fear shut his eyes, fear of the splitting of wood and the terrified looks of dying men as they fell headlong into the swallowing sea. This uncontrolled death far from the controlled manner of holding a dagger in his hand unnerved him. He cracked one eye and saw an unbelievable sight. Many of the mariners, those who were not bleeding or mangled on the deck, smiled and threw up their arms in victory. The triumphant shouting cut the air in a deafening cry. He lifted himself to the ragged railing and beheld the Armada scrambling northward in retreat and the English navy following hard at their sterns with Sir Francis

Drake taking the charge. Thankfully, Kit discerned his ship banking toward the mouth of the Thames where the Queen waited for news at Tilbury.

The moon peeked from behind the dissolving storm clouds and glinted over the horizon as the ship glided near the shore at the fields of West Tilbury. Kit gladly took his leave and felt his footing once more as he stepped out of the skiff onto the grassy bank. He walked up the hill and looked across the encampment. As far as he could see, soldiers, horses and fires dotted the field. In the midst, the shimmering silk tent of Elizabeth the First glowed with her royal standard perched at the peak and popping in the wind. He took a step forward and paused when he heard the whinny of a horse over his shoulder. He turned and his sight filled with her presence.

Elizabeth sat upon a white Andalusian, her red hair streamed down her back and a polished breastplate across her chest caught the glow of the moonlight. She dismounted and held out her hand to Kit. He fell at his knees and kissed the back of her fingers. Without a thought in his head, he let his lips linger for a moment. She slowly pulled her hand from his grip and touched her fingertips to his unshaven chin.

"Master Marlowe, we see you survived the adventure. We are glad of it."

He kept his stare at the hem of her skirt, noticing the hint of a leather soldier's boot peeking out from below the embroidered kirtle.

"Yea, your Majesty, 'twas quite a sight to behold." Kit lifted his stare and caught her smile. "As are you, my Lady, in the moonlight."

Elizabeth cocked her head and lifted her narrow eyebrow. "O, you are bold, Kit Marlowe! You know our General, the Earl of Leicester, would have a dagger to your neck to hear you flatter us with such impropriety."

Kit stretched his smile wider. "Forgive me, your Majesty. I am no threat, I am but a simple poet, after all."

She laughed, and the sound made Kit think of a warm spring bubbling over rocks. "O, nay, sir, you are anything but simple. Master Sidney was more the simple poet who had aspirations of a soldier. You, however, are a soldier with ambitions as a poet."

Kit huffed. "You are wrong, my Lady. I have never been a soldier. My heart has always loved words more than killing, more than anything in this world."

She lowered her eyes in curiosity. "Anything, Master Marlowe? Words make poor bedfellows as we ourselves should know very well." She laughed again. "O, we are all soldiers of sorts, sir, even I." She gestured in a wave across the fields. "So I told them all. I may have the body of a weak and feeble woman, but I have the heart and stomach of a King. I meant what I said when I told them I would live and die amongst them."

Marlowe kept his eyes upon her regal profile and her proud eyes gleaming across her loyal subjects gathered before her. *What a beauty she was in her youth, what a beauty she still is,* he mused.

"You will not have to die, your Majesty, for if my eyes did not deceive me, the Armada breaks and races to the North."

Her head jerked toward him and her eyes filled with joy.

"Forsooth, Marlowe?"

"Yea, my Lady, the truth."

She took a deep breath. "And did you acquire the knowledge you needed to fill a play?"

Kit bowed. "I did, my Lady, and will tuck it away until needed. Already I have inklings of ones that will amuse you."

She brushed a lock of his hair over his ear. "Good news, then, sir. You may return to London and we will give word to Master Tilney to approve the production of your next play."

His brow creased in confusion. "But, your Majesty, my patron and your councilor, Lord Burghley, assigned me to tutor his ward, the Lady Arabella Stuart."

She huffed and pursed her lips before answering. "Ha! That little weak chinned girl who they think to groom for our throne? Very well, Marlowe, but we are giving you an order to be scanty with your teaching. We will never make her our heir, so all your knowledge will be valueless upon her." She brushed her finger over his cheek once more. "Besides, I think to keep you near me, Kit Marlowe, for you have quite drawn the interest of the Queen."

Act Four

1590 – 1593

XXIV

William dangled his legs over the edge of the stage, his eyes burning and watering in the summer sun. A single page fluttered in his trembling hands and he let go a sigh. Burbage plopped down beside him and slapped him on the back.

"A letter from home, Will?"

William nodded. "Yea, 'tis just a note from my mother to let me know how the children are doing. My boy is five years old now, you know?"

Burbage wrinkled his mouth in empathy. "Do not worry, Will. Perhaps soon you can return to Stratford to see the boy. I am sure your family appreciates the coin you are providing to them, besides what man can say he is taking care of his family and pursuing his dream at the same time?"

William folded the letter and wiped the sweat from his brow with the back of his sleeve. "I know you are right, Richard. All I can do is hope Hamnet will forgive my absence."

Richard nudged him. "Is that all, Will? Your frown shows there is more to the letter."

William crumpled the paper in his fist. "Yea, there is more. 'Twould seem my father is still railing about the denial of a coat-of-arms from the College of Arms here in London, even after all these years."

Richard chuckled. "I would not think he still felt a right for it. Pray, I mean...."

"I know what you mean, Richard, and you are correct. Since my father's dismissal as alderman, he has taken up the job of an old man sour at the world and barking his regrets. Still, the dream of being a gentleman tingles there on the tip of his tongue." William sighed. "How different am I, then, of my father? I used to swear 'twould not be the same for me."

"O, but 'tis different for you, Will. I mean look at you. Five years of apprenticeship, first with Leicester's Men, then the Queen's Men. You have traveled far and wide across England: Kent, Dover, Rye, and even in Plymouth when the beacons were lit during the Spanish Armada raid. And surely you remember our performance at Greenwich for the Queen?"

William bent his lip in a smirk. "Yea, I know what you are doing. You are trying to ease my conscience with this talk."

Richard bellowed a laugh. "Is it working?"

William joined him in the humor and changed the subject. "Very well, friend, you have convinced me. Pray, tell me, what are we readying the stage for?"

Richard looked over his shoulder as a couple of stagehands swept the boards with ragged rush brooms. "O, I think the troupe has settled on Kyd's tragedy, but another thought has been tickling my brain. You know the inn at the Black Bull?"

"Yea, I do."

"I am thinking of a performance of Faustus there come Hallow's Eve. Perhaps you can be my eyes and check out the stage there. If my memory serves me, 'twill be a cozy dark place to conjure such a devilish play."

A chill raced up William's arm. "Well, I hate the play. You best find another actor to play it, for I will have no part of it. Get Alleyn, for he seems to relish any part Marlowe writes. Give me a good comedy anytime and a bit for a dog. Those are the kind bringing the groundlings with their pennies."

Richard leaned back on his elbows and sighed. "You are wrong, Will. It seems of late tragedy is filling the seats. I think it be a sign of the times we live in."

William shrugged. "Yea, 'tis odd. One would think the common folk would have enough blood, gore and sorrow from the platforms of Tilbury and Bridewell. Anyway, I will do your errand and go to the Black Bull. I took up lodging close by there, anyway."

"What? Will you not stay with us here in Shoreditch?"

William pinched his nose and made a sour face. "Nay, for I cannot take the smell of the city ditch and the bevy of cut-purses crowding the streets around the Theater. The area around Saint

Helen seems to be more to my liking and as clean as a London street can get."

Richard extended his hand and William shook it. "Then I will see you this eve as we begin rehearsals on Kyd's play."

On the other side of the city wall from the venality of Shoreditch, William entered the world of Bishopsgate with its crowded inns and taverns jetting three and four stories over the streets. He passed the arched gateway through a jam of carters clacking along the cobblestones, some carry black coal and chopped wood, others laden down with heavy barrels and the smells of heady beer, fresh milk and sweet hay. The lanes packed with every sort of face, from the poor woman begging at the corner, to the ruff-collared gentleman exiting his coach to take lodging at the Angel, the largest and most accommodating of the Bishopgate Inns. William found himself literally rubbing shoulders with a stretch of human society. He stopped in front of the Black Bull and gazed up at her common appearance. She, like her neighbor The Green Dragon, opened up along a narrow passage off Bishopsgate Street and into a courtyard where the ostlers waited to take a traveler's horse.

William continued through the courtyard, winding down until the passage opened up to an inn yard perfect for an outdoor play. He measured the space with his strides and counted the number of torch holders on each of the archways surrounding the square. Thirty strides by thirty, square. *Small, but adequate for a quaint crowd*, he thought, *perhaps more of a well-paying and affluent crowd traveling from the continent seeking entertainment, as well.*

He walked back up the lane and asked one of the groomers for the ale room. The man pointed toward the front of the courtyard on the opposite side from the stables. William took a crown from his pocket, pushed open the door and perused the crowded room for an empty seat. He viewed an open stool at a table with two other men, a red-headed shifty-eyed man and the other, a gentleman in a slashed green doublet, gray stockings and pointed beard.

William walked over and bowed. "Forgive my intrusions, sirs, but I found myself sweltering in this midsummer heat and would beg that I sit for a moment to take a pint of ale."

The gentleman stood and gestured for William to sit.

"Are you a traveler, sir," the gentleman asked with a flowery air.

William flicked his hand to the barmaid and ordered a pint. "Nay, sir, I am not. I am Will Shakespeare, a player with Lord Strange's troupe. I came down from Shoreditch to consider this inn for a performance in October and acquired lodging down Winding Lane near Saint Helen's church."

The man's eyebrows arched. "Ah, a fellow artist and neighbor! My name is Thomas Watson. I am a poet and acquaintance with Lord Strange. And this here is another of your neighbors, Robin Poley."

Robin bowed his head as William guzzled the beer. William wiped his mouth and asked, "Are you a poet, as well, Master Poley?"

Robin laughed. "I am whatever will fill my pockets with ducats."

The three men chuckled and Thomas continued his inquiry. "You say that you are seeking the Bull for a play. What play are you going to enact?"

"Burbage wants to do Marlowe's *Doctor Faustus* on Hallow's Eve," William replied.

Thomas' eyes widened. "Ah, Christopher Marlowe! Now, there is a man and a writer of the most excellent caliber."

William frowned. "I know, I know, so says every man within the acting circles."

William noticed Robin lowering his gaze toward him. "You do not think much of Master Marlowe, sir?"

The barmaid poured another pint and William sloshed the beer down his throat. "Think much of him? Honestly, I do not know him very well. I met him once, a while ago, at the Mermaid Tavern, but did not have the opportunity to acquaint myself with him, except that I noticed men treat him like a god here in London."

Thomas raised his mug. "And so should he, for his plays and poems have the touches of a muse in them and his blank verse marks the beginning of a mighty time for play writing. He is the first man among us, I warrant you, and if he continues to scrawl out these meaty plays and sonnets, then I predict generations will know him."

Robin snickered and looked to William. "Forgive my inebriated friend Thomas. His accolades go far beyond loving the man as a writer."

Thomas sliced his gaze at Robin. "Watch your implications, Poley. Yea, I love Kit Marlowe, but only as a man would to whom he owes his life." He turned back toward William. "He saved my life a year ago. Have you heard the story?"

William downed another pint. "Nay, I have not."

Thomas adjusted in his seat and smiled as Robin buried his head in his hand and exclaimed, "Not again!"

"Well, 'twas nearly over a year ago. Kit took lodgings near Wayside Cross in Shoreditch. He met me at the Mermaid after a performance of his Tamburlaine at the Curtain theater. 'Twas a merry evening and many players and poets drank and caroused well into the night. Thomas Kyd was among our group as well as Sir Raleigh. Kit, Thomas and I could barely make it back to Shoreditch. 'Twas quite a sight, the three of us singing and laughing and falling in the streets. When we came up to his lodging house, a man came out of the shadows around the corner of Hogs Lane brandishing a sword. He flicked the blade at my back, causing me to tumble to my knees and Kyd fled into the dark. He is such a boy at the sight or prospect of blood. Anyway, when I looked up, Marlowe stood between the two of us with a dagger in his hand. I did not know the man with the rapier, but Kit's eyes wrapped around him with a purpose, as if the swill in his brain evaporated into a resolve. Being unarmed, I cowered in the doorway and listened. The man lunged and Kit flicked him away as easy as a horsetail pops a fly.

The man bit his thumb and ripped the side of Kit's cloak with the sword and said, 'Do you know me, Kit Marlowe?'

Kit answered, 'Yea, I know your beady eyes, William Bradley, and see the strings Baines pulls to make your dance. He is such a coward that he cannot think to face me himself. Pray, then, you bite your thumb to me in his stead.

Bradley laughed in a low sinister whisper and continued the word play. 'Yea, an Italian insult from your Jesuit friends and here is my fiddle stick to make you dance. Baines is not a coward, but very clever, for he knows to keep his hands clean and whom to pay for such deeds.'

And Marlowe bit back, replying, 'And he will turn on you as quickly if there is an advantage in it.'

Bradley flew forward with a plunge, tripping Marlowe with his foot as Kit ducked his head from the blade. Then Bradley spun around to face me and pointed the tip at my face and said, 'Art thou now come? Then I will have a bout with thee!' Marlowe ran at him, throwing all his weight against Bradley's chest and sending him backwards into the street. Their blades clanged and whipped in the night air, and their cries and jests brought a pack of people from their beds. They fought back and forth along the lane. Bradley sliced Kit's hand and, then, Marlowe grabbed hold of Bradley's arm, wrestling him to the ground and elbowing him in the face. 'Twas a fatal shot, for when Bradley's hand flew to his broken nose, I charged forward to wrench the sword from his hand. Marlowe's dagger glinted in the moonlight as he lifted it high over Bradley's head and buried the point deep into the pocket of his eye. Two kicks of his foot and he was dead. Before the crowd gathered closer, I pushed Kit away from the man and took up the dagger in my own hand to save the man who saved me. Marlowe spent two weeks in Newgate Prison for his murder and I, six months."

Robin chuckled. "And to think Master Watson holds no ill will for having to stay longer in that same prison for a murder he did not do."

Thomas nodded in agreement. "Yea, and would do so again. 'Twas a small price to pay to the man who saved my life. Bradley would have torn me to shreds, for as you can obviously see, I am not a fighting man."

"But why only two weeks," William asked.

Robin answered. "'Tis the reward of being a favorite of Her Majesty."

William huffed. "And yet, methinks there is more to this story. Why would Master Bradley tell Marlowe that he gave him an Italian insult from his Jesuit friends? Why would something like that matter to a playwright? And this man, Baines? Why is he so bent on killing Marlowe, if, again, he is only a writer for the stage?"

Robin cleared his throat and William, unmistakably, caught a hesitant look pass between the two men. "You are very inquisitive, Master Shakespeare, about matters not pertaining to you."

William sipped on his fourth pint. "I have my reasons, sir."

Thomas leaned forward. "Ah, Master Shakespeare has a story about Kit Marlowe, as well. Pray, tell us."

A prickly knowing burned in the back of William's mind, something telling him to be cautious, but the ale seemed to loosen his lips and he found himself spilling the matter. "I have always had my doubts about Kit Marlowe. I would swear to this day he was the reason my cousin found his way to the torturing platform of Tilbury. I have heard the Queen's secretary, Sir Walsingham, has a ring of spies infiltrating London and the countryside for Catholic sympathizers. I have no proof, but my gut tells me Master Marlowe is one of those spies."

Thomas laughed loudly and slapped his hand on the table. "S'wounds! Then account me as the King of France! Marlowe a spy? Not bloody likely."

William scratched his chin. "Then what of....."

Robin interrupted. "Master Shakespeare, you are new to London, so you would not be privy to the festering sewage of her criminal network. Baines is a man whom you would do well to avoid, for he seeks new naïve flesh to feed upon, anyone he may step upon to reach the heights he aspires to, which is below the feet of the Queen. He tried with Marlowe, and after seeing he could not fool him, he turned on Marlowe and now seeks a way to bring him down. My advice to you is to keep your mind to the stage and away from these knaves wallowing in the dirt of London. You would do well if you made friends with Kit Marlowe, for any alliance with him is paramount to commanding the favor of those that patron him, namely, Lord Burghley and our dear Queen Elizabeth."

William looked down into his pewter mug and swirled the beer. "So I have heard many times over. 'Twould seem Christopher Marlowe is the spider at the center of a very large web."

Thomas lightened the mood with a rattling airy laugh. "And he will very likely be at the performance of his Doctor Faustus you are seeking to perform here at the Bull. I hear he always attends his plays, so perchance you may make your acquaintance with him there."

William brought the edge of the mug to his lips and whispered in his mind.

Maybe they are right. Maybe 'twould be well to form alliances with this spider before a hand crushes him against the windowpane.

XXV

K it rolled over and threw back the blanket covering his sleeping companion. Aemilia's dark skin glowed like rich clover honey and her thick dark hair cascaded down her back and pooled beside her on the down-filled mattress. He traced his finger down her spine and she giggled while a thousand tiny goose pimples rose on her flesh.

He met her more than a year previous after a drunken night with Thomas Kyd in the inn district of Bishopsgate. His mind swarmed after a performance of Faustus at the Black Bull Inn. The night edged with spirits, being Hallow's Eve, and he hid behind a pillar to watch the performance. The groundling's faces glowed orange in the torchlight and there among them, the sly form of Richard Baines leaned against an opposite post from him on the other side of the stage. Never before had Kit felt a part of his own play, even more so as Alleyn, in the part of the warped Faustus, conjured the imp. Kit felt Baines' eyes bearing down on him across the crowd which made his skin crawl so he darted his eyes away from Baines, back to the stage, only to light upon another man glaring at him to the right of the platform. He saw Will Shakespeare studying him as if he were delving into his innermost thoughts.

What is this bewitching madness...?

Kit grabbed hold of Kyd's doublet and pulled him from the crowd. The streets breathed alive with old pagan lore, masked men and women, festive ribbons and crackling bonfires, cackling laughter, drumming, songs and drunken brawls. Kit felt relief wash over him as he escaped from his own play and those delving eyes of the man who hated him and the other who appeared to know his future.

They hopped from one tavern to the next, guzzling beer, betting on a bear-baiting and losing six crowns after the bear mangled five dogs, and finally arrived at the doorstep of Aemilia Bassano, the beautiful Italian Jew of Shoreditch and secret courtesan to Lord Hunsdon, the Queen's cousin.

But only to line her purse with coin for her lover could not maintain her extravagant taste, she would always declare to Kit. It was such a night, Kit recalled; a night when Thomas fell asleep on her floor, words of sonnets filled his brain and Aemilia unlaced her gown while standing before him in the candlelight.

Now, a year later, he still found his way to her doorstep. He pushed aside the hair covering the back of her neck and kissed the skin behind her ear. She smiled, her straight teeth revealed like perfect pearls between her tawny lips, and she spun over, cocooning her legs in the sheets and around his warm body. He kissed her hard, almost ravenous like a starving man.

She giggled and tangled her fingers in his hair, then raised a finger to his lips to stop him. "Kit, will you write a play for me?"

He nibbled on her fingertip and released a sigh. "O, Aemilia, you inspire many characters in my plays, but I did not come here for words."

She stuck out her bottom lip in a pout. "But, Kit, 'tis the only payment I require of you."

He shaped his hand over the curve of her hip, the cool sheet wrinkling between her skin and his. "Ah, yea, and 'tis the only thing of value I have to give."

She threw her head back while he placed a dozen kisses up her neck and jaw. "And I hope I have inspired you."

He laid his head beside her on the pillow and caressed her cheek.

"Inspired me? Yea, Aemilia, you are Calliope in the flesh. My mind swarms with strong, beautiful women that will grace the stage with resemblances to you. Shall I tell you?" Her eyes lit up, and she nodded. "Very well, then. My play, *The Jew of Malta,* is nearly complete. You are my Abigail, the beautiful Jewess who will be the death of the men loving her. And the others are here in my head, waiting silently in their turn to dance from my quill."

Aemilia giggled. "What are their names, Kit? Tell me, please!"

Kit took a tendril of her dark hair between his fingertips and spun the curl around his finger. "Sweet Jessica who betrays her Jewish father and converts to Christendom for love of a Christian man. I think to place a character with the name of Bassanio as a clue to you. And more: a lady of Venice who falls in love with a man displeasing to her father, only to have the man fall into a jealous rage and strangle her in the end."

Aemilia frowned. "So much tragedy, Kit; must you follow this vein?"

Kit rolled onto his back and gazed up at the ceiling. "In truth, my dear lady, I find I cannot pen words without taking from my life. Tragedy, revenge, manipulation, schemes, strategies, and dissembling, all tools I have seen and used to protect those who protect me. And my comedies are merely relief mingled with irony and innuendos."

She reached over and touched his cheek. "So are my thoughts so frail and unconfirmed, Kit. The follies of this world chain me as well. You think I wish to live this kind of life? But my experience, purchased with many tears, has made me see a difference in things. My sinful soul has paced too long the fatal maze of disbelief and too far from the Christ that gives life."

Kit shook his head. "Ha! Will you win my soul with your words, Aemilia? With prejudice against your race you think to convert to something better, and yet, I have seen religion used as nothing but a childish toy. I believe there is no sin but ignorance and say so in my prologue. Methinks I oftentimes write my own fate in my own words. Hodie tibi, cras mihi."

She leaned over and kissed him gently on the mouth, quieting him with a soft hush. "No more words, sweet Kit, forgive me for urging you so."

He grabbed hold of her arms and spun her to her back, crushing down on her and devouring her kisses. For a moment, her delicate sighs and the rustling of the sheet were the only sounds in the still room. He shuddered as he ran his hand across the small of her back, and her velvet skin warmed under his touch. She grabbed his other hand and placed his palm over her belly, pulling him down to whisper in his ear.

"Kit, I am with child."

He chuckled as he looked into her sudden sad eyes. "And

what, pray tell, does that have to do with me?"

"Only that this may be the last time we are together, for when I told Lord Hunsdon he received permission from the Queen for me to marry her court musician, Alphonse Lanier, with a promise of well keeping, for Lord Hunsdon thinks the child to be his."

"And what do you think?"

"I think I would be a great fool not to take this offer, for it secures a future for me. And yet, the child could be yours."

Kit shook his head. "Ha! Your Jewish affections seem to switch if you hear the possible rubbing of two coins together. I cannot give you anything but words and I told you so from the beginning. Take your problem to your apothecary, Simon, for I hear he is potent with cures to rid an unwed girl of an unwanted babe. O, but I see the answer in your eyes, Aemilia, for never before has a nobleman seeded you. So, I am cast aside?"

The door burst open, crashing against the wall and toppling a small table in the path. Aemilia gasped, grabbing the sheet to cover her body and Kit jerked upright against the headboard. His eyes adjusted in the candlelit room, thinking to see Lord Hunsdon raging in the doorway. Instead, Thomas Kyd's pale face and wide eyes formed. Kit grabbed a pillow and threw it at him.

"S'wounds, Thomas! You gave us quite a fright, I could have killed you, man!" Kit's fear morphed into irritation. "What means you bursting in on me like this? Can you not see I am preoccupied?"

Thomas leaned his hands on his knees and his words mingled with panting as if he ran a great distance to find him. "Forgive...... me, Kit. I have..... been searching everywhere.... for you."

Aemilia reached over on the floor, grabbed Kit's clothes and held them out to him. Kit slid the billow-sleeved shirt over his head and frowned at Thomas. "See what you have done? Now my lady seeks to send me away. The news better be worth why you seek me, else you will have my fist in your gut."

Thomas took a deep breath. "O, 'tis the most profound of news, my friend."

Kit sat at the edge of the bed and pulled on his boots. "Well, go on."

Thomas walked near to him, placed a hand on his shoulder, and whispered in his ear. "Kit, Sir Walsingham is dead."

A low ominous tone resounded from the bells of Saint Paul's Church, dignified, yet simple, according to Walsingham's wishes. The moon peeked her sad eye over the dark towers. The light sound of weeping drifted along the north aisle as Kit followed the torchlight glowing in the dark gloom of the Gothic church. He leaned against the screen separating the choir from the aisle and peered around at the drawn faces, the flames licking shadows across their sad expressions. Burghley and the Queen stood like quiet sentinels while Sir Francis' wife and daughter touched their fingers to their lips and on the brow of the cold corpse of their husband and father. There stood by very few to bid him farewell. Kit knew he was ill of late, but suspected he would find a way to cheat death in a clever way. Even Walsingham could not escape the surety of his mortality, and now his death sent fear racing through the spy circles and many of his former provocateurs already fled the country or took refuge with other protectors. Rumors of King Phillip's joy upon the news drifted from mouth to mouth. Kit knew exactly what he himself felt, pure and utter happiness.

As the wife and daughter backed away, he impulsively approached the bier. Burghley came up to his elbow and whispered, "I thought not to see you here."

A smile crept across his face. "Did you not? I came to make sure 'tis not staged to fool the fools of Rome." He reached across and placed his hand on Walsingham's chest. "Tell me, Lord Burghley, how long do you think he will lie here before he rots? Not long, methinks, for to my mind, he is rotten already."

Burghley pinched his arm. "Go to! You ought not speak so ill of the dead and the one who has protected you all these years."

Kit ignored him and leaned forward as if to whisper in Walsingham's ear. "Where be your taunts and tricks now, Master Walsingham? Ah, you are quite chap-fallen now, nor can you raise one crooked finger to bend me to your will. I am done with you. The cat mews no longer as the mouse scurries away."

Kit turned to face the Queen. He bowed low before her. Elizabeth extended her hand, to which Kit grabbed with a complete lack of propriety. He let his lips linger there, tasting the white powder dusted on her skin.

She snatched her hand away and reproved him. "We are not amused, Master Marlowe, for we are not as merry as we once were. Come, walk with us into the air." She stopped and placed her hand on Mistress Walsingham's shoulder. "Our hearts are with you, dear lady. We will miss him greatly for the protection he provided to our England. Methinks there is not another living who can replace him." The lady curtsied and Elizabeth motioned to Kit and Burghley. When they reached the steps to the church, she turned on Kit and glared.

"How dare you act so cavalier about the man who not only has protected your Queen, but who brought you to the heights you now enjoy? Do you think for a moment we would have bent our notice to a penniless nothing from Canterbury without his urging?"

Kit lowered his eyes and spoke, flavoring his words with flattery. "I beg your pardon, my Queen and my muse, for I am but a poet and have not the skill of your flowery gentlemen of Court."

She looked to Burghley, her sternness melting for a moment. "You think Burghley to be flowery?"

Kit looked up and answered. "Nay, sweet lady, but every bud has a beetle trudging along the path filling its belly with the flowers in the path."

The Queen smiled, her white caked face gleaming in the moonlight and the humor cracking lines about her mouth. She followed Kit's lead.

"Burghley, Marlowe calls you a beetle eating up my flowery gentlemen at Court. First Dudley, now with an eye on Essex, who next? Shall it be my Marlowe?"

Burghley lifted his hand in denial and smiled. "Your Majesty, I do nothing of the kind. I give my opinion but shall always stoop to thy command."

She pursed her lips and then blew a puff. "Sometimes you give your opinion too freely, Lord Burghley. I shall miss Walsingham. The two of you balanced each other so well. Now there is just you." She looked to Marlowe. "Master Marlowe, here you see a man who does not claw at my feet, a man who does not tally the number of links in his lineage to my house to see if he can become a claimant to my throne, nor has he ever applied for the job of a suitor to breed within his line a royal heir. He is a true servant and loyal friend."

Burghley bowed as Marlowe spoke. "Indeed, your Majesty, he is most dear to my heart as well and has saved even me on many occasions. I am indebted to this man and by serving him, I serve you."

She acknowledged Kit with a smile, even taking her fingers and caressing the soft shadow of a beard on his chin. "You are clever, Master Marlowe, and we have enjoyed your plays of late, as well as the secretive work you have done. We shall leave the two of you to discuss further our cause in the Netherlands." She mounted her coach, paused and looked back over her shoulder. "You have my permission to visit me in my apartments where you will share with me some of your pretty words."

Burghley huffed as she left them. He walked near to Kit, watching the clever wrinkle of his smile settle upon the words. "Remember, Kit, it will not be your pretty words that will continue to win her heart, but the continued protection of her realm. Even more so now that Walsingham is gone. Rome will see this as an opportunity, thus we must maintain what he began."

Kit chuckled. "Burghley, a woman is a woman whether Queen or courtesan. I have not known one won over with blood rather than words. The Queen holds my future in her hands, yes, but I am released from the bonds Walsingham shackled about me. I have devoutly wished for this consummation, no longer bound up in blood and darkness, but bursting the dam with a flood of ink and my name whispered in awe wrapped up in my words. I swear history will not remember me as a knave, spy, nor murderer. That is what I long for, Burghley, my true self and name. I have a whole school of tongues in this belly of mine, and not a tongue of them all speaks any other word but my name."

Burghley grunted under the weight of his form as he sat on the edge of steps like an old gargoyle guarding the entrance to a church. "I warned you of this, Kit. We are in the presence of the Queen for her security only and what she bestows or takes away is her God-given right. We are not here to advance our own state. You may not have to answer to Walsingham anymore, but I am still the patron bending the favor of the Queen in your direction. I fear you are being corrupted by the wrong examples."

Kit chuckled again. "Examples? Who, tell me?"

"Raleigh? Essex? Baines? Who knows whom else? Each of these names invokes images of those clawing at the Queen's feet for none other than their own elevation. Look at what it did to Dudley, the one who had the tender ear of the Queen, now dead and gone midst the falling out with her. We are an impatient lot, we humans, and history proves this true. Instead of waiting on God for the answers, we push forward, planning and scheming and most often to our own demise. I have told you from the beginning you must have patience, Kit. Patience and all will come right. Impatience breeds rebellion. I sense it in those around you and I pray not to let it affect you."

Kit walked into the street and knelt near the water trough of the city ditch. His reflection stared back dark and faceless. "Why am I in this fray? 'Twould have been enough for you and Walsingham to come to me at an early age and say, 'Hillo ho ho, boy, thou art a witty poet and we wish for you to amuse the Queen', instead of 'with your clever mind we wish for you to do this and that and then you will have your reward.'"

Burghley laid a hand on Kit's shoulder. "I know this troubles you, but one cannot step from the stake without feeling the flames. Let the fire created by Walsingham die down and the embers smolder, and like the phoenix, you will rise from the ashes."

Kit looked up into Burghley's face. The old man's gray eyes flickered something like love, yet something else shadowed the affection. Kit's brow wrinkled as he searched for the word hiding like a mischievous child in the corner of his brain, then springing out from the hiding place to give a scare. The word sparked like a flint. Death. He grabbed hold of Burghley's arm.

"Soon, this must happen soon, else I fear it will be too late."

Burghley's fondness faded into an aggravation. "Christopher! I said patience and I will have patience. There are things still to do. The Queen's life still hangs in the balance until her line secures. Catholic factions fester like the plague, growing and spreading the older she gets with no heir. They bide their time waiting for her last breath, and when she does, they will spring to action with their teeth set to grind England to the dust. I am sending you to Flushing where you will do as always. Delve into the underbelly, carouse with knaves, do whatever necessary to infiltrate these factions, for it seems they use the proximity of Flushing to funnel their funds and their plots. Perhaps this will be the last time for the use of your skills as a provocateur."

Kit shrugged and dropped a pebble into the waters. He watched the rock sink and settle in the murky darkness at the bottom. "Very well, my Lord, I shall leave with the morning tide."

Burghley cleared his throat. "There is one other matter. 'Tis the matter of Richard Baines."

Kit narrowed his eyes. "What of him? There has been little talk of him of late."

"Indeed, but a man such as he is like a bear that hibernates, sleeping and biding time until the first thaw, and then raging forth with hunger. He has been about, seeking the veins of other powerful men like a leech. Men such as he we must watch, and if ever they find a willing host, the poison spreads and multiplies until a dangerous weakness forms that can overthrow a kingdom."

Marlowe's heart perked upon the thought. "Pray, tell me, has he found this host?"

Burghley scratched his chin. "Perhaps. There is something afoot even within the Star Chamber itself, and I fear our Archbishop of Canterbury may be the host Baines is seeking."

"Whitgift? But why would Baines seek him out?"

"Whitgift holds the power on the council to wield a torturous hand. If Baines could convince him it is in his best interest to root out those close to the Queen, those who may be influencing her down a wrong path, well, then Baines will have found a different path to glory. He tried with Walsingham, but Francis saw his weakness and stupidity immediately; he tried with me, but he lost my trust when he failed with his assignment in Rheims. So, he goes a different way, and I fear someone will fall prey to his cunning."

Marlowe sat on the step next to him, lowering his voice to a whisper. "And if Whitgift does fall prey, what can he do? What kind of man is he?"

Burghley sighed. "Unfortunately, dear Kit, Whitgift has the power to use any means in his hand to smite any in his path. We have had our fights even, and if he could, he would use it against me. He hates men such as Raleigh and Dudley because they held the favor of the Queen and because of that position, they hold a semblance of power. He hungers for that, as does Baines, and unfortunately, as does Essex. This triad of men, Whitgift, Baines and Essex, need a watchful eye as they try their hand at catching the Queen."

Marlowe mused for a moment. "Hmm, Whitgift, with witchcraft of his wit and with traitorous gifts. O wicked wit and gifts having the power so to seduce and win to his shameful lust the will of my most seeming-virtuous Queen. This will not do, and I can see now, Burghley, where my mind must lie. If I can deliver unto my lady's hand a threefold branch, she will snap it and my reward will be great."

Burghley laid a hand upon Kit's shoulder. "Caution, my boy, for the Archbishop's hand is quick with torture and his favorite method is the rack. It will take some time to delve quietly."

"Time, yea, time, that too is not my ally...."

Burghley interrupted. "Tell me, do you have an idea how to go about this?"

Kit's lips curled up in delight. "Somewhat. First, is to seek the company of those whom Whitgift might want out of the way, and fortunately, I am already acquainted with Raleigh. What else can we do?"

"This perhaps... I am reinstating Baines as a spy to go along with you to Flushing. Do you remember the first mission I gave you?"

"You mean the one where I spied upon your son?"

"Yea, the very one. I want you to perform something very like that upon Baines. What his advantage is or what his motives are, are still in question. The essence of my reasoning is this: I do not trust the man, and he knows too much about the groundwork laid by Walsingham and I fear if he does not gain his advancement, he will switch sides as easily as breathing. Do you know what this would mean?"

Kit nodded and sighed. "It means that he can reveal names to any Jesuit assassin who asks. And, as each provocateur silences, 'tis one step closer to the Queen."

"Exactly! Therefore, my dear Kit, take caution and to thine own self be true. We will rout out this rat if that is what he reveals himself to be."

Kit stood up and kicked his toe against the edge of the step.

"Very well, your Grace, but I swear to you, this will be the last time I am this dead Walsingham's poppet."

XXVI

R ichard grabbed up his goblet and slammed the wooden cup into the mouth of the hearth. The wood splintered and the residual wine sizzled and crackled in the flames.

"I despise Christopher Marlowe!"

The Archbishop looked up from his writing desk and stroked his fingers across his pointed chin. "Calm yourself, Baines, for if I can teach you anything, is that mildness heaps fiery coals upon the head of your enemies. Sit and tell me what is raging in your mind. After all, did you not tell me you rode straight here from London to speak to me?"

Richard Baines leaned forward in his chair, warming his hands in the fire and his bare toes curling in the heat upon the marble hearth in the private chambers of the Archbishop of Canterbury. He looked about the room, his eyes glinting upon the shimmering velvet curtains, the fine silver candelabras on the mantle, the golden goblet on the writing desk, and then, lastly, on the gilded ring on John Whitgift's forefinger. Whitgift sat at his desk, a squatty wrinkled toad upon his scarlet lily pad croaking out continuous words as Baines hesitated to answer.

"I can hardly believe 'tis already the thirty-fourth year of our Queen. We have seen the end of Mary of Scots, the Spanish Armada defeated before our eyes, and the end of Walsingham. Now is a new time, Baines, a time for purging and a time for fire. No more of this quiet and sinister darkness Walsingham wrought. No more of secretive spy rings and bookcases of files. This is a time for other means. Perhaps this touches close to the things you would like to tell me?"

Baines lowered his eyes to appear humble to the priest. "Yea, your Grace, for you see, I had nowhere else to turn."

He looked up and caught a faint smile on the Archbishop's lips. "Go on, my son, for your words remain safe here within this church."

Ah, Richard thought, *flattery warms the color of his fat cheeks.*

"Pray, your Grace, that you might hear of the travesty laid upon me. I acquired a release two days ago from Newbury Prison where I spent four weeks in the most deplorable conditions any man may undergo. And for what? For reporting a truth to Lord Burghley."

The Archbishop's eyes flashed upon the mention of a fellow councilor of the Star Chamber. He grunted and scooted his chair closer to Baines. "And Burghley imprisoned you for telling the truth?"

"O, yea, sir."

The Archbishop leaned forward. "Tell me, my son, what is the nature of this truth?"

Baines felt giddy inside. "I will tell you all, your Grace, in hopes you will ask God to right this wrong done to me and with the power you wield on the council you will bring retribution to those hiding lies."

"I will judge it fairly, my son."

Baines settled in his chair. "May I confess to you first that I was a provocateur for Sir Walsingham during the time he lived? His first and foremost loyalist. 'Twas always to me he turned when sniffing out any Catholics plotting against our Queen, but 'twas not long before a conjurer appeared on the scene quite hypnotizing Walsingham, Burghley and the Queen away from loyal men like me."

Whitgift scratched his chin. "This Christopher Marlowe that you spoke of?"

"Yea, your Grace. He is very potent with such ways. He even entertains the crowds with his play of a man who conjures a devil to grant him great powers, wealth and women."

Whitgift smirked. "Yea, I have had many complaints from people of this play, as well as his Tamburlaine."

"O, your Grace, 'tis not just his plays that we must fear, for Walsingham made him a spy as well, and what is more, Burghley and the Queen both patron him. I know he seeks his own ambition, for three months ago Burghley came to me and requested I take up another mission. He sent me to the Netherlands with a report of another faction of Spanish Catholics plotting to counterfeit coins there to bestow upon King James of Scotland, in hopes he would think Elizabeth sent the money via her blessing through the Spanish Ambassador. A ploy to ply James into their good favor and mayhap turn his thoughts back toward the Catholic Church. Burghley even thinks that King Phillip hopes to marry his daughter Isabella to one of James' future sons."

"And what, pray tell, does this have to do with Marlowe?"

Baines smiled and swallowed his victory. "I caught Marlowe counterfeiting right along with those men. Smelting and stamping coin for his own pocket, even giving consent to help them in their plot. Straightaway I went to the governor of the Dutch town, Sir Robert Sidney, and reported the matter. 'Twas not three days and guards arrested him at a pub near the waterfront, charging him with treason and counterfeiting."

Whitgift arched his eyebrow. "Ah, a crime punishable by hanging. But how came you to be in prison, then?"

Baines wrinkled his mouth. "'Twas my own folly, I suppose, for if I had not wanted to be there to see him fall, 'twould not have given him the opportunity to point his finger and implicate me, as well. He even went as far as falling upon the commendation and favor of the governor's deceased brother, Sir Philip Sidney. The governor had no choice but to clap me in irons along with him. He straightaway sent us to London to face Burghley. As quick as snapping your fingers, Burghley penned us both in Newbury. He raged against me, his gray face flaring blood red and all for believing his beloved Marlowe. He dismissed me from ever showing my face before him again, after all of my faithful years, sentencing me to four weeks in prison. Marlowe only spent three days, and this Burghley's attempt at not showing favoritism."

Baines lowered his head into his palms in mock sorrow. "I do not think I will ever forget Marlowe's demonic smile the day of his release. He passed by my cell glowering through the bars. I think he means to destroy me entire."

Whitgift stood and waddled toward the fireplace, taking the poker in his hand and heating the end within the hot coals. He lifted the hot iron before his face; the sizzling glow crackled as it cooled.

He turned his bulging, frog-like eyes toward Baines. "Have you ever smelled burning flesh? Some say 'tis a putrid smell, but I think not, for in the means is a cleansing, a method to reach men's souls. 'Tis a powerful tool to use in weeding out truth and, yet, many on the Council do not feel the way I do. Walsingham's ways are fading quickly upon his death, and still Burghley has the Queen's ear. 'Tis a shame, for she is soft where she needs to be hard. If she continues in this vein, then a tolerance will continue to grow for the Catholic side. There should be no tolerance for Catholic, or for heretical and atheistic demonic views in this country. I have told Burghley this, and yet, he taunts me at every turn, calling for patience and charity. 'Tis not a time for patience, 'tis a time for a fire that heats metal, turning it into a liquid so the scummy dross skims off the surface to make it pure. I only wish to protect the Queen, and yet, she continues to turn to men such as Burghley."

Baines continued to smile, twisting his fingers over his mouth to hide his delight. "And men like Marlowe and his magical cunning. There are even others, you know, others she turns to, ones that could topple all she has worked for. All that you, the protector of our spiritual health, have worked for."

Whitgift jabbed the poker into the flames and watched as the logs fell.   "Indeed? And what would you want to reveal such names to me?"

Baines wanted to laugh at how easily his plan fell into place. "Want, sir? O, only to remember me when you receive your reward from the Queen. There is much I could tell you of the men surrounding our beloved sovereign Elizabeth."

Whitgift twisted the ring on his finger, then, slowly removed the bauble and held it out to Baines. Baines' hand trembled as he took the gift in his fingers and let the light from the flames sparkle along the etchings in the golden circlet.

"Speak, Baines, and this shall be your first reward."

Baines sat back and placed the trinket in his pocket. He took a cleansing breath and began. "Have you heard of a group called the School of Night?"

"The School of Night? Nay, I have not. What is it?" Whitgift took the chair from the desk and sat in front of Baines, leaning forward in curiosity.

"'Tis something I only recently learned about from a former classmate of mine at Cambridge. 'Twas formed at Cambridge and has developed quite a following here in London among certain men who consider themselves above the law and, might I add, above religion. They have a saying amongst them: 'Black is the badge of hell, the hue of dungeons and the school of night.' I hear they seek a higher truth, one built upon philosophy and science and, dare I say, perhaps necromancy? There is one among them who even calls himself the Wizard."

Baines saw Whitgift's mouth moving back and forth, as if he gritted his teeth. "And these men seek to place themselves above God's laws who does forbid such things? And among their throngs are ones in the Queen's favor? O, she must know of this, for by their magical cunning they might influence her on a wayward path. Who, tell me, are these wicked names and we will smite them?"

The taste of Marlowe's name tickled his throat and giddiness surrounded his heart, and yet, this time he needed to be cautious. This time the knave would not escape calumny. Baines feigned to laugh aloud at the cleverness of his plan; how he would use the Archbishop to fulfill his desire.

He opened his mouth, swallowing first to bury Marlowe's name, and let another breath out across his lips. "Sir Walter Raleigh, my Lord, is among the throng."

The Archbishop bolted up, his chair toppling over behind him.

"Raleigh? That braggart pagan pirate?" He walked to the window and stared across the cloister to the commanding spires of the Cathedral. "For so long now I have seen a lustful desire in the Queen's eyes when he enters a room. First, 'twas Dudley, yet he fell easily under his own stupidity; but now, this wayward seafarer with his black eyes and dark manner has her favor. I could never figure out his hold on her, but this, this quite explains it. Who else? Is this Marlowe among the coven?"

Squirming in his chair, he held Marlowe's name within. "There are many others, sir, but I think to topple the top of a tower, one must first remove a chink from the bottom. Even further to the bottom below Master Marlowe."

Whitgift turned to look at Baines, his eyes glowed in the

firelight.

"You speak well, Baines. You are a clever man and serve the Queen well. How shall we try it?"

Baines stood and walked to the door. "Let some time pass, your Grace. Let these knaves settle into a peace, a peace that will ensure a laxness, which will in turn give us the fuel we need. In time, I will send word to you to have someone arrested who, I am sure, under a certain means of pressure, will reveal details and names of those who seek to undermine Elizabeth's throne and church by these paganistic and atheistic practices."

Whitgift bowed his head to him in approval. "Get to it then, and I will wait for your word." He then raised his hand to pause Baines as he placed his hand on the latch. "I have another thought. If we could find a man to use as our eyes, perhaps someone unknown to these men, someone we could fill with dreams of protecting their Queen, 'twould benefit us even more in this pursuit."

Baines bowed and curled the corner of his mouth. "I will keep my eye open for such a man, your Grace."

Baines left Canterbury, racing against the biting wind toward London. Just before midnight, his horse's hooves clopped down the soured streets of Cheapside. He reined the mare and hopped off before the doors of the Mermaid Tavern, his nostrils stinging under the weighty smell of ale and tobacco. Baines slithered into the public room, keeping to the shadows, spying with a watchful eye for Marlowe's face. He frowned, noticing the playwright's absence. Then, as he downed a mug of beer, he recognized a former acquaintance sitting alone at a table across the room. Baines approached.

"Well, if it is not Marlowe's old friend. How are you, Thomas Kyd?"

Thomas looked up, his eyes glazed with drunkenness. "Richard?"

"It is indeed. Shall I sit with you?"

Thomas motioned for him to sit. "How is it that I find you here at the Mermaid? I thought you had not the stomach for players and poets, Master Baines?"

"Nay, not so much for the stage-talk as for the other affairs spoken of in the dark. You know what I mean... religion, politics, court affairs, gossip that does fill the poet's sonnets and the player's stage."

Thomas lifted his mug and held the cup near his mouth, sipping and licking the foam from the edges with his tongue. "To what end, Richard, for you have gained the reputation that the only reason you need knowledge is to use it some device. Marlowe told me of your little fray in Flushing."

Richard chuckled. "Come now, Thomas, 'tis been too long for us to suspect one another. Can I not simply want to know what my old friend has been doing of late? Your play, how goes it?"

Thomas sat the mug down and rubbed his thin sallow cheeks with his fingers. "Old friend? Nay, Richard, that we have never been, nor do I see a future for such friendly feelings. Pray, though, you have caught me at a lonely hour. My brain is full of ale and I would talk to the devil himself, methinks. My play is doing well and has received proper accolades. I feel the many nights I spent wrangling with my tragedy creeping upon me. I did not sleep well as I wrote, but Kit tells me such is the way of a writer. Sometimes I marvel at how he does it with such ease. Have you seen any of his plays?"

Richard squinted at Thomas. "Nay, I have not, but I heard of his success. Three and more plays performed in five years and with such lofty patrons, then his pocket must sag with coin. Does he visit the Mermaid often these days?"

Kyd shrugged. "Nay, not so much anymore. When I have seen him 'tis always in the company of Raleigh or Thomas Hariot or Ingram Frizer. He has not much use for his former friends, except when they have something he needs."

Baines noticed the bitter slice in the words. "You sound cynical, Thomas. Has he used you of late?"

Thomas' thin shoulders drooped, as his countenance seemed to melt before Richard's eyes. "Perhaps I should not speak of him so. He is a great playwright and has much on his mind. Happiness filled my heart when he came to me to request lodging, and in hopes we could reacquaint ourselves like we did when I first met him all those years ago. Yet, as I said, he is often busy writing and other things. You should see his portfolio. The bindings strain under the volume of writings he has yet to bring to fruition. He caught me looking at them one day and blasted upon me like a roaring bear, snatching the papers from my hands and clutching them to his breast. And between his days at his desk, I hear he is of much use to Lord Burghley and the Queen. O, Richard, you should see one of his plays. They are brilliant."

Baines found Thomas' weakness. "So, Thomas, I gather you are not familiar with the gatherings Marlowe attends? The same one Raleigh supports?"

Thomas huffed. "You mean the School of Night? Nay, I do not attend."

Baines leaned forward toward Thomas. "But you know of it and what they speak on?"

Thomas looked up from his ale, pausing for a moment to Richard's questioning. "Why are you interested, Richard? You have never sought out Kit's company before. All of us know well how you feel about him."

"People change hearts all the time, Thomas. Look how easily the common folk switch their faiths. 'Tis amazing what a spell in prison will do to a man. Perhaps 'tis time for me to mend the past with Marlowe. Do you know where I could find the meeting?"

Thomas held up his empty mug. "For another pint I will tell thee all."

Richard motioned to the barmaid and ordered up another round, placing a crown onto the table top. He leaned in to listen as Thomas began.

"They will meet here within the hour and to be honest, 'tis mostly of nothing they speak. 'Tis not at all the mystical fellowship the rumors speak of, but more a meeting of thought, wrangling out the meanings of philosophy and science. Sometimes just a recitation of a new sonnet or lines from a play and more often mere nonsense accentuated by card playing, beer guzzling and wenching. To my mind, a group of pompous bellows puffing air. They have never sought out or listened to anything I have to say."

Baines smiled and sat back in his chair. His words whispered out, low enough so Thomas could not hear. "Then I will wait, and perhaps will find the food to bait my trap."

XXVII

The fog rolled across London like a worn blanket, thick, yet patchy, and unable to protect against the cold. The last of the February snow melted into slush along the byways as March crept in on the back of never-ending downpours and misty chills. Kit stood framed in the doorway of Thomas Kyd's lodging house in Norton Folgate with his cloak wrapped over his hand and across his nose as he stared into the street. A dozen or more fat rats scurried along the city ditch in front of the creaking wheels of the death cart. Already, in one day, the house across from him delivered up three corpses wrapped in dingy white sheets and stacked near the door for the plague-bearer to gather up and add to his burdening weight. Kit cursed the stench, yet could not keep his eyes from the sight of death.

Thomas, having warmed two cups of mulled wine over the fire, handed Kit a cup and urged him from the doorway. "Kit, please, close the door for I do not wish the red death to creep over my threshold."

Kit slammed the door and held his stomach. "S'wounds! The smell is worse than rotting eggs!"

Thomas sat in front of the fire and stretched out his legs. "'Tis the sulfur used to disguise the stench of death, methinks. The odor permeates London and I hear the disease is ravaging her like a fire."

Kit sat next to him and sipped the wine. "Yes, and Tilney closed the playhouses for fear of spreading. Burbage, Alleyn and all the troupes have left for the countryside. These are dark and ominous days, Thomas, and I fear 'tis not only the plague shadowing London. Something in my soul bespeaks doom."

"O, come now, Marlowe, I have heard you speak the same

way for months now, ever since the performance of Faustus. Why do you not refresh your mind with a comedy? I know your portfolio overflows with first drafts awaiting revision."

Kit stood up in a sudden motion and slammed his cup onto the oak mantel. "I need time, Thomas, and yet, my mind keeps telling me the sand is thinning through the hourglass. Like the breath of a wraith on my neck whispering I may not see my thirtieth birthday come next year."

"Is wraith in the form of Richard Baines," Thomas questioned.

Kit leaned against the mantel and cut his stare to Thomas. "Most like, my dear friend."

"Then why do you not just find a way to kill him?"

Kit creased his brow. "Despite what you or anyone else may think of me, killing does not come natural to my hands nor my mind."

Thomas shrugged. "O, I was not thinking of you, Kit. Surely there are ones with whom you rub shoulders who could perform the job and call it an accident."

"You mean those in my acquaintance of the School of Night?" Kit glared at him in irritation as Thomas nodded. "Thomas, you do not know what you are saying. The School of Night is a gathering of intellectuals, not of murdering knaves. 'Tis the one place where I can escape all the plotting, scheming, blood, politics and religion, and sit with fellows wishing nothing more than to enhance our minds with poetry and prose. You know, 'twould do you well to join us one evening to see for yourself."

Thomas shivered. "Nay, you will not see my face there. There is something about your companions that gives me a chill, especially Henry Percy."

Kit chuckled. "You mean because he calls himself the Wizard Earl? You ought not to speak on things you know nothing about, Thomas. Percy is a good man, an intellect of the highest degree, and we have had quite a discussion on philosophy and science tempered by our ale. I would think you would snatch the opportunity to expand your mind, thus expanding your sources for future plays."

Thomas pulled a blanket tight around his shoulders and leaned toward the fire. "Nay, count me out, Kit. You do not realize the rumors swarming through the London streets of your meetings.

Whether they are true or not, the taint will remain. I would rather keep clear of any hint of atheism or treason against the Crown."

Kit huffed. "And do you not realize the demon behind such talk? Richard Baines would do anything to sully my name."

Kit jumped as a pounding on the door reverberated through the room. He walked across and grabbed hold of the latch, opening the door to reveal a small boy holding a letter. Kit took the paper from his fingers, broke the seal and read:

'Christopher, you must attend me without delay, coming promptly upon receipt of this letter. There is something wicked playing about your name and I must meet with you before the other members of the Star Chamber hear of this matter.

Lord Burghley'

"See, what did I tell you? O, Baines will have his day, Thomas, but not at my hands. He thinks to tighten his fingers about my throat, but I will delve one yard below his mines and blow him to the moon. Watch yourself, Thomas, for he is very cunning and will try to use any around me as pawns in his game. I must be off."

Kit tied the cloak tight around his neck, lifted the hood over his head and ran out into the fog, swirling the dragon's breath behind him.

℘ↄ☙

Lord Burghley leaned over the former desk of Sir Walsingham as Kit threw back the door, puffing and panting from his sprint to Westminster. Kit laid the cloak on a chair and slumped onto the window bench. Burghley closed the door and grunted across the floor, sliding a chair near as Kit drew circles on the wet frosted panes of the window.

"Well, I am here, Lord Burghley, but if you think to tempt me to another mission, then you are wasting your time."

Burghley gruffed. "Then why did you come, Marlowe?"

Kit sat up and faced him. "Because your letter said something wicked played about my name and my name of late is becoming quite known here in London for the thing I always wished, as a playwright and not a provocateur. I do not wish anything to damage that."

Burghley ran his stubby fingers across his brow. "That will be quite difficult to do, Christopher, considering your past. Men can run from their past, but inevitably the talons will rip down from above without warning."

Kit pounded his fist into the cushions. "Nay, 'twill not do! Walsingham's death was the end of my past."

Burghley held up a letter in front of Kit's eyes. "And yet, Richard Baines is still alive with a cunning he never displayed whilst in Walsingham's service. I think the hatred for you is driving him to different depths. If ever he hated the Pope the way he hates you, the whole church would have toppled with the blast of his breath. Do you know what this is?"

Kit took the letter and perused the words. At the end, Kit handed it back to him and snickered. "Nay, I do not know what this is. 'Tis the words of a simpleton, a child even. What is it?"

Burghley raised his eyebrow, his face shadowing in seriousness.

"This is nothing to snicker at, Christopher. He hammered the bitter libel to the door of the Huguenot church here in London and has caused patches of rioting in the streets. Many are placing the blame for this at your door, thinking your recent fellowship with a certain atheistic group is raging your words against those French refugees whom our Queen vowed to protect."

Kit snapped his fingers. "Ha! The School of Night is far from atheistic. 'Tis the work of Baines, for surely any reasonable man can see these words are a poor imitation to mine. Amazing that a knave like Baines can flavor the libel with words like 'Machiavellian' and 'Paris massacre' and 'Tamburlaine', and the people clamor to believe this of me. 'Tis a wonder humanity leans toward believing bad of a person instead of good, especially if a slight morsel is fed to them."

Burghley huffed. "Only when a person's past taints with such, Marlowe. Unfortunately, many know you were part of Walsingham's circle and this libel puts you in a very precarious position. You continue to hide that by writing your plays, and yet...."

"And yet," Kit interrupted, "the bloated corpse keeps rising to the surface. S'wounds! Seems I am forsworn no matter how hard I fight against it. What do I do?"

Burghley scratched his chin in contemplation. "Methinks for you to keep quiet and low for now. Did I not hear Walsingham's nephew extended his patronage to you since his uncle's death?"

"You mean Thomas Walsingham? Yea, he has, and has invited me to his country home in Scadbury."

Burghley pursed his lips and surmised. "Then perhaps 'twould do you well to take him up on his invitation for a time. Leave London while this plague rages. Take the time to write and let this matter fade. I will do what I can to quell this matter with the council, but I know when Whitgift gets wind of the libel, his teeth with clamp down like a dog on a meaty bone. Even now he plies me with pressure to execute the man accused of penning the Marprelate letters against him. I think you may know the man holed up in the Tower."

"I do? Who is it?"

"I think from your early days at Cambridge you knew a Puritan youth named John Penry."

Kit stood up and faced his gaze out the window. "John Penry? To be sure? I knew a youth of that name but have not seen him since, but I did know him as a young man of purity and grace who doted on my words in those younger days. I cannot imagine him penning such words against the Archbishop, but as these fell times are proving, I have been wrong about many men and women. All except for you, your Grace. You are as steady and true as the mighty Thames."

Burghley stood and wavered upon his crooked feet. Kit crooked his hand under Burghley's arm and steadied him. "Nay, Christopher, not as mighty as I once was. Go along, for I need to rest my bones. I will keep you abreast of the news and will report all of this I have told you to the Queen. She has an interest in you, as well, an interest far surpassing anything Baines or Whitgift may do. Do not forget that."

Kit bowed and left the room. He knew Burghley would keep his word by telling the Queen, but as far as her interest in him, Kit knew her mind as fickle as any woman or any women he had ever known. He wandered the hallways with his mind in a fog, drifting between Burghley's words, Baines' taunts, and the memory of his fellow peers toasting him at the Mermaid.

As close as his ultimate success seemed, the glory still felt intangible like trying to grasp the edges of the horizon with your fingers. He sighed and looked up, noticing his wanderings led him to the east corridors of Whitehall. As he ambled through the snatches of sunlight piercing through the arched windows, a soft delicate sound drifted along the hall. He followed the tinkling melody, pausing in the shadows as the last door at the end of the hall opened and closed. Lady Sidney, Philip's widow and Walsingham's daughter, closed the door behind her and scurried along the hall, never noticing his shadow stretching long across the floor. The music continued on the other side of the door luring Kit with a feeling he had not felt in many years.

He turned the latch and cracked open the door, just enough to see a lady with soft golden ringlets tumbling down her back, dressed in a pale blue gown and sitting at the virginals playing a merry tune. He knew her at an instance as he entered the room with cat-like steps and leaned forward against the back of a small tufted couch to listen. Kit's heart surged and filled with the sights and smells of spring. The flooding feelings of a fifteen-year-old boy rushed upon him and his mind swirled with the memories of that summer at her estate in Salisbury. She stopped in mid-stanza, almost as if she sensed his presence, and slowly spun around on the bench to face him. He caught his breath when her blue eyes rested upon him and he let her name caress across his lips.

"Mary."

She did not soften her stern expression. She remained stoic as he drank in her every detail and he trembled as her voice filled his ears.

"Ah, Master Marlowe, I did not think you were at Court. I have not seen you before the Queen as of late."

Kit could not hide his delight at seeing her, nor did he want to. "And you have been much absent from Court, as well."

She pursed her lips. "Yea, since my brother's death I have not had much use for such matters. Other things preoccupy my time at my home in Wilton."

Kit smiled, thinking to ease her stone face. "Of course, my Lady. I have heard from Thomas Kyd that you have become quite the patroness and inspiration to many of our poets. But did I not tell you once you were a muse?"

She looked away from him, brushing her fingertips over the

last keys on the small harpsichord. "Thomas is a kind man and a fine writer. As for you, Master Marlowe, I know you are receiving the acclaim my brother always knew you would receive. 'Tis a pity you thought so little of him that you could not have written three lines to bemoan his passing."

Kit felt the jab to his heart. "My Lady, 'twas not from uncaring that Philip died without my notice, but I was away on an assignment with Her Majesty's secretary, Sir Walsingham, and no one bothered to inform me of his death. I am truly sorry for your loss and always have been. I would not be the man I am today, nor have the knowledge needed to write such plays, without the patronage of your brother. If there is ever anything I can do for you, Mary, to make amends for your thoughts against me, please, I beg of you, to give me the command." He walked near to her and took a tendril of her hair in between his thumb and forefinger. "If my memory serves me, then you know, and have always known, of my affection for you."

She held out her hand, and he fell upon her fingers with a dozen kisses. "Ah, Mary, dear Mary, I did not think to hope I would ever see you again in private. Too long, 'tis been too long...."

Mary pulled her hand away and cut her stare toward the settee before the hearth. She extended her hand as a young stranger rose from the seat and crossed the room toward her. Kit stepped back, startled, and purveyed the delicate youth before him - the sharp chin, the brown curling hair, the piercing blue eyes.

Mary raised her chin and spoke plain to Kit. "One would think my purpose has been clear all these years without any word, Master Marlowe. I am at Court with only one thought and that is to acquaint my son with Court life. Christopher, this is my son, William Herbert, the third Earl of Pembroke."

Kit bowed as William spoke in soft, airy tones. "Sir, 'tis a pleasure to meet you. My mother speaks often of you. She has told me and shared with me much of your work and I had hoped to meet you. Now it seems fate has brought us here together. I am sure you know our family does much to support the gifted poets of our time and I have always wished to offer myself as a patron."

Kit looked to Mary, confusion filling his mind and sarcasm flooding his words. "So, Lady Pembroke, you have never had any thoughts to seek me out? You thought only to display your son's money to the poor wretched and mediocre rhymers who would clamor to receive his patronage?"

Mary's face shadowed in reverence as a Madonna in a painting. "What more could a poet want? Perhaps my son looks to patron you, Master Marlowe, someone far from mediocre; and if that be the case, I do beseech you to give your consent to him."

William waited for a moment and extended his hand. "Excellent notion, mother, and I give it most heartily, sir. Your talent deserves many patrons, but as it is, I shall be your first and foremost."

Kit remained silent and perplexed as Mary took a sheet of vellum from a nearby desk and placed the paper on the table. She dipped a quill and held it out to William. "William, write out your consent to Master Marlowe. I did not think this would proceed so easily but as my son said, fate seems to have brought us together. Here, sign and seal with your mark."

William looked at his mother. "Surely, Mother, my handshake will suffice betwixt gentlemen."

Mary pounded her palm onto the table. "You are a tiresome boy! Can you not indulge me? Pray, sign the paper and honor your oath to patron him. Be done with it."

As William signed and handed the paper back to his mother, Kit's mind whispered. *There is more to this, I see it in her eyes.*

Mary looked away from Kit's studying eyes and she walked toward the window. Kit could not keep his eyes from her, even as her son opened a portfolio on the floor and recited his favorite Marlowan verse. The boy puffed up his chest and extended his arm in front of him, facing his mother.

"Is this the face that launched a thousand ships?"

She turned and smiled at her son. Kit's heart soared upon the sight of those perfect pink lips curving into a moon-like slice. "Christopher, my son knows all of your plays like rote."

"Indeed he does, my Lady."

William snickered. "Perhaps one day under my commission, you will compose a sonnet or two for me, or even a play like this one. My mother is always encouraging me towards marriage, to continue our family line and heritage, so perhaps one day you will give me some pretty lines for a prospective lady. Your sonnets are lovely, Master Marlowe, yet I adore your Faustus. It is so terrifying and yet, so human. I believe all men attend to the thought of immortality."

"You are correct, William," Marlowe answered. "I see your teachers feed you well on the bread of Plautus and Aristotle. Your father must be proud of his witty son and the things he has learned."

Mary dabbed her fingers to her nose and released a sigh with her words. "Yet, there are things he does not know, nor do you.... nor does anyone." She paused, closed her eyes for a moment and took a deep breath before training her gaze directly on Kit's face. "My son is correct when he says that men, and women, attend to thoughts of immortality. Even more so the closer they arrive at that fateful date with death. So often the fear of what lay beyond spurs a person to right the wrongs done in their lifetime."

Kit watched her face soften, and the sunlight sparkled upon a line of tears welling in her lower lashes. Her eyes, still, never left his as she continued. "I did not think to see you again, Christopher.... actually, even thinking to continue to avoid you for the rest of my life.... but, it would seem that God has brought us so suddenly together, the three of us.... here.... in this room." She paused and breathed deep once more. "And methinks, he is urging my soul to undo a wrong.... to undo a lie of my youth." She let go a nervous and awkward giggle. "You see, my wild youthful days have made me quite the religious woman in my aging years, and now, upon the Lord's will and my eternal soul, shall I undo this coincidental reunion."

William looked up from the pages scattered on the floor into her telling face. "Mother, what is wrong? What are you saying?"

Mary steadied her shoulders and spoke. "What I am saying.... what I need to tell.... is this. I do pray your father will be proud of his witty son and the things he has learned." Her gaze went from her son's face to Christopher's eyes. "William, here is thy father. Christopher, look at thy son."

Her eyes revealed no jesting. William rose from his place on the floor and stood with his mouth gaping open. "Mother, what do you mean? What are these words?"

The words swarmed into Kit's ears and he felt dizzy as she confirmed her answer.

"Just as I said, William. Master Marlowe, William is your son, born nine months after the summer you spent at Wilton, born the year of the great earthquake that rumbled across this island." Kit could not move, he could not speak, and still the words tumbled from her lips. "Christopher, did you really think so ill of me all those years ago to imagine I would consummate my marriage to Lord Pembroke without a reason? What could I have done, except what I did? And now, look, your son is an Earl."

The blood drained from Kit's face and he cut his eyes toward the boy, who stood in shock between them. William's eyes flashed confusion and his mouth formed an astonished circle. He swayed and Kit reached out to steady him with a hand at the boy's elbow. William gritted his teeth and snatched his arm from Kit's grip.

"Get away from me," he screamed as he glared at his mother. "This is not true."

Mary straightened, firm in her stance. "Yea, my son, it is and I am sorry."

"You are lying! How dare you snatch my birthright from me just to ease your conscience, and clap my blood to this man?"

Mary raised her fingers to her lips to hide the trembling. "And yet, a moment ago, the poet entranced you."

William's words bit hard. "Yea, as a poet, not as a father. I will never acknowledge him; you do know that, do you not? I cannot, else all that I have will fall apart." He turned and pointed his finger into Kit's face. "And you, standing there with a hint of affection in your eyes. Leave it be, for if ever you give the slightest hint we are of the same blood, then I will blacken your name and bury you so far beneath my feet that nary a soul will ever believe the slightest suggestion that such a knave could be my father."

He ran from the room and slammed the door so hard the windows shuddered. Kit's eyes trailed from his newly found son back to Mary's face. She could not look up for the tears streaming heavy down her cheeks. Kit swallowed his confusion of emotions.

"So, I was right all those years ago when I asked you if you were with child. Mary, why did you not tell me sooner?"

"For what purpose, Christopher?"

Kit displayed the irony with a crooked smile. "For what purpose does it serve now? Except that you may live the rest of your life in holiness whilst thrusting that sin upon me to carry with the rest of my mistakes. You know he can never acknowledge me as his father, you knew it before you spoke, and I am caught in the same net, as I cannot ever reveal him as my son. How can I blacken his name, especially when mine own is in the midst of scandal and he a child of state?"

Mary bit her lip and blinked away the droplets in her lashes.

"And yet, he has signed and sealed his word and consent to patron you."

Kit blew a sigh through his nose. "O, Mary, you are so naïve still. Paper and the words written upon them are fragile things, easily changed, easily burnt and easily forgotten. You have always been so impulsive and I see age has not softened that hue." He looked back toward the door. "He is a lovely boy, Mary, and the thought of having a son quite stirs something I have never felt. He is your looking glass and recalls the April of your prime. We shall see, shant we, how our past indiscretions and this day's confession will continue to haunt our future."

XXVIII

The day turned out a failure. Kit wandered down the corridors of the palace, finding his way like a sullen man stuck in a maze of despair. Within just an hour, Marlowe won and lost a son. He left Whitehall consumed with the familiar hurt of despised and rejected love and sought out the attention of his admirers at the Mermaid Tavern. Sir Walter Raleigh and Henry Percy greeted him in the street as he entered. Marlowe affected a smile as Raleigh slapped him on the back.

"Walter, you look like a painted peacock with your scarlet cloak and tufted collar. Your purse indeed overflows with commendations from the Queen."

"Indeed, Kit, our lady is very generous, would you not agree? For I know she has showered her favors upon you as well."

Kit huffed and waved away his question. "I wish not to speak on her, for her favor is a thing to tread upon carefully, like most women. Give me some good dragon's milk and let me drown out thoughts of that weaker sex."

The three men swept into the public house in a flurry of velvet, feathered caps and starched ruffs. Marlowe looked around Raleigh's shoulder and saw Richard Baines conversing with his chamber mate, Thomas. Kyd's face floured pale as he caught Kit's glare.

"Thomas, are you so poor in companionship that you would seek out the likes of Baines?"

Richard's stare sliced through the air like a rapier as he interrupted Thomas' response. "And are you so poor in companionship that you would seek the company of a pirate?"

Raleigh joined the conversation, taking up a table behind them and ordering a round of ale. "Come along, Richard, for we wish for some jovial words, not these dark moods mixed with deep meaning. Drink up, lads, for tonight I am bent on seeing the bottom of the barrel."

"I am with you, Walter, for this day fills with too many sorrows already," Kit concurred.

Kit smiled and left Richard skulking. He sat at the table with Walter and chugged a pint, and then another. A half hour passed as Kit sat across from Baines, taking turns cutting daggers with their eyes. Richard Cholmley joined the group as did Thomas Heriot. As the night progressed, the ale flowed, the laughter grew louder, and the words more rank and senseless as the topic leaned toward the plight of England's soul. Kit stood and swayed toward the wall and leaned upon the shoulder of Raleigh.

He lifted his tankard in the air. "Friends, a toast to a new writer in our midst, a man of infinite jest who can set the whole table in a roar with his clever words and innuendos. Why, he has caused rioting in the streets with his latest creation." He tilted the tankard toward Richard Baines and downed the drink in one gasp.

Raleigh laughed and slapped the table. "Ha, Kit! Surely you do not refer to Baines here, for all of us know full well how illiterate the man is. If'n he is a writer, then Heriot here is a prophet!"

Kit belched and motioned to Thomas Heriot. "Well, then all know it to be true, then Prophet Heriot! Baines is the creator of a most excellent libel whose poison begins a quiet sleep and death here in London. And Moses was nothing, but a juggler compared to our dear Heriot here, who being Sir Walter's man, can do much more than he."

The room crested in an uproar at Marlowe's sarcastic words. Kit continued slurring along on his comical drunken spree. "... And what is more, if I was to write a new religion, as Baines is trying to do, I would undertake both a more excellent and admeeeer..... admirable method. What say you, men?"

Everyone at the table clinked their mugs in a toast, spraying beer along with their spitting laughter. Heriot answered in jest. "And I say that all that love not tobacco and boys are fools!"

The group hushed as they all looked to Heriot. Kit belted a laugh and raised his cup. "Well, then, Thomas, our drink is the poison that doth bring forth many truths from our mouths, although in your case I would not have so hastily answered!"

Kit's words raised the laughter and the drinks once again. They drank deep into the morning, drowsing in the drunken words of nothing. Baines pushed his mug away and looked about the room at them all quietly sleeping with their head tucked in their arms or body splayed on the floor where they fell. All except for Kit Marlowe and Thomas Kyd. Kyd left earlier in the evening and Kit propped upon his hand, watching Baines. Baines slithered from the room, turning once to look at Kit, and smiled a demonic smile.

Baines' words filtered through the morning air, tickling the inside of Kit's ears like a prophecy, as he pointed at him with a crooked finger. "I have you, Kit Marlowe. I have you at last."

Kit blew his tongue across his lips, spraying a shower of spit. "Go to hell, Richard Baines! You have nothing and if you speak of the libel you wrote, 'twas a clever plot, to be sure, but I am one step ahead of you."

A maniacal laugh eked from Baines' throat. "O, I have just begun, Kit Marlowe."

Kit stood and followed Richard out of the pub. As he stood in the shadow of the door frame, he saw Richard taking hold of Cholmley's arm, pulling him into conversation as they sauntered down Friday Street. Kit wondered if Baines' next move was afoot by whispering into Cholmley's ear. He waved for a coach and headed to the flat he kept with Kyd near Shoreditch.

When Kit opened the door to the flat, his eyes focused on a strewn about mess: chairs overthrown, papers askew and not a sign of his flat mate. Kit stumbled into the garderobe and heaved the contents of his stomach into a wooden bucket, collapsed onto the floor and fell into a deep drunken sleep.

The day passed away as Kit slept fitfully, tossing and turning upon bloody dreams. He bolted straight up as the door opened and Thomas trudged into the room. He sat opposite Kit with his cloak hood covering his face.

Kit yawned and stretched, rubbing away the crusty sleep in the corner of his eyes. "Where have you been all day?"

Thomas shook his head and Kit noticed his shoulders trembling. Kit reached across and took him by the arm.

"Thomas, look at me. What is wrong?"

Thomas raised his eyes. The hood fell back from his head, revealing deep red and purplish wounds around his eyes and brow. Marlowe stood and ripped the cloak from Kyd's back and discovered his shirt in bloody shreds, his flesh peeking through the thin fabric with deep, scalding slashes, a trademark of the Archbishop. Thomas raised his right hand before Kit's eyes. The raw flesh festered with boils like tender meat dipped in steaming water.

"O, Kit, I am undone! I have spent the morning in the steel clutches of an iron maiden. Then, when her ripping metal teeth finished feeding, they dipped my hand in scalding water. Shall I ever pick up the quill again?"

Marlowe brushed his fingers through his hair and grasped his throbbing head. He ripped a strip from the linen sheet on his bed and wound the material around Thomas' hand.

"Thomas, who did this to you? And why?"

Kyd whimpered, his frail form collapsing on the bed next to Kit.

"They have subdued me, Kit, and I can feel my soul quite broken."

"But why, Thomas? What was their gain?"

Thomas raised his weeping eyes until Kit could see the answer. "Christopher, forgive me. Please, forgive me. I am a weak man. There were papers, you see, that they found among my writings. Atheistic ramblings that would have sent me to the Tower. You know they were not mine, Christopher. I had no other choice but to give them what they prodded me for."

Fear sprung upon Kit like the familiar breath of a wraith and he backed away from Kyd, his feet shuffling through the papers about the room. Kit's eyes darted about, forming the sense of what was happening. He gathered up his cloak, his portfolio and ink bottle, looking over his shoulder as he opened the door.

"Et tu, Brute?"

Thomas' wails followed him as Kit ran into the street and called for a coach. "Take me to Scadbury in Kent in all haste."

$$\mathcal{SO}\mathcal{QR}$$

The late afternoon sun broke across Kent, flooding the green rolling hills and casting a glow over the hedged pastures and black-faced sheep. The red-bricked walls of Scadbury shone like a brilliant beacon in the gathering fog.

Thomas Walsingham leaned over a dish of scones and spiced wine at a table in the garden midst the jasmine blossoms aching to burst their scent over the arbor. Walsingham's servant introduced Kit into his company. Thomas looked up and greeted him with a harsh glare. Kit shivered at the resemblance the man shared with his late uncle, the narrow dark eyes and slender face.

"Pray, Master Marlowe, what brings you thus to Kent without prior warning?"

Marlowe hesitated, unsure of trusting even this man. "Thomas, you invited me here after your uncle's death. Do you not remember? Lord Burghley said he would send word ahead that I am to take a rest here in the country to write and we could think of no better place in the world than Scadbury."

Walsingham huffed. "Are you sure you do not seek refuge from thine own troubles? I have received messages from Lord Burghley that the Queen commands a word with you and to tell you so if I were to see you."

Kit stuffed a scone into his mouth, noting Thomas' words biting with displeasure. "A word? Words, you mean. Words, words, words. 'Tis never quite just a word with our Majesty, is it, Lord Chamberlain?"

"Not unlike yourself as of late, Marlowe. Seems your many words are getting you into trouble."

A growling anger surged in his stomach. "Bah! What does it matter anymore? I seem unable to voice the very words that are important without more being read into them than necessary or without more being required of me or words applied to me which are not even mine. The Queen commands a word of me? A whole volume I have given her and that pompous ass Burghley. I have often wondered what more do they want from me."

Thomas slathered some clotted cream on his scone. "I have never heard you speak so harshly about the man who has saved your life on numerous occasions and still seeks to do so. You know the Queen thinks it to be deeper than just a matter of the production of a few plays."

"Deeper, indeed. She knows where my heart lies, I have never given a moment's doubt about that to her; but the question comes to mind, do they know or are they seeking to plant something there that does not exist to boost their own ambitions?"

"They, sir?"

Kit leaned forward and narrowed his eyes at Thomas. "You are very quizzical today, Thomas. You know very well what I mean. They, yes, the entire bloody Star Chamber starting with the Archbishop who is probably lining the pockets of Richard Baines, as well as the still prying claws of Rome. Protestant or Catholic, I do not see why I have to care anymore. And why does everyone seem to care about me? Pray, I have done a few favors for the Queen, and now I wish they would let me be. I choose my side at this point in my life, my name, my plays.... and that is all."

"Some would mark that down as borderline atheistic, Kit. 'Tis important because those the Queen favors deal with scrutiny. 'Tis not our side but her side, which bolsters the whole country, politics and religion, which is a protection for the state, as well as a protection for you."

Kit slammed the remainder of his scone onto the plate in disgust.

"Yea, so I have been told my entire life. So many things are being believed of me these days, and I will only receive protection if I continue to choose the right side, which is only the Queen's side. I have nothing wholly for myself."

"True, but the Queen herself has given you her word...."

"Nay, as I said, I give her my words all the time and I refuse to let the Church of glorious England or her Virgin idol, or the Pope and his Church, or self-seeking ambitious mediocre men in this realm to continue to tear my life apart. I want to write, Thomas. I want my words to breathe and live on the stage. That is the legacy I want to leave and is my right. I am ready to tell the Queen that all of this is over. She can just find herself another favorite and I will make my own way to see my plays to the stage. I am so tired of all this nonsense at Nonsuch."

"'Tis a little late for that lament, Kit; and you did not think it to be nonsense when first my uncle recruited you."

Kit balked at the word 'recruited.' "Are you serious, Thomas? Recruited? Nay, not I. They bought me as a slave and being so young, did I have a choice? And yet," Kit buried his face in his hands, "my soul accuses me daily as the seller and methinks there were days earlier I could have found a way out. I kept saying it was a means to an end. To have my work promoted by the highest authority in the land and in return, to sniff out a few Catholic rats? I mean, who would refuse such an adventure? 'Run a few errands for me,' is what she would say. That is what she called them. 'Just a simple errand here and there, my darling Kit, and I will make thee a household name.' O, what a foolish figure am I."

Thomas leaned back in his chair. "Foolish enough that you did not recognize the rat right in front of you."

Kit's brow wrinkled. "You mean that early time when Baines first confronted me at Cambridge? Is that what you mean?"

Thomas dunked the last scone in a dish of lemon curd. "Yea, the very man. I heard Whitgift arrested Thomas Kyd two days ago and held him at Bridewell. He then introduced him to the crunching thighs of the Maiden to make Kyd reveal the source of the seditious papers found in his lodging. Burghley received an indicting note this morning from that same Richard accusing you of treason and atheism and said a witness to this truth will emerge when called into question. Tell me, Kit, where were you the night before?"

Kit felt his thoughts ripping open and the silly drunken words from the night at the Mermaid tumbled out. He clasped his forehead with both hands as if to keep his skull from cracking wide.

"Yea, I know of what you speak. Thomas returned to our flat yester morn, having given up the name fed to him by Richard Baines. They squeezed him until my name piddled out, so thus begins my march toward death."

Thomas' manservant approached, wringing his hands. "My Lord Walsingham, there are some men for you at the door."

Thomas looked up, his mouth full of crumbs. "Who is it, man? Bring them forth."

A chilled sensation crept up Kit's back as his destiny unfolded before him and the tiny hairs at his neckline stood as the Queen's guards entered the garden. Baines walked between the two red-coated men, his face glowing in victory.

"I am here to fetch thee, Christopher Marlowe, on the

demands of our Lord Archbishop, to be brought before the Star Chamber to answer questions on treason and sedition."

Kit's heartbeat quickened. "And who are you to bring me thus?"

Baines smiled. "I am new marshal to our Lord Archbishop and will bring you hence."

"Ah, so thou hast found the host. I am arrested then?"

Baines crooked his smile like a demon feasting upon a fallen soul.

"You are, and you are to follow me and present yourself tomorrow morning."

Kit's throat dried. "May I ask, on whose confession am I being questioned?"

Baines gloated. "O, shall I tell thee? The Star Chamber has the written word of Richard Cholmley, who confessed 'twas you who bent his ear toward atheism. And 'twas on the word of Thomas Kyd. He wept like a baby when Whitgift twisted the screw that tightened the iron jaws around his body. It did not take much to break him for his lily flesh tore easily under her teeth."

Kit bolted from the chair and rushed upon Baines with his fist pulled back. The guards charged and restrained Kit as he spat his words into Richard's face.

"'Twas easy for you to select a gentle soul like Kyd to bend under your kind of pressure! Tell me, Richard, when did you place the papers in Kyd's lodgings?"

Baines continued to smile. "Why, Master Marlowe, I do not understand what you mean."

Thomas walked near to Kit and whispered in his ear. "Go, Kit, and let justice prevail. These charges will die away, Burghley will see to it and the Queen has promised your protection."

Kit stormed out with the guards and as he mounted a horse, Baines stoked the fire. "And if you think to rely on the old man, Burghley will not save you this time, Marlowe, for I have it on good authority that the old man's gout has him bedridden. He will not be with the counsel, so you will be quite alone before the Archbishop. However, I am sure it may go well with you if you reveal the next name in this treason group. There is one the Archbishop is longing to hear."

Kit spat on the ground, splattering the spittle across Baines' silk shoe as he mounted his horse. "I will give nothing to you!"

Baines shrugged and spurred the horse. "'Tis no matter, for my purpose comes to fruition. Thou wilt see the block in either case."

Marlowe rode in silence in the gloating wake created as Baines squared his shoulders, lifted his chin and parted the crowds on the way back to London. Kit sensed the arrogant words swarming in Richard's mind. As they approached Westminster Hall, the seat of the Privy Council, Kit reined his horse close to Richard.

"Pray, tell me, have you conjured how you will bend you knee to the Queen as you present my head on a platter? What accolades do you expect? An estate, a knightship, or perhaps another gilded ring?"

Baines glared down on him. "I wish only justice done, and fellows such as you and your slanderous and atheistic views scourged from this land."

Marlowe's words seethed out between his clenched teeth. "Since when did you become so religiously and politically inclined? Since Whitgift let you suckle at his dug?"

Baines dismounted and pulled Marlowe from his saddle. The guards surrounded the two men and Baines let him go, crooking his mouth in a sadistic grin. "Guards, take this scum in before our Lord Archbishop."

The Star Chamber convened and all present except for Lord Burghley. Marlowe stood before them and noted the faces: Whitgift, Puckering, Buckhurst, and Lord Derby, all accounted for, dressed in their scarlet robes of State and seated on the dais before him. Marlowe found a smile as he noted how the performance resembled a play: the stage, the players, Baines lurking to the stage left as the author; and he, standing as a groundling in the pit. Marlowe raised his eyes, remembering the last time he beheld the star-pocked ceiling; then, just a boy, a boy full of ambition and fear and longing. *Not so different as a man,* he realized.

Whitgift began. "Sir, I shall read the charges before you and you will remain silent. We bring you hither before the Council of the Star Chamber for your blasphemous writings and traitorous sayings against our beloved England and our Queen. We have libels of yours, signed under the name of one of your characters, prompting violence in the streets of our fair city. Do you deny this?"

Marlowe brushed his stare to the ceiling and sighed. "Begging your pardon, Lord Archbishop, but if it is indeed signed by one of my characters, do you not know my characters are imaginary creatures created for the stage? How could such an airy one have signed so weighty a page?"

Whitgift leaned forward, his nostrils flaring. "Master Marlowe, we shall have none of your wit here. As the creator of the character Tamburlaine, then 'tis thine own signature. Dost thou still deny this?"

"Again, sir, anyone could have signed the name Tamburlaine, for 'tis easily written."

Lord Derby spoke up, his large jowls quivering with his words. "We see the game you play with us, sir, but we are not moved. You have yet to proclaim your innocence with proof."

Marlowe crossed his arms across his chest. "Proof? What proof do you have that I wrote anything or say the things this council accuses me of?"

Derby answered. "We have three witnesses to your seditious tongue and that is enough to put your head upon a pike. Richard Baines spelled out how he went to the home of Thomas Kyd, your lodging place, and discovered papers there of a most blasphemous nature." He held the papers up in the air before him. "Shall I read some statements? Here: *Moses was but a jugler and that one Heriot, being Sir Raleigh's man, can do more than he; that the first beginning of religion was only to keep men in awe and fear; that I, Christopher Marlowe, have a good right to coin as does the Queen of England,*" and another, "*all they that love not tobacco and boys are fools.*"

Kit's thoughts raged as he looked across at Baines. "Ha! Sir, these are lies! They are creations of the foul mind of Richard Baines!"

Whitgift interrupted. "Then, you say these comments never fell from your lips? And take care how you answer, Master Marlowe, for remember we have witnesses against you. Are you not fellows with a group called the School of Night?"

Marlowe held his tongue, breathing deep to cool the hotness in his face. "Sir, what will a man not say when pumped full of strong ale? 'Twas nonsense spoken among friends. The School of Night is nothing more than a platform for intellectual men to drink heavy and spout nothing. Surely, any man can relate to such an experience."

Whitgift's beady eyes squinted. "Nay, sir, not every man. We have witnesses against you, Marlowe. Baines gave us Thomas Kyd's name, whom we first accused as owner of the papers and we arrested; and he, in turn, confessed the papers belonged to his chamber mate, you, Christopher Marlowe. And another fellow, Richard Cholmley, has also confessed how thy private counsel persuaded him to atheism. How do you answer this?"

Kit looked across again to Baines, who gloated in the corner of the room. "A man will say anything suggested to him upon the fear of the rack."

Whitgift interjected. "Why would Thomas Kyd, who hath claimed to be thy friend, accuse this same friend of such things?"

"Again, sir, what things would you say if an ax hovered above your neck?"

Whitgift sat back in his chair. "So, then, thou hast no proof of thy innocence? No statement at all?"

Marlowe took a deep breath. "Only this: a pound of flesh do you seek and you will have it, for you give credence to a knave. I may as well go stand upon the beach and bid the main flood bate his usual height or question with the wolf why he hath made the ewe bleat for the lamb. I may as well do anything most hard as seek to soften that which hardens. I do beseech you, make no more accusations, use no further means, but with all brief and plain convenience, let me have judgment and the knave his will."

Whitgift's eyebrow rose into a hairy arch. "'Twould go easy with you if thou wilt confess the names of those in thy company who dost sway thy will."

Like the spark of candlelight, Marlowe sensed the meaty carcass for which Whitgift's scavenger eyes searched. Burghley said there was more to the matter between Baines and Whitgift, and at the heart of it was the next links in the chain to the Queen—Raleigh and Essex.

Marlowe answered. "Nay, Lord Archbishop, let it end here. There is not a soul that carouses the streets of London that hath not spoken something ill against these bloody times you wield. Shall you chop of the heads of every citizen of this country?"

The Archbishop slammed his hand on the table. "So be it, then! We shall see if thou wilt feel the same when thy judgment speaks. Christopher Marlowe, we hereby sentence thee for treason and sedition, and thus taken to Bridewell and...."

The doors to the council chamber pushed open and the familiar click of a cane across the stone floor silenced the Archbishop. Lord Burghley took his seat at the council table with a gleam in his eye as he peered across at Kit.

"Pray, tell me, Lord Archbishop, will you pass judgment without my input? I have the Queen's ear, and she distresses over this arrest. Are all in agreement to send this boy to the block?"

The council members exchanged glances and shrugs, and Burghley took the cue.

"Marry, it might suffice to let this pass with Master Marlowe being required to present himself before noon each day to this council till his demeanor softens to your request, Lord Archbishop. Perhaps with a merciful hand, you will find out the matter that you seek."

Whitgift growled in his throat as the council members all nodded in agreement. Burghley tapped the table with a gavel. "Then, let it be said, that you, Christopher Marlowe, in punishment for the supposed libelous letters and atheistic writings, must address the Privy Council each day at eleven o'clock in the morning until you supply the names of those in your company subverting loyalty to the State. If within ten days you do not supply a name, then Lord Whitgift will administer whatever means necessary to extract them. Do you understand?"

Kit bowed before the council, suppressing a smile and the urge to look at the defeated eyes of Richard Baines. Burghley finished, "We dismiss you, Marlowe. We will see you again upon the eleventh hour tomorrow. If you fail to attend, we will search you out and it will be the Tower for you."

Marlowe lowered his head and backed out of the Chamber. As the doors closed, Burghley's messenger approached and handed Kit a note. He opened the parchment and read:

'Christopher, you are to attend us at Nonsuch this evening. The trap springs and we must discuss how to play this.

E.I.R.'

By the late evening, Marlowe stood before the Queen and Lord Burghley in a private room at Nonsuch Palace. Elizabeth stood at the window, tapping her fingers on her chin.

"We wonder, Lord Burghley, that more men are not as you. Is it so little a thing that we made John Whitgift our Archbishop of Canterbury that now he seeks more power?"

Burghley grunted. "Your Majesty, his thirst for torture seems to outweigh any thought for his position. I fear he wishes to rout out those close to you so he may bend your ear toward his favor."

"So it seems," she acknowledged. "My father had the same problems to deal with in Wolsey. Wolsey saw himself as the power behind the throne, and then again, with Cranmer; but in the end, their ambitions were their undoing. It will be the same in this matter, but until then, what shall we do with you, Kit Marlowe?"

Kit sat in a chair near the Queen and he turned up his eyes to her in adoration. "Hide me away, my Lady."

Burghley spoke up. "A mere hiding will not do, for Baines and Whitgift will continue to seek you out. Just the other day, Whitgift pronounced a death sentence upon a man who sought clemency from me, a man whom you know and whom we spoke of before, John Penry. The same will be for you, Kit, if we do not maneuver this game."

Marlowe continued to stare at the Queen. "John Penry is to die? Dear Lady, can these proclaim guilt even if the one accused is innocent? Shall you let this fate come upon your favorite playwright?"

Elizabeth did not return his look. "This is not a simple matter, Christopher. We have given authority to the Star Chamber to administer punishment where it sees fit. Do you think we will do more for you when it was our own signature sending our kinswoman and anointed Queen to the block? These are games men play and they look for ways to point the finger at our throne. Who is it they seek? Raleigh? Essex? Perhaps even Burghley? Nay, we cannot save you, but we can delay. Time must pass and all these matters will unravel themselves. Perhaps we can undertake a banishment, which should quell the Archbishop's hunger and give us time to uncover his true ambition and plans."

A sharp pain seized Marlowe's heart. "You mean banishment in jest, my Lady?"

"Nay, not so, for if you stay in England, Baines will find you and continue to mold ways to capture you, thus giving your head to Whitgift."

Burghley nodded. "This is well, my Queen. Perhaps we will send him to your cousin, James Stuart, in Scotland."

The Queen pointed at Burghley. "See there, Christopher, how everyone around us waits for the days after we breathe our last breath? Even Burghley here finds the need to make plans. He is trying to winkle a way of persuading us to proclaim James as our heir, even now, in the midst of your dilemma. What do you say to this, Kit, shall you to Scotland go?"

Marlowe frowned. "Ha, banishment! Be merciful and say death, for exile has more terror in his look, much more than death. Do not say banishment for fear that word will follow me like a plague about my house."

Elizabeth finally looked into Kit's face. "Yet banishment easily reverses, my Kit, death does not."

Burghley's eyes gleamed with approval. "This is well, your Majesty. How shall we play this?"

Marlowe stood and turned his back to her. "Speaking of such, if I live my life in banishment, then what of my plays? Have I given my life to the protection of this throne only for you to throw me into exile and my plays cast aside? I told you before, my Lady, that I have plays upon plays waiting production upon your word. Shall all the blood I have spilled to keep my Lady safe, all be for nothing?"

Elizabeth walked to the window, musing upon the rising moon.

"Perhaps we can place someone as your proxy, a man who with a bit of coin to line his pocket will hold his tongue to this masque. Perhaps a small unknown actor even, who can come to London to perform a mighty act, stepping into your shoes as a master playwright. Only, the plays will be yours, sent hither to him by secret messenger. Poley would suffice in this matter, do you not agree, Lord Burghley?"

"Yea, your Majesty," he replied, "this would do well. Marlowe, have I not heard you speak of a clever actor you met once in Stratford during your mission upon Arden?"

Marlowe interrupted. "Yea, his name is Shakespeare, but no

one knows him to be a playwright. It will be as if by magic that he suddenly writes, and besides, if I am only exiled for a time, then continue to present my plays in my name and when the time comes, herald my way back into England. Even in this notion, my heart aches. I say again, death would have more of a pleasing air than to have this man handle my words."

Elizabeth turned to him. "Then death you shall have, for you are correct. If we announce your banishment, then Whitgift's mind will remain with you. We wish for him to turn his mind toward his true cause. I have determined, in short time, we shall have your death, and I will author your resurrection when this matter passes."

Burghley rose. "Death and resurrection, my Lady? What means you?"

Elizabeth smiled as Marlowe turned to hear the answer. "You are a playwright, Christopher. Write us a play about your death and we will set the actors in position. Perhaps give us a scene with witnesses to your death, yea, that will work nicely. And we shall use my own coroner, as well, and all paid and sworn upon their own heads before me that I will be the only one who will have the glory of the resurrection and revelation before John Whitgift."

Marlowe scratched his chin. "A play of my death? So after ten days, I shall meet my untimely end and this player from the banks of the Avon will usher my words into England masked in his name and form until my muse doth herald me back into the living flesh? This will mean if ever I step back onto England's soil in my own skin, Whitgift and Baines, or whoever else taken into their company, will send me to my true death."

"We like this well, my Lady," Burghley interrupted as he watched Kit's face turn pale. "Leave off the wrinkle on your brow, Kit, for it will not be long. Men such as Whitgift rush headlong into their destiny. Perhaps only a month or so, and it will give you the opportunity to explore Scotland and the continent as a holiday with plenty of time and money to develop your plays."

Elizabeth took Kit's hand. "We will have Lord Burghley arrange this masque, the players and the place. As for you, take one of my coaches to Warwickshire, fetch the man, Shakespeare, and bring him here to Nonsuch. We know enough about his kin, methinks, to seal his mouth shut on this matter, and I am sure with his pocket filled with gold, he will submit to anything. Go, have him here before tomorrow night and we will meet again in this room."

Marlowe's heart sank. "Do I have no other choice? Is there nothing other we can do?"

The Queen's eyes remained resolute.

Act Five

1593 –1594

XXIX

Dusk settled on Stratford and the glow of firelight warmed the night air, casting shadows across the cobblestones from the leaded windows. The smoke from the chimney tops drifted and melded into a hazy ghost fog, creeping into the night sky. Through the approaching darkness, a coach ambled down Henley Street, stopping twenty strides away from Shakespeare's door.

The coach door swung open and a dark figure pulled the cloak hood about his face. The horse stamped his hoof against the stones and blew out of his nostrils, his breath creating a blast of warmth circling in the cool night air. The stranger stroked the horse's mane with a gloved hand and steadied him, then turning and strode across the street to rap against the door frame of the quiet house. A moment passed, and he heard footfalls nearing the door. The door opened and a woman's face cut through the darkness. She looked older, more wrinkled, but recognizable to the stranger.

He spoke, keeping his face in the shadows. "Is this the house of William Shakespeare?"

The woman's nose wrinkled as she rubbed her wet hands in her apron. Like little doorsteps, her children gathered about her skirt. "And who wants to know at such an hour?"

The stranger chuckled and continued. "A friend, dear lady, 'tis all. I have a message for him from his fellow players." He pulled back the hood, just enough so she could see his face. "Do you know me, Mistress Shakespeare?"

Anne screwed her eyes and backed away, scurrying the children into the room. "Nay, I do not know any of William's actor friends, and do not wish to."

She closed the door, but he placed his hand on the latch.

"So, then, this is his home, and you must be his shrew wife,

Anne?"

Anne's lips twisted in a sardonic grin. "Ah, this is what you have heard of me? Well, 'tis no matter, for I will take it. It takes a shrew to live with an actor. What do you want of him?"

"Could you call him please, it is very urgent I speak to him."

She looked over her shoulder into the room. "He is busy. Come back in the morning."

"If I could, dear lady, I would not be here now. 'Tis at the Queen's command I stand here. See here, I have letters from her."

Anne's countenance fell and her eyes filled with fear. "The Queen? We have done nothing wrong.... we are good subjects to her..... faithful Protestants. What does she want with William?"

The flicker of candlelight cut through the darkness as William stepped into the doorway. "Sir, is there something I can help you with at this time of the night?"

The stranger motioned toward the garden. William pushed Anne aside and stepped into the night air. Again, the stranger pulled back his hood until his face lit up in the moonlight. Marlowe felt clever with his disguise: his hair trimmed close above his ears, wet and slicked back; his clean shaven face now thick with a bristly beard courtesy of an expert costumer in the Shoreditch hovels; and his voice, raspy.

"Do you know who I am?"

"Nay, should I," William answered as his eyes perused over Marlowe's face.

"Yea, you should, because from this day forth I will have a tremendous impact on your financial situation for the rest of your life. You see, William, I know everything about you. You are William Shakespeare, the son of an illiterate tradesman counseled before the Star Chamber because of his refusal to support our Queen's church. You married a woman nine years your senior, whom you now despise; and you have three children whom you struggle to support on a player's salary."

William squinted his suspicious eyes. "What do you want from me?"

"O, 'tis not I, you see. You have caught the attention of an illustrious muse. Our dear Queen begs a favor from you and she means to compensate you well."

"Please, sir, I beg your patience, but I do not understand."

Marlowe gazed up at the moon. "You rub shoulders, do you not, with a certain playwright named Christopher Marlowe?"

"Kit Marlowe? Yea, we are, as you would say, in the same circles."

Kit smirked. "In some of the same circles, but not all. Are you aware of the favor the Queen bestows upon him?"

William fidgeted and wrinkled his brow. "Well, sir, we are a humble folk. We hear rumors, but to know for certain, well I am afraid that I cannot claim."

"I am sure you know enough. As of late, Marlowe has made himself quite useful to the Queen, but a situation has appeared which needs your assistance."

"Mine, sir? But how could the Queen know of me?"

"Marlowe saw you perform once and spoke in great regard to the Queen of your acting skills; also, she needs someone quite unknown and, how shall I put this, well, someone devoted to our Queen's English Church." Marlowe paused and added a prod to the request. "Unlike your father."

Shakespeare rubbed his mouth with his fingers, his tongue suddenly dry and pasty. He knew of his father's secrets. Catholicism was lifeblood to those in Stratford before the Reformation, but now, he saw this man scanning for any signs of betrayal in his words. Like the apt actor whom Marlowe commended, he played his part to perfection. "Pardon me, sir, but I still do not understand."

"Your Queen requests your presence tomorrow evening at Nonsuch. Need I explain anything further? Your hesitancy reveals something... perhaps you are not as devoted to her as she thinks?"

William took a deep breath and lifted his chin to look straight into Marlowe's eyes. "Of course, I am, sir."

"Then pack your bags and kiss your wife and children, for a different muse seeks you now."

"You want me to go with you, now?"

"Yea, now, and we must not tarry. The Queen expects you at Nonsuch thus we must make the first Inn by midnight. Secrecy must be at the very core of this retreat from Stratford."

William looked back at the house and saw Anne's shadow hovering near the window at the back door. "Secrecy? Then, what do I tell her?"

Marlowe huffed. "Tell her naught of what I have divulged this far. Only this: Her Majesty commands of you a performance and she allays your absence with this." He held out a small velvet pouch and turned the contents over into William's opened palm, revealing a mound of gold coins. "From the latest harvest of Spanish treasure, and it will continue to flow to your dear wife, Anne, and the children, as long as you continue to please the Queen."

William gazed back at her shadow. "Will I see them again?"

Marlowe shrugged. "Who can say?"

William's thoughts licked like tongues of fire in his brain. His blood surged with the drama of the request. *The Queen wanted him? And now, he, William Shakespeare, would be the man? The one to whom this illustrious muse now winked her secret eye? And now, how could he, a simple actor, refuse his heart's desire? How could he refuse the passion of performing and conquering the heart of this most perfect Virgin of England?* Thoughts of Anne paled in the glow of Elizabeth.

"Begging your pardon, sir, but may I ask in what capacity the Queen requires my service?"

"An actor, Master Shakespeare… as an actor to perform a play at her command."

"Indeed? And what is the subject? Something of Marlowe's?"

Marlowe's eyes cut deep through the night air. "More matter with less art, Master Shakespeare. I am done with your questions. All questions answered in time. My Lady awaits." He waved his hand, and the coach rolled up near to them. "I will await you here only briefly. I would hate to return to Nonsuch without the Queen's newest favorite."

William's heart stirred again. The decision cleared.

Anne's mouth wrinkled with agitation as he stepped through the door and into the candlelight. Over her shoulder, the children already fast asleep, tucked beneath a blanket and near enough to the warm orange coals in the fireplace. His heart tugged, but not near the tug when he thought of this adventure. He said nothing as he gathered several breeches, two white shirts and doublets, and stuffed them into a wool sack. As he brushed the dust from his boots, Anne wrung her hands in her apron. William took her fingers and placed the velvet pouch into her hands, holding them for a brief moment.

"The Queen commissions a performance from me. I am for London tonight."

"Tonight, William, so late? Can she not wait for all of us to come tomorrow?"

He let the answer settle in his eyes. He squeezed the bag in her hands. "There will be more where this came from."

Anne's eyes turned cold. "Ah, so now I see your conscience, eh, William? This will always be the way of things for us, will it not? 'Tis always the stage before me."

He knew his eyes betrayed his thoughts. *How can it not be this way, Anne, when every ounce of blood running through my veins throbs for the stage? I contented to act when I could and be a husband when I should. Yea, my greatest performance to this date is this marriage.*

A small hand tugged on his doublet and he knelt down to look into his son's eyes. He ran his fingers through Hamnet's straw-colored hair and a lump formed in the back of his throat.

"Father, are you leaving?"

William took Hamnet's face in his hands and he caressed the boy's small pointed chin with his fingers. "I am, Hamnet. You must be the man of the house for a time. You know that I am an actor and I must go when called, just as before with the Chamberlain's Men. 'Twill not be for long, I promise."

Hamnet smiled, but William could see the paleness shadowing his son's cheeks. "You will write to me, father?"

He mussed the boy's hair and stood. "I will, Hamnet; I promise."

Anne enveloped Hamnet in her arms and waited at the door. William did not acknowledge her upturned cheek as she sought a kiss. The door of the house on Henley Street closed behind him and he stepped into the waiting carriage. Settling in across from this stranger to him, he closed his eyes and listened to the clop-clop of the horse hooves against the stones. When the sound changed to the soft grainy sound of dirt, he knew they passed Clopton Bridge and were on their way toward London. The darkness enveloped the carriage, but the words between him and the stranger burst like little blasts of enlightenment... in hushed spurts, yet heavy with meaning like a wool cloak on a wintry

English night.

About an hour into the ride, the stranger leaned forward. "So now, William, to the meat of the matter."

"Yea, sir, pray tell. Who is to author the play in which I am to perform?"

"You are, sir."

William chuckled. "Me? I am no fool, I can write well enough, but I am no playwright."

The stranger's face came into view, cutting the darkness beneath a stray moonbeam like an ancient ghost bearing dire news. "Ah, but you are a worthy actor, sir. All men can pretend to write, as I have seen in recent days, and the pretense can have profound effects. You will suit her well enough. She indeed wants an actor, and the play will be the stuff of legends for history to come. You shall be the lead actor."

William's mind swirled with accolades, imagining the groundlings cheering and swooning. "Legendary, you say? Is it something of Marlowe's, then? Has he written something new and I am to perform it?"

Marlowe sat back, his face disappearing into the darkness. "O, yea, 'tis something touching Master Marlowe, but patience, my dear Shakespeare, patience, and all will reveal."

The carriage cut through the night, the horses galloping at a heart-pounding pace. William could not sleep. His mind swirled with excitement and the adventure of not waking up another day in Stratford. The rocking of the carriage lulled his secret companion into a deep sleep, thus William took a moment to discern the man's features in the passing glow of the moon.

He looked about the same age as himself, twenty-nine, to be exact. He bore the same brown hair with no traces of gray, clipped close to the head. William peeked through the opening of his cloak which revealed the deep rich colors of a burgundy doublet with gold buttons and black velvet slashes. He looked down at his own dingy brown one and fingered a tear at the pocket. His eyes went back to the man, taking note of the fine buckled shoe and stockings; then lastly, to his ungloved hand resting upon his thigh.

The man's fingernails clean and his hands, white. A signet ring on his left forefinger faced downward toward his palm to conceal the seal. William leaned forward in the darkness and squinted, noting a birthmark branded on the top joint of the man's forefinger. He adjusted his eyes once again until the mark cleared to reveal the definitive stain of ink.

The horses whinnied and snorted as the groom slowed the carriage. William peered out the window and the yellow glow of firelight through the inn windows appeared. The sign above the door squeaked in a gentle breeze: the Black Boy Inn.

William reached across and nudged the sleeping man. "Sir, we have reached Banbury. Should we stop for the night?"

The stranger roused and pulled his cloak tight around his shoulders. He rubbed his eyes and glanced toward the inn. "Yes, this will serve us well. We should be able to make London by late today."

They ambled down the cobblestones, past the hedge wall and through the front door where the innkeeper held a rush torch to greet them.

"A room for ye mates?"

Marlowe motioned to William. "A room for him and a bowl of stew for us each."

The innkeeper lifted the torch into a holder affixed to a timbered post, the smoke creating a gray haze along the plastered ceiling. William followed the stranger's lead and sat at a nearby table. The stranger slid a gold coin to the edge of the table, to which the innkeeper snatched the prize up and bit the edge between his brown teeth. He smiled and bowed.

"Very good, sir, and will there be anything else? The room is up the stairs and to thy left."

The stranger shook his head and waved him away. "Nothing else. Leave us be."

William took up his ale and steadied his stare across the lip of the tankard as he drank. The man remained silent, so William prodded.

"Will you not tell me who you are, sir?" The man sipped on his ale, with no motion to answer him. "Are you a poet, sir?"

The question prompted a cough from the stranger. "Why do you think I am a poet?"

William pointed to the ink stain on the stranger's finger and Marlowe laughed. "An ink stain does not mean I am a poet any more than catching one fish makes one a fishmonger. All you need to know is I am a pawn sent hither to collect you."

Silence prevailed once more and William fidgeted. "Sir, begging you pardon, but did I not hear you say that 'twas Kit Marlowe who recommended me to our Queen?"

The stranger downed his ale, held his chest and burped into the air.

"Yea, he did."

"Pray, tell, when did he see me? Do you know?"

The stranger leaned forward. "I do know and will tell you after you tell me a story."

"What should I tell you?"

"O, anything but to the purpose, Master Shakespeare. Why do you not tell me how you came to be an actor when your family is so low-born?"

William smiled. "How, indeed? Well, there are children who kneel before their fathers and say, 'I will be ruled by thee' and truly mean what they say with their hearts, and there are those who learn to kneel and say as if playing in a game. I am the latter, thus acting became rote to me."

The stranger snickered. "Not unlike those who attend church."

"Yea," William agreed. "You see, from an early age, I learned to act from my own father. He is a poor man with his sights set on lofty things; the first, of which, was my mother, Mary Arden. My father said to me that on my birth night he pulled back the arras from the window and held me up to the moonlight. He announced to the world that I would be the one to ascend to glory and bring back England from its wonted way."

The man leaned his cheek upon his hand. "I recall a familiar scene in which my own father saw the pulpit in my future, swearing to the sky that my sermons would reign over England. Do you suppose all fathers believe such of their sons?"

William thought about Hamnet. "I do not know, but I suppose sons hold the future their fathers wished to have. They hold the legacy, but, as for me, I never wished to go down the path my father wanted."

The stranger laughed, again. "Pray, tell me, when first you noticed the hypocrisy of your father?"

William scratched his chin as his mind brushed back through

the memories. "I believe I was eight or so, maybe even younger. My life filled with watching this man play a game of compromising and ascending. Each time he compromised his convictions, he gained another position; yet all of us knew well what he truly believed. He was intent on teaching me things not taught at the Big School. He took me to his worktable one day and sat me in front of him. To this day, I can smell the pungency of well-oiled leather and it brings the day to mind. I do not know why I recall this to you now."

Still a stranger to William, Marlowe's face eased to a calm understanding stare, remembering how easily persuasion moved William into trust and words, and recalling the days Walsingham taught him a procurer's ways.

"Go on, William, for I have many things to share, as well. What is ale for than to relax a man to loosen his mouth? Besides, you do not know me now, but when I speak of our similarities, you will see that I am a friend and our lives are mirror images."

A prick of hesitancy swirled in his stomach as he saw the flicker of something in the stranger's eyes. He paused for a moment and Marlowe took the cue and prodded more. "I promise, William, your words will be tenable in my silence. I have served the Queen for many years and hold a secret I will share with you first to show my good will. You have a trusting face, Master Shakespeare, and perhaps you will hold my secret, as well?"

William breathed deep. "Of course, sir; of course."

Marlowe lowered his gaze. "Then, here it is. I am bound in servitude to the Queen for all the indiscretions of my own family and their connections to the attempts to put Mary of Scots on the throne. Even now, after all the years from her execution, I fear they are still plotting; and I, out of fear for their lives, remain here to secure favor from Elizabeth's hand to keep them from her notice. I often wonder about my slave life if not death would be easier."

William sighed. "Ah, good sir, I thank you for your candor and you are correct, we appear to be mirror images. I wonder about my own family. Tell me, do you remember Edmund Campion?"

Marlowe leaned back in his chair. "Indeed. There are not many in Warwickshire or in England who have not heard of this famous Jesuit. He plucked strings among the countryside who still favored the old church."

"Yea, you are correct. Marry, my father was among those who heard him. As we sat at the worktable that day, long ago, he reached within his shirt and revealed a small parchment. The lettering bold and handwritten by a skilled hand, definitely not by my father's hand, but it revealed my father's mind. I can remember feeling anxious as I read, but still as the actor that I am, I let my father speak on it. He asked me if I knew the writing."

"And did you know?"

"I did, indeed. 'Twas a testament. I knew these words were not my father's words, but they were Campion's ravings. He met the man at my kinsman's home, Edward Arden. I told him to destroy the papers, but he stood and asked me if I would have him denounce his very soul, to which I declared that I would have him live. He extended his hand and said he would have his son beside him. He asked me to take his hand. It all seemed like such a game, a play with so many characters vying for center stage, all puffing their own soliloquies; and yet, each no greater than the other. It sorrowed me, but I knew I must play my part. I asked him if I did not take his hand would I still have his approval..."

Kit looked away, his face shadowed in the darkness of the night. He interrupted William's story. "And he told you no, that you would not have his approval."

William eyes widened in surprise. "Yea, that is exactly what he said. I told him it was done then, that he never had known me, but one day all would know my mind. And if there be a God, he alone would judge me soundly. Silence is the key. Someone may assume you compromise if you are silent, and yet, you may not have done so at all. If I am useful to the Crown and silent, then no one will take notice I have not sworn; and because I am useful, they do not care."

Marlowe huffed and shook his head, astonished at the ease of Shakespeare's pliable nature. "You need to be careful with that kind of thinking. Usefulness has a limit. Take what happened to Sir Thomas More, not so long ago. He thought silence was the key, yet it did not keep his head from the block."

William smiled. "Yea, but he was not an actor; he was a religious man, was he not?"

Marlowe chuckled. "Yea, indeed, outward religion is a precarious nature. You know, William, all the world is a stage and

all the men and women merely players. They all have their exits
and entrances, and one man in his time plays many parts. I think
you will indeed be most useful to the Crown."

William prodded. "How, sir, can you tell me now?"

"Too many questions, William, and too little night left. I will
be faithful, for now I am tired. Revelations require a rested mind,
so get to your bed. We will have the journey for the rest of the
words."

With that, Marlowe stood and disappeared through the front
door and into the night air. William brushed the stray tendrils of
his hair away from his eyes and rubbed his brow. *How can I
possibly sleep?*

William sat upon the bed and stared out the leaded panes of
the window. A delicate rain drizzled against the glass like music to
his ears. He thought of the days of sitting in Schoolmaster Hunt's
room listening to the rain as little raps tapped out a tune while the
words of Hunt faded away under the wet song. The rain always
mimicked William's dreary mood, that is, until the players came to
town. Book learning and words were not among his favorite things
unless they were words on the stage.

A play held his attention like nothing else. As the days passed
within the beam and plastered walls of the King's School in
Stratford, he learned to be a consummate player. His teachers did
not see beyond his mask, being only happy that he was always
tidy, in attendance, and polite; but knowing he would never excel.
Latin and Greek flowed choppily across his lips, yet to an
undiscerning ear and unstudied eye, no one was the wiser; and no
one seemed to care.

William took this to heart each evening as he laid his head
upon his pillow. Something stirred inside him like an untouched
love. His quiet secret, a secret he dare not tell his father, for he
always enraged over this fancy idle dreaming of costumes and
painted faces, of pretend swordplay, and false speeches. The stage
was the world where William could speak as he never had at home.
He bent to the urging of Melopmene and Thalia as they laughed
and danced and hid their faces with the masks of tragedy and
comedy. The two beautiful sisters nudged him like a nagging voice
since the day he dreamed of them in Arden's forest when they
promised a reward to him. And now, the fruit of that promise

seemed almost in reach.

Marlowe recommended him and his chest swelled with pride. Somewhere Marlowe saw him perform, perhaps when he was in London before and he saw a gifted actor with the extraordinary ability to take flat black words from a beige parchment page and lift them into life in all the color and imagery befitting them. He could take the word 'baker' and have the audience smelling scones and meat pies before Act Two, or he could take the word 'fire' and the groundlings would have sweat upon their brows. The stage was his love and there he would play his part, not becoming a shadow of a man in a glover's shop. This was his ambition, and he would see it through.

&OCR

The morning rain came and washed away the dark hue of night. A spring bluebird perched on an elm branch outside the window greeted William's eyes. *'Twas a good sign,* William thought. He buttoned his doublet, pulled on his boots and hurried down to the public room. William hailed the innkeeper, to which the man brought a plate of hard dark rye bread and cheese. The innkeeper wrapped the food in burlap and motioned toward the door.

"Your strange friend slept in the carriage last night. He bade me to give you this for your travel and said to tell you to come quick for thy lady awaits."

William opened the door and plopped down onto the leather seat across from the stranger, his mood as giddy as the day. The stranger curled toward the corner, wrapped his cloak tight and bound the hood around his face. He tapped his knuckles on the ceiling and the coach jolted to a start.

William unfolded the food and tore off a chunk of the bread with his teeth. He found his voice along with the chewing.

"I barely slept the rest of the night for the excitement. Did you sleep, sir?"

"Sleep? I cannot remember the last time I truly slept."

William continued his happy stare. "Indeed, I can imagine a servant to the Crown has many nights of unrest."

Marlowe smirked. "You are in a merry mood. Do you think this journey will lead to your happiness?"

William stretched his smile wider. "Marry, yea, I do, indeed."

Marlowe turned to William, settling his back against the side of the carriage and stretching his legs out across the seat. He watched William from beneath the shadow of the hood, noting the sparkle of adventure in his hazel eyes and the way his lips turned up at the corners as he ate.

"Pray, tell me, William, what would a man do to save his life? What would you do? Would you continue to compromise as you spoke so forcefully about last night? To sell yourself, to give up something dear to spare your bones? Perhaps to save someone you love?"

William snapped his middle finger and thumb together. "In a snap, sir."

Kit looked out of the window. "Then our Queen has found the correct man. Now, then, I shall tell you about this quest."

William wrapped up the remainder of the bread and leaned forward toward this stranger to him, his eyes sparkling and anxious for the revelation. Marlowe breathed deep and began.

"'Tis true Marlowe hath seen you perform and again, 'tis true he recommended you to the Queen. Now, to answer your question of when. Do you remember the winter of 1583?"

A cloud passed across the sun, shadowing William's face in gray.

"Yea, I do, 'twas ten years ago and an ill time for all in my family."

"Indeed, 'twas a winter of discontent, not just among your family, but for the Queen. Warwickshire swarmed with unrest and at the core of it were rebels, one of whom you spoke of last night."

"Campion?"

"Yea, Campion, and Robert Persons, and John Somerville, who is a kinsman to you through your mother's family, the Ardens. Arden himself proved to be quite the staunch Catholic and a thorn in Robert Dudley's side. Elizabeth gave Dudley the commission to rout out Catholicism in Warwickshire and the surrounding counties of Kenilworth. He did so with full force, using at his disposal the craftiness of Burghley and the pawns of Walsingham. Do you know on what I speak?"

William's stare fell to the floorboards. "I do, sir. 'Twas whispered throughout the townships that Walsingham had his spies in every nook and cranny."

"Then you will know how the story unfolds. From the time the Queen visited Kenilworth, Arden brazed his hatred for her. He denounced Dudley, calling him an adulterer, refused to wear the Earl of Leicester's livery on the day of her visit. Dudley waited patiently, waiting for the right moment to spring to action... the moment when there would be no doubt in sending him to the block. And it happened in the winter of 1583, when Somerville railed against the Queen, running through the streets brandishing a pistol and calling her a heretic. He plotted to assassinate her. 'Twas as if the links in the chain melded together. Somerville linked to Francis Throgmorton, a suspect in a plot with the Queen of Scots against Elizabeth; in turn, Somerville's father-in-law was your relative, Edward Arden."

William fidgeted in his seat. "Seems you know quite a lot about my family, sir, as do I. But what does any of this have to do with me or the reason I am here with you?"

"I shall tell you. I can tell from the wrinkle on your brow that the day of your kinsman's arrest troubles you greatly. Tell me why."

William remained silent and Marlowe continued.

"Perhaps because 'twas you who revealed the last detail to one of Walsingham's spies, the last nail, so to speak?" Marlowe waited a moment more for a response from William, and then finished. "I will confess then to you my part." He held out his hand and lifted his forefinger before William's eyes. "I am a poet and playwright. You guessed correctly."

The stranger before William reached up and pulled the hood from his head, revealing a newly shaved chin and telling eyes. William choked upon the last of the bread in his jaw.

"You.... you.... Marlowe?"

Kit answered, "I am the very man."

William's cheeks flushed red. "Sir, I know not what to say.... 'tis an honor, sir, to acquaint with you."

"You may love the playwright, yet still you do not recognize me even without my disguise, do you? Walsingham was correct all those years ago, 'tis amazing the secrets one can learn behind the guise of a mask. Your suspicions have been correct, as well, all these years." Another pause, and then Marlowe plunged the dagger of truth as swiftly as when he killed. "Think back to that winter, Master Shakespeare. 'Twas I, sir. I was the spy who sat at the table with you the day of the performance at Burbage's tavern, the minstrel who ate a meal in your very home. And there is more.... do you remember the boy who played mills with you at the festival in Kenilworth all those years ago.... a boy named Harry Le Roy?"

Williams's words bubbled out across his astonished oval mouth, the heat rising in his neck as his suspicions from long ago sparked fresh from the embers.

"Yea, I remember. Even then you thought to deliver my kinsmen to the Queen." A dewy film collected in the corner of William's eye. "And to think I have now revealed all of those things to you last night about my father. To you, one of Walsingham's men, and now you take me to London to rack me and reveal my own father's treason. What a smooth liar you are."

Kit glared into William's face. He sat for a moment in silence and then turned the corner of his mouth upward in a grin. "Ah, sir, you need to look to yourself at how easily I ply you with words. You give up your heart and soul for flattery, not unlike your father, sir. I may have lied to you about who I am, but not about the reasons for taking you to London. And yet, you are caught, William, and the Queen will use you accordingly. Your free revelation has fixed your destiny, for if you reveal anything transpiring in the next few months, I will have your father's head."

William's lip trembled with hatred. "I do not understand, sir."

Kit leaned his head against the velvet curtains of the window and closed his eyes. "Patience, William, and ease the daggers you feel towards me. After this day, you will have your revenge, for your reward shall be at my expense. You shall be the greatest player of all times and seasons. You shall be the means to my end."

XXX

Marlowe and Shakespeare's carriage entered the Northwestern gate of London called Newgate and passed by Greyfriar's Inn. Marlowe peered out the window as the carriage passed through the streets of Cheapside, bumping along the cobblestones as it wove in and out of the crowds of the living, the dying and the dead. A group of children held hands and skipped in a circle, their tiny necks encircled with sewn pockets of flowers held with a string. Marlowe sang along in a whisper the tune filtering in through their passing coach.

"Ring around th' rosy, pocket full of posies... ashes, ashes... we all fall down."

Kit cut his stare to William as the driver turned right onto Gracechurch Street and ambled in between the towered walls of London Bridge. Marlowe pointed to the ramparts and chuckled, "No heads today."

Marlowe noted William's grimace, perhaps remembering when his cousin's head decorated the towers. Fifteen more miles and they entered the fortified gatehouse of Nonsuch Palace. William's eyes flashed wide at the spectacle cast in creamy stucco, the tall octagonal towers flanking each end of the massive structure and rising ten stories above the ground. Henry the Eighth's arrogant need to rival the great French palace of Chateau du Chambord.

"An excessive palace for an excessive King, do you not agree," William asked.

Marlowe tilted his head in agreement and curved his lip in a smile.

"Indeed, sir, and such a good character for a play. Perhaps I shall write of him one day, and perhaps you shall perform him. 'Tis truly amazing that such an excessive King led to such a change in our times and created such an amazing lady as our good Queen Bess."

"Am I to meet her this day," William questioned like an eager schoolboy.

"You are."

"And what shall I say... what shall I do... what..."

Marlowe leaned forward and captured William's worried stare. "William, you are an actor. Do what you do best; act."

The carriage halted and the tired horses stomped and blew. Shakespeare covered his eyes to the glaring sun as he stepped from the coach. Marlowe extended his hand to present him to Lord Burghley, who awaited them in the courtyard.

William bent forward at the waist as Burghley spoke.

"We have been awaiting you, Master Shakespeare. We have heard much of your prowess on the stage, yet the Queen confesses she does not remember you in your performances with the Queen's Men at her residence in Greenwich. Perhaps you can dissuade her doubts about you and show her the man to whom Marlowe has acclaimed."

Shakespeare kept his stare to the ground. "Sir, I will endeavor to do all our Lady wishes."

Marlowe nodded his head to Burghley. "Sir, will you see the player well bestowed? We have had a long journey."

Burghley motioned for Shakespeare to follow. "Come along, sir, and rest for a bit. The Queen is impatient to speak with you. We will have a dozen or so lines this evening from you, so prepare well for the Queen has an astute ear to whether or not a man is a good actor. As for you, Master Marlowe, do not forget your appointment with the Star Chamber this morning."

Shakespeare looked to Marlowe with a look of concern.

"Ease your mind, William. I will come within the hour to your chamber and give you the lines to say. Just remember, Her Majesty inclines well to eyes full of mystery and soft flattering words."

William stood in the anteroom of the Queen's private apartments, his heartbeat echoing deep in the recesses of his chest. He recited the lines Marlowe gave him, letting them roll on his tongue and whisper across his lips until they flowed natural and unrehearsed. He bowed, and bowed once more, practicing the depth, the pointing of the toe, the humble gestures of the arm, and filled his mind with confidence. The doors opened and Marlowe stood at the entrance.

"Are you ready?"

William took a deep breath. "I am, sir."

Marlowe sighed and stood to the side. "Then, let it all begin."

William entered the room, absorbing the surroundings into his memory: the flickering flames of each candle in each iron candelabra running the length of the long narrow room and the yellow glow casting shadows against the warm paneled walls. At the end of the room, below the blast of the purple canopy enveloping a massive velvet arm chair, sat an image in gold. Elizabeth bedecked in glimmering silk, with her delicate white hands resting with authority on the chair arms, and her white face haloed with angelic-like wings stretching out from her back with her eyes fixed on the actor before her.

William approached and bowed with his toe pointed perfect, with one arm across his stomach and the other outstretched to one side. Elizabeth laughed and the deep tones from her throat resonated in the chamber.

"'Tis a comical bow, I must say, Master Shakespeare."

He rose quick. "I am sorry if I offend your Majesty."

Elizabeth raised her hand for him to stand before her. "Nay, thou dost not offend, 'tis merely amusing. Now, before we lay aside laughter and take up the matter of our meeting, I would like to hear a few lines from you. Speak, sir."

Shakespeare closed his eyes for a moment, sinking into the depths of the character Marlowe conjured for him. In the deep wells of darkness, he brought forth tears, lifted his arm, pointed to Elizabeth's hands and began the lines.

"Speak, gentle lady, what stern ungentle hands hath lopp'd and hew'd and made thy body bare of her two branches, those sweet ornaments, whose circling shadows kings have sought to sleep in, and might not gain so great a happiness as have thy love? Why dost not speak to me? Alas, a crimson river of warm blood, like to a bubbling fountain stirr'd with wind, doth rise and fall between thy rosed lips, coming and going with thy honey breath …"

Elizabeth raised her hand to cease. "Stop! What is this, something new?"

Marlowe approached. "Yea, my Lady, 'tis something wild and full of tragedy. The stage will fill with blood."

Elizabeth glared at Marlowe, boring into him with a stern stare. "I will have none of thy politics, Marlowe. Why can you not write something merry for us?"

Kit frowned. "Shall I give the Queen my quill as well as my mind, so she may write it herself?"

Elizabeth stood, her face flushing red, as Burghley stepped toward Marlowe and Shakespeare reared back in amazement at Kit's bold words to the Queen.

"How dare you speak to me thus! 'Tis a favor that we keep you alive, sir, for the love shown to my throne and our protection, as well as the true gift we see in you. We would not silence the thing God hath given you, but for your saucy mouth we might prolong the agony you will feel for this masque we undertake. If we sense in your words that you are forgetting your benefactor, we will turn on you like the raging wind. Is this clear, Master Marlowe?"

Marlowe bowed, yet set his mouth in defiance. She turned her attention back to the actor. "Master Shakespeare, whereon does your own loyalty lie?"

William's dry tongue tumbled over his words. "Dear Lady... my Queen... with only you."

Marlowe flavored a huff with sarcasm as the Queen continued.

"Easily said as you stand before us, but not so easily done as portrayed by members of your own family. You know we lopped off your kinsman's head for disloyalty, and monthly we receive reports from Warwickshire of thy own father in the lists of those continuing to refuse to attend my Church of England. Pray, then, how shall we trust you?"

William bit his lip. "In truth, my Lady, I do not know what to say. My feelings for my family are like rainwater running over the surface of the ground, gushing forth but quickly dispersing. My feelings for the stage surge as deep as the regal waters of the Thames. Let me act, my Lady, for you. Grant me your favor as the greatest player of all times, and my loyalty will steel."

"Well said, Master Shakespeare, we like this manner well. Shall you swear to it?"

"I shall, my Lady, by the blessed moon."

Elizabeth pursed her lips. "O, swear not by the moon for she is inconsistent. She changes each month in her circled orb, so will thy loyalty prove likewise variable? Swear by something with meat in it."

"What shall I swear by?" William looked around the room until his eyes rested on Marlowe's slight smile.

"Swear by your father's neck," Marlowe answered.

William bowed. "So be it. I swear by my own father's neck."

Elizabeth tapped her fingers on the arm of her chair. "Very well, 'tis done. Pray, tell me, Shakespeare, has Marlowe told you all to what you now swear?"

William looked to her, then again to Marlowe. "My Lady, he told me I am to act in your favor."

The Queen tapped her fingers on the chair arm. "So, then, Marlowe has not told you about the play?"

"No, my Lady, he has not... does it matter, for I will most willingly act whatever character I am given."

The Queen smiled. "It may matter after you hear all, but it matters not now that you have forsworn. I will tell you, Master Shakespeare, to what you have lent yourself. Your service in this regard shall not only be for my amusement, but for service toward Marlowe. Recently, a knave named Richard Baines brought charges punishable by death to our darling playwright and provocateur."

Burghley interrupted. "Richard Baines has always had an agenda against Marlowe, and as the years have progressed, the agenda reveals itself. He is Marlowe's nemesis and seeks his end, preferably by death. He is a coward, for he does not with to sully his own hands, but wishes to bring this about through someone else. On more than one occasion have I saved Marlowe from the devises of this man."

Marlowe turned his back to their conference, and their voices trailed away as his stare drifted out the window and along the wind with a delicate dandelion seed. He watched the seed dip and soar, tumble high into the air, and then crash across the pebbles and crushed under the boot of the Warders making their daily circle around the grounds. He shuddered as Shakespeare's voice trickled back into his ears.

"Pray, then, my Lady, why not just have him arrested?"

Elizabeth answered. "'Tis a tangle, Master Shakespeare, for you see, this idiotic man has attached himself to our Archbishop of Canterbury, and, methinks, to our Lord Essex. The Archbishop sits on the Star Chamber and has authority, given by me, to root out anyone who speaks against the Crown or the Church of England. How would it look if I, the head of the State and Church, took measures against our own Star Chamber for a mere playwright? Thus, you see the dilemma, for we protect those loyal to us. Christopher is my darling and has done us a great service for the protection and amusement of our throne. These things we do not dismiss lightly, for loyal men are a precious commodity in these dangerous times."

William shrugged. "But, you know this man to be a liar?"

Burghley spoke. "Aye, we believe Baines has an agenda for the demise of Marlowe, but Archbishop Whitgift has one, as well. Two day ago, the Star Chamber arrested Marlowe and charged him with treason on the word of Baines, yet we feel this matter is deeper than just Marlowe and Baines. 'Tis a stepping stone, if you will, to a weightier cause. This cause will only reveal with time and patience and with the protection of Master Marlowe until these matters unravel. This is where we require your skills and why the Queen hath asked for your fealty under pain of death to your father."

The Queen lowered her eyes at William with an inquisitive glare. "Tell me, Master Shakespeare, will you enact a performance that will ultimately protect the man who gave up your kinsman to death?"

William lifted his chin. "In truth, my Lady, 'twas I who revealed Edward Arden. Even so, Walsingham suspected Arden's allegiance to the old Church for secrets bubbled forth in Warwickshire. 'Tis my passion to act, and if an act is what my Lady wishes, then I am here to grant all."

Elizabeth smiled. "Very good, then let us speak on this masque."

"A masque, my Lady? Of what nature," William asked.

"O, Master Shakespeare, 'tis of a nature delving into intrigue; one which will play out upon the platform of all England under the eyes of her people and directed by my hand. Simply, 'tis this: we will have you take lodging here in London and join yourself to a company of players and when the time comes, you will present a new poem or play written by your hand unto England."

Shakespeare's brow furrowed. "What, my Lady? Written by my hand? But, as you said, I am merely a player. Marlowe assured me 'twas not a play written by me that you wished."

"Quiet, Master Shakespeare, and you will hear all. Indeed, you are a player and we wish for you to enact the part of a playwright; in particular, the part of Christopher Marlowe. Now, to the crux of this play. This time tomorrow, before the midnight bells of Westminster peal across the night air, Kit Marlowe will enact a death scene, and you will step into his shoes. Of course, 'twill be an act, for you see, Marlowe is still of use to us, politically and artistically. Marlowe will leave the country for a time to pursue our political agenda and his artistic wares, but we have promised him payment for his good service and we will continue to patron his plays. We cannot do so in the sight of the Archbishop, for fear he will hunt Marlowe down and kill him. You will receive Marlowe's plays via messenger, pen them in your own hand and give them your name. See, 'tis a simple thing, with coin to fill your pockets and a step leading to greater things after the play is complete. Can you not hear the crowds, Shakespeare, when you bow before them? Hear the cheers and swoons for this great actor who fooled a nation and protected the greatest playwright of all time? When I reveal all, I daresay your name will mingle with Marlowe's for eternity for this mighty service you have given to your Queen."

The Queen stood and walked across to Marlowe. She touched her fingers to his chin and he looked to her. "My darling Marlowe, leave off these sad eyes. 'Twill not be for long, I promise. We leave you now for the two of you to talk and rehearse the next scene."

Marlowe slumped onto the pillows as Burghley and the Queen exited the room. His eyes caressed over the painting splashed across the ceiling. Kit drew William's stare as he pointed up toward the mythic images.

"Look, William, the painting is of Narcissus gazing at his reflection." William's eyes scanned the painting above them, following the scene as Kit continued. "William?"

"Yes?"

"Do you think there is providence in things such as this scene above us?"

"The painting?"

Kit's voice trembled upon seeming prophetic words. "Yea, the painting. See how he gazes upon his reflection, captured by it, forevermore to look upon his image, but never again to possess it. The image was not the man himself, and now as the world walks by the self-named flower, all they see is a flower. Is there anyone who stops to remember what became of the man?" William remained silent. "You remain silent and I wonder why?"

"You search for things not there, Marlowe. This is just a painting, and I am silent for I am just an actor. Give me the words to say and I will play this part."

Kit smiled, sensing the irony. "Play this part, you will, and if you are the stuff of legends, then the entire world will believe my words are yours." The sorrowful look in Narcissus' eyes held him for a moment more. "Still there is a pause about my heart and I suddenly fear to tread this path... William?"

"Yes?"

"When the time comes, will you promise to give back my words to support the Queen and my resurrection?"

William closed his eyes and jangled the coins in his pocket. "'Tis not your words I want, Marlowe. Our regal Lady says she will pay me well. When I die, I shall see the word Gentleman after my name. There are things in life, Christopher, of more worth than words can ever buy."

Kit mused on the thought. "My words and my name are the only valuable things I have ever possessed."

William plopped down on the throne chair and draped his leg over the arm. "'Tis very like a tragedy."

"What is," Kit asked.

"Your life, Marlowe. To trust a stranger with something valuable and to have faith that he will tender your treasure dearly, and then return it to you unscathed, is a faith I have not seen in this world."

Kit's voice echoed a breathy laugh. "Do you say this to shake me, Shakespeare? Trust and faith are not words inhabiting my speech, nor my life. Do I trust you? Nay, I do not. Do I have faith my Lady will be true to her word? I do not. I believe in my words only and the life and breath I give to them. They alone shall be my legacy and when returned to me, then shall I have my own glory. And they shall return to me, or my own hands will do the slicing… do you get my meaning?"

William narrowed his eyes at Kit, as Kit stood and placed a leather portfolio to his breast and, then, on the table next to William. Kit watched him as he untied the bindings. William's fingers ran across the first page, his lips mouthing the words placed there by Kit's quill.

"Venus and Adonis. What is this, Marlowe?"

"This shall be your first act, the firstborn of the heirs of this invention, and registered under your name. Learn the words well, William, and with each new act I give you, copy in your own hand, take them to a scribe, a good one like Thorpe in Bridewell, and have them registered. Wait two weeks after my false death, for I wish the poem registered on the Earl of Pembroke's birthday. Keep these safe in this portfolio, for these are my release and proof that these words are mine. Here, take this letter, as well, for you will need to seek a patron. I have written to the Earl of Southampton. He will serve you well after I am taking advantage of my idle hours with some graver labor."

"Southampton? But why not the Earl of Pembroke? I hear his family are great patrons of the arts."

Kit closed his eyes, his thoughts raffling through the images of Mary and his son. He knew Mary will recognize Venus' words as her own.

"Nay, he will not be your patron. He will know the writings are from me, but fear not, neither he nor his mother will reveal what they know. There are secrets lying beneath secrets the Countess and her son will take pains to keep hidden. You need not concern yourself with any of these matters, and I will say no more of that matter to you."

William turned the pages, his eyes drinking in the words. "You are hiding clues to your identity?"

Kit sighed. "Fear not, for 'tis a tangle, William, and shall be yours now. These are your words, and the world will ponder the message in relation to you only. Yea, my plays and sonnets will be a message, and those having eyes will see. Again, I tell you not to fear. Those in lofty heights will never descend to unravel the matter. Instead, everyone will think you brilliant to weave words not connecting to your life. The hidden clues will be a puzzle for years to come."

"You mean until the day our Queen reveals you are the true author."

"Yea, until that day." Kit extended his hand. "Take my hand, Shakespeare, as a gentleman's agreement. We shake this spear and the masque begins." Marlowe sensed no hesitancy in the pause between his words and the taking of his hand. "William, do you give up yourself so eagerly?"

William smiled. "Dost thou?"

As they shook hands, Kit cursed in silence as he felt his soul drain out of himself, down his arm and into this actor who transformed before him like a scrounger. He wanted to grab hold of the portfolio and run out of the doors.

William's words grounded him. "Kit? The Queen and Fortune binds us forevermore, you and I. Two men seeking the heights of ambition. 'Twas Fortune's hand led us to meet all those years ago as boys at Kenilworth."

A sharp pain sliced through Kit's heart and mistrust brushed his thoughts from the look upon William's face. His mind wrestled with the words: *Victory? Glory? Greed?*

As William exited through the paneled doors, Kit's legs weakened. When the latch clicked, he fell to his knees, his fingers tearing into his hair as his heart tore from his chest. He shrank down to the floor and his trembling sobs crushed and weighed down upon his face. He gave away the children birthed by his muse and knew not when he would see them again.

XXXI

The tenth day since the sentencing came and Kit wrung his
hands. Dusk rolled in dreary and heavy like the fog coming
off the Thames, a fog holding many secrets. Kit closed his eyes for
a moment as he leaned against the door frame of the house next to
Mistress Bull's home. Even as he rubbed his brow, he could not
erase the image of Shakespeare taking the portfolio in his hands
the night before in the anteroom at Nonsuch. He felt trapped within
the confines of this prison, leaving all trust to this man and to his
Queen. He edged closer and hid in an alleyway as William Danby
approached the back door.

"All is ready, Danby. The front door locked, the room upstairs
ready. I counted twice: four goblets, four chairs, and a heavy
wooden chest in the room with the wooden shutter on the window
bolted shut. Much counts on your discretion and your aptness as a
well-paid player. The lines are for you and the direction of the
play. Follow them well."

Kit sank back into the shadows of the alleyway to listen,
knowing well the stage direction and words afoot inside Mistress
Bull's dwelling.

Eleanor, sitting silent by the fireside, waits for the rap on her
door. A light tap echoes through the sparsely lit room. She opens
the door and Danby, the Queen's coroner, speaks. All following the
marks of the play.

"Mistress, he lay 'round the corner. We must need to take him
in for the plague cart will be 'round soon."

"How long has he been dead," she asks.

"Since two o'clock yesterday and the rigor takes hold. I will
hold off the inquest until tomorrow to give the muscles times to

slacken and the chilled air should keep him well. Has anyone been about this morn?"

She looked to her left and to her right. The dense fog hovered with nothing visible within a few feet. "Nay, not even a rat."

Marlowe smiled in his hiding place. He knew to whom she referred. Rumors stirred that Baines followed him, but as of now, his beady eyes were not piercing the mist.

"Stay here, Mistress, I will carry him," Danby said.

Marlowe watched from the shadows as Danby disappeared into the fog and returned withal cradling a dead body like a child in his arms. A crimson cloak shielded the mortised body, and the hood hid the face. Mistress Bull reopened the door and stood to the side to let him pass. As she did, the fog swirled and the death wagon halted in front of them. Danby leaned against the doorpost and lowered his head to shield his face.

The wagon keeper, Harry, smiled a gappy grin, his greedy hands pointing at the body in Danby's arms.

"Have you a body for me, sir?"

Eleanor walked between the plague bearer and Danby. "Get along, Harry, there is none here for you."

Harry's nostrils squeezed shut and he smelled the air. "I smell death and your friend looks quite stiff."

Eleanor took him by the arm and moved him into deeper fog. Her voice took on a whimsical tone. "Come along, Harry. My friend has had a bit of strong ale and is sleeping off the sting. Now, get along, I say, and let the poor gentleman bed his drunken head."

Harry scratched his gray-bearded chin. "Gentleman, you say?" He cut his eyes back at Danby and nudged Eleanor on the arm with his elbow. "There be a shadow about your house, Mistress." He smelt again and tapped his temple with his forefinger. "I know these things. I know death."

Eleanor pushed him on his way. The wheels of the wagon squealed under the weight of the bodies it bore. Danby raised his eyes to meet hers and the fear spoke clear. She patted him on the arm.

"Never fear, dear Danby, Harry is not one to worry on. His mind decays with plague and forgetfulness. I daresay he will not remember the sight within the next block or so."

"'Tis not he I worry on, 'tis Baines. His eyes are everywhere."

Eleanor pushed a puff of air between her lips. "Harry? Not bloody likely. He only relishes the death march he makes each day. I cannot think he would make a good spy for Richard Baines."

Danby shrugged his shoulders. "Very well, if you are certain. Now, let us get our most still Lord Faux-lowe to the chamber."

The room stilled in the morning air. Shadows formed in long fingers as the sunrise seeped through the cracks of the shutter. Danby tucked the body into the chest and looked about the room.

"Remember well your part, Eleanor. Only you are to receive the gentlemen into this room and lock the door behind you."

"Sir, one question I have that Lord Burghley did not answer for me. What shall I do if any other of my regular visitors stop for my scones or for a room? What shall I do? Turn them away? Would that not cause suspicion?"

Danby rubbed his chin and contemplated. "Feign plague sickness or whatever, anything to keep Baines from learning aught." He took her hand and kissed the top of her fingers. "Adieu, my lady, it has begun."

Danby left through the back door, pausing once to lift his eyes and nod to Marlowe. Marlowe pulled his cloak hood about his head and walked to the adjacent doorway. He turned and saw Mistress Bull through her window, seated again at the fireplace. She took up a basket and a sock to darn. Marlowe kept his vigil and station, using his spy tactics and patience to watch the faces in the crowd. The morning fog lifted and the sounds of the city grew.

Six o'clock: the soft padded feet of the torchbearer and the glow of the night's torches snuffed out.

Seven o'clock: the wagon wheels thundered toward the marketplace. James, the fishmonger from the nearby pier, takes a load of fish from the early morning's catch and lays them side by side; John, the baker, passes along the street and the smells of loaves and scones fill the air as he pushes his cart along the lane; and then, Priscilla, a widow, finds a cozy spot in a corner and opens her basket filled with beeswax candles and wooden candleholders to sell. Marlowe stops John and gives him a penny for a scone.

Eight o'clock: the city stirs with conversation, laughter, dogs barking, children playing and the continuous pounding of horse hooves and carts across the cobblestones. The roadway outside

Eleanor's house saw continual use, being easy access to the waterway, the waterway being easy access to the world, thus Mistress Bull's ale quenched many a thirsty stranger and her rooms lent to many a weary friend. Many times she lent her fireside tables for Marlowe and his mates to take a bite of Shepherd's pie, a drink of ale and a gamble with a deck of cards.

Nine o'clock and his innards churned. He held out his hands in front of him and noticed the tremble. He closed his eyes and breathed deep, remembering well the hours he spent waiting and watching for the devils of Rheims to reveal themselves. As he released the anxious air and opened his eyes, Robin Poley stood at the back door biting his thumb, a sign that all was well and proceeding as planned. Marlowe joined him and Robin rapped on the door. Eleanor opened the door and Poley spoke his lines, loud enough for any ears to hear.

"Lo ho, Mistress, have a room for us?"

She turned with a smile to greet Poley and Marlowe, cutting her eyes to two young boys sipping on ale at a front table. She whispered to Marlowe.

"Watch them, sir. They claim to be players seeking you, but I think it odd they think to find you here. Could be pawns of the rat."

Marlowe set his eyes on the two boys as he strode across the room within a short distance from their table.

"Actors, are you," he asked. The boys nodded, and he continued.

"What are your names?"

The taller spoke for them. "I am Henry, and this is Robert, sir. John Baker said we might find you here. We want to play your Faustus, sir. I have practiced the demon's part many times, and we wished to seek you out."

Marlowe huffed a laugh. "Ah, you are too young to think you could portray such evil, but give it time." He turned and shook his head toward Poley. "Give it time, right, Poley? Live in this godforsaken Londinium long enough and you inevitably will learn how to play the part."

Poley gave him a hearty belly laugh, nodding in agreement.

"Well spoke, Kit, and no truer words could ever be uttered. Now to my lady. Mistress, say you have a room for us? I met Kit in the byway on my way to the port. I am to board in the morning for the Daneland and thought to take the evening here."

Eleanor curtsied and reached into her pocket for the key. "I do, my Lord, this way up the stairs."

Poley motioned to the boys who kept their eyes upon every movement of Marlowe. "You two, there, come help me with my carton, else a knave will tote it away."

The boys followed him to his carriage and lifted a heavy wooden chest from the berth, followed him up the stairs and laid the trunk within an arm's reach of the door. Eleanor scurried them back down the stairs to their table. She cut her stare and glared at their glowing faces. Marlowe and Poley entered the staged room, dragging the chest behind them.

Marlowe cracked open the door to watch the scene, speaking the next act to Poley. "A few minutes more and Frizer and Skeres will arrive. The two boys in the main room, they are not part of this play, but we may use them for our own purpose. Listen, Eleanor's lines are next."

She yelled up the stairs. "I will have none of your tomfoolery, Kit Marlowe. The first sign of a fray and you will be out on your arse."

The boys giggled like entranced scullery maids, nudging each other with their elbows. Eleanor turned her attention back to them.

"And I will have none from you, either! Drink up your ale and be on your way."

Five minutes passed and two raps came, one at the front door and one at the back. At the front, Ingram Frizer; and at the back, Nicholas Skeres. Frizer removed his hat and extended his hand to Skeres.

"Well now, Nicholas, how are you for an afternoon of card playing? Shall we join the others and wrestle for the reckoning?" Frizer smiled and Eleanor motioned for them to go up stairs, but first, darting in front of them to block their passage.

"Pray, my Lords, my house is a gentle house. Let Marlowe not cause a disturbance here, for he is known for his raucous card playing."

Skeres placed a hand on her shoulder. "Patience, dear lady, and let us pass. I meant only that we would play for the bill. Surely you would not deny us a pleasant game of cards among friends and for us to pay for enough ale and food to line your own pockets."

Marlowe heard the lines flow easy with the two boys as witnesses, yet Eleanor hesitated. The moment she stepped away, all the planning, the scheming, and a secret all swore to take to their grave would pass. Everyone gave their oath, sworn to Elizabeth the First, and upon their own hidden secrets, not to reveal anything transpiring before or after this day; swearing to the only person who would ever have the glory of the revelation and the only one who set the play in motion, Marlowe's enthroned muse.

Kit saw the hesitation and cleared his throat. Time was of the essence. The ship which was to carry away Poley and his "precious" cargo, sat in the harbor preparing to embark in the evening and the Star Chamber would already be astir about Marlowe's irresponsible absence this morning. Eleanor stepped aside, following the men from behind, and she opened and shut the door with the solitary key.

As the door shut, all moved into motion. Time ticked by as the sun made a quiet sojourn across the English sky, sometimes bright, sometimes hidden behind a drenching cloud, and soldiering on toward the final act. The four men exchanged glances and busied themselves. They talked of nothing and yet, everything: of London, of the Queen, of her suitors, her favorites, her heirs, and yet, in all the words, what lay ahead of them burned like cinders in their brain. No one said a word of what was to come.

Hours passed as the four of them supped on hearty mutton and roasted leeks. Dark ale and brandy wine flowed down their throats as slick as the words sliding up, and they slept and walked, with each taking a turn on the terrace. Lastly, after the last scattering of betted coins disappeared from the table after an afternoon of card playing and Whist, the moon shined her silvery head over the dead body they removed and positioned like a rag-a-muffin on the bed near the window. Poley lifted the arm and dropped it, making sure the mortised muscles slackened after a day and a half from the man's death.

Poley spoke first. "Well, lads, shall we drink over this body?"

Skeres and Frizer took their goblets, yet Marlowe faltered as he stared at the corpse. "Who is this?"

Poley answered. "Danby said 'tis someone named Penry, John Penry, methinks. Some Puritan who caught the wrath and the rope of Whitgift. Burghley saw to it that the man fitted this play, for even his family did not know of the death."

Marlowe shook his head and leaned close as if to whisper in the dead man's ear. "So, dear Penry, I did not know 'twas prophecy I spoke to you so long ago, that if we exchanged cloaks, you could pass as me. Those long forgotten days when we were nothing more than boys with eyes full of the future. Now, in your death, you will save me? Indeed, I knew this man from Cambridge. He used to dote upon my writings and now see how still he sleeps. How death falls across him like hoarfrost; how he patiently awaits to bid my soul to the grave. There is something in this that remembrances shall spring forth in words."

Poley laid his hand on Kit's shoulder. "Do not fret upon this, Kit. He is but a shadow, a resurrection, if you will, to more glory. He is your stepping stone from here to there."

Frizer pointed at his face. "Yet, did you notice, 'tis not a well likeness of Kit, even his neck bears the marks of hanging. How will we perform this, even with Danby's help?"

Skeres knelt and put his hands about the man's throat. "See here, very much like the markings of strangling. One of us will have to confess we strangled Marlowe in self-defense."

Kit felt the irony. "Hands about my throat to silence my words; yet, we must add something more. Have you never heard that death's a great disguiser and you may add to it?"

A gloom settled in his stomach. Marlowe removed his doublet, breeches and boots and traded with the dead man. He pulled the dagger from the sheath at his belt and added to Penry's face with a gash and opening at his eye.

"Now, our stature the same, our hair the same, his clothes are now mine… now look to the brawl."

He turned to face Robert Poley, Ingram Frizer and Nicholas Skeres. "It is here I turn direction to the three of you, my fellow provocateurs. I owe you my life, and because of your silence, my words will continue to flow. Our Queen binds us all, for inasmuch as any words reveal the secrets of this prison house, we are all bound to the block. She will have our heads, know you this?" They all shook hands in agreement. "For the greedy hand of my muse will continue to seek my words. My life has been a succession of buying and selling, and all for advancing my art and ambition. One would think it should come easily now, but alas, it does not. Let us have at it, boys."

Marlowe yelled out and overturned the table, the cards and coins scattered to the floor. The four men wrestled and stomped, tossing bedclothes and spilling beer. Marlowe punched Frizer square in the nose. Frizer stood over the corpse of Penry, letting the fresh blood flow fall upon his face, his doublet and the floor.

Ingram took Marlowe's dagger, smearing it with his own blood and dropped it on the floor. The four men looked about the room. Kit hid behind the door as the final act completed and he waited for the next entrance as Eleanor's lines came next.

The moment she heard the chairs crack and the silence following, she hurried herself up the stairs. "I told Kit Marlowe not to cause a stir in my house. Sit you down as you have done all day, you boys, and I do not need you getting into the mix."

Mistress Bull played her part to perfection. The door opened and there on the bed, the bloodied body. She wavered and grew pale, fanning herself with her hand and a perfectly acted deep moan rose from her throat. She staggered back down the stairs, grabbing hold of the boy Henry's shirtsleeve.

"God ha' mercy! He... he... it cannot be..."

Henry looked to the door, just as Poley himself stumbled from the room. They caught each other's look. "Come here, you boys. Come at once!"

Henry helped Eleanor to sit, and they moved toward the upstairs scene. Poley stood to the side to give the boys a view. Robert grabbed Henry's arm, the uneasiness of a dark dream creeping upon him. The boy's round and bulging eyes twitched upon the unimaginable words.

Poley grabbed Henry's arm and handed him a message. "You two, go at once to this address. 'Tis the kinsman to Marlowe and there you will find Lord Danby, the Queen's coroner, taking dinner there. Go quickly and tell no one of this sight. The Queen must know of this first, do you understand?"

Robert found the words in the trembling of his throat. "This is.... Marlowe?"

Poley lowered his eyes, enacting defeat. "We have apprehended the assaulter and have him bound. 'Twas a fatal blow, I fear, and all for the foolishness of the reckoning."

Henry turned and looked at Robert, his countenance full of sorrow.

"The world has lost him, Robert. Marlowe is no more."

Poley took them hard by the arms and led them down the stairs and to the front door. "Get you to the Queen's coroner. The Queen is within the verge of this murder of her favorite, and she must hear of it first. She must not receive this news second hand. Go quick, do not dally."

Marlowe came out from his hiding place and ran to the terrace. He peered over the edge at the two boys. Henry fled to the coroner, yet Robert paused for a moment and headed in the opposite direction. Marlowe turned to his mates.

"Our fear speaks true, methinks. The younger boy is dashing to report this to Richard Baines. We must hurry."

Eleanor went to the window, opening the shutters to keep a look out for Danby. Marlowe walked to the large wooden chest and opened it, looking into the hollow as into a coffin.

"Here shall Marlowe die. When this lid closes, then Marlowe is no more. I will arise across the ocean in another suit and another face. My name buried where my body is and live no more to shame nor me nor you."

Skeres extended his hand and helped him step into the chest. "'Tis only brief silence, Kit. You will, like the phoenix, rise out of these ashes. When you do, we will all report you and your cause aright to the unsatisfied."

Marlowe looked at Nicholas. "You would do well to tell your master Lord Essex to watch Whitgift and his own neediness of the Queen's favor. Raleigh has already found his way back to the seas, away from those watchful eyes, and see what it now has done for me?"

Poley sighed and placed a hand on his shoulder once more. "Kit, there is something you should know. You know that I have my ear upon the whispers of London since we were both boys. 'Twas just before my coming to Deptford that I paused for ale at the Mermaid and saw Baines skulking in the corner of the tavern, seeming in a celebratory mood. He bought a round of drinks for the lot, so I moved closer to him, hiding myself in the shadows. 'Twas not long before his loose drunken mouth spilled out the reason for his humor. I heard him say to some nobody, without speaking your name, that he revealed several names and aliases to a group of Rome's henchmen, and that by morning, if the Star Chamber did not have the one knave he sought, then Rome would."

Marlowe wavered on his legs. "Is this true? Then my name is spreading like fire among those assassins. And the same for all of you, you all must scatter. I will never feel safe, even after the Queen's revelation, to show my true face in England again. O, this is a tragedy!"

Eleanor went to his side and caressed his arm. "Nay, 'tis but wild and whirling words you feel, just fancy is all. We will all stand with you when your Lady reveals all. Her word doth assure your safe return and protection from Rome."

Frizer, still holding a bloody rag at his nose, interjected and held out his hand. "Here's assurance, Kit, and we all anxiously await your being settled. 'Tis but a brief time for Baines will come to his end and your words will continue to make their way across waters and onto the stage."

Marlowe gazed once out the window, seeming to drink in the last rays of evening moonlight as the moon slid behind a storm cloud. "I will rise like the phoenix, but still, I feel ill about my heart."

Calliope formed in his mind and whispered familiar words for the second time in his life: *If your mind dislike anything, obey it.*

He looked down into the darkness of the chest. "One would think there is special providence in the darkness beneath my feet., so like the fall of a sparrow."

Poley beseeched him. "Forgive me, Marlowe, but we must to the ship without delay."

Kit lowered himself into the chest and Poley closed the lid over him. Poley and Skeres carried the cargo to the back door and called for a wagon. Poley's man came and loaded the chest. Within the hour, Marlowe emerged on the ship as a new man and a new alias: Monsieur Le Doux, a Frenchman bound for Scotland and the continent.

Act Six

1616

"The earth can have but earth, which is his due;

My spirit is thine, the better part of me:

So then thou hast but lost the dregs of life,

The prey of worms, my body being dead,

The coward conquest of a wretch's knife,

Too base of thee to be remembered."

Sonnet LXXIV

XXXII

William Shakespeare lifted his pewter tankard in the air and toasted the phantom groundlings before him. He glanced about the stale quiet room and watched the barmaids as they scurried about, washing down tables and moving the dirt about the floors with tattered straw brooms. Just an hour ago and the Mermaid buzzed with players, poets and minstrels clinking their tankards and sloshing their laughter and thoughts back and forth. Now, the Tavern stilled. The dim glow from the candlelight cast an eerie haze, yellowish-brown against the plastered walls and the haze clouded his eyes. He lowered the tankard, missing the table and sending the remaining ale in a brown stream across the boards.

He tilted his head and propped his cheek against his opened palm, his fingers tangling in the curls falling from his receding hairline. As he closed his eyes, the fire within his brain swelled. A snort opened his eyes, and he looked to his left. Ben Jonson lay sprawled on his back on the floor near to him, the brown stream of ale puddling in his curly black hair. William squinted and noted him through the drunken fog in his brain. Ben's head twisted to the side, smashing his left cheek against the trestle bench leg and creating an imbecilic pool of saliva in the corner of his mouth. The drool rattled out with each exhale, running down into his ear and dripping in steady drops onto the floor.

The sight amused William, yet he could not even find the

strength to laugh. A shadow moved close and took William by the arm, pulling him up on his wobbly legs. He gazed up, seeing another familiar face.

"Michael Drayton, where have you been?"

Michael blew out a small laugh. "I have been here with you, William. I have paid the bill, now get you to home and a bed for you."

William paused and pointed at the large blob of a man slumbering in his drunkenness.

"Look, 'tis Ben."

Michael peered across the table and chuckled. "Indeed, Will, 'tis Ben. 'Twill be better for us both to let him sleep where he fell, else 'twill be like baiting a bear."

William found the chortle in his throat, along with the bile of too much ale bubbling forth. He swayed and spat as Michael held him upright. They shuffled out of the tavern and the warm stagnant air settled on William's fevered brow, pasty and stale. His innards churned within him. Friday Street shadowed as dark as pitch since the torch-lighter often excluded lighting the torches of the rank alleyways of Cheapside.

Michael pulled his cloak close around Shakespeare's shoulders and whispered. "Come along as quick as you can, Will. 'Tis not a night to be walking the streets in East Cheap with the rush torches burned out. I fear more for our persons than for our purses."

They traversed slow through the ins and outs of East Cheap, down the bank of the Thames and over London Bridge to Southwark, pausing at intervals for William to retch out the contents of his hot innards. The torches of Southward glowed, setting ablaze the circle of the Globe Theatre.

William lifted his head, steadying his balance and outstretched his hand toward her. "Ah, 'tis my lady and my love."

He toppled over into a heap at the edge of her tar-beamed and plastered gown. Michael knelt near to him and unfolded his crumpled friend. He gasped as he touched his fingertips to William's forehead.

"William, wake up. Come along now and I will send for the doctor. You have had too much drink and your brain burns with it. William!"

Michael shook him until the delirium eased away and he lifted him to his feet. Another few steps and they reached the doors to the Globe. Michael lifted the latch and pushed his way inside, dragging the sagging William in his clutches.

For a moment, William's countenance rose, seeing the stage rising to greet him. He stopped in the midst of the penny pit and slowly spun around, his feet shuffling through the fresh strewn hay. The moonlight glowed through the opened circle of the arena and fell across the stage. He bowed before the raised platform and soaked in the regalia of her marble painted columns and gold-dusted cymatium. He swayed to the left and Michael took him hard by the arms, pushing him forward to the doors at the side of the stage. Michael helped him to a couch and draped his cloak over him. He lit a candle and illuminated the room in a yellow glow.

"Sleep, William. I will stay with you till morn and will fetch the doctor come daybreak. Perhaps the night will ease the burning in your brain."

William's eyes closed, but the fever gnawed at him. Faces flashed vivid in his mind: Elizabeth the First, Anne Hathaway, Anne Whatley, and then, Burbage as Macbeth, as Prospero, as Titus. He twitched with each vision. And a face from the past loomed before him and rose like a smoky spirit.

William moaned and spoke his name in the delirium. "Marlowe... O, Marlowe..."

Michael leaned forward, placing his hand upon William's brow.

"What is it, William? What of Marlowe?"

William fixed his eyes on Michael and spoke through a dry throat.

"Ah, Michael, he is dead."

Michael wrinkled his brow. "Yea, Will, he is dead. You know this, remember? 'Twas long ago. Peace, now, and sleep. Do not think on these things."

A tear burned in the corner of William's eye, and he held the stare into Michael's face. "Michael, do you have a son?" To which he affirmed, and William's body deflated into a sigh. "I had a son, but alas, he died."

William closed his eyes and fell into a fit of sleep. A boy of eight ran in and out of the shadowy dreams and William ran after him, weaving in and out of the golden stalks of corn, across heather fields and down the muddy banks of Shottery brook. The boy's voice sang clear as the bubbling of the water across the rocks.

"Catch me, father!"

William caught him up in his arms, spinning and laughing until they collapsed onto the fresh mossy grass. The boy rolled near to him, side by side, and took William's hand in his, palm to palm. William gazed at his fair-skinned boy, the love burning in his heart.

The boy looked up into his face and smiled. "I am your son."

William smiled. "Indeed, Hamnet Shakespeare, you are my son. You will carry my name into posterity."

Hamnet frowned, his youthful mind jumping from one subject to the next. "Mother saith I must go to school, that 'tis long past since I was to go. What say you, father?"

William looked up into the clouds and thought for a moment. His father had been right; he was none the worse for leaving school. He learned much through business and numbers came easy to him; ciphering and adding, buying and selling; a skill he learned more from his father than from the King's School. He set his jaw and spoke. "You like not the thought of school?"

"Nay, sir. Grandfather says I can learn more from him than keeping my nose in a book. He said that he told you the same when you were my age."

William chuckled. "He did, indeed. There was quite a row between your grandparents over my schooling. He sent me to fetch water from the well, but I sat near the window and listened to them. Your grandmother's face reddened as a cock's comb and she stamped her feet, saying she would pack the children off to Snitterfield if he would not let me go to school. She said, 'I will not have him set his foot in this world without schooling.' And your grandfather snarled back, 'Why should you vex me? Have I not given you all you would wish and done it all by signing my own name with a simple cross?'

She answered back, 'The boys his age have already cut their teeth in books. He will be forsook if you deny him this.'"

Hamnet smiled, intrigued by this tale. "And then, what did grandfather do?"

William took Hamnet's hand and smacked his fist into the

boy's palm. "He pounded the table, sending the goblets to the floor, and declared, 'I breed a sound mind and good sense. Even if he never speaks a Latin verse, I will warrant he is made of bigger stuff. I will teach him to grasp the tail of opportunity when it wags his way.'"

Hamnet's brow knitted together. "But, father, you went to school?"

"Yea, I did. Your grandfather relented, yet he said, 'We will have you here to school here in Stratford, the King Edward's School, where you will learn to mark your name with more than a cross, but remember well what I teach you. You will learn more of what you need in this world by putting yourself in the right places at the right times, instead of putting this,' he tapped my head, 'into a book.'"

Hamnet giggled and tapped his father's forehead. "Then I shall be like you, father. I will to the King's School for mother, but will learn more from you."

A moment passed in silence as they watched the gentle drooping branches of the willows dance and tickle across the surface of the water. Hamnet turned to his side, propping his head upon his hand, to stare into his father's face. "Father?"

"Yea, boy?"

"Grandfather also says that 'tis not important to go to church, that 'tis a creation of the bastard Queen, and he could teach me a thing or two about the true faith, and..."

William scooped up Hamnet into his arms, clasping his hand over the boy's mouth. "Hamnet, these are things you must not say. Your grandfather is an old man who makes up stories. These are things a boy your age needs never to learn."

"A boy needs never to learn..." William mumbled in his sleep.

The night air cooled the fever upon William's brow and his dreams melted away upon the first rays of sunlight. Michael Drayton awoke with a start as the door to the dressing room burst open. Ben Jonson stood in the doorway, his burly frame filling the expanse and the odor of the night's fray filling the room. He guffawed and scratched the hair on his head, his fingers catching in the matted tangles of ale and saliva.

"William Shakespeare, you left me in my puke and now I come to take back my honor!" He shoved William in the side with the ball of his booted foot. William stirred and opened his eyes while Michael defended him.

"Ben, hold, he is very ill. The ale stung him last night, and it sits very bad with him. All night he tussled with a feverish muse."

Ben smiled, his jolly cheeks quivering. "As did I, Michael, and quite the lusty muse was she." He knelt near to William, placing his fingertips against William's brow. "Indeed, he has a fever."

Michael shook his head. "There were many times during the night he spoke, but the words fell disconnected. Several times he spoke of his son, and then of Marlowe, and then words of betrayal."

Ben slapped William's cheeks. "William? William, wake up!" With no response, Ben looked over at Michael. "'Tis very strange. He has of late spoken to me many times of his son. 'Twas such a tragedy to lose such a treasure. And he spoke out loud of Marlowe?"

"Yea, many times."

Ben scratched his chin and the course sound beneath his fingers echoed in the room. "Yea, 'tis very very strange, but I suppose to lose someone like Marlowe and then, to lose a son, well, what it may do to a man's mind is a peculiar thing."

"Ben, I am not as sure as you of this matter. The matter of his son I can see, but he barely knew Kit Marlowe. Kit died two weeks before William took up with Pembroke's Men."

Ben twirled his mustache between his forefinger and thumb, squinting in Michael's direction. "Hmm, 'tis true what you say. We shall wait and let our friend wrangle out the meaning to us. Look, he stirs."

William bent at the waist and pulled himself to an upright position. He raised his eyes and focused upon the two men seated before him. He leaned forward, raising one hand toward the ceiling and the other upon his head.

"O, this distracted globe within this distracted Globe. My head reeks with fire." He caught Ben's puzzled stare. "How did I traverse this path from the Mermaid to here? Have you sat with me all this while?"

Ben chortled and slapped his friend on the back. William swayed and moaned beneath Ben's bear-like swat.

"Nay, you left me in the dust of the Mermaid. I woke to the clutches of that drabber Blanche straddling my purse." Ben smiled. "Well, 'twas not all bad, except our night's escapade with drink and whores has left me near penniless. 'Twill be back to my quill and paper for the rest of the month to fill my purse again. S'wounds, Will Shakespeare, you will not tempt me to the Mermaid again with your smooth sayings. Of course, how could I refuse, knowing full well none of you, but I, have any sense and it will be my intellect smoothing the course for all of you. And now, Michael speaks of your frightful nightmares… so here I am to hear all."

Michael laid a hand on Ben's arm, signaling for an immediate halt to his words. William forced a sad smile across his lips. "Ben, you are my Mercurtio. Thou talk'st of nothing. These dreams you speak of are what fires my brain. I fear some consequence hanging in the stars has begun a fearful date with this night's revels and expires the term of a despised life, which closes within my breast by some vile forfeit of untimely death. He that hath the steerage of my course, direct my sail!"

Michael's smile left his face as he shifted himself onto the divan near to William. His words shrouded with the things he heard during the night.

"William, no more of Romeo's speeches, 'tis these dreams you speak on we wish to disclose to you. You speak of untimely death, of consequence, of setting your course toward revelations, and then, during the night, you echoed your son's name over and over, and then leapt upon Marlowe's name, moaning and crying, and falling upon words of betrayal and death. I told Ben these things this morning before you woke and we are here as your friends to help you unravel this mystery."

William felt as his if his veins opened and his blood replaced with an icy snow. Michael grabbed hold of him around the shoulders as he swayed. Ben continued the interrogation. "William, you speak crazed words, names and faces swirling in your fevered mind. Speak to us, William, for our ears are bent."

William managed a pained look into Ben's face. "Speak to you my words? If only I could." He gave up the stare and reclined back against the couch. "Ben, take me home."

Michael stood and reached his hand out to William. "Come along. I will help you to your lodging house."

William shook his head and looked again to Ben. "Nay, not there. I am for Stratford, for I am weary of playing another man's life. 'Tis time, my dearest friends, for this soul to walk a day in my own shoes. I am tired..."

Michael creased his brow. "He is not in his mind, Ben. He cannot leave London. What of the Globe? What of the plays to come? There is no one to follow him." He turned back to William. "Nay, Will, you cannot leave us empty. Your stage is here, your groundlings. What will we do without your words?"

William closed his eyes. "My words? You have never had my words. You have never known me and I fear never will after these days." He opened his eyes, praying Ben could see the pleading there. Ben agreed with a nod.

"Come along, Michael. We will let William sleep awhile more." He pushed Michael to the door, pausing once to lean near to William's ear.

"I will get you home to Stratford if you promise to unravel this matter to me."

William closed his eyes and whispered a morsel of revelation to Ben. "Ben, do you remember when Marlowe died?"

"I do. 'Twas an ill day for the stage, yet he brought it upon himself. He was a brash and insolent irreligious rogue."

William rolled over on his side facing the wall. "His death brought forth my birth day."

Ben chuckled. "William, you are swine drunk and will squeal away nonsense until the poison flushes out. Come along, Michael. Let us away whilst he sleeps. We will be back in the morning, Will."

Upon the clicking of the latch, William rolled over upon his back and looked about the prop room. The sunlight crept in and danced in thin strips through the cracks of the oak door. His eyes focused and took in the characters about him. The costumes of the Tempest lay in a pile in the corner: Miranda's diaphanous sea-colored dress, the wings of Ariel and the black woolen mantle of Prospero. William wheezed as the fever and the anger swelled.

"O, might Prospero, how clever you concealed yourself. Perhaps too cleverly, for no one yet knows our secret. And now you have put aside your mantle and left me quite undone. There is nothing left for me but to leave London; for if I stay, then they will want more of me and without you, I am nothing. But remember, I have your magical book, your conjured words and have skill enough to see them affixed to my name, which I will do if you push me. What else do I have anymore but your words?"

His eyes and mind drifted from one play to another. He stood and ran his fingers along the racks of costumes: Macbeth's Scottish tartan cloak, Antony's armor, Caesar's laurel crown, and Hamlet's sword. Trundling along the wall, his fingers traced the rough plaster until, at last, he grasped the curtains leading to the stage. A familiar feeling spread over him as if he waited for the hush of a waiting crowd as the author took the stage. Burbage spoke of the feeling, but none since Marlowe struck such awe as Shakespeare did when he pulled back the curtains.

His brain swelled with adrenaline. A pause, a breath, and he snatched back the curtains. He placed his hands upon his hips and strutted across the stage, walking back and forth, pausing, swaying, breathing, and last, collapsing near the trap door reserved for the bowels of hell. His eyes scanned the fake blue heavens of the stage across to the blue sky above Bankside framed in the perfect circle of the roof. He looked again at the heavenly mural, finding the secretive laughter in his throat.

He lifted his hand and pointed to the faux sky. "I remember the painting, Marlowe! Narcissus gazing at his reflection… Ha! No one remembers what happened to the man!"

He pulled himself up to a sitting position and beheld the phantom crowds before him. Some smiled, some frowned, and some leaned upon the stage. He held out his arms to them.

"'Tis a new play. I hope you enjoy this comical tragedy. 'Tis the chameleon's dish, crammed with nothing but airy promises. Men are deceivers ever… but wait, those lines have been spoke here before, but you see, dear London, 'tis all I have. There are no more words for he has silenced his quill. He thinks that by his silence I will have to reveal him, but I will blow him at the moon… Ha!"

He stood, his knees wobbling beneath the weakness and fever, and bowed before them as he spoke another line.

"'Tis a winter's tale beginning my life, beginning his life; for you see, we were kindred brothers born in the same year. Two houses, both alike in dignity in fair England where we lay our scene, one in Canterbury and the other, Stratford. Can you see us? We met, Kit and I, but there were things abreast in secret that I was unaware of. A pawn was I, but perpend, I learned a thing or two from my father. I learned to grab hold of opportunity when it wagged my way. And now, here I stand, the owner of this theater, the owner of his words and the reason for his prolonged exile. O, you frown at me?"

He pointed his finger at the accusing ghosts and thundered his voice to the third level of the seats.

"I am no different from any ambitious man! Yea, I was the means to his end!"

"Then hate me when thou wilt; if ever, now;

Now, while the world is bent my deeds to cross,

Join with the spite of fortune, make me bow,

And do not drop in for an after-loss:

Ah, do not, when my heart hath 'scraped this sorrow,

Come in the rearward of a conquer'd woe;

Give not a windy night a rainy morrow,

To linger out a purposed overthrow."

Sonnet XC

XXXIII

Marlowe lowered the quill as a resounding knock echoed through the room. The door creaked open, and a messenger stood framed in the doorway of the piazza, fiddling with his cap.

"Shakespeare is dying, my lord."

His words rang clear in Christopher Marlowe's mind like the bells clanging from the spires of the Sistine Chapel. Marlowe's heart pounded, halfway between fear and joy. The parchment page he wrote upon trembled in his shaking fingers. He released the page, and it fell to the floor and his gaze drifted out the window as the sun rose over Rome. The city flashed domes of gold and rich hues of piety; a creamy carved marble wonder reflecting religion in the sparkling vein of the Tiber River. Those prophetic waters flowed past the window as a daily reminder that he is here, exiled, and Shakespeare is there, prospering.

The smell of ripe olives on the Mediterranean wind, the wafting aroma of good oil, good wine and prayers did not move his heart, nor did the heralding white doves on the windowsill cooing the arrival of another spring day. Yet, with each increment of light, hope rose in his heart. The possible spurred him, and the words: *Shakespeare is dying.*

A poet is forever hopeful, he mused. *When did I lose my hope? Have I ever had that word in my heart? Yet, hope weaves like a silent thread through the tapestry of my words, yea, hoping, nay, praying the threads reveal the picture of my name.*

He leaned out the window and whispered, out of the earshot of the messenger. "The truth shall set me free. Today I shall take back my life and my name with my own hands. Shakespeare will not die with my words on his lips. His name teeters on the brink of immortality. Walsingham peeled away my name long ago, like a ribbon of skin from a caraway. How was I to know? I was just a boy, ignorant of the value of a name. Now as death rattles my own aching bones, what have I to lose? The readiness is all to die as I wish. To die with a true reckoning. The demon will not collect payment here in this blood-lust city filled with soldiers of Christ and phallic towers. My bones crave English soil."

Marlowe cut his stare to the man. "Do you have anything else for me? A portfolio, perhaps?"

Christopher's heart sank as the man shook his head. The man seemed an ordinary sort, he noted: thin, wiry, a good stereotype for roles such as the fidgety Osrick, yet something lingered behind the man's eyes which gave Marlowe a moment of pause. Kit perused the fellow's belt to search for the leather sheath holding a dagger and found none.

Christopher blew a puff of air between his lips. "Nay, of course, that would have been too easy. Then your visitation is for a different purpose. Are you here to kill me?"

The messenger creased his brow and laughed. "Nay, my lord, why would you say such a thing? I am merely an actor with the King's Men sent hither to you with this message."

For so long, fear ruled Marlowe's heart and even his actions. Skeptical of every man and afraid of the demons in the shadows, those Jesuit assassins assigned the singular task of finding every known pawn of Walsingham and smiting them; especially the task of finding the phoenix and setting him aflame. Twenty-three years of hiding since his fake death in Deptford and his enemies still fed on the rumors that he lived. They still sought his true death, and now, here he hid right in the midst of them. He learned a thing or two about hiding in plain sight and revealed this through his characters Viola, Romeo and Portia, all hiding behind masks in the midst of enemies. His life reflected in his work as he hid behind a mask of words.

Yet, he wondered, *why has no one seen the truth?*

He glanced back down as a black spider appeared at the edge of his table. With quiet resolve and habit, he lifted the pewter candlestick and tilted until two large drops of wax splattered across the back of the creature. While the spider struggled, and the messenger gasped, Marlowe lifted his heavy lids to view his infirmary prison.

Here is my prison house, this white unblemished room aching for ink.

So much whiteness ready for ink from a quill: the fluttering linen curtains, the bed sheets, and even the pillow propped up against the white-washed walls. Yet, mingling with the purity of the Ospedale room at Santo Spirito were always the dark things crouching in the corners: a singular mahogany desk adorned with a bottle of ink and the blackness of an oak seafaring trunk, the very chest which carried his life in younger days now hunched at the foot of his bed like a silent spirit filled with secrets.

The messenger fidgeted again and Marlowe questioned him further. "You are very like Osrick from the play *Hamlet* as you fiddle with your cap and deliver dire news. Your master, Shakespeare, does he wait for a reply?"

"I have played Osrick, my lord, and yea, he does wait."

Marlowe huffed again. "Then let us pray fell death will show patience. Stay awhile, I will be faithful."

Marlowe pulled the chair out from his desk and sat; and, as a second habit, took a piece of parchment and an unused quill from the drawer and placed them on the table before him. For a moment, a lump formed in his throat and his mind drew as blank as an unblotted page. He closed his eyes as fear seized his hands and his fingers curled in retreat. Stretching his left hand, he took the ink bottle in his grip, bringing the mouth near his nose. He breathed deep, taking in the pungent aroma of gall ink; the sweet perfume of the muse, Calliope.

Before dipping the quill, he rested his hand on the Bible at the corner of the desk. Raleigh would laugh at him to see that book within his reach, and yet, many false accusations swarmed about his name; false labels such as Atheist, Blasphemer and Betrayer. *What about the titles of Playwright, Bard and Poet?*

Marlowe believed in God, but not the one of Rome or England's making. After seeing the hypocrisy and bloodshed from both sides, he merely rejected the titles of Catholic or Protestant. He learned the game of compromise and that for each thing you do for someone in power results in your gain until you achieve what you desire most in life: recognition, approval, and yea, sometimes power itself. Yet, this greedy little trinity bore a high price; and like most of her courtiers, Marlowe mewed like a wide-eyed kitten greedy for the royal teat of the Queen to dole out her milky favors, yet too young to recognize the bitter taste of wormwood in the suckling.

He fingered the gilt-edge pages and like predictive tidings, the pages fell open to the seventh book of Ecclesiastes. The words leaped from the page as piercing as a dagger in an assassin's hand.

Marlowe's bottom lip quivered as he read aloud. "A good name is better than precious ointment; and the day of death than the day of one's birth. Tell me, sir, to whom did Shakespeare send you?"

"To you, sir, Monsieur Le Doux."

Prickly irony seethed in Marlowe's heart at the man's answer. "Le Doux? Of course, for what more could I have hoped for? I sold cheap what I held most dear, my own name."

His hand brushed across the Bible, the table and rested upon a tightly bound leather portfolio. He took the ties between his left thumb and forefinger and pulled slow. The parchment pages within exhaled from their corseted confinement.

He lifted the leather case before him, letting the book fan open. As the pages settled, the words drifted from them and filled him with such pride. His faith swelled in the creation, these words born to him by his muse, these originals in his own hand. He scanned the page before him and smiled upon the words of Hamlet as only a father could upon a most precious child.

He sensed the quiet sardonic laughter curdling behind his tongue as he considered the cleverness of his cryptic hand farming three letters to hide his name: Marley to Hamlet. So many of his characters reflected his faults and qualities, from the wit of

Benedict to the darkness of Faustus and the ambition of Macbeth.
So the life of a writer, to illuminate the audience with a cast of
imaginary players to move the groundlings, make them weep, stir
them to anger or sweep them away in love. Ultimately, he owned
the joy as he stood in the wings of the theater to watch their faces:
fingers to their lips, chests heaving from the momentary climax of
pain, or guilt, or knowing that in a brief three-hour slice of life,
they witnessed the invention of a human.

He paused from his amusement, feeling a slight twinge of pain
deep within his heart. "Tell me, messenger, have you seen the
plays of Kit Marlowe upon the stage?"

"Only his *Doctor Faustus,* my lord. The players rarely
perform them nowadays for the penny-stinkers clamor for
Shakespeare's words; so we oblige them, for in that, we all get
paid."

"Shakespeare's words? Ha!"

Marlowe laid the portfolio gently on the table. He brushed his
hand through his thin gray hair and cradled his head upon his palm.
His fingers ran across the maze of wrinkles upon his brow. The fire
in his brain raged as he read aloud Hamlet's words.

"There is special providence in the fall of a sparrow..." He
paused and considered, daring the single tear in the corner of his
eye to fall. "Twice in my life I saw the fall of a sparrow, first as a
boy and, again, as a man. The latter was a moment I stepped from
the threshold of the lodging house near Finsbury Fields. A figure
stood like a specter near the end of Holywell Lane banked in fog,
yet his eyes pierced the mist like a dagger. My eyes fell from the
stranger as my foot crunched upon her tiny bones. She was so
small, so fragile and her feathers askew as if she had given up in
mid-flight."

The messenger lifted his gaze to the blue sky peeking through
the trellised arbor over the doorway. "And the first, my lord?

Marlowe sighed. "The first? 'Twas mine own doing. I killed
the innocent bird perched on the branch of a tree with a slingshot."

"God was watching, my lord."

"Was he? I have seen nothing in my life to give validity to that
thought, sir. Methinks on that day I did nothing but kill innocence,
my own innocence, for afterwards change invoked change onward
to my soon impeding death. I did that, not God. Pray, tell me,

messenger, what would you do if someone stole something from you? Would you not move heaven and earth to change it, to receive a reckoning before you shuffled off this mortal coil?"

The messenger shrugged. "I suppose, sir, 'twould depend on the value of the thing stolen."

A sweet thought formed in Marlowe's mind. "Then you shall have your reply to Master Shakespeare, sir."

He dipped the quill and scrawled an answer.

I defy augury. Shakespeare, prepare your soul, for I return forthwith.

As Marlowe bowed over his desk to seal the note, a creeping shadow fell over his shoulder. He lifted his eyes just as the candlestick bore down at the back of his head with a crack. Marlowe shuddered with the sound of pewter against bone and he slumped to the floor, knocking the ink pot over as the messenger folded the letter and picked up the portfolio.

"Shakespeare thanks you, sir." He lifted the portfolio before Marlowe's eyes as he retreated through the door. "Indeed, your original words are a valuable thing. No need to spoil the lie now, is there, Monsieur Le Doux?"

A wail stirred in his gut and crawled up his throat as he clamored toward the retreating man. His fingers smeared the blood and ink spilled on the floor. Darkness overtook him as the words tumbled out across his parched lips.

"Run and hide, sir, for I know what it is to kill a man. Warn Shakespeare, if you will, for I am coming quick! I will have my reckoning!"

"O, how I faint when I of you do write,

Knowing a better spirit doth use your name,

And in the praise thereof spends all his might,

To make me tongue-tied, speaking of your fame!"

Sonnet LXXX

XXXIV

William awoke to the light sprinkling of rain on his face. A passing shower left the stage dewy wet and the penny pit transformed from a dusty hovel to mushy slop. William rolled over to his side toward the empty benches in the terraces and the words in his mouth tumbled out in a soft rumble.

"The means to his end. The means to his end."

In the haze of his vision, a large figure pushed through the entrance doors and squashed through the mud toward him. William wiped the rain from his eyes and spoke to the stranger.

"Who goes there? Friend or foe?"

Ben Jonson walked near to the stage and leaned upon the edge, his eye level with William's face. "A friend, dear Will, and a foe. Are you still fevered?"

William extended his hand and placed it on Ben's shoulder. His voice caught on the sadness forming in his throat. "Ben, I was a means to an end, that is what he said."

Ben reached out and felt William's forehead. "Yea, I see you are still raging. Come along, Will. I have a coach and will fetch you home. Perhaps your son-in-law doctor will see you set right."

Ben disappeared to the stage left and returned with a cloak and blanket. He pulled William to the edge of the stage and wrapped him tight. As they walked across the pit, William's heart pounded. He stopped and looked over his shoulder, leaning heavy upon Ben's arm. His eyes shadowed over with a watery veil.

"'Twill be the last time I see her, Ben."

Ben lifted him up under his armpit and released a reluctant

chuckle.

"Nonsense, Will. You will rest at your home in Stratford, regain your disposition and within a month, I daresay you will pound these boards again."

William leaned against the coach as Ben closed the doors to the Globe. The rain fell in large sopping raindrops penetrating the wool cloak about William's shoulders. He closed his eyes, and the tears mingled with the rain as he heard the latch lock to the theater. Steadying himself, he pushed past Ben and laid his cheek against the wooden doors. He lifted his hand and traced the grain of the oak and the raised nail heads with his fingertips. His body and thoughts clung to her and he lifted his gaze, as he backed away, until her form filled his eyes. Through the fever, the rain and the sadness, he swallowed hard and kissed his fingertips to bid her adieu.

He swayed and Ben caught him up in his arms to lead him to the open door of the coach. William lay across the cool leather of the seat and listened to the rain pound on the roof. They rode in silence through the streets of Southwark, across London Bridge, one last time through Cheapside, past the Guildhall, until lastly, they made their exeunt through the Northwestern gate of the city. The cobblestones changed to dirt, the stone fortress walls surrounding London fell away, and the landscape transformed into forests of oak and elm and yew-fenced meadows dotted with sheep.

The rocking of the carriage lulled Ben and William into a dreamy sleep. About an hour into the ride, midst the rattling snore coming from Ben's throat, the clopping of the horse hooves and the rising humid fog after the rain, William woke. He pulled back the curtain from the window and filled his gaze with the colors of the English countryside: heavy luscious hills gorging their greens with the cool spring shower and fields of green rye with their new popping heads bent and drunk with the same liquid. He breathed in the blue sky and felt the acrid filth of London melt away, yet still, in the depths of his gut, a fire brewed. Some dark secret boiled in the crucible and seethed to reveal itself; the kind of secret that feeds on a man, eating his bowels and festering in his heart.

"'Tis a difficult thing to keep something hidden," he whispered, "when all the holy vows of heaven plead for it and all a man can do is hold on by his fingernails and suffer in his soul, crying for mercy. Even when time seems to give assurance in passing. O, Marlowe, where art thou? Are you hiding beyond the trees? Will you be reclining near the fireside in my Stratford home? Have you seen my retreat from London and now, are you laughing and calling the groundlings forward in my Globe to tell the world my secret? Nay, our secret? How shall I hold on to what you gave me and not lose my own name? I pray the Earl of Pembroke's plan comes to fruition. 'Twas fortuitous he crossed my path. Ha, Marlowe, you thought to hide your name in the sonnets, but your witty boy figured out the ruse."

William closed back his eyes and mused over the encounter with the Earl.

William never traveled to Salisbury before, but when he received the letter requesting his presence before the Earl of Pembroke, he went in haste. He stretched his legs out in the coach and soaked in the aroma of the fresh rain as it bathed the rolling sage-hued hills. His soul felt very satisfied with money in his leather purse, a fine saber at his belt, the soft silk touch of a plum-colored doublet and the shiny, oiled sheen of his new leather boots. His skill as an actor led to many more things, as the Queen promised: new houses in Stratford, part ownership of the playhouse in Southwark, the awarding of a coat-of-arms to his family to which brought a father's approval, the admiration of paupers and princes, mongers and Earls; all quite daft of the fact that he, William Shakespeare, was merely a page on which the masterful Marlowe wrote his plays.

The thought of Marlowe's name made William squirm. Thirteen years to this day passed since the day Kit transferred the portfolio into his keeping. The first year or so, all went according to the plan, then Burghley succumbed to his failing health and died with no revelation of Marlowe's whereabouts. Marlowe's letters to him filled with agitation and worry, as it became apparent that the Queen forgot him, especially after the performance of Richard II. Elizabeth hated the play and felt the full on attack of Marlowe's words insinuating the deposition of the monarch. Marlowe morphed into a scorned man, seeking revenge against his muse's delay in bringing him back to England which lingered past a decade. *The play took the stage at the Globe and Lord Essex, using Marlowe's play as his proxy for the instigation of a rebellion against her Majesty, took the fall; and yet, Elizabeth's words hinted at another secret conspirator.*

Shakespeare heard the rumor whispered that she uttered, 'I am Richard the Second, know ye not that? He conjures characters from those he knows, but he that will forget God will also forget his benefactors.'

William knew to whom she referred, not to Essex, but to Christopher Marlowe whom Richard Baines accused of 'forgetting God' before the Star Chamber. She warned Marlowe if he played in this way, forgetting the hand holding his future, she would turn on him like a wolf upon a lamb. Therefore, she let it pass and all of England, in fact, bought into the ruse; not only buying it but also becoming quite comfortable with the man Shakespeare. The corner of William's mouth turned up in a smile.

His coach approached the gatehouse of the bastion. A gentleman clad in a creamy brocade tunic stood waiting for him at the door, the feather in his cap dancing on the breeze blowing off the riverbank.

William bowed after he exited the coach and the man waved him inside.

'I apologize for all the secrecy and the hastiness of my message, Master Shakespeare.'

'You are the Earl of Pembroke?'

'Yea, forgive me for the lack of decorum. I sent away all my servants today. My mind is much upon other matters of late, and the matters I must discuss with you presently. I thank you for coming so quick. Come, we will to the anteroom of the west tower and pour out these matters with a tipple of brandy wine.'

The two of them wound through the cloisters of Wilton House. They came to a bleak whitewashed chamber furnished with a simple table and two chairs, lit only by the tall narrow sliver of an archer's window. The Earl filled two tankards from a pitcher of heated brew at the hearth and the two men sat.

'First, let me say and commend you for your excellent plays. 'Tis a superb dish served when visiting Court. You have quite the gift.'

William bowed his head. 'From you, sir, 'tis quite the honor.

There are many, as you know, among my contemporaries who would feign to hear such words from a Pembroke. Your noble name carries weight among poets and playwrights alike. May I ask, are you to commission something from me?'

'Master Shakespeare, if I were merely to commission a work from you, 'twould easily serve at Court in London. Can you not tell from this secret liaison there is more to this matter?'

'Pray, my Lord, I can.'

'Then you answer well, for the matter I wish to discuss touches the circulation of your sonnets. 'Tis very strange, for I have read most all of them and I sense a deeper meaning there. Tell me, when you wrote them, were you conjuring them from nothing or was experience the teacher behind your heavy heart?'

William fell into character. 'Well, sir, can any writer truly say whether a muse blesses him or if it is his own history that speaks, without disclosing the secrets of his heart?'

The Earl laughed. 'True, so I will tell you why I ask. Your sonnets are like a puzzle aching for a solution. You dedicated them to a Mr. W. H., so you can see why the initials would spark my curiosity. I know in this enlightened age we live, 'tis not uncommon for hidden messages, clues even, to mingle themselves among a poet's words. The quill is a mighty thing, often used to sway men's souls and change thinking, would you not say?' William agreed and the Earl continued. 'Tell me, did you know Master Marlowe before he died?'

The spark of Marlowe's name sent a chill down Shakespeare's back. He lied, 'Pray, sir, not well. We briefly met, only a few days before his demise in Deptford. 'Tis a shame, though, for I would have liked to know the man.'

Herbert huffed. 'Do not esteem him so highly, sir, for the man was an atheistic bawdy rogue. Pray, shall I tell you why all the secrecy and the questioning of your sonnets? 'Tis this: when I was a boy, a mere thirteen summers, Master Marlowe happened upon my mother and me at Court. This poet and paragon who created a new way of writing entranced me. His words spilled out upon the page as if he merely dictated the words of the muses, and then, in an instant, all my adoration of him ceased. My mother announced to us both that I was the product of this poet's seed thrust upon her one summer he spent at Wilton House. Marry, yea, I see the shock in your eyes. For the free revelation knocked me from a noble birth to the rank of a bastard. What is more... his bastard and sullied by the mud drying upon his name. And again, there is more. Before my mother's religiously inclined confession, she had me sign a statement saying I would patron Marlowe when called upon to do so. This I did, signed and sealed with my mark. Upon his death, I forfeited the deed, and yet, I cannot help but see the signs of his writing and words among thine own sonnets. Can you explain this?'

Shakespeare paused before answering and let the variable answers form and weave in his mind. The answer settled clear, and he replied.

'Marry, yea, my Lord, I can explain all. Attend thine ear upon a marvelous tale for the end is near, and you as a patron and a poet may very well like to collaborate upon this work. The opening line is a crowd-catcher: Christopher Marlowe is alive, well, and living in Rome this very day. And the well-rounded characters spoke their lines with finesse: Queen Bess, who authored the ruse to protect one of her favorites, the actor seated before you playing the part of a playwright, and Marlowe's former savior, Lord Burghley, who might have heralded the protagonist from exile, but alas, both the savior and the author are now dead, leaving the player to act on his own accord.'

The Earl stood from the table. 'Is this true? But how and why do you now tell me?'

William slouched in his chair. ' Tis a matter of business, 'tis all, my Lord. Marlowe sold the very thing he held most dear. His words are now mine and all of England speaks my name in his stead. The Queen forgot him and in her fickle mood found new favorites. In the last days of her life there were heavier matters to attend to than whether she should bring back a simple playwright from the dead. Marlowe wrote letters upon letters to me, and yet, all I had to do was answer with this: I am bound to the Queen's will for I am her subject and cannot press her upon matters she herself finds unimportant to disclose. We swore to this masque.'

'You swore to it? Tell me all. Why did this happen?'

'You know the Star Chamber charged Marlowe for seditious letters found in Kyd's lodging house and upon the word of Richard Baines. 'Twas only a matter of delay, for you see, Baines and the

Archbishop would have tortured Marlowe, even killed him, in an attempt to weasel closer to the Queen's affections. She whisked Marlowe away, and the Queen paid me well to continue ushering his plays into the country. But now, I find myself in a very different situation. Our new King James knew this Marlowe only through his alias from his brief visit to Scotland after his faked death, and has no reason to bring him back. I have often asked myself, would England wish this tainted man back upon her shores? All of it has become a game of mills. Marlowe pleads, sends letters and shows up on occasion in disguise, even at his own plays and the King's Court, and yet, the one thing he desires is drifting away from him like a bottle on the ocean waves. Shall you be the one to pluck him from this watery grave and uncork the secrets?'

The Earl stared out the window. 'Who else knows of this? What of those attending him that night in Deptford?'

'It has been thirteen years, my Lord. All the players, save for myself, are dead. Even Baines, whose clever libel began this masque. Although he never gained the favor of the Queen, I hear he died with a smile upon his lips, perhaps thinking he succeeded in destroying his nemesis.'

The Earl turned, his forefinger tapping upon his lip. 'So, the question is, shall I use my noble influence to reveal this story to our King and sway him to bring Marlowe back from exile, thus sending you back to the simple state of a common player and me, to the rank of a bastard; or do I keep my word and patron the works my mother had me swear to?'

William frowned. 'What of that, are they not the same?'

Herbert smiled. 'Nay, they are not, for you see, his works are thine and bear your name only. If I keep him in exile, then no one will ever know the secrets of my birth. Does he still send works to you, to this day?'

William shook his head. 'Nay, he does not. I have many yet to play and publish. Three years have passed, the year of Elizabeth's death, since the last of his works came to me. I think with her death he is taking the only step he knows against me and that is to cease his writing. The last three he sent to me: the Tempest, All Is True, and Two Noble Kinsmen, all hold the same cryptic devises he has used his entire life. Prospero, his Italian name for Faustus, lays aside his magical mantle, thus does he tell me he is laying aside his quill. The Kinsmen play is not even complete. In addition, the All Is True play, with its themes of reconciliation, well you can guess what that means. If you could hear the speech uttered by Katherine of Aragon, it smacks of Marlowe's voice calling out across the ocean.'

'Hmm, do you not fear he will come back to England and after you?'

William shrugged. 'What will he do? Kill the only man who can substantiate his claim? If he kills me before I confess, then he will simply rot in jail for the murder of the fair playwright, William Shakespeare. They will think him a mad fool with his uttering of being Christopher Marlowe. Nay, he needs me to save him, besides, from his own letter methinks he is already bent towards madness.'

'Do you have no conscience toward this deed? No thought of God?'

William raised his tankard. 'Nay, I do not. To use his words: conscience doth make cowards of men. Give me the slick boldness of a pint of ale and I will push forward in this pursuit despite his pleas.'

'So, still he pleads with you for he knows until the King recognizes him or you confess, he loses everything.' Herbert extended his hand. 'Then I will strike hands with you, sir, and promise to keep the dog at bay. Rome still seeks to dash those who have murdered against her, and perhaps Marlowe still fears even this. When the time comes, Shakespeare, I will send a final blow and I give my word backing the plays and sonnets in your name.'

Ben awoke with a loud smack of his tongue against his lips, the slobber glistening upon his beard like dew. He pushed back the mass of black curls from his face and focused his eyes.

"Thou art awake, Will. How do you feel?"

William kept his stare out the window. "Like a festering canker."

Ben snorted. "Well, 'tis good then, for this is thy disposition of every day."

William pulled the blanket close to his breast. "So says the pot to the kettle. You speak for yourself, Ben, for my cause is this fever that will not release its fingers from my throat."

Ben looked to the floor of the coach. "Would I be amiss to say thy fever is heart-rooted? I am a poet as you, William, and can see the muse's ardor in a man. What words can I say to extract the poison?"

William let go an ironic snicker. "A poet such as me? You are a poet such as me? I think not."

Ben's shoulders squared. "Nay, you are correct, I am better." His words brought a smile to William's face. "See, what would you do without me, Will?"

William looked into his friend's eyes. "You are a true friend, Ben. What will you say about me when I am gone, I wonder?"

"The same thing I say to your face, my friend; that you know very little Latin and less Greek, and yet you can write a line without a blot or redo which puzzles my mind. If truth be known, I wish a thousand of your words blotted out. You are as tiresome as your words, too perfect to believe. The sources of your quill flow from the sugary banks of the Indies and dost make me sick of thy company."

William smiled a little more. "Then why do you accompany me?"

Ben guffawed, his large belly rolling beneath his doublet. "Did not the gentle Romeo need Mercurtio, the clever soul whose wit and intellect far surpassed his friend. I fear for your safety, for men such as you, with your fancies and temperate eye, cannot see the rock that may stumble your progress. Men such as you need allies such as me to block, to lunge and to slice. See how I make your fevered heart rejoice? You need me for that as well. We will have you to your former self before we reach Oxfordshire."

The smile fled from William's lips as he stared out the window.

"My former self? That seems like an age ago. When was I ever my former self? Before London? Before the Queen's Men? Before Anne of Shottery?"

William leaned forward and buried his mouth into the scratchy wool of the blanket, his thoughts seizing his gut with a cough leaping from the depths of his chest. The ache held fast as it pounded and hacked until William collapsed onto the floor of the coach.

Ben lifted him onto the seat next to him and felt his forehead.

He reached within his own doublet and pulled out a leather flask, opened the seal and urged William to drink.

"How fares you, my friend?"

William shrugged against the seat. "Very, very ill, my friend. Ben, are you truly my friend, my Horatio even?"

Ben chuckled. "Unfortunately."

William smiled and stared back out the window. "Then will you keep my secret and not think ill of me? I must tell someone before I die, else the fires of hell will stoke double for me."

Ben leaned forward. "Whatever fires this fever, Will, I will keep it."

William grabbed Ben's arm, shaking with desperation, as his voice trembled. "Ben, are you a true friend? Will you seek my legacy even after I have died?"

Ben leaned near to William. "I am known as a rough man, Will, but I do love thee and will honor thy memory this side of idolatry. What you speak to me will die with me and I will see your name painted among the stars."

He squeezed Ben's arm. "Swear to it."

"I do swear."

William closed his eyes and relaxed. The color drained from his face as the secret clawed up from his heart, through his throat and settled on his tongue. He lifted his lids and stared deep into Ben's eyes.

"It is done, then. I shall tell you all, even using his words. This is the night that either makes me or fordoes me quite."

Ben's brow creased with lines. "His words? You mean your words, Will; the fever makes you quite forgetful."

William breathed deep and spoke, releasing the demon. "Nay, Ben, they never have been my words. They belong to Marlowe. I fear something dreadful when we reach Stratford, something afoot like the breath of a wraith hissing and waiting for me. If I speak not of this to you, I fear I never will. Marlowe... Marlowe, thy name is like daggers unto my ears."

Ben affirmed the same feeling. "Daggers unto many ears, Will. History and his own foolishness scorched his name with the plastering so long ago of his libel upon the church doors. I have my religious doubts, as do all of us in this time of upheaval, even sprinkling my own writings with the salt of questioning, but to do what Marlowe did, blasting his atheistic views and dancing about as if no one would notice, was insanity. 'Tis no wonder Frizer murdered him."

William felt the sickening humor rising from deep within. A small snicker escaped until his body shook with a diseased laughter mingled with coughing fits and watery eyes. Pain settled across his face like a shroud. Ben reached across to steady him, but William held up his hand to stop him.

"Murdered? Aye, of course, you think him murdered, and this is where my fear lies." William's voice trembled. "Ben, Christopher Marlowe is alive. Frizer killed no one that night in Deptford. The Queen spirited him away and I am his proxy, his page, ushering his words into England all these years. I warrant he waits for me in Stratford to reclaim what he lost."

Ben pushed back the mass of curls from his eyes and let the words settle in his ears. He looked to the floor, then out the window, then again to William's resolute face. "Alive? What means thou? His grave is in the churchyard of Saint Nicholas. The news of his death raged through London like a fire. This fever is making you quite mad."

William sat back and shook his head. "Nay, dear friend, I am not mad. I shall tell you more on this, for you will be my surety after my death. If you love me, then listen. Marlowe *is* alive. He will laugh upon my funeral bier and bury me for I have something belonging to him, something dear I promised to give back to him long ago. I have his words, copied in my own hand, the same as when I used to copy my fellow schoolmate's lessons at the King School. Even then, the quill never felt like it should in my fingers, not for writing anyway; but I could transform it into a sword or play the part of a writer. My schoolmate, Alfred, sat near to me and I used to watch his eagerness with the quill. He would bite his bottom lip and lean forward upon his open palm as if to steady the weariness of a tired brain. I learned to mimic him like a mirror image and we would sit side by side with our quills moving in harmony.

Then, one day I slid a farthing onto his desk. He looked at me and could guess the meaning in my eyes. He resisted at first, but the taste for payment became more of a reward, so I monthly supplied him with a coin and he indulged my secret. Schoolmaster

Hunt never guessed. I would catch him watching me from time to time, but he would only smile and nod in approval. 'Twas my first taste of the success of opportunity, so when presented with the chance again, I did not hesitate."

Ben could not raise his stare from the floor as he listened in silence. William continued. "Ben, Kit Marlowe is alive. I have been his proxy since his death is Deptford. All of the plays, poetry and sonnets are his words, not mine. The Queen paid me well, and I am protected by noble men who sought to stamp out all traces of Marlowe. How else did you think I acquired my holdings in Stratford? Upon an actor's salary?"

Ben's mouth formed a circle. "Forsooth, William? 'Tis the fever that speaks."

William shook his head. "Nay, Ben, 'tis not the fever, 'tis truth. The day after Marlowe's faked death, the Queen summoned me. I stood before her with a knowing smile, and she asked me if I heard some ruffian killed her dear Marlowe in a tavern brawl. I knew she tested me and I continued with the masque. She gave me a pouch of Spanish gold and commissioned a play for Greenwich come Twelfth Night. I wandered through the halls of Nonsuch quite unsure of how I felt about the whole matter. Then, a figure stopped me in the courtyard. 'Twas Archbishop Whitgift. To my surprise, he remembered me."

"Remembered you? From when?"

William lifted his eyebrow. "Quite ironic, you might say. Whitgift signed by marriage license to Anne Hathaway when he was Bishop of Worcester. I remember him saying then that he might do me a good turn when he reached his pinnacle. 'Twas as if Fortune lowered her hand over me and directed my course. I confessed all to Whitgift, thinking if I rid my soul of the lie I could continue without any guilt. I did not know until later of Whitgift's own plan against Marlowe."

"But I do not understand. Why would you have guilt?"

William looked away from him. "Because, Ben, I knew when I agreed to the plot to save Marlowe's life, and to be his proxy, what that could mean to my future and my fortune. I knew I had to keep Marlowe from ever coming back. Whitgift gloated upon the knowledge and we set upon a second plan to fix both our destinies. I continued divulging Marlowe's whereabouts and Whitgift continued setting traps for him in the form of pressure from Rome's spies. Richard Baines was most helpful in the plan, all the way until his own untimely death. And the Earl of Pembroke, my patron, hated Marlowe, as well, for his own reasons which I swore to never utter. I surrounded myself with men who despised Christopher Marlowe, thus insuring my success and giving me the revenge for his deeds upon my own family."

Ben shook his head. "Forgive me, Will, but I cannot believe this."

William leaned against the side of the coach and closed his eyes. "I know confusion fills your mind, but my head is pounding and the words are draining me. Death is all around me now, I can feel it. This journey is my cortege. Let me sleep and I will tell you more."

"What potions have I drunk of Siren tears,
Distill'd from limbecks foul as hell within,
Applying fears to hopes and hopes to fears,
And losing when I saw myself to win!"
Sonnet CXIX

XXXV

The darkness behind Christopher's lids blanketed in red. He moaned and sat up, holding his hand over the throbbing gash on the side of his head. Touching his fingers lightly over the wound, he eased the blood-matted hair away and gazed around the room as the memory of what transpired crept back into his pounding brain. His lip quivered. The messenger vanished on the breath of the morning air and the words, 'Shakespeare is dying' floated back to the surface with each heartbeat.

The puddled blood and ink on the floor stuck to his fingers. He held his hands up to his face and feigned a smile at the irony.

Blood and ink, my legacy. 'Tis a tragedy that would make the groundlings wet their eyes.

He wanted to laugh and cry at the tapestry of his life. A comic spin made it easier to accept the sadness, easier to accept the inept winding of the river flowing through the levies of the world stage. Too many people raised and lowered those gates in his life, completely unaware or perhaps uncaring of the times he almost drowned or when they left him sweltering in a drought.

"And all of them dead," he whispered, "and I am still flailing like a gasping carp in the mud."

He grabbed the side of his desk, lifted himself to stand, and ran his fingers over the empty space where his portfolio had been.

"I am such a fool to have trusted him! And such a coward… when did I become such a coward?"

Deep in his memories, Walsingham's words echoed.

When all who protect you are gone, I foresee you becoming a coward of a man, hiding behind your feeble words...

Christopher shuffled his bare feet across the cool limestone. He turned the latch, opened the door, and the sun blasted through the arches and across the tiny blue and white mosaic tiles of the palazzo floor. Looking in each direction, to the right a long passageway stretched with a pattern of red-painted paneled doors leading to the other rooms of the infirmary and two white-clad nuns standing at the end of the passage, their light Italian voices whispering in the breeze as they held their hats on their heads from soaring away like birds with outstretched wings. He watched them until their angel feet padded away and they disappeared around the far corner. As he looked again to the left, the passageway extended another twenty feet and curved sharp to the left. He walked near to a servant boy, who slept against the stone banister, and tapped the chair the boy sat upon with the side of his foot. The boy snorted and roused, wiping the saliva from the corner of his mouth.

"Signore Le Doux! I am sorry, sir... sir, you are bleeding!"

Christopher placed a finger on the boy's lips and looked over his shoulder in the direction of the nun's departure. "Hush, now, Benvolio, for I have a service for you to perform and you must do it quickly. Come into my room."

Benvolio went inside the infirmary room and Christopher followed, looking again to the right before closing the door. He sat upon the bed and spoke, dipping a rag into a bowl of water and cleaning the wound on his head.

"Benvolio, I need for you to take this money and book passage for me on the next ship bound for England. Next, I need you to send a cart for my things tonight after all have retired to sleep." The boy nodded. "Very good, now go. I will wait for your return."

The boy left and Marlowe exhaled a sigh. His heart pounded as he thought of England. Closing his eyes, he wiggled his toe against the cold stone floor, imagining the feel of the sandy beaches of the English coast, and he tilted his head back to imagine the sounds. The phantom seagulls cried and the roar of the waves surged against the beach before the chalk walls of Dover, all filling his ears, and then, further inland, his spirit soared through the green hillocks and sheep-dotted pastures, on to the crowded streets of London where the ravens cawed and the royal walls of Whitehall rose like a beacon to a weary traveler.

Many years passed since Christopher saw his homeland, three to be exact. 1613, the year Shakespeare's Globe burned to the ground during the performance of Henry VIII. Marlowe chuckled upon the memory.

Yea, that was a good memory. Shakespeare's dream brought to nought. Has it really been so long since the gentle mist blowing off the Thames has dampened my cheek?

Southwark buzzed with excitement that day. A passing shower doused the streets, leaving the people steamy and rank in the summer heat, yet they crowded into the playhouse, oblivious to the fetid smell of mud, sweat, straw and urine. The colossal O, Shakespeare's Globe theater on the banks of the Thames, opened wide its doors with the herald of the Master of the Revels posting a placard on the wall for all to view.

Kit leaned against the timbered beam near the door and read, his heart shadowing over in anger.

'Come all and see a new play by William Shakespeare: All Is True, presented by the King's Men with all pomp and ceremony, telling the true story of King Henry VIII and Anne Boleyn. To be held this day, 29 June 1613.'

Kit's fingers curled in anger as he resisted the urge to rip the placard from the wall. He bit his lip and mingled into the crowd, paid pence to be among the groundlings and pushed his way to the far left of the stage. The play began and Marlowe's heart sank as he watched the eyes of the people. The crowds wept upon Katherine's speech, hissed at Lady Boleyn, and cowered in awe at the imposing Henry; all the proper expressions for which he had hoped. He stayed a tear in his eye, knowing at the conclusion of the play the accolades would not be for he, but for Shakespeare. Yet, here he was, the true author, hiding like a banished humiliated creature among the poor, filthy, plague-scarred people of England. One more act and they would call for the author, and Shakespeare would strut out onto the stage. 'Twas more than Kit could bear.

As the scene fell away to the conclusion, Kit raised his gaze to the stagehands wheeling in a small cannon toward the end of Act Five, Scene Four, and perching the weapon high above the stage in the window of the solitary bird's nest platform within a stone's throw of the thatched roof. They tilted the barrel high, directing the mouth toward the opened circle of sky above the theater, packed the mouth with a dabbling of fine sifted gunpowder mixed with a portion of sand to give the semblance of a cannon blast without the dangerous results. Kit felt half-way pleased that the direction of the play yielded such lofty props to excite the crowds, and then, his mind wrapped around a delicious thought as his eyes fixed upon the cannon.

A few more lines and the player Chamberlain, the porter and his man will exeunt from the stage, he remembered. Then, they will light the cannon, sound the trumpets and all the noblemen bearing christening gifts for the player babe Elizabeth will pass about the stage. Kit knew 'twould be easy during the chaos of the changing of scenes to use his spy-like skills to traverse the back stairs to the cannon perch and drop something like wadding into the mouth.

Would it work? Could I behold Shakespeare's mighty circular dream, the thing precious to him, crumble into ash?

Kit pulled his mantle hood closer about his face and reached down into the straw strewn about the pit and gathered up a handful of the paper playbills the crowd cast aside. He glanced up, slinking along the side of the stage and dipping behind a curtain opening at the back, mindful of the eyes and direction of their stare. The Chamberlain's words and the blare of the trumpets entranced the crowds, all unaware of the vague creature tiptoeing up the stairs. The two stagehands leaned over the perch with their eyes fixed upon the stage, waiting for their cue. No one noticed the shadowy hand dropping the angle of the cannon, nor the fingers stuffing the wad of balled paper into the shaft. Kit crept in silence down the stairs, melding into the backstage commotion and back into the crowd. He weaseled his way to the entrance of the theater.

'Even now,' he snickered, 'I have not lost the movements of a spy.'

A moment's hush fell across the people as the sound of the lit fuse sizzled in the air and merged with the triumphant music heralding the fake royal babe. Kit paused and gazed over his shoulder, just as the cannon fired. Many in the pit shouted in shock and fell to their knees, some in wonder, and others in fear. Kit just smiled as he watched a single fiery page float upward on the thrusted wind. Higher it rose, swirling and drifting, until it rested on the dry crisp thatch of the roof. All of the audience admired the

babe on the stage, the image of their former Queen in infant form,
bellowing out her royal commands even then. No one, save for Kit,
noticed the flame flaring and eating away the straw. He pushed
open the doors and ran west down Maiden Lane, tucking himself
into a shadowy doorway on the corner of Horseshoe Alley within
view of the theater. The idle smoke caught the air and the tender
roof burst forth in flames.

Two gentlemen charged past him from the Hart Tavern,
pointing toward the building and yelling, 'Lo Ho, look! The Globe
burns! Open the doors! Open the doors!'

The screams crested and the panicked people poured from the
enclosure, surging, trampling, crying and fleeing. The Globe
became the stage, and the groundlings gathered in horror among
the elm trees of Winchester Park as the flames ran the ring of the
theater. Layer by layer, sizzling and popping, she crumbled and
fell. Through the heated glow and the filmy smoke, Kit watched as
Shakespeare ran from his collapsing dream in disbelief and fell to
his knees at the image before him.

Kit strode toward him and willed his stare through the smoky
haze. He paused within a few feet of William and watched as this
thief beat his chest and the ground, cursing and wailing. Sooty
tears blackened and streaked across William's face and the image
of this crushed man sent giddiness swelling in Kit's body. William
raised his head and through the thickness of the heat and ash,
their eyes met. The words in Kit's brain flowed out like a heralding
trumpet across the air, yet, to the stricken crowds skirting about
him, only silence. Silence, save to all except William, who saw
Kit's mouth move and form the whispering words.

'Do you know me, even after all this while? Even in my
disguise? See, William, Shakespeare, what greed hath wrought
you? Shall you be immune to the consequences of sin, retribution,
reckoning and the wages due for taking away my life? 'Twas not
only money you sought but also the glory and approval of all
around you. Pray, tell me, William, how does it feel to have
something precious taken away from you? Will you, even now,
turn back from this way and bring me back from exile?'

Kit kept his eyes upon him as William edged forward,
crawling on his hands and knees. The sight amused Kit. Two men
emerged from the crowds and lent their hands to help William to

his feet. Kit recognized the older man by his formidable chin and curling red hair as Richard Burbage; the other, a stranger to him.

Once William stood on his feet, the stranger threw back his dark cloak and gazed over his shoulder in Kit's direction. His stare pierced and delved, and he sniffed the air like a hound on the scent of an elusive fox. Kit's amusement ceased as fear froze his body. The protection of his disguise suddenly felt inadequate as the man's eyes fell upon him. The vaporous heat blurred his vision and the man's eyes seemed to glow like the demon shadowing him. Through the thickening smoke, the man appeared to morph into the image of Baines. Kit hid his face with the sleeve of his cloak and mingled into the gawking crowd. His pace slowed as he ambled around the glowing remnants of the theater, quickening his step past Bear Garden until he sprinted to the docks of Moulstrand. Ten to twelve ferrymen gathered near the docks and along the banks of the Thames to watch the blushing orange of the flames tinge the walls of the brothels and inns of Southwark.

Marlowe shook his head and huffed. "That is when I called for a boat and made my escape. Yea, I did become such a coward without the protection of Burghley and the Queen. And now, with such wrinkles upon my brow, what more do I have to lose?"

The night came slow as the sun sank low and the golden crown of Saint Peter transformed into a bright silver cap reflecting the reflective light of the moon. Christopher sat motionless. He readied for the journey to come. His ears strained in the silence, filtering the sounds and waiting for the cue. Distant laughter from the street and a cry of 'Lo Ho,' the deep tones of the bells of the basilica as the moon reached the midnight hour, and then, lastly, the rumble of cart wheels against the cobblestones.

Christopher raised his eyes to the door. The door latch turned and Benvolio's voice whispered through the darkness.

"Signore, I am here."

The door pushed open and Benvolio walked in with another boy following. The boys bowed before Christopher.

"Signore, this is my friend, Balthasar. He is here to help me carry your things."

Christopher held out two more florins and the coins glowed in the moonlight.

"All is in order, then?"

"Yea, Signore Le Doux, all is how thou requested. Thy ship leaves on the morning tide. Here are thy papers."

The boys carried the chest to the waiting cart. Christopher looked a last time across Rome, pulled his hood down across his eyes and walked down the passageway of the palazzo. With each step, he felt a heartbeat in his ears. With each step, he remembered the lyrical meters of his imaginary muse and the music of blank verse transforming into iambic perfection. He stopped for a moment, his eyes tracing the tiles of the hall until they rested on the image of his imaginary friend framed within an arch, the moon casting an aura around her copper tresses.

"Where have you been," he whispered. "I am going home, Calliope, the place wherein you blessed and cursed me. Are you happy? I will regain our children and my name."

She blew him a kiss.

Marlowe, bent at the waist and leaning upon a stick, his head still pounding from the blow, ambled with the two boys through the maze of Roman streets: west along Via Paola, south along Via Guilia, snaking along the Tiber and moving onward to the western port of Fiumicino. Only two pair of eyes gazed upon him and two voices spoke to him as he passed and he marked them. The first, the dark-haired Bianca of Via Paola, her home and Inn hidden in an alleyway on the Northern-most side of the Florentine Church. Here within the shadow of the dome, as the night crept along, she sat on the holy steps and lured strangers to her bed, both laymen and priests alike, for their need for lust and her need for money knew no religion.

He paused and watched her different aspects in the moonlight: her face, her form and the place they filled within the pages of his plays. Christopher nodded to her as he passed and she beckoned him, lifting her skirt to display her lily leg and bending her lip into an entrancing smile.

He held up his hand in refusal, speaking to her this last time.

"Nay, sweet Bianca, your bed is not a stopping point on this journey. My true love awaits and I must hasten to her side before my breath runs out."

Her smile fell away. "A journey? Thou art leaving me behind? Shall I no longer have the company of thy witty words?"

Christopher smiled. "You shall always be with me, for you see, I wove you into my words and you shall be immortal. Every man will wonder where is this sweet goddess whose lips they long to kiss?"

He walked near to her, leaned forward on his cane and brushed his cracked lips against her tender cheek. Taking her hand, he placed five florins in her palm. He bowed to her and walked away, looking down the shadowy Via Guilia.

Before him the piazzas lined the cobbled streets like majestic monuments to their artists: Raphael, Sangallo and Michelangelo. Their arches and ivy-covered balconies rising and falling like the steady breath of a sleeper dreaming of white marble gods and cobalt mosaics while soaking in the aroma of freshly painted frescoes inspired by God himself. Marlowe released a sigh. He always felt pity that the lusts of the Church laid the foundation for such a beautiful city. From the day he stepped his foot within her gates, he perceived her deceptive true intent hiding behind lily-white hands and pious smiles; so like Bianca perched on the righteous steps of the church prodding her flocks with a wink of her eye.

He traveled southward down Via Guilia, pausing once before the palazzo of Raphael. Many a night he came to this very spot, a lane across from the gardens where the tall narrow cypresses stood sentinel, and would stare up at the balcony. Here stood the birthplace of his Juliet, her name springing from the name of the street. Many years ago, he spotted a maiden on the balcony, her head tilted to the right as she rested her cheek upon her hand. Her blue-black hair cascaded down her shoulder and danced on the evening breeze. As he watched her, a band of boys ran down the lane, raising their voices in a witty aria and playing their lutes, all the while hiding their faces behind golden masks trimmed with festive ribbons and bells. He watched as they disturbed her quiet counsel with the moon, laughing and blowing her kisses while pleading with her for a night of revelry. But she was just an innocent maid, a maid whose cheek flushed red in the glow of the moonlight. Calliope blessed him that night, a sleepless night, yet when the sun rose the next morning, Marlowe laid down his quill and dusted the final page of his beautiful tragedy of that balcony-perched maiden.

He continued on after his musing, mindful of the moon and her melancholy sojourn across the sky, and hastened to get to the ship awaiting him. He hurried along, five city blocks down the Via Guilia, past the church of death where the skulls embedded in the facade glare out upon unsuspecting passers-by with the smile of finality, a knowing smile, a smile of destiny, a smile remaining with those who stop to stare as if to say 'thou wilt be with me soon.' Marlowe's aged limbs found quickness as he passed the steps to the church, never stopping to stare or to give those beckoning pale bones satisfaction in his nod. He looked to the starry blanket of the night and whispered words as he passed. They were familiar ones once uttered by Walsingham.

"Thou know'st 'tis common. All that live must die, passing through nature to eternity."

His eyes drifted downward from the heavens to the small arched bridge crossing the Tiber, the Ponte Sisto, and saw his imaginary friend once more, seated like a perched angel on the pediment of the bridge. Before her, on the ground, a shriveled little man sat shivering. Marlowe rubbed the wound on his head and wondered if he dreamed.

She motioned for him to approach, speaking to him as he cautiously walked near. "If it be, then why seems it so particular with thee?"

Marlowe stopped a few feet from the man, still the little man made no movement. He was small, frail and worn, and his skin pulled taut like a drum over the suggestion of a skeleton. Christopher looked over his shoulder toward the skull church, but the darkness swallowed up the faint outline. He looked again to the man. The man's clothes wasted away with his flesh and the holes exposed ribs, back and arms. Marlowe took another step, and the man looked up, his ashy face looking in the direction of the sound. The man's cloudy eyes searched for an image in the darkness. Lifting his hand, he seemed to hear another sound as he echoed the muse's words to Marlowe.

"If it be, why seems it so particular with thee?"

Marlowe felt the breath of death running up his back and down his arms. He answered. "You can hear her, old man?"

The man's face widened, his grin stretching and revealing bluish gums. "I hear you, sir. All that live must die... thou know'st to be common… I ask you why this seems particular to you in your tone… look at me, 'twill be a common thing for me soon."

Marlowe looked past the old man at the image of Calliope sitting on the bridge. She cocked her head, waiting for an answer. He obliged.

"Seems, sir? Nay, you are correct, it is; I know not seems. 'Tis not alone my inky cloak, good sir, nor windy suspiration of forced breath, no, nor the fruitful river in the eye, nor the dejected 'haviour of the visage, together with all forms, moods, shapes of grief, that can denote me truly. These indeed seem, for they are actions that a man might play, but I have within which passeth show, these are but the trappings and suits of woe."

The man laughed, the breathy huffs puffing out from the depths of a diseased lung as if each exhale to be his last. He pointed a finger at Marlowe's face as Marlowe pulled the cloak hood tighter.

"I know you, Signore. Before this cancer sucked my bones, I played this part on a stage here in Rome. 'Tis well known across the continent from those distant shores of England, even my own homeland. Death comes for me soon, and if I could see, my eyes would tell me death comes quick for you, as well."

Goose flesh tingled on Marlowe's neck. "Nay, sir, you do not know me."

"I do, for in my blindness, I see all men who fear death. I sit here in darkness, both day and night, for they are indistinguishable to me, like the blackness of the pit we succumb to in the end. Will you have anything with you in the place which binds us all that will be any more than what you have now? We are all mortals, sir, on this journey from birth to death, some of us closer to one than the other. Tell me, what are you seeking as you cross this bridge?"

Christopher looked again to the muse who stared down into the river, her reflection absent in the flowing waters below. His brow wrinkled as he pondered this parley, but still he answered. "My name, sir. I am seeking my name."

The man's raspy cackle echoed across the waters. "No forgiveness? Every man seeks forgiveness in this pious city full of priests."

Marlowe shivered and pulled his cloak tighter about his shoulders.

"Who are you, sir?"

The man lifted his sharp shoulder blades in a shrug and held out his hand, the bony fingers wriggling to Marlowe. "The blind leading the blind. Sir, sweeten my hand with a few coins for this is what I seek from those who cross."

Marlowe placed two florins in the man's hand and stepped onto the bridge. The man's breathy cackle settled in Marlowe's brain and, as he passed across the bridge, he heard the man blast the muse's words once more to the night air.

"What's in a name? That which we call a rose by any other name would smell as sweet."

Marlowe paused at the top of the arch and gazed Northward down the Tiber. He looked to his right, but the fog rolling off the water swallowed up the man and the muse. Far in the distance, through the haze, the orange glow of torchlight burned in Saint Peter's Square. There they burned continuous for any pilgrim who made his journey there by day or night.

Marlowe whispered. "What's in a name? My name, my words, by W.S. will not smell as sweet, nay, not to me. The torches of Saint Peter's burn bright tonight and I wonder, why do they journey there? For redemption, for absolution, for their name before God? Yea, indeed, I will have this pilgrimage and I will have my reckoning. Then, and only then, shall I not fear that undiscovered country from whose bourn no traveler returns. Now, back to my steady steps and my waiting vessel wherein I shall command, Westward Ho!"

On the other side of the bridge, the two boys sat upon the cart, their eyes fluttering with the weight of sleep. Marlowe approached and nudged them.

"Come, the night is well along and we have many miles ahead of us before we sleep."

Time passed quick and the rising sun silhouetted the three of them against the hazy glow of light surfacing from the horizon. Marlowe sniffed the air as he watched the darkness of night melt away. He smiled, remembering the vision of Hamlet's father smelling the morning air, announcing he must be quick for 'the glow-worm shows the mattern to be near.' Marlowe knew he must be quick, as well, yet still he stopped beneath an olive tree on the hillside overlooking the coast of Fiumicino.

The shadow of night moved away like clouds over the terraced landscape until the rosemary dotted hills warmed. A slight breeze rippled over the sweet stalks.

Rosemary is for remembrances, whispered in his mind, as his eyes followed the wind rising and falling, swelling and cresting through the herb, down into the vale and against the side of the ship rocking in the harbor.

The boys curled beside each other to his left, sleeping on the ground with stones as pillows. Marlowe laid on his side, removed his cloak and balled it beneath his head, just enough to keep his eyes affixed to the ship in the distance. A moment's rest before his journey across the sea.

This would be his last voyage and his sea legs ready. He recalled the first time he felt the hills and valleys of the ocean at eight years old, tossing and turning his youthful stomach until he retched blood. Walsingham laughed at him and Nicholas Faunt teased him for his weakness. Only Philip Sidney looked on him with an understanding eye, but then again, Philip possessed a gentle poet's soul. Kit found his sea legs later, after many voyages to the mainland of France, Germany, Denmark, Italy and the Netherlands, all in service of Her Majesty by the demand of his master, Sir Walsingham. Marlowe almost felt grateful for the travel, for in it he found an eye for new cities and new characters unfolded within his plays, even grateful at times for the tragedy, the hypocrisy and the blood. All of it translated into masterpieces the world eagerly ate up.

But those grateful times were few, clouded as they were by the shadow of a lost life. He lost any chance to run along the village streets as just a mere boy, or skip a stone across the flowing waters of the Thames just for fun. Those were idle childhood games for ignorant illitcrate boys, not the bloody games played between Catholic and Protestant pawns, the young brilliant geniuses used and molded according the will of Walsingham.

Marlowe looked again to the two boys across from him. Peace glowed on their dirt-smudged faces, a restful sleep whose dreams were perhaps of paper boats and puppies. He envied them. He thought of the old man at the bridge who spoke of men's lives being closer to one end of life than the other, birth or death. The boys had a world awaiting them and he wondered what kind of men they would be, what kind of decisions they would face, what kind of betrayal would shape their lives. His envy turned to sorrow knowing that in a fleeting moment, they would change. They too would struggle on weary limbs searching for the boys they used to be to no avail. He wondered, as well, if they would remain friends or if the greedy hand of jealousy or greed would eat away their hearts and set them at odds against one another.

It had been so with Baines, for he blamed Marlowe for all of his failings. Marlowe shook his head, chewing on the thought of how different things could have been. How easily Baines could have leaned the other way if ever the Queen had acknowledged him with a slight smile. She did not, and so he never learned to play the game proper.

That is, not until all those protecting me slept that eternal sleep. How like fate to maneuver Baines and Whitgift into Shakespeare's path, and to remove Burghley and Elizabeth. Those companions part of the masque were like flies living for a day and dropping to the windowsills. Burghley, the Queen, Poley, Frizer, Skeres, Danby and Mistress Bull: all dead. Their mouths forevermore silenced with no fulfillment of the promises they made.

Christopher sat up and wiped his hand across his eyes. The memory of Baines drifted away, for the moment, as he beheld the ship again in the distance. He stood and pulled his cloak about him and turned to face the two boys. Their dewy faces shone with morning sunlight, innocent and fresh, and eager for their payment. Marlowe untied the leather pouch hanging from his belt and poured out ten florins in the palm of his hand. The boys held out their quivering palms.

Marlowe counted out two coins each and watched their eyes flash and their smiles gleam. He took another singular coin and held it up to their faces. He tossed the treasure high in the air. At that moment, the boys lost any care for friendship as they ran and scrambled, slugged and bit, yelled and cried for the extra coin. Even as Marlowe traversed the terraces with his cart to the waiting ship, he could hear their cursing.

He did not look back as he walked across the dock of Fiumicino. The sea-weathered boards squeaked under his feet and the gulls squawked and circled high above his head. Marlowe hid his face from the crowds, always mindful to speak in French and keep his eyes lowered, even though he doubted anyone would recognize him as the vibrant young playwright and provocateur of two decades ago.

He gave his papers to the man at the gangway and a young cabin boy came and helped him lift the chest onto the ship. All proceeded well. The sky forgave, the waves lay at peace and Christopher's heart readied. He walked to the front of the ship, the bow pointing to the West, toward England, and he breathed in the salty air.

"Or I shall live your epitaph to make,

Or you survive when I in earth am rotten;

From hence your memory death cannot take,

Although in me each part will be forgotten.

Your name from hence immortal life shall have,

Though I, once gone, to all the world must die;

The earth can yield me but a common grave,

When you entombed in men's eyes shall lie.

Your monument shall be my gentle verse,

Which eyes not yet created shall o'er-read,

And tongues to be your being shall rehearse

When all the breathers of this world are dead;

You still shall live – such virtue hath my pen -

Where breath most breathes, even in the mouths of men."

Sonnet LXXXI

XXXVI

William stared out the window as the familiar landscape of
Warwickshire unfolded. He let his mind drift away, for a
moment, as his heart soared in the green castle-like forest of
Charlecote.

William reached in his cloak pocket, removed a letter and
handed it to Ben. "Before we reach Trinity Church, look here at
part of my proof, dear friend."

Ben unfolded the pages and read:

'W.S., 15 June 1605 - *My muse is gone. All my charms are
overthrown, and what strength I have is mine own, which is most*

faint. Now, 'tis true, I am here confined by you. Let me not dwell in this sterile promontory by your spell, but release me from my bands with the help of your good hands. Gentle breath of yours my sails must fill, or else my project fails, which was to please. Now I want spirits to enforce, art to enchant; and my ending is despair unless prayer relieve, which pierces so, that it assaults mercy itself, and frees all faults. As you from crimes would pardon'd be, let your indulgences set me free.

Thy quill, C.M'

Ben folded the letter and handed it back to William. "These words are from your Tempest."

William huffed. "From his Tempest. Can you not see with your own eyes this writing in his hand? Are you so stubborn a man so as not to believe tangible proof?"

"'Tis not that, Will. If indeed this man is alive and supplying you with these works, then, where is he now? Why has he not taken back what is his from you? Forsooth, if a man took away my words and gave them his name, his belly would feel my dagger."

William breathed deep and clutched the velvet fabric of his doublet in his fingers as a pain shot through his heart. "In truth, Ben, this shadow that follows me from London is one of flesh and blood, I fear. He is coming, I can feel it. Death is close on his heels. This fever clenching her fingers about my throat is a guilty conscience, brought on by heavy drink and advancing age. I always thought time would ease my worry, and yet, to hold on to the lie, wanting so to bury it with me, has become a struggle for my everlasting soul."

Ben leaned forward and took William's arm. "Pray, tell me, you think Marlowe is indeed coming after you after all these years?"

"Yea, I have a sense of it. I received a message a few days ago that a trusted conspirator who knows of this secret sent hither to Marlowe's hiding place to put an end to him. The message told that the deed was done, but there is no proof of it. Perhaps 'tis nothing but the vaporous sensation a man has when he knows death is galloping toward him. I do not know what to cling to any more, Ben."

Ben's stare fell to the floor. "Perhaps faith, William, is the only thing left to a man before he dies. But think not on that, you will recover your wits here in the countryside."

The coach rounded a curve and ran parallel to the Avon. William lifted his head and gazed across the treetops. Within his sight, the tall spire of Trinity Church appeared through the elm trees. He leaned from the window, yelling to the coachman.

"The church there, take me to there."

The lane narrowed to a small walking path dotted along with cobblestones and moss, and the sunlight pierced through the elm trees like small beacons of God's glory. Ben helped William from the coach, nearly carrying him to the doors of the church. William took a deep breath and willed himself to stand, biting his lip as the sweat trickled down his brow. He grabbed Ben hard by the shoulders.

"Leave me here. I wish to enter alone."

Ben sighed and walked back to the coach as William laid his hand on the church door latch. A click and a push and he entered, his steps slow and pained. He closed the door and turned, leaning upon the door and soaking in the memories of the days he spent here, the days he forgot and the days he cursed. All exactly as he remembered as if the memories stilled and puddled within the stream of time; and yet, a thickness hovered, a slow melancholy lay like dust across the floor. Dried autumn leaves lay untouched along the stones, blown in through the broken stained glass. William swirled his cloak about him, brushing through the leaves and dust, and gazed downward into the chancel. One step, then another, then another, until the weight of the fever drained him and he collapsed before the altar. He did not try to move, but lay there with his face chilling against the cool limestone floor and the dust caked on his sweaty cheek and brow. He closed his eyes and shivered.

"Here below me is where I shall lie eternally, my feet toward the East to wait until the sounding of the trumpet, until his voice calls and I stand once again. Where shall he send me? Shall I taste the sweet bread of everlasting life or the stinging melting heat in the bowels of the earth? O, dear God, forgive me! I have stolen another man's life to save me from the mediocrity of mine own. How shall I repent now, now that death lies like a shadow next to me? I cannot give him back his life, it is spent. If only a week passed, even a month, but two decades plus three gave my heart another home. How irony dost fill me that his own words do inform against me, blasting me at every turn, shaking an accusing finger even now. Shall I speak them? Why can I not find my own words to accuse me; why should your words, Kit Marlowe, whisper in my brain?

'O, my offense is rank and smells to heaven. It has the primal eldest curse upon't, a brother's murder. Nay, not murder in the strictest sense, but indeed, I have taken his life. Pray I cannot, though inclination be as sharp as will. And indeed, what form of prayer can serve my turn? Forgive me my foul deed? That cannot be, since I am still possess'd of those effects for which I took away his life: the glory, the money, my name, my houses, my theater, and plays upon plays. May one be pardon'd and retain the offense?

What then? What rests? Try what repentance can, what can it not? Yet, what can it when one cannot repent? O wretched state! O bosom black as death! O limed soul that, struggling to be free, art more engaged! Help, angels! Make assay! Bow, stubborn knees, and, heart with strings of steel, be soft as sinews of the newborn babe! All may be well and yet …"

William rose onto his knees, his body shaking from the force of the words.

"O… O… O, Marlowe leave me be! His words fly up and my thoughts remain below; words without thoughts never to heaven go. This church holds no forgiveness, 'tis an empty shell, a skeleton of remembrances and tombs."

The tiny hairs on his neck stood erect as the sound of shuffling footfalls echoed across the tiled floor. William turned his head until his eyes bent their stare across his shoulder.

"Marlowe?"

A crippled caretaker approached with his hat in his hand and the lines of decades etched into his face. He leaned forward in a humble bow.

"Begging your pardon, sir, but can I assist you?"

William crawled across the floor and pulled himself up onto the steps of the altar. "Who are you?"

"I am Timothy, sir, caretaker and gravedigger of Trinity."

William paused and scratched his chin. "And who pays for your service, sir?"

The man shrugged. "Well, sir, 'tis mine own inclining, but I am sent a small pension since the day of young Hamnet Shakespeare's death from his own father, to look after the plot where his family shall rest ．"

"And have you met the man who pays you?"

The man fidgeted with his hat. "Nay, I have not. He has not been to Stratford since the time Hamnet was a little lad, gone off from his family and scrounging in the sewers of London, I was told."

"So, I have heard, as well. And you saw his son buried?"

"O, yea, sir, I dug the hole. 'Twas the plague death, sir, and he was buried quick. His father gave no thought to coming to his own son's passing, but 'tis no matter. All comes right on judgment day, eh?"

William flinched as he gazed across at the plots he secured before the altar in the nave. "Why is there no plot marker for his son?"

"O, sir, Hamnet 'tis not buried here. I suppose of a guilty conscience the man bought up these plots after Hamnet's death thinking God would have to look down with favor upon these stones. The boy lay buried somewhere in the churchyard. 'Tis no marker for the playwright's son."

William urged the man closer with a gesture. "Here, take this money for your pains and for your service."

"My service, sir?"

William pointed to the first plot. "There you will dig a grave, six foot deep. Begin it soon, for Master Shakespeare will end his journey there before many days, methinks."

The man took the purse. "You are a friend of Master Shakespeare, sir?"

William lifted his eyebrow in an arch. "A friend? Nay, I hate the man."

The gravedigger spat on the ground. "You hate him yet you would pay to see him well bestowed."

"Yea, for you see, I lie. I do love the man too much, methinks."

The man shrugged as he turned away. "Thou speaks strange, sir; but thy money is enough to send me to fetch my spade. I thank thee."

William bowed his head and placed his feverish brow upon his palm. "O, Hamnet, my son! Is there nowhere I may kneel before your monument and beg for your forgiveness? I cast thee aside to follow Marlowe, to follow my own ambitions. I did indeed become my father, the very thing I swore my family would never see. O, the paths we stupid humans choose, thinking we have a lifetime to fulfill all our hopes and dreams, to correct wrongs and meld our lives into the shape of perfection. And then, like a whisper, 'tis breathed and 'tis gone. Nothing I do now will alter the life I chose. Hamnet is gone. My young life snuffed out and my old before long, and what will live after me? Nothing. My name, Shakespeare, will die after me, lost forever upon the death of my beautiful boy. O, what was all this for?"

William pulled himself to his feet, the muscles in his neck straining from the pain. He shuffled down the nave and turned into the arm of the North transept, feeling for the door leading to the graveyard. An anxious need shot through his body as the sun glinted through the rising fog and across the gloomy markers. His legs found urgency as he ran through the field. Then, just as sudden, his body faltered, and he collapsed in a weeping heap among the stones, his right hand slamming across the ground and sending his signet ring tumbling into the yew bushes. He dug his fingers into the dirt, pulling at the weeds and roots and flinging them into the air in his search. He growled like a mad animal, fighting against life and death, choices, mistakes, and all the earthly sins plaguing a man.

Ben heard the ravings and ran through the churchyard until William's figure formed before Ben in the misty fog. He grabbed hold of William's arms and pulled him close, wrapping his arms about William's shaking body. William lifted his face to heaven and let out a sigh from deep within his bowels, the depths of a broken man. Then, he whispered, his voice cracking as if the breath in his lungs vanished.

"Ben... I know not where he sleeps. No one... no one does. I failed him. Money he had... and a house with a fire... but no father. He had no father."

Ben lifted William, his frail form crumpling into Ben's arms.

"Come, dear friend, we will get you home. I have sent for the solicitor and for your son-in-law. Do not fear, Shakespeare. I am your friend and will not leave thee."

"Your love and pity doth the impression fill

Which vulgar scandal stamped upon my brow;

For what care I who calls me well or ill,

So you o'er-green my bad, my good allow?"

Sonnet CXII

XXXVII

As the shores of Italy shrank away to the horizon, Marlowe kept a vigil with the dark deep blue depths of the Mediterranean Sea. The waters lifted the ship gentle as the bow cut through the swelling breaks. An airy mist kissed his cheeks until they were cold and wet. His mind crested like a happy sea-boy playing among the ocean of his plays where many times the sea played a part in dashing Viola's ship to pieces, bending to Prospero's hand, parting the French and the English in the narrow Channel, and the swelling Adriatic. Hamlet took arms against a sea of troubles and now, he, Marlowe, would do the same and hull through the wild sea of his conscience.

As the ship broke out in the sea room, past the shoals and rocks, the sailors hoisted the sun-bleached sails. The cloth flapped against the wind, then inhaled and filled like a proud man's chest.

There is no turning back now. My mission and course set. My life is before me, or could it be my death? Exile has been a scurrilous thing. Banishment in jest, to begin with, somehow latched on to my life like a cockle feeding upon the rumors. Who scandalized my name? Who spread the lies across the length and breadth of England to the point that everyone believed? Shall I believe the idiot Baines set all in motion when he could not fulfill any assignment given to him in the past? And Shakespeare, as well? Did Baines attach to him, or was this all his own inclining? One step back upon the shores in my own skin would have caused my death, nay, will still cause my death, perhaps. So, why now do I go?

He pondered to himself and let the words troll across his lips as the waves rolled against the sides of the ship.

"Why do I go? 'Twill be my death if discovered in mine own skin. Why is this visitation different? I have visited many times before in many form, as a Frenchman, an Italian and others. But now I return as myself and now I feel pigeon-livered. Is this noble that I have suffered the slings and arrows of a calamitous life, the whips and scorns of time, the oppressor's wrong, the proud man's contumely, the pangs of despised love, the law's delay, the insolence of office and the spurns that patient merit of the unworthy takes? Nay, 'tis not noble, but cowardly. Now shall I my quietus make, gain my reckoning, reconcile and repent before my last breath, for I fear it comes quick."

His chest tightened, and he held his hand across his heart. Beneath his fingers, he felt the rattle of his breath as he coughed. Still, his words seethed across his tongue.

"Conscience has made me a coward as I bore the insults of Baines, the despised love of the Countess, Elizabeth's delay in clearing my name and in the insolence of her office-holders, Burghley and Walsingham. They forgot me as I sailed away from England like a string dangling from a hem, too insignificant to notice and easily cut off. Pages and pages I wrote for her, plays and poetry mingling within the cryptic and coded clues spelling out my name. Those having eyes blinded themselves. They admire Shakespeare and the lie is easy to believe. Seems my own propaganda speaks against me."

He lifted his chin and braced against the bracing wind, looking intently at the horizon. "I am coming, Shakespeare, and will rise like Hamlet's father, like Banquo's spirit at the banquet table, and I will expose this iniquity."

Marlowe turned with his back to the railing and gazed across the deck. Many of the passengers gathered to enjoy the journey, soaking in the warmth of the spring sun. He noted them all: sailors in their weathered brown sea-gowns, Lord and Ladies bejeweled in the colors of the earth, deep sky blue, meadow greens and wheat-kissed gold; and all laughing and conversing, their voices blending with the ocean roar; and then, pocked among the crowds stood one black raven of the Church.

Marlowe blew out a disgusted huff and caught the stare of the tonsured monk. The man lowered his head toward him and smiled, even as Marlowe narrowed his eyes to look upon him with a devil's stare. Marlowe's mind filled with words and he whispered them, even willing them on the wind toward the monk.

"O, what plans does Rome have against King James? Many a man such as you have I killed, and many a man such as you have I seen kill, all the while smiling that sanctimonious smile with one hand in the holy font and the other in blood."

The monk looked away and Marlowe's thoughts washed over him with a realization.

What makes a man decide to kill, even in the throes of piety? What makes any man traverse the path he takes? What of myself? Could I have not simply refused the path Walsingham set before me, or was there blood lust in me, as well? I sold my soul for another four and twenty years, to see the glory of my work expounded. Am I so different from Master Shakespeare then, or these monk-assassins?

A woman walked between Marlowe and the monk, the sunlight catching on her fiery red hair. Marlowe's fingers wrapped around the smooth curved rail, as he felt a familiar pain deep within his chest. His words tumbled out once more.

"O, how differently things could have been. I might now lay in my deathbed with my dearest love encircling her arms about me, but alas, you look at the path before you and say, 'Nay, I shall go this way, not that, for this way looks pleasing and straight,' and then, at the bend, you fall from the cliff and there is no turning back. How many times must I fall from the cliff? Nay, not this time. The demon shall not come to take me or shred me to bits. I repent and Calliope herself will right this wrong."

A low rumble echoed out across the calm waters of the ocean, bringing Marlowe out of his dreamy stance. He looked up and perused the earthly canopy. Fluffy clouds reached into the sky like heavenly castles, gray-washed and ominous. Far in the Western sky, in between the breaks of clouds and sunlight, a sheet of silver fell from the dark sky, and then, a flash and roll of thunder, a warning of things about to come.

Marlowe retreated to the safety of his cabin just as the first raindrops pelted and spotted the dusty boards of the deck. All those on deck ran for cover except for the brave sailors clamoring up the ropes to drop the sails.

In his cabin, he listened. The thunder rumble grew louder until the ship shook to the core. The table in the middle of the room shivered. Marlowe removed his cloak and laid it across the simple wooden bed. The sea chest, his constant companion, sat awkward-like near the door, moving a few inches each way to the rocking of the ship like a living thing taunting him and teasing him. He pushed the chest hard beneath the bed to where it remained silent and still. And, still, Marlowe's stomach churned.

"Nay, I will not think on thee. You are my funeral bier and I will not think on thee."

Marlowe removed the dagger from his belt and whittled away on the bony end of a feather until it curved into a point. He held it in his teeth as he reached in his cloak pocket and took out a bottle of ink. He uncorked the stopper, closed his eyes and ritually let the pithy smell fill his nostrils. As his eyes opened, he sensed his imaginary friend sitting near the end of the bed. He did not look at her, but only smiled and greeted her.

"Welcome, Calliope. How like you to go back to England where you did first kiss me?" He thought he heard her whimper. "Nay, sweet muse, be not afraid of Jove's mighty rumbling. We will be safe. A week in the crossing and we will meet the chalky shores of Dover. Now, to my work. I pray for your kind help, for my quill aches for a requiem epitaph for Shakespeare, one that will weave my spirit into the words with clever codes of my name. Something in my soul says he does not have many more days. Foul whisperings are abroad. Unnatural deeds breed unnatural troubles. Infected minds to their deaf pillows disclose the heat of a mind and I pray I arrive in time to soak up the revealing truth. Help me, dear Calliope, for 'twill be my last dagger for this Judas."

A laugh rolled out of his chest and mingled with a cough. He took the quill from between his teeth, dipped and scrawled out several lines. The ship rolled across the rain-kicked sea. The storms worsened, pitching the wooden vessel within a maelstrom. Remembrances of words crept across his tongue as Calliope kept watch over him. She mouthed the words as he spoke them.

"Now would I give a thousand furlongs of sea for an acre of barren ground, long heath, brown furze, anything. The wills above be done! But I would fain die a dry death."

Thou will die a dry death.

Marlowe opened his eyes to her and his brow wrinkled in deep furrows. "Fine apparition, 'twas that prophecy you spoke? You said the same to me once long ago whilst I stood on the deck of the *Nonpareil*."

She smiled and looked away from him, the vision of her fading away as a light rap came upon the door. Marlowe walked across on wobbly legs, balancing himself from the rise and falls, and opened the door. The monk stood in the hall, holding himself steady against the door frame. Marlowe's stunned look quickly fell to the man's hands to see if he held a dagger. The man only clutched a pearl beaded rosary, entwining the jeweled idol in his fingers. Still, Marlowe's heart skipped a beat as if death stood at the door.

"Signore, many of the guests have gathered in the dining hall to pray. I am sent hither to bid others to come."

Marlowe released a breathy laugh and answered him in Italian. "I thank you, but my aged legs are better resting upon my bed. These days my knees complain if I bend them in prayer."

Marlowe tried to close the door, but the monk stepped over the threshold and bowed his head. "Then I will say one for thee here."

Marlowe's eyes squinted in puzzlement. "'Tis not necessary, sir."

"'Tis very necessary, for every man should prepare his soul for heaven. Think if the ship tears apart from the storm and we fall into the sea; wilt thou die without confession?"

Marlowe continued to hold the door open. "Confession to you? I shall give none of my words to you or to anyone else ever again. My words are the one commodity I alone can possess. I should have learned that long ago. My last words shall be mine and mine alone."

"But surely you would have your soul fit for …"

"For heaven, sir?" Marlowe spat on the floor. "Nay, I have seen your heaven and the whips and fires you put people through to get there. I have even tasted the sweet breath of a muse who spoke of a different path to heaven, but the honey from those lips became the song of a siren. So many times those higher offered heaven, only to snatch their hand from me. This time I shall take it with my own bare hands. I shall not leave my fate in anyone's clutches."

The monk pulled a chair out and sat, his face falling in and out of the shadows as the lantern swayed over the bolted table. Marlowe closed the door and stumbled to the bed.

The monk questioned him. "I take it then, Signore, thou art not a religious man?"

Marlowe's face screwed up in a laugh. "Religious man? I received holy orders in Valladolid and before then, studied in Rheims. I warrant I know the verses better than you."

The monk lifted his left eyebrow. "So, thou art a priest? I could not take it from thy clothes and thy manner."

Marlowe removed the dagger from his belt and placed the blade on the pillow next to him.

"'Tis not these weeds that denote me truly, just as many such as you hid deeds behind the facade of a scratchy wool gown while hiding your sanctimonious smiles 'neath a hood whilst you dropped your rosary and took up a dagger."

The young fair-haired monk smiled and narrowed his eyes. "Thou speak as a bitter man and thou listen to rumors and lies."

Marlowe stood, leaning forward on the table to look the monk square in the eyes. "Rumors? Lies? Nay, I have seen the deeds with my own aged eyes. You are a young faith-bitten fool, but one day you will know the amount of blood Rome drinks. The fat Cardinals glut themselves with the liquid."

The monk's mouth sagged in a frown. "Now thy voice flavors with the accent and acrimony of a French Protestant."

"No, I am not a Huguenot, for even the other side washes their lily white hands in the same liquid. Tell me, does God require such quenching? I do not believe in such a God."

"Then thou speaks as an atheist."

Marlowe's countenance fell as he sat back on the bed. "So it has been said. To be such is a scandal upon one's name and thus, I hold that tattoo upon my brow. Tell me brother, how shall a person cleanse their flesh and their name before God and make it fresh as a babe?"

The monk held out the cross in his finger. "Kneel, kiss this cross and confess thy sins and I shall give thee absolution."

Marlowe smirked, his voice resounding in sarcasm. "Ah, as

easily as that? Then, tell me, brother, how shall you give me absolution founded upon a church that will not confess its own sins? When did you hear the Pope supplicate for forgiveness for breaking the commandment 'Thou shall not murther' or 'Thou shalt not bear false witness'? Shall I go on?"

The monk remained silent, his face shadowing over with a strange innocence. Marlowe continued.

"You know not what to say to this, I see the doubt in your eyes. You are young, yet, I wonder… what would you undertake to ascend to the heights of the church? Would you murder for it?"

The monk's words whispered out. "Murder for the church? 'Tis unheard to mine ears. No one has ever spoken of such deeds to me or asked such things, and yet, you are saying you know of such holy men who have done this?"

"Ah, yea, murder most foul, as in the best it is. I could tell you tales that would harrow up your young soul. Stories of Queens and Bishops, spies, plots and intrigue. Of Elizabeth, Walsingham, Burghley, Mary of Scots, French and Spanish Kings, Armadas, and yea, of your precious Pope. But let that be, I shall not speak on it, for even in confession the stain holds fast. There is no reclaiming my soul; it has been sold unto hell." Marlowe held up his hands before his eyes, opening his palms and stretching out his fingers. "Out, damned spot! Here's the smell of blood still and no perfumes of Arabia will sweeten this little hand. What's done cannot be undone."

The eyes of the monk perked up. "I know that, sir, 'tis from a play that I saw once in London. 'Tis from Master Shakespeare, I believe."

Marlowe's mouth turned up in an ironic grin. "Indeed? A monk who delights in the plays? 'Tis very strange, but you know the plays well?"

"Some, sir, but not all. Many of the monks disapprove of them but I find it helps to know the minds of the common people, thus helps to lead them to God."

"And, how, sir, is your Latin?"

"'Tis a native tongue to me, for I trained at the Vatican."

"Then, tell me the meaning of 'Si una eademque res legatur duobus, alter rem, alter valorem rei.'"

The monk rubbed his brow. "Yea, I know the translation. It

means if one thing is bequeathed to two persons, one of them shall have the thing itself, and the other the value of the thing."

"Yea, I have the thing and he, the value of the thing. So many times, I scattered the clues. I hid them in songs, in sonnets and soliloquies; yet never once did anyone notice. Every word doth almost tell my name; do you know on what I speak?" The monk shrugged as Marlowe stood and opened the door for him to leave. Marlowe motioned for his dismissal. "Brother, I do not need you here. I am an old man and have not the strength to illuminate you on the secrets of my heart. I do not seek forgiveness or consolation; what I seek is beyond your giving. I thank you for your pains, but remember what I have told you. One day the church will ask you for a deed that will make you question your faith. How will you answer? Will you give up the dearest thing you believe in for the quest of the glory? Think on it, brother."

The monk bowed and backed out of the room, the glow of the candlelight shining across his shaved head. Marlowe's fingers curled and, for a moment, he felt the tingling desire for the blade within his hand. Something deep inside whispered to him as the monk skimmed his stare across the tops of his lids and the left corner of his lip turned up in a smile.

Goose flesh tingled up Marlowe's arm. *What is this look, this visionary glance? Is it the allusion of Mephistopheles? Shall I kill him now? To what purpose? O, how the taste of blood doth salivate upon my tongue! Nay, for once in my life I shall leave it be. Close the door and let him pass. Perhaps this one is truly innocent.*

Marlowe slammed the door shut and turned the key in the lock. He gasped for air and stumbled to the bed. Sweat gathered on his brow as his mind ran hot with fear, with words and with guilty deeds racing before his mind's eye. He pulled the blanket beneath his chin and squeezed as Calliope's hazy image appeared across the room. He spoke to her.

"How did it come to this? This falling off? My wordy children hide like shamed creatures, seeking the company of the adopted father they have known, and abandoning their true one. Why, Calliope? I only sought to keep them sheltered and well fed or else the world would never know them. Shall I continue to run after them and beg for their forgiveness, seeking my repentance? How did it come to this?"

The vision of her dissolved into a watery shape, morphing and coming again into view, this time in the shape of the ghostly form of Thomas Kyd, his yellowed eyes peering through his blood caked brown hair. Marlowe caught his breath and touched the wound on his head.

"What has this injury done to my brain?" Marlowe shivered as the image raised a finger and pointed toward him. "Avaunt," Kit cried. "Quit my sight! Let the earth hide thee! Thy bones are narrowless, thy blood is cold; thou hast no speculation in those eyes which thou dost glare with! Never shake thy gory locks at me! Thou were a tortured friend. Yea, 'twas thy doing and now shall I sleep and remember thy betrayal? Thou were a weak man, a Brutus, and I have lived my life in exile on thy doings."

Kyd's ghost vanished and Calliope walked across the room and sat at the end of the bed. Marlowe sighed.

"O, heaven and earth, must I remember?"

"And I will call him to so strict account,

That he shall render every glory up,

Yea, even the slightest worship of his time,

Or I will tear the reckoning from his heart."

(I Henry IV, III, II, 152)

XXXVIII

Deep in the night, Marlowe's coach stopped at the Tabard Inn on the outskirts of Southwark to refresh the horses. The driver tapped his whip against the side of the coach, awaking the sleeping Marlowe. The horses, changed and suited in the common chinks of coach tack, snorted and blew as Marlowe watched them through the carriage window; their dark and velvety coats blended into the midnight air. The coachman clicked his tongue and tossed the reins, and again, they were off toward Warwickshire.

A somber mood of reflection fell across him as the moon peeked from behind a passing storm cloud which covered the landscape of London in a white foggy glaze. All on the ship survived the tumultuous crossing, and each dispersed on separate paths; yet, not before the monk paused on the beach and cast his dark eyes and prophetic smile in Kit's direction.

Marlowe shook his head to rattle away the disconcerting thought. He directed his gaze back and forth across the thatched and tiled rooftops, the familiar haunts of his life. The Cathedral of Saint Paul towered above the stacked houses of Blackfriars, casting a religious shadow over the tavern where he had spent many a day writing, drinking, debating, and drabbing. Sadness collected around his heart, slowing the beat to a methodical painful thump within his chest. He held his hand to the spot and closed his eyes as he leaned his brow against the window frame.

This is the last time I shall see you, my lady, my London. I have come home to taste your honey lips I have missed, but only

*now to drink your form in sips. Yet, even you betrayed me. You
cast me aside for that masked player and revel more in the false
tale than in truth. Have you not always been such a fickle thing? A
shrew when it suited you and bending like a reed to the current
blowing in from the surrounding countryside. Yea, even you were
a dark lady to me, covering your fair face with a black mask as a
lady of the court does when flocking to the public theaters,
disguising intent and rank and identity to me, shameful of my
presence. I gave my life to your protection and like a strumpet, you
forgot me and bedded another. Why... why... why? And your
ordained mistress, Elizabeth, the leader of you, took you by the
hand and lulled you into this deceptive peace. 'Twould have only
taken a word from her, a single line, even I could have written it
for her. A simple thing to write, such as 'Marlowe is alive, bring
him home,' or 'Marlowe writes Shakespeare's plays' or any quaint
thing that would have been the key to the chains I am bound in
since I was a boy. Did my name ever cross her virgin mind as she
laid there upon her deathbed?*

He closed his eyes and dreamed of the sad day thirteen years
ago as the coachman spurred the horses.

*All of England sat in silence upon the whispered hush that
Her Majesty drew to bed. The citizens of London walked about like
sad wafting spirits drifting on the air, waiting for the dreaded
words, the tolling of the bells, the snuffing out of the candlelight in
the window at Whitehall Palace. Kit blended into the arena of the
city, taking on his familiar disguise of a Frenchman, and awaited
a different word: a summons, a reprieve, anything to announce his
release.*

*The crowds gathered in the streets of Surrey and in the
courtyard of Richmond Palace, and the nobles took their station in
the Grand Hall, straining their ears upon any whisper, their
tapping fingers and worried brows wrapping around the
speculation of the succession. Kit melded among them, watchful of
those he must avoid. He slipped behind a column, just in time to
see Richard Baines lurk into the room and position himself within
view of the stone steps leading to the Queen's apartment.*

*Kit conjured the scene of the death chamber as he leaned
against the column. There she lay, propped up against the creamy*

satin pillows, the delicate fake curls of her wig flashing a shocking
orange against the scarlet curtains hanging from the canopy
above her, bedecked in her exiting clothes of gold brocade and
silver thread, crimson bows across her breast, her fingers
twiddling with the royal coronation ring embedded in her swollen
forefinger. A rumor circled that she stood at the window in silence
for two days as if she contemplated the pictures of her past, her
arthritic fingers resting upon her cracked pale lips; no food, no
water and no words crossed them. Yet, Kit imagined her turning
and smiling, radiating the aura of the muse who inspired him, and
extending her hand to announce to the room and all of England
that her one true servant, her darling, Christopher Marlowe, was
alive and must come before her before she took her last breath.
And that Shakespeare was merely a well-paid player to protect this
beloved favorite. Marlowe imagined the shock in Whitgift's eyes,
the look of failure in Baines' face, and the admiration of England
as they welcomed home their prodigal son. Yea, all the proper
people in attendance: the ladies-in-waiting, the new Lord
Chamberlain, Robert Cecil, and, of course, the one who had
procured himself into her favor, Archbishop Whitgift. The thought
struck Kit that of all of the faces hovering about her deathbed, not
a one among them of her true loves. No Essex, no Dudley, no
Burghley, no Walsingham; all preceding her in passing off this
mortal coil and now waiting like a line of angels for her to take
her everlasting throne. Kit snickered in his throat.

'Or like devils heralding her descent. Yet, dear lady, here I
am, for you to brink back from the world of the dead as you
promised. Bring me back as you fly across the Styx.'

Kit watched as Baines wrung his hands and smacked his lips,
waiting for the Queen's call and the giving of one last favor upon
him. Kit found the anxious look on Richard's face amusing and the
thought that, for this moment, both waited for the same thing: a
word from the Queen.

All the faces in the Hall turned as one guard, already dressed
in mourning clothes, approached the top of the stairs and walked
near to Lord Cecil. Cecil leaned his ear toward the youth and the
crowd paused in a reverent hush. Kit stood straight and readied
himself for the summons; but then, an unthinkable thing cascaded
down the stairs like the tumbling waters of a waterfall, breaking

and dashing across the rocks until they settled into a clear still pool—the whisper.

Kit watched as the message flowed from mouth to ear, quickening and surging until it rested on the lips of a gentleman near to him. He leaned forward to accept the words into his own ear, anticipating the revelation of his name. The gentleman cleared his throat, and the words brushed across Kit's ear.

"'The Queen is dead. They say the last word she spoke was Robert Dudley's name.'

Kit flinched, his eyelashes batting against his skin as he tried to blink away the realization of the words. His thoughts stumbled out in snatches.

'Did she... was there... nothing more?'

The man reared back from him. 'You mean the succession? Look, the Lord Archbishop stands ready at the top of the stairs. We shall hear more.'

Whitgift strode out onto the landing, his face lowered in a mock humility. He held up the coronation ring and spoke, lifting words from Marlowe's own works.

'Our beloved Queen, Elizabeth the First, of the royal house of Tudor, is dead, and as befitting such a Queen, who loved the arts, we speak. Though of her death our memory be green, with mirth in funeral and dirge in coronation, we do announce her wishes that her cousin Scotland mount the throne.'

The voices and cries mingled together like out-of-tune instruments blasting and wailing, lilting, cooing, and weeping. Kit stood in disbelief as the crowds surged from the palace and out into the streets, carrying him along like a leaf on the wind. The muscles in his throat seized shut and his eyes stung with a harsh sadness, and the air moved about him as if time fell into a void, taking with it all hope. The same feelings swept over him the day Burghley died. That day shrouded his future but did not bury it, although he did then fear without Burghley's encouragement, the Queen would edge away from her promises to him. His fear happened, even more so after he sent a letter to Lord Burghley the week before his death. The page contained one simple line:

'Where is my reckoning? C.M.'

To which, Burghley answered back with his own frank style of words.

'I cannot force her hand. B.'

Which Kit knew as utter nonsense. There were plenty of times he had seen both Burghley and Walsingham play the game of persuasion, directing the royal person down a path in a way she imagined was her own inclining. They had done so with the affair of Mary of Scots, with Robert Dudley, with Lord Essex, and now, even with himself. Kit felt tossed upon a turbulent sea, jubilant at the headwinds given him when Walsingham died, for Sir Francis would have kept him on that dark path of blood, and pained at the maelstrom created upon Burghley's death as it began the swirling vortex now concluded upon Elizabeth's last breath. He watched as a black flag skirted up a wooden stake above the turreted castle keep. As the cloth inched along, Kit's face drained of feeling and he fell to his knees.

England darkened with mourning. Kit fell to grieving, yet for an entirely different reason. All hope for the man he was, for this banished man, would now lay most still in a tomb, unable to release her promise and her love upon her most favorite playwright. Her only words had been for that man, Robert Dudley, and not a one for Kit Marlowe. With his one heart, he wept and cursed.

The coachman paused before taking the horses across London Bridge. "Sir, we are to Southwark. Are you sure you do not wish to sleep out the night here at the Inn?"

Marlowe opened his eyes, pushed back the curtains from the windows and gazed out across the fields. The boxy outline of the row houses and inns near the Thames focused into view in the moonlight. A cloud drifted away from the moon, flooding the scene like a lantern, and there, within his sight, stood the majestic circular walls of the Globe Theatre.

He answered the driver. "Nay, sir, I do not. We shall continue on to Warwickshire. Tell me, though, is that the Rose I look upon?"

The driver leaned forward from his perch and squinted. "O, sir, methinks 'tis the Globe."

Marlowe lip twitched upon the name. "But, sir, I thought the Globe burned three years ago in the summer of 1613 during a performance?"

"Yea, it did, sir, but 'twas rebuilt with incredible speed. Only three years and the crowds gather there again to see the mighty plays of Master Shakespeare and others in his company."

Marlowe frowned and whispered, "Indeed, seems I am thwarted at every turn."

Marlowe pressed his forehead against the side of the window frame, supporting the weariness sweeping upon him as they passed through the streets of London. His former joy of reunion with his homeland melted away into a pool of depression. Calliope's wordy breath caressed his ear as she snuggled near to him.

"Calliope, I am journey-bated and now you seek to fill my mind with former words? Go away! God forbid that made me first your slave! I should, in my thoughts, control your times of pleasure or at your hand the account of hours to crave, being your vassal, bound to stay at your leisure! Why do you torment me with more words? Can you not see I am weary with toil? By day my limbs, by night my mind, for thee and for myself no quiet find!"

His imaginary friend, his faithful lifelong companion, touched her fingers to his chin and urged him to look at her.

Why do you journey, my darling?

Marlowe closed his eyes and allowed this airy conversation. "You know why! To reclaim the lost seed, our children! Do you not weep for them? Nay, I gather you do not, for your flighty and adulterous ways bore you hence to Shakespeare's side as he gave them life on the stage. Did it not make your sisters happy? Did Melopmene and Thalia frown and laugh at the sport he made with my words? They did not care that the words did not originate from his mind and hand. They cared only to inspire his lips as he spoke them and his hands as he directed. Leave me be, Calliope, I am sick of thy company. I would be happier today without women in my life."

Calliope reared back from him, dropping her hand from his face.

Your heart has changed. Where is the brilliant boy whose virgin mind I once kissed?

Kit growled at her and swept his hand through the air as her form swirled away like a vapor into the night air.

"Changed? I have changed? Nay, my purpose is the same now as it ever was. 'Tis not I that changed, 'tis the world around me.

Would you sleep content to let William Shakespeare bear my words to his death and give me nothing for the nights of unrest I gave you?"

He could still hear her voice deep in his mind.

Do you still seek glory for yourself, Christopher Marlowe? All things will come right in the end. Do you still not trust, even now?

"Nay, I do not! Trust thee? I have trusted too many creatures in my life and all of them have betrayed. Now I shall trust myself and my own hands. 'Tis something I should have done long ago instead of bending and waiting for all those around me to give me my reckoning. I said leave me, for I no longer have use of you."

A gradual sadness filled the air in the coach as she spoke.

I will leave thee, Christopher Marlowe; but know this, without my help, this will all come to naught. I leave thee with thy solitude. Farewell.

The night air chilled as a misty rain began. Christopher felt her leave him as if the dermis of his skin peeled away in a sheet. He seized his chest and gasped as the air in his lungs disappeared like a man falling from the boughs of a tree and landing on his back. The breath returned, and the fear settled. Marlowe touched his fingers to his cheek as he realized his mind voided of all thought—blank like an empty page. A deep throbbing pain churned in his stomach. He clasped hold of his cloak as the fear swelled, dotting beads of sweat across his forehead. He squeezed his eyes shut, and he shuddered at the void within him as the simple thoughts of a common man eked out across his trembling lips.

"Where are you? Forgive me… forgive me."

His eyes sprung open when he realized he could not remember the rhythm of a sonnet, the sweet lyrical meter of a poetic line, or the meaty meaning in a soliloquy. All the skill vanished with the silence of Calliope's voice. Marlowe shoulder's shook and his teeth clattered together, as a different voice filled his mind: his own accusing words mingled with the only line left for him to remember, a line from his Faustus just before the demon came to collect his due.

O lente lente currite noctis equi! Cut is the branch that might have grown full straight and burned is Apollo's laurel bough that sometimes grew within this learned man.

His stomach heaved as he cried out like an orphaned child.

"Am I going mad? Calliope, leave me not!"

He opened the door to the coach and flung himself out onto the roadside, rolling and collapsing into the muck. He scrambled to his feet as the coachman reined the horses to a halt. Marlowe ran into the darkness, his eyes scanning the night sky for a suggestion of her form. The coachman bolted from his perch and sprinted after him, catching hold of him within thirty feet of the road.

"Nay," Marlowe cried, "lay off your hands! I must find her! I must ..."

The coachman held Marlowe fast, even as he struggled and wept.

"Sir, what is this madness? 'Tis a wonder you did not break your neck tumbling from the speeding coach. Come, sir, I will help you to the seat. Surely these were night terrors that sent you in such a stir."

Marlowe grabbed hold of the man's arm, his senses puddling like the soft rain collecting on his shoulder. "How far are we from Warwickshire?"

The man helped him mount back into the coach. "Sir, 'tis still night. We have this and the morrow and another change of horses before our wheels touch the cobblestones of Stratford."

Marlowe wiped his brow with the edge of his cloak, smearing the wet mud in a streak. He raised his hand and waved. "Lay on, man, lay on. I thank you for your help, now here let me rest. When we are close, wake me, so I may look upon my betrayer's home."

The coachman climbed back to his perch and snapped the whip, spurring the horses onward. Marlowe curled into himself, his aged bone creaking and aching from the fall. He felt tired and drained as he closed his eyes. The thoughts in his mind sputtered in disconnected snatches instead of the beauteous and melodious cascading of a poetic waterfall. The thoughts of a simple man broke his heart.

I am dying... I am lost. Shakespeare will be my release... yea, he will give me back my words... then, she will return. Yea, then all will come right. Yea, then shall my reckoning come...

"When a man's verses cannot be understood,

nor a man's good wit seconded with the

forward child understanding,

it strikes a man more dead

than a great reckoning in a little room."

(As You Like It, III, III, 9-12)

XXXIX

The moon silvered in the clear night sky, glowing in the serene waters of the Avon as Christopher Marlowe's coach ambled across the lane crossing Clopton Bridge. Marlowe tapped the roof of the coach at the arch of the bridge and opened the door.

"Here, sir. I will walk from here." He handed the coachman another pouch of money. "Here is another purse for your pains. I thank you for your speedy delivery. Leave my trunk at the Inn and tell the innkeeper that a gentleman, a Monsieur Le Doux, will come shortly to fetch it."

The coach sped away, leaving Marlowe standing on the bridge. He looked to the left and to the right, one path leading away from Stratford, the other leading to the heart. Making his way over the wall, he scaled down the rocks into the reeds at the bank and ambled along with the flow of the river, gazing once to catch his reflection in the waters. He held out his hands before him, his pale skin catching the ghostly shadows forming from the moon streaking a glow through the trees. The patterns imitated the stains of blood.

"Shall I kill again? Silence this betrayer and take back my name? O, Calliope, will you not come back and direct this final act?"

A breeze blew, rippling across the waters and rustling the tree branches across the way. Marlowe's eyes strained in the darkness as he prayed for her image to form. A deeper blackness cloaked over his eyes as a dark cloud strayed across the moon. He dropped his hands and continued the journey along the riverbank.

A moment's reprieve in the cloud broke and Marlowe's eyes rose to meet Trinity church rising before him, glowing in the momentary light. He frowned at the symbolic meaning that his feet would lead him to retry repentance. He looked to heaven, his poetic words still silenced, and raised his fist to the sky.

"What good has faith been to any man? What faith is true? Catholic? Protestant? Of what shall I repent to? Nay, my purpose is set. I knew from the day I left Rome where my faith lies. I do not repent this course, nor do I forgive the betrayers. Cast your eyes down upon this Shakespeare. Will you bless his damned deeds? Will you forgive him?"

Marlowe stilled his breath as if waiting for an answer. The rhythmic sound of a spade violating the earth broke through the piercing silence. Marlowe followed the sound, pushing through the doors of the church and he gazed down the chancel into the nave. There, before the altar, an aged man dug into the ground and whistled a happy tune. The top of his gray head peeked over the ridge of the hole.

Marlowe walked near, but kept to the darkness. The old man tossed his spade onto the tiles of the church and pulled himself from the grave. Marlowe spoke, recalling lines from his play.

"Whose grave is this, sirrah?"

The old man smiled, his teeth gaping and brown. "Mine, sir."

Marlowe looked about him, searching for Calliope. The gravedigger's form reminded him of the old man seated at the Ponte Sisto bridge in Rome. He continued.

"I think it be thine, indeed, for thou liest in't."

The man laughed. "You lie out on't, sir, and therefore 'tis not yours. For my part, I do not lie in't, and yet, 'tis mine."

"Thou dost lie in't, to be in't and say 'tis thine, 'tis for the dead, not for the quick, therefore thou liest."

The man chuckled. "'Tis a quick lie, sir, 'twill away again, from me to you."

Marlowe grinned. "You are sharp, sir, and shall I continue the play? I will ask what man dost thou dig it for, and you will say for none; and for what woman, none either; and again, for whom, and thou shall say for one that was a man, sir, but, rest his soul, he is dead."

The man wriggled his finger at him. "Yea, all of us know Master Shakespeare's plays, but as for dead, nay, he is not."

"He is alive, then? Master Shakespeare?"

"Yea," the man answered as he wiped his brow with a cloth. "Yea, for a bit, but I heard the talk, as talk spreads rapid in a small town. I saw the doctor, his son-in-law, John Hall, racing down the street toward New Place, when I went to fetch my dinner. I saw his daughter and his wife standing in the doorway, nary one of them with a look of sorrow on their faces. 'Tis no matter, for all of his wrongs will come right soon enough."

Marlowe reached into his pocket and removed a parchment page from inside his doublet. "Indeed, sir, a reckoning approaches soon. Do you know a mason that will set this to stone? I wish to pay for a monument in remembrance of this Shakespeare."

"Yea, sir, I can have it done."

Marlowe handed him the page and the last of his coins. "Then, get to it, man. I have a journey to complete."

Marlowe turned and sauntered out of the chancel, pausing once as the man's voice whispered through the church. "And why do you journey, sir? Will you not stay for the memorial?"

The skin on Marlowe's arm prickled as if an angel brushed by him.

"You know why I journey. Did you not ask me the same when I saw you seated before the holy waters of the Tiber? I seek my name, old man."

The gravedigger chuckled. "Before the Tiber? Nay, you did not see me… but if thou seeks thy name, why dost thou not kneel here before the altar? I will brush away the dirt so you may kneel."

Marlowe wrapped his cloak about his arms. "Nay, I will not kneel," he yelled, as he charged back into the night air.

As he made his way along Mill Street, a dark figure shadowed him and crept along hidden beneath the cloak of night. The blade of a dagger flashed in the moonlight clutched between the stranger's fingers.

Shakespeare pulled the covers of the bed up under his chin. The chill rose to his chest and his heart pumped with an icy coldness, slow, tired and strained. He laid beneath the quilt his

mother stitched and the vision of the Guild Chapel within his sight
through the window of his home at New Place.

John, his son-in-Law, dampened his head with a wet cloth.
Ben stood near as John questioned.

"This fever, it has continued all this while, since when you left
London?"

"Yea, it has," Ben answered.

"This is very like the sweating sickness of so long ago,
methinks. Can you not think of no other cause that might have
brought this on?"

Ben shrugged. "I came upon him after we spent an evening at
the Mermaid."

John's brow furrowed. "Indeed, then 'tis quite likely the poison
of a viperous ale. If it does not break…"

William opened his eyes, his vision hazy and blurred. He
reached out for Ben. "Ben, what hour is this?"

"The sixth hour nearest to dusk."

"And the day, my friend?"

"'The twenty-fifth of April, Will. You have slept in your fever
since we arrived here to New Place."

William sighed deep. "Ah, the same day I came into this
world. Pray, tell me, Ben, what kind of day is it?"

Ben looked out the window. "'Tis a glorious day, Will; a
spring day like none other. There is a slight breeze blowing off the
sweet waters of the Avon catching the tendrils of the willow trees
and bending them like a prayer. If you breath deep, your nostrils
fill with honey clover and heather mingling like perfume in the
fields of Charlecote."

William raised his hand. "Enough, Ben, for this type of poetry
sits ill upon your rough manner. Indeed, 'tis a fine day to rest. John,
how is my daughter?"

"She is well, sir, as is your wife."

He grabbed hold of John's arm. "Will they come to see me?
No, wait, I see the answer in your eyes. 'Tis no matter. I do not
blame them. I do not blame her, for I did set a table of hatred,
rejection and resentment and bid her feed upon it. I was an absent
man to my family. John, bid them to forgive me, I pray you."

John turned toward the door. "I will, sir. I will come again this
evening to check on you. Ben, will you stay with him?"

"I will, sir."

William closed his eyes. "Ben, look there to your left on the desk and retrieve my quill and paper, for I wish for you to add to my bequests and make sure the solicitor receives these papers."

Ben uncapped an ink bottle and sat at the desk near William. "I will do this for you, friend, but 'tis foolishness. 'Tis a fever you will recover from, Will. You are leaning toward the road to death as you pen your will, for a healthy man waits at his leisure to do such things."

"As you said," William answered, "a healthy man does not do such things, and this I am not."

William leaned forward and hacked into his blanket. The maddening pressure within his brain flexed with each cough and the fever surged and rose again.

"Take this down, Ben. To my daughter, Judith, one hundred and fifty pounds of lawful English money paid to her this way: one hundred pounds in discharge of her marriage portion within one year after my decease, so shall it be for deliberately marrying that knave Quiney. All else, including my home in Stratford, to my daughter, Susanna, and her heirs for the entirety of their life. Then to my kinsfolk, my sister Joan, twenty pounds and the house in Stratford whereon she lives. There are others, as well, the solicitor knows of already. Ten pounds to the poor of Stratford to ease my conscience, and my sword, my gilt bowl, and the like have names attached to them. Shillings to buy remembrance rings for my fellows John Hemmings, Henry Condell and my dear Richard Burbage. There, that is enough."

Ben cleared his throat. "Will, what about Anne?"

William huffed. "Indeed, why should I mention her now upon my death hour. 'Tis a coldness I have kept for her since the day I left Stratford, why should I warm to that name now? Nevertheless, 'tis enough the law grants her right to one-third of my estate as a matter of course, so she will lack for nothing. 'Twill be the mention of her name in my will she will seek to grind her teeth upon after I am a corpse in the ground. Will I give her satisfaction?" He paused for a moment and thought. "Very well, I will give her what is hers. To my wife, Anne, I leave unto her the second best bed only, which she brought forth from Shottery and can take away again. Are you satisfied, Ben?"

Ben held up the leather portfolio thick with sonnets and plays. "Only this, Will, what of your writings, your mighty works penned and played upon England's stages? Will you not have me gather them up, bind them and commit them to posterity?"

William turned his head away, his gaze falling back into the flickering shadows of the sun peeking past the tapestry over the window. "Pray, Ben, tell me, how shall I gave away that which is not mine. Do you see these airy things within my reach? Are they here in my possession? Shall I convey this nothingness to your keeping? Have you been deaf to the confessions of my heart, determined to stay the course of this bold lie I have lived? Nay, set it not down upon my testament for I fear the black words would leap from the page and strangle me in my sin, accusing me before mine own eyes that I claim what is not mine. Leave it be."

Ben stood and placed a hand on William's shoulder. "Very well, for now, but I will not let this matter rest. Think on't. I will leave you to sleep for a while whilst I go to Burbage's Tavern for some food to eat. Will you be well?"

William sighed and rolled over to face the window. The sun melted into the horizon, filling the dusk with the springtime hues of pales oranges and pinks blending into the wispy clouds. William kept a vigil out of the window and the hours passed as he took turns between sleeping and staring. His hot thoughts fleeted across the images of his past and always coming to rest upon the picture of Hamnet frolicking along the bank of the Avon. The sunset and the past dissolved and blurred into the hours of night. The fever seized hold of his heart, arching his back into a moment of heat and cold surging through his veins. He flung his head from side to side, wrestling with death as the wraith sought to snatch away his breath. He grabbed hold of the sides of the bed, clinging to life, as he feared...

"That undiscovered country from whose borne no traveler returns," a voice spoke in the darkness.

William's eyes sprung open as the creeping feeling of another presence filled the room. He spoke a question into the air.

"Did I speak aloud?"

A figure, shrouded by a black hooded cloak and banked in moonlight, answered him. "You did, and the words were not of your making."

Shakespeare released a groan from deep within as the man untied the cloak and let it fall to the floor. He raised his hand and pointed to William. The man spoke.

"Is it a ghost you look upon, Shakespeare? Am I human or an apparition come to accuse you of your crimes; you who did take my life?"

William's lip trembled. "Marlowe... Marlowe... have you come to send me to my grave?"

"All things in proper order, William. I come to claim what is mine. You swore to me long ago 'twas not my words you sought, but only to line your purse with coin. When did it change, sir? Perhaps when you saw the registered pages of Venus and Adonis distributed among the streets of London emblazoned with your name, or perhaps the first time the groundlings swooned for more than your acting, calling out for the author to bow before them, or maybe the day you strutted Twelfth Night before the Queen at Greenwich Palace and she extended her hand to you, smiling a knowing smile as the secret your shared passed from eye to eye. I heard she grew to be quite fond of you, but did I not teach you that, as well, on how she would bend her favor to a daring look and a pleasant voice? And then, 'twas so easy a thing to deceive King James, for he knew nothing about the masque. O, you played this well, William, as you banked upon the hope that I would fade away, that those seeking to kill me might discover my hiding place, which would send your name into posterity and silence me forever. Well, sir, here I am, in the flesh. I am no specter sent to haunt thee. I have blood coursing through my veins, hot with intent. Deliver unto me what I ask for and I shall leave you to die in peace."

William rubbed his brow, damping the back of his palm with sweat, as his eyes fell to the portfolio lying on a chair near to him. Marlowe caught the look. He seized the book and untied the bindings. His soul sighed as the pages and words filled his sight; and yet, the manner of writing was not his own.

"What is this," Marlowe asked. Shakespeare remained silent. "These are copies in your hand. Where are the originals I bid you keep? Where are my originals your man stole from me in Rome?"

William rose to a sitting position, his voice soft and full of fear.

"They are gone, Marlowe. I feared to keep them. I committed the originals to the flame."

Marlowe glared at him and he grabbed hold of William's right hand. "Then, all remaining is this. Confess your deed before God and before our King and release me from my bonds. Here, I give you pen and paper. This time you shall write your own words."

Marlowe scrambled to the desk and lit a candle. He removed a single sheet of parchment and slammed the ink bottle onto the desktop. William reared back from him as Marlowe's teeth clenched and he growled the demand.

"I will have my reckoning, sir! Signed with ink or with blood, William, I care not how 'tis performed."

The corner of William's mouth twitched. "Marlowe, cowards die many times before their deaths. The valiant never taste of death but once. Of all the wonders I yet have heard, it seems to me most strange that men should fear, seeing that death, a necessary end, will come when it will come."

Marlowe's hands balled into fists and his face reddened. "O, you call me a coward? Yea, I have tasted death before, but you are a fool to think you are valiant. You who cannot use his own words to counter me. I know my own Caesar's speech."

William made no movement of submitting, sending Marlowe into a frenzied roar. Christopher charged at him, tearing away the blanket and sheets as he clawed at Shakespeare's fragile body. Marlowe grabbed up William's linen nightshirt, crumpling it in his fingers, as William shrunk away from the angered touch. Marlowe shook him until William lifted a crinkled hand, his voice cracking like the dry branch of an aged oak tree.

"Marlowe... mercy! I have not the strength to fight you... nor the ability to right all that has passed. My signature would not bring your life back to you. I see your brown locks dulled in silver and your skeleton wears a wrinkled weed. We are both old and have lived a life born on the back of sin. What could I do now that would bring back the youth of wrong deeds righted?"

Marlowe slammed him against the headboard. "What could you do? Give me my name, William Shakespeare! My bones are sound enough even now to live another five or ten years from your deathbed. Time enough to thwart the demons of my past, time enough to…"

William lowered his eyes. "Time enough to be a father to a son? To glorify your name and hope that all your children will welcome you with outstretched arms? Pembroke will not have it so."

Marlowe released William's shirt. "Pembroke? What of him?"

William took the cue and played his hand. "Did you think me so stupid a man that I would not figure out the secrets of your sonnets? Then, an interesting thing happened the month the sonnets were completed and registered. I received a message waxed with the seal of the Earl of Pembroke asking for my presence at his home in Salisbury. 'Twas a revealing visit to both of us, as you can imagine."

"He told you then? You know he is my son?"

"Yea, but he will not acknowledge you, else he falls to the state of a bastard. He gave me his word that if ever 'tis revealed that he will accuse you a liar and will support the publication of a folio of all your works in my name."

"What? He knows?"

Shakespeare leaned forward in the bed. "He knows and is the one who sent the messenger to find you in Rome. Obviously, he failed in his attempts to silence you forever."

Marlowe backed away, stumbling over the cloak he dropped on the floor. The deep hacking cough returned upon him as he blindly reached for the desk chair and sighed.

"O, but he did not fail to snatch the last of my words, which he will never release from his ransom."

William almost pitied him. "Look at us, Marlowe. Old men who have lost sons and lost lives, scrounging for the few crumbs left to us before that eternal rest. What more can we hope for?"

Marlowe lifted his gaze toward him. "To die with thine own name, William Shakespeare, for 'tis the only one I will ever have. Will you cling even now to what is not yours?"

"Not mine? 'Tis the only life and name I have known, as well. Yea, 'twas a stolen one, but did I not wake every morning to my task? Did I not pound the boards upon the Globe and the Blackfriars and the Rose, the comedies before the Queen, the tragedies before the King, biting my nails and hiding in the dark, under candlelight, to copy your works in my hand? 'Twas the only life I have, Marlowe, and now you would have me do the very thing you yourself cursed? Give up the name I have and reduce my state to a scoundrel and knave?"

Marlowe pounded his fist against the desk, his voice straining in desperation until every nerve ending in his body trembled. "'Tis not yours! What, is this a quandary? Nay, 'tis a simple confession. You are a well-paid player, Shakespeare, nothing more. I will have my reckoning or I will have blood!"

Marlowe's stare softened, flying past Shakespeare into the vacuous air, as Calliope's hazy figure glistened in the candlelight as she stood in the corner near Shakespeare's bed. Crouched at her feet, her two sisters hid their faces behind gleaming golden masks, frowning and smiling at the scene before them. Calliope tilted her head, her lips turning down as if she stared upon a dead loved one.

Marlowe directed his words to her, the wound on his head throbbing once more. "Do you not come your tardy son to chide that, lapsed in time and passion, lets go by the important purpose of this visitation?"

"What is this madness, Marlowe," William questioned as he raised up in his bed and pondered Marlowe's struck eyes.

Shakespeare's stare hardened as a strange shadow, hidden beneath a dark cloak, slipped into the room from the doorway, tiptoeing behind the oblivious Marlowe and touching his fingertip to his lips to silence William.

Marlowe gasped as the shadow seized him from behind, placing the sharpened tip of a naked dagger to the pulsing vein below his jaw. Marlowe's body froze, and still he could not take his eyes from his imaginary friend in the corner, even as the shadow spoke familiar Italian-flavored words to him.

"So, 'tis you I am dispatched to kill. What irony that we sat across from each other on the same ship from Fiumicino. I could tell you thought me so young and stupid that I did not know the amount of blood my master drinks. I know it all, Signore Le Doux, or rather, should I say, Christopher Marlowe, and all the church accomplished for a righteous cause. I hear that many times you slipped from the fingers of Rome, yet God remembers. Thou shall reap what thou hast sown. The phoenix rose only to find the flames once again. Have you prepared yourself, for I shall rip you to shreds for the innocent martyrs thou hast killed? Rome's cause is still the winning back of England's soul. Even now, we prepare to bring down your Protestant King James."

Shakespeare remained motionless as Marlowe eked out his answer.

"'Tis you, the monk? I spared your life in my chamber, and now I do repent my momentary folly. Who dispatched you?"

"O, 'tis a tasty morsel! Baines fed my master many rumors that you still lived until the day of his own death, as did Whitgift and Pembroke, but my dispatching came from another anonymous source."

Marlowe caught Shakespeare's stare. "Ah, William, so you learned to play the part of the provocateur, as well."

The monk continued. "Yet, you kept slipping through our fingers. I almost had you that day in Southwark when the Globe burned, but you were still clever and young enough to escape. Rome never forgets those who take odds against her, and now, with your death, thus ends all Walsingham wrought. Now, shall you eat this blade!"

Calliope's words filtered through the air into Marlowe's ear, unheard by all other ears except his.

'Thou knew it must come to this. Thy life is a tragedy, Christopher Marlowe. Thou wilt have no reckoning in this generation, nor the next, nor the next, for thou knowst God bestows blessings upon those who value their name before him, not to those who carelessly discard it. You were the sparrow God saw fall all those years ago, Kit, but herein is your fault: even now at the end of your days, all that thou seeks is the glory from men. Three times on this journey did he give thee a chance to beg for forgiveness, and three times did you fail. O, Marlowe, if thou hadst given ear to me, innumerable joys had followed thee. But thou didst love the world...'

Her voice flowed off the monk's tongue, as he squeezed the dagger tighter into Marlowe's throat. "And now must you taste hell perpetually."

She answered: *'O, thou hast lost celestial happiness, pleasures unspeakable, and bliss without end. Had'st thou affected sweet divinity, hell or the devil had had no power on thee. Had'st thou kept on that way, Marlowe, behold in what resplendent glory thou had'st sat in yonder throne, like those bright shining saints, and triumphed over hell! That hast thou lost. And now, poor soul, must thy good angel leave, the jaws of hell are open to receive thee.'*

Marlowe grabbed hold of the monk's hand and struggled to tear the dagger away as Calliope's ethereal shape vanished before him. He caught Shakespeare's fevered glare.

"Shakespeare, give me my reckoning! Tell me my name will not fade to naught after this bloody death! I have become mine own character Faustus, selling my soul for another four and twenty years to see my art expand; and now, this devil who hath his hands about my throat will rip me to shreds. O, that time might cease, that midnight never come. Fair nature's eyes, rise, rise again and make perpetual day, or let this hour be but a year, a month, a week, a natural day that Marlowe may repent and save his soul to see his words bath in the waters of his name. William, I am dead... thou lives... report me and my cause aright to the unsatisfied..."

His voice squeaked, gurgling out his final words as the dagger popped through the fatal vein. "Drop, drop, drop... goes the candle wax..."

The monk released him and Christopher bent forward, clasping his hands about his throat. Slowly, as the light faded, he raised his hands before his eyes and soaked in the last colors of his life. His legacy, red and black, blood and ink, forever brandished upon his fingers. He stumbled forward, catching his fall across the bed where Shakespeare stared in amazement. Marlowe clasped him by the shoulders as he coughed, spraying a shower of red across William's chest. No more words brushed across his lips, only a slow bubble of blood gurgled from Marlowe's throat and saturated the bed around Shakespeare.

William cocked his head, his head dropping in sadness as Marlowe's eyes closed.

"Marlowe, forgive me... for as you know, the rest is silence."

Marlowe's hands softened from their grip and his lifeless body slid from the bed, leaving a streak of crimson cascading onto the floor. Shakespeare raised his eyes to the monk who still stood in the room with the dagger poised. The monk lifted the blade with the tip tracing a path toward William.

"Now, we come to you. I know nothing of you, but somehow I sense you are mixed up with this man. Art thou ready to follow him?"

A fleeting memory passed through William's mind: the memory of his father twirling about in the nave adorned in his scarlet robe. His father's face gleamed in happiness as he taught his son to play the game. William marked the words in his minds. *If you play the game right, then you will have thy heart's desire.*

William leaned forward and folded his hands before him, palm to palm, finally falling into a character of his own making. He answered.

"Dear brother, 'tis correct I am mixed up with this man, for you see, 'twas I who sent you to dispatch him. Please, give me thy blessing, for this murderer sought to kill his last Catholic. I humble myself before thee."

The monk lowered his blade and narrowed his eyes.

"What is this? 'Twas you? And thou art a child of Rome?"

William bowed his head in a mock humility, even as the fever pounded his brain. "Yea, I am."

The monk walked forward and placed a hand on William's head.

"Then I give thee my blessing. The phoenix now burns in everlasting fires and shall nevermore rise from the ashes. This deed shall be forgotten."

William peered once more out the window into the night sky. The clouds parted, heralding a wondrous velvet blanket pocked with twinkling stars. Shakespeare did not see the dark assassin slink away into the night, nor did he greet Ben's wondering face as he returned from the tavern; his eyes only caressed the tender suggestion of moonlight haloing the Guild Chapel tower. He sniffed once, spoke a line and closed his eyes.

"Brief, let me be…"

Ben stood stunned in the midst of the silence of the room. He surveyed the bloody mess. He turned Marlowe's body over with the toe of his boot and gasped as he recognized the aged playwright. The door creaked open and John Hall entered with his fingers touching his lips in amazement.

"Ben, what is this? What happened?" John rounded the bed, his own boots brushing against the still and bloody corpse on the floor. "Who… who is this?"

Ben's hands trembled as he gathered up the papers and the

blood-soaked blankets strewn about the room. He looked across at William, noticing the peaceful smile stretching across his friend's face, and he found the words.

"I suspect we will never know how this game finished, but this bloody sight must remain silent between us, John. This man on the floor is of no account and will vanish from our memory. No one is to know of this, and 'twould do well to leave off a report of this day in thy records. All that will be known is that England's sweet swan of the Avon has flown. I will go to Trinity church and have the gravedigger dig a deeper grave, one that will hold two men and all of these bloody secrets."

Ben Jonson walked near to William and leaned over the actor's resting body. He ran his fingers over William's brow, now cool to the touch.

"Has the fever broken," John asked.

Ben wiped a tear from the corner of his eye and whispered, "Yea, it has cracked his heart. Never fear, William, my friend, for I will write thy name upon the stars. All thy pained secrets that thou hast carried throughout thy life will follow thee to the grave. I swear that I will not reveal it, but will publish that thou were a good man, though flawed like us all. You will be not of an age, but for all time."

Terminus hora diem; terminat Author opus

Afterwords

Calliope kissed Christopher Marlowe's lips and sucked back the artistic breath she breathed into him at an early age. She sighed as Ben Jonson and John Hall lowered his shrouded body into the muddy pit dug for William Shakespeare.

'There he will lie,' she cried, 'twelve feet deep. His bones crushed and hidden beneath the elegant carved coffin carrying Shakespeare. No reckoning for this sparrow and not a single human tear nor hallowed prayer to bid his crossing.'

The darkness of the hole in Trinity Church gaped open to receive his body, swallowing all his hopes of reclaiming his name. Calliope brushed away a tear and remembered the beautiful boy she met on the banks of the Stour River. He showed such promise in those early days, the day before mortals snatched away her dream of a prodigy.

Walking over to the newly chiseled epitaph, she traced her fingers over the words as she read them aloud:

> *'Stay passenger, why goest thou by so fast,*
> *Read if thou canst, whom envious death hath plast*
> *With in this monument Shakespeare, with whome,*
> *Quick nature dide whose name doth deck Ys tombe,*
> *Far more, then cost: Sieh all, Yt he hath writt,*
> *Leaves living art, but page, to serve his witt.'*

Calliope laughed like the bubbling of water over rocks. She turned to her sisters who hovered near and plucked the strings of her lute.

'*Marlowe kept clever to the end, and yet, he did not realize he wrote his own final destiny. For any who dare tear apart these words and grave, they will find Marlowe's name and body within. Methinks, though, that generations will pass by these stones with blind eyes. And look, Ben Jonson added his own poetic curse to protect all these secrets:*

> '*Good friend for Iesus sake forbeare,*
> *To digg the dust encloased heare:*
> *Bleste be Ye man Yt spares thes stones,*
> *And curst be he Yt moves my bones.*'

'*O, what fools these mortals be,*' *Calliope sang.* '*Shall we away, for if my senses do not deceive, I spy another bright youth staring out his window with dreams of a story.*'

Thalia smiled and asked, '*Forsooth, sister, do you forget your darling Marlowe so soon? Tell me, what be the new playwright's name?*'

Calliope raised her eyes toward the rising morning sun, her form vanishing with her words.

'*Ah, dear Thalia, methinks Marlowe's name will blow away like the chaff under the rolling pestle of your ambitious Shakespeare. I am done with playwrights for a time. Give me an artist who dreams only of telling a story and not for fame, perhaps of the sounder sort. My mind skips away to this new one quite easily, and he goes by the name of Milton... John Milton...*

A Conversation with D. K. Marley

There have been many novels about Shakespeare, why did you feel it was important to write about this particular topic?
Yes, there are many novels on Shakespeare, expounding the continued belief that he wrote the plays and sonnets attributed to him, but this novel gives wing to the possibility of someone else being the writer.

So, this novel is of historical importance?
I would rather say it is of historical interest. I am not a historian. Even though I love doing research for my novels, my passion is fiction and a story like this that is rich with intrigue and theories, well, it is the stuff historical fiction writers dream about. Both characters, William Shakespeare and Christopher Marlowe, have a world full of questions surrounding them. There are endless avenues any writer can traverse when it comes to these two men.

What made you want to write about Marlowe and Shakespeare?
The first time I visited England in 1997, I took a tour of the Globe Theater and there in the museum was a wall dedicated to the five other men who may have written the plays, a thought I had never imagined before. To this day, I truly don't know why Marlowe stood out to me, but I took out my notebook and began writing notes about him, knowing a story was there.
When I came back home and started researching on the Internet about the possibility, I came across some amazing discoveries. The more and more I delved, the more the theory sounded plausible. Given the fact that Marlowe was already a

playwright and had access to far greater resources than Shakespeare ever did, the idea had merit, but the problem was the issue with his death at the age of twenty-nine in Deptford.

When I came across Peter Farey's discussion, the problem resolved and all of my questions melded together into one solution: he never died, but was exiled. This was truly a sixteenth century case of conspiracy and identity theft. The idea of a crime novel or suspense was quite interesting to me, even something on the line of Dan Brown's books, but in finding my own voice, historical fiction felt more like home, especially the time period of the Tudors. The Elizabethan era has always been my favorite period and I love tackling the job of weaving a bit of the old language with our modern tongue. While I tried to stay true to history, I did use artistic license, such as the additions of the subplot of Marlowe's imaginary friend, to round out a writer's torture who is plagued with a "muse," as was Marlowe who was referred to as the "muse's darling."

My grandmother gave me my first book of the complete works of Shakespeare when I was eleven years old. The language, the history, and the style of writing has intrigued me ever since. During my school years, I immersed myself into English Literature, even acting the part of Calpurnia in Julius Caesar when we studied that play.

There will be many who scoff at the idea that Shakespeare was merely an ambitious actor who stole the works of Marlowe; how do you approach this?

Of course, there will, and I expect that, but again, I do not claim to be a Shakespearean scholar or historian. Yet, sometimes the simplest of explanations lean more toward truth than elaboration. That is why I used the quote from Francis Bacon, who himself is another candidate for writing the plays - "The forbidden idea contains a spark of truth that flies up in the face of he who seeks to stamp it out."

There may be a spark of truth to the idea that Shakespeare did not write the plays and there always will be those who wish to stamp out debate.

This is the same kind of wall the writers and men of ambition and progress, those of the "School of Night" faced during the

Elizabethan era. I have been to some delightful debates over the years discussing the question of Shakespeare's authorship, the first and foremost being the lectures held at the Globe Theater in 2007.

There is even a petition people can sign on the internet called the Declaration of Intent for the Shakespeare Authorship Debate, although the site supports Edward de Vere, the Earl of Oxford, as being the writer, which is fine with me, for any support for anyone other than the man Shakespeare shows I am not alone in believing that this actor from Stratford was not the man who wrote such eloquent and astounding verses; and yet, I am not against those who do believe.

The question reminds me of a small episode where this very thing took place. I was standing in a group at the first debate held at the Globe and a gentleman looked at me when he discovered I was a Marlowan, and said, "O, you are one of those. I suppose you believe he was exiled." Very calmly, I replied, "Well, you have to admit that the idea makes for a great story, and that is what I am, a story teller."

What kind of evidence is there that Marlowe survived the tavern brawl in Deptford? And what evidence is there against William Shakespeare being the writer?

To me, Marlowe was as a brilliant writer as he was a spy. A man who could create such astounding characters, even if you only attribute those we know about – Faustus, Tamburlaine, Edward – shows he had the ability to form well-rounded characters. Walsingham was known for recruiting boys of genius at a young age for the underground spy ring, so a boy of Marlowe's caliber, a boy and man who could morph characters, would have fit into Walsingham's plans. It would not have been a difficult thing for Marlowe to do as a writer, for oftentimes writers use this technique for getting into the minds of their characters.

What kind of questions should a person ask who is looking to do some research on this topic?

1. Do we know Marlowe survived the death in Deptford without a doubt? No, but tell me this:
2. Why was one of the most beloved playwrights of his day, before Shakespeare, buried in a common

churchyard?

3. Why did the Queen provide her own coroner for the inquest when she herself was not within the verge of the murder, and then give instructions that no one delve further into questionings about Marlowe's death?

4. Why was Marlowe with three other well-known spies instead of presenting himself before the Privy Council at eleven o'clock, which was his punishment for the supposed seditious writings found in Kyd's apartments?

5. Who is the mysterious man known simply as Monsieur Le Doux during those years Marlowe would have been dead?

6. Why do we not hear anything about Shakespeare's writings until after Marlowe dies?

7. Who is the Mr. W. H. to whom the sonnets are dedicated?

8. Who is the "dark lady" of the sonnets?

9. What kind of education did the two men have?

10. What is the secret riddle of the epitaph above Shakespeare's tomb?

11. Why was his grave dug twelve feet deep instead of the normal six foot?

12. Why did Shakespeare's son-in-law, Dr. John Hall, leave off any mention of the day Shakespeare died in his journal?

There are so many questions, I could go on and on. If a person holds up all of these in relation to Shakespeare, the questions loom; and yet, when I held up each of these questions to Marlowe, all the answers, for me, fell into place.

Shakespeare did not have the education for such lofty writing, he did not have the background and there is no evidence of his having traveled. Even his friend, Ben Jonson, railed him on his lack of languages. Also, maybe just to me, but I thought it odd, there is no mention of his writings, or any books he may have had in his possession for his own research, in his will. For those in favor of Shakespeare, I am sure they will say it is because the plays belonged to the playhouse and the actors, but still, to me, there is a question.

There is no doubt Shakespeare was an ambitious man and a brilliant actor, and considering the time period he lived with poverty and sickness so rampant, a man might do anything to make sure of the survival of his family, the legacy of his name and his own ambition.

When you read some of the sonnets, many of the ones I have quoted in the novel, the desperation of a man writing the words resounds. Clearly, the sonnets show a man desperate for someone to recognize the hidden clues, clues that smack of the life of Marlowe, not Shakespeare. It was a common practice in those days to hide clues or riddles within writings, so this style of writing would not have been unusual for Marlowe. Also, he had all the means available to him to undertake a masque to save his own life – the money, the backing, the patrons, and a favor from the Queen herself, who was known to take great pains to protect those who protected her.

Any final thoughts on the Shakespeare authorship question?

Yea, simply this – an early American author, Napolean Hill, said, "All great truths are simple in final analysis, and easily understood; if they are not, they are not great truths."

31398330R00233

Printed in Poland
by Amazon Fulfillment
Poland Sp. z o.o., Wrocław